ACCLAIM FOR SARAH E. LADD

"Beautifully written, intricately plotted, and populated by engaging and realistic characters, *The Curiosity Keeper* is Regency romantic suspense at its page-turning best. A skillful, sympathetic, and refreshingly natural author, Ladd is at the top of her game and should be an auto-buy for every reader."

—*RT Book Reviews*, 4½ STARS, TOP PICK!

"An engaging Regency with a richly detailed setting and an unpredictable suspenseful plot. Admirers of Sandra Orchard and Lis Wiehl who want to try a romance with a historical bent may enjoy this new series."

—*Library Journal* ON *The Curiosity Keeper*

"Ladd's story, with its menace and cast of seedy London characters, feels more like a work of Dickens than a Regency . . . A solid outing."

—*Publishers Weekly* ON *The Curiosity Keeper*

"A delightful read, rich with period details. Ladd crafts a couple the reader roots for from the very beginning and a plot that keeps the reader guessing until the end."

—SARAH M. EDEN, BESTSELLING AUTHOR
OF *For Elise* ON *The Curiosity Keeper*

"My kind of book! The premise grabbed my attention from the first lines, and I eagerly returned to its pages. I think my readers will enjoy *The Heiress of Winterwood*."

—JULIE KLASSEN, BESTSELLING, AWARD-WINNING AUTHOR

"Ladd proves yet again she's a superior novelist, creating unforgettable characters and sympathetically portraying their merits, flaws, and all-too-human struggles with doubt, hope, and faith."

—*RT Book Reviews*, 4 STARS, ON *A Lady at Willowgrove Hall*

"[E]ngaging scenes of the times keep the pages turning as this historical romance . . . swirls energetically through angst and disclosure."

—*Publishers Weekly* on *The Headmistress of Rosemere*

"This book has it all: shining prose, heart-wrenching emotion, vivid and engaging characters, a well-paced plot, and a sigh-worthy happy ending that might cause some readers to reach for the tissue box. In only her second novel, Ladd has established herself as Regency writing royalty."

—*RT Book Reviews*, 4½ stars, TOP PICK!
on *The Headmistress of Rosemere*

"If you are a fan of Jane Austen and *Jane Eyre*, you will love Sarah E. Ladd's debut."

—USAToday.com on *The Heiress of Winterwood*

"This debut novel hits all the right notes with a skillful and delicate touch, breathing fresh new life into standard romance tropes."

—*RT Book Reviews*, 4 stars, on *The Heiress of Winterwood*

"Ladd's charming Regency debut is enhanced with rich detail and well-defined characters. It should be enjoyed by fans of Gilbert Morris."

—*Library Journal* on *The Heiress of Winterwood*

"This adventure is fashioned to encourage love, trust, and faith especially in the Lord and to pray continually, especially in times of strife."

—*CBA Retailers + Resources* on *The Heiress of Winterwood*

A Stranger at Fellsworth

Books by Sarah E. Ladd

Treasures of Surrey Novels

The Curiosity Keeper

Dawn at Emberwilde

Whispers on the Moors Novels

The Heiress of Winterwood

The Headmistress of Rosemere

A Lady at Willowgrove Hall

A Stranger at Fellsworth

SARAH E. LADD

THOMAS NELSON
Since 1798

A Stranger at Fellsworth

© 2017 by Sarah Ladd

Published in Nashville, Tennessee, by Thomas Nelson. Thomas Nelson is a registered trademark of HarperCollins Christian Publishing, Inc.

Thomas Nelson titles may be purchased in bulk for educational, business, fund-raising, or sales promotional use. For information, please e-mail SpecialMarkets@ThomasNelson.com.

Library of Congress Cataloging-in-Publication Data

Names: Ladd, Sarah E., author.
Title: A stranger at Fellsworth / Sarah E. Ladd.
Description: Nashville: Thomas Nelson, [2017] | Series: A Treasures of Surrey novel; 3
Identifiers: LCCN 2016053266 | ISBN 9780718011857 (paperback)
Subjects: | GSAFD: Christian fiction. | Love stories.
Classification: LCC PS3612.A3565 S73 2017 | DDC 813/.6--dc23 LC record available at https://lccn.loc.gov/2016053266

Printed in the United States of America

17 18 19 20 21 LSC 5 4 3 2

I dedicate this novel to George
in loving memory

Prologue

She shouldn't be listening. It was not polite to eavesdrop. But the daunting temptation was too much to bear.

Annabelle Thorley pressed her thin frame against the rough plaster wall just outside her uncle's private library. She leaned close to the paneled door and strained to hear the hushed conversation within the chamber.

Under normal circumstances Annabelle would not care to listen to a conversation between her mother and her uncle, but a chilly autumn drizzle had forced her to abandon her painting in the garden, and boredom now compelled her to seek another form of entertainment.

Her mother's laughter traveled through the wall and rose above the rain's incessant pitter-patter.

Annabelle frowned. Her mother's laugh did not sound like a happy one, like the one she used when she was amused or surprised. It was the high-pitched, shrill sound she made when she was nervous.

Annabelle looked to her right and her left to make sure no one would witness her snooping, then settled back against the wall to learn the source of her mother's discomfort.

Her uncle's words were low. "Rumors of your husband's business failings, not to mention his sharp temper, are far-reaching, Mary.

1

As your brother, I feel I must intervene on your behalf. So I ask you directly: Is Thorley in trouble?"

Annabelle tightened her grip on her painting box and bit her lower lip. Why were they talking about her papa?

A pensive silence trailed the pointed question, then her mother finally responded. "I admit he is a different man than the one I married, but one thing has remained constant: Robert is a determined individual, with lofty ambitions and exacting expectations. Nothing incites chatter more than success, so please bear in mind that the tales you hear are merely rumors. They will fade, as gossip always does."

Annabelle sensed the hesitation in her mother's tone. Mama would not talk negatively about Papa. Such a tactic was not her way. Instead, she would dance around the subject, like the Christmastide street performers Annabelle had seen prancing dangerously close to open fires.

Her uncle's voice lowered. "Lofty ambitions can cause even the most scrupulous man to crumble. I do not trust him, Sister. I never have and I never will. I am uncomfortable with your situation, and if I am to be completely transparent, I fear for you and your children."

Her mother huffed. "For heaven's sake, Edmund. You speak of him as if he is a monster."

"No, not a monster, but the more we know a person, the more acquainted we become with his character. You are hardly the first woman to fall in love with a man and marry, only to find he does not possess the character you believed he did. That is why my door is open if you or your children are ever in need."

"Thank you, but that is not necessary," Mama snapped. "We are quite safe."

"But are you happy?"

At this, no response followed.

Annabelle bit her lip. Why would her mama not be happy?

True, her papa's voice rose from time to time, and his face was often red, but his outbursts seemed to have little effect on her.

Annabelle gathered the courage to peek through the half-open door. She glimpsed the back of her mother's pale-blue silk gown and the pearls woven into the ribbons adorning her chestnut tresses. Annabelle inched farther to see her uncle's profile, his straight nose so like her mother's . . . and her own.

She bit her lip and assessed what she could see of the chamber. Mama would call it simple. Papa would call it impoverished. A worn woven rug covered most of the rough-planked floor. Dusty books haphazardly occupied several of the shelves lining the walls, and a single large desk stood in the center of the room. Motes balanced in the thick air, illuminated by the gray morning light seeping in the dirty windows. Her mama and uncle were seated in two faded chairs next to the fireplace.

How different it was from her home in London.

Uncle Edmund stood from his chair. Not wishing to be discovered, Annabelle straightened and turned, but her paintbrushes slid from the top of her mahogany watercolor box and tumbled to the floor. The resounding clatter echoed through the silent space.

She froze.

Sounds from the library ceased.

Sharp footsteps snapped toward her, then stopped.

Annabelle held her breath and looked up.

Uncle Edmund's tall frame filled the doorway, his expression stern. He pinned her to her spot with his keen gray eyes. Did he use this same displeased expression with his students? Her tolerant governess would have turned a blind eye to her indiscretion and sent her on her way.

"Annabelle. Come in."

Annabelle locked eyes with her mother's hazel ones, silently pleading with her mother to intervene. But she did not.

Her uncle cleared his throat. "We are waiting."

Annabelle retrieved her paintbrushes from the floor and forced one foot in front of the other. She stepped near the fire . . . and closer to her mother.

Uncle Edmund returned to his chair by the fire and settled himself. "Tell me, child. Are you in the habit of listening to other people's conversations?"

Annabelle shook her head.

"I know your mother has taught you better manners than to respond to an adult by merely shaking your head. So I'll ask you again. Are you in the habit of listening to other people's conversations unannounced?"

Annabelle's mouth dried. "No, sir."

"I didn't think so." He leaned back in his chair. "How much did you hear?"

She swallowed. "Not much."

"I will take this opportunity to remind you that it is unladylike to listen to private conversations without making your presence known."

"Yes, sir."

Several moments of silence lingered, and Annabelle braced herself for more reprimands.

"We've not had a great deal of time to visit since you have been here."

Her shoulders relaxed slightly when his tone softened.

"It amazes me that you have been on this earth for these nine years and this visit is the first I have seen of you. I've no wish to lecture you, but I would be remiss if I did not correct you in this instance."

Annabelle eyed him with care. She could not decide if she liked him or not.

He inclined his head to the center of the room. "Follow me to my desk, child. I should like to give you something."

At the prospect of a gift, Annabelle's interest increased.

Uncle Edmund pulled open a side drawer and retrieved a tiny carved statue. "When you arrived, I knew this should be in your possession."

She stepped closer, reached out, and accepted the trinket. It was an intricately carved hunting dog, painted with browns and blacks and small enough to fit in her palm.

"This belonged to your mother when she was about your age. She gave it to me when she tired of it, and I've had it ever since. I couldn't bear to part with it. Now I think it should be in your possession, do you not agree?"

Maybe her uncle wasn't as frightening as she thought. "Thank you, sir."

His angular face softened. "Perhaps whenever you see that, you will remember you have a friend in Fellsworth. Do not forget it. Now run along. And no more eavesdropping."

Annabelle curtsied and quit the room, still uncertain whether she liked her uncle or was frightened of him.

Chapter One ────────────

*A*nnabelle gasped at the sight that met her eye as she passed the parlor door. Her steps slowed. Her eyes focused.

A strange man, clad in workman's attire of dirty linen trousers and a shabby tan coat, hoisted her mother's teak writing desk.

Annabelle balled her fist at her side. "You there. Stop this instant!" she ordered from the corridor, employing her most authoritative voice.

But the massive man paid her no heed. Once the desk was balanced on his shoulder, he reached for the matching carved chair.

Her shoulder clipped the door's frame when she marched into the bright parlor. "I said stop. Put that down immediately!"

As she drew closer to the man, he turned to face her, annoyance evident in the firm set of his wide jaw. "You say something?"

Heat rose to her cheeks at his irreverent tone. "Yes, I said something. I demand you return those items to where you found them before I call for the magistrate."

The man's low, gritty laugh ignited her anger further. He shifted his weight, and his dirty boots squeaked on the polished floor. "You? And who are you?"

Annabelle jutted her chin up. "I am Miss Annabelle Thorley, and I will not be spoken to in such a manner. Now do as I say and leave my home at once."

"Are you Mrs. Thomas Thorley?" he demanded.

"I am not. I am Mr. Thorley's sister. But that is my mother's desk, so return it to where you found it."

His bushy eyebrow lifted in amusement. He lowered the chair, pulled a piece of paper from his faded waistcoat, extended it out as if reading it, and then crumpled it in his thick fingers before he returned it to his pocket. "My orders come from Mr. Thomas Thorley, and he says this desk, and the rest of the furnishings in this chamber, are all to go to auction."

Without another word he pushed past her, leaving the scent of brandy and filth in his wake.

As the meaning of his words sank in, dread trickled through her. Thomas intended to sell their late mother's belongings. Annabelle had known her brother was in financial distress, but this?

Sensing she was fighting a losing battle, she scurried to a cupboard while the man was out of the room and scooped personal belongings from it. A book of verses. A miniature portrait Mama had painted of Papa. The odiferous man might be a barbarian, but she would not allow him to leave with her mother's letters. Irritation blurred her vision as she clutched the precious mementos to her chest and rushed from the room.

Annabelle marched down Wilhurst House's narrow hall to the back of the home. There was no question in her mind.

Thomas needed to answer for this.

Annabelle found him in his study, as expected, but instead of sitting at his desk, he reclined on the settee beneath the window with his arm over his eyes.

She discarded her treasures on a small side table, stomped toward him, and poked his arm. "Wake up, Tom. Merciful heavens, it is late morning and here you are, sleeping."

He grunted but made no movement. "I don't recall asking for your opinion on how I spend my time."

Annabelle ignored his snide remark and pulled the curtains

open, allowing the bright summer sunshine to spill into the chamber. "There is a man in the parlor removing furnishings. He said you instructed him to do so, and I told him there must be some mistake."

Thomas heaved a bothered sigh. "No, no mistake."

Frustrated at his lack of interest, Annabelle poked him again. "Get up and make them stop."

Thomas eased his bloodshot eyes open and pulled himself up from his reclining position. He swung his boots to the polished floor, yawned, then tugged at the snowy-white cravat hanging around his neck. "I can't stop them from taking what belongs to them."

"What *belongs* to them?" Annabelle shook her head. He was not making sense. "Tom, those are Mama's things."

He held out his hands, as if to display the fact that he was out of options. "It's quite simple. I owe money, but I don't have any money. I am paying them in kind and then they will leave me be."

Annabelle pressed her lips together while choosing her words. Crossing her brother on such a topic would only lead to more arguing. "Wilhurst House is my home too. This is the home our parents shared. Perhaps if you were to include me in some of the decisions, I could—"

"Include you?" He snorted, his pinched face reeking condescension. He jumped to his feet. "Belle, this home, and everything in it, is mine, not yours, as are all the debts, the unprofitable business dealings, and the plethora of problems Father created before he died. So no, Sister, I'll not include you. Not until I somehow manage to work my way out of this monstrosity of a mess."

He was correct. The home and everything associated with it now belonged to him. She had no right to them—not her mama's desk, not the paintings in the hall, not even the trinkets in her bedchamber.

She eyed Thomas as he lifted a glass of amber liquid to his lips and tossed it down his throat. Reprimanding him for indulging at this time of day would do more harm than good, regardless of how wrong they both knew it to be.

After several moments, he filled his lungs with the study's stale air and forced his long fingers through his dark, tousled hair. He fixed his hazel eyes on her with the same intensity that their papa used to, and she braced herself for the hurt that would inevitably follow. "In the future you will remember that these are my issues to solve. Not yours. I do not need, or want, your interference."

The sharply hurled words stung. Annabelle swallowed, her anger shifting to discouragement. She softened her voice. "I am concerned, 'tis all."

He pointed his finger at her. "All you need concern yourself with is the ball at the Baldwins' this night. Cecil Bartrell will be in attendance, and I expect you to encourage him. If you do as you are told, hope might exist for us yet."

Annabelle's stomach clenched. The mere mention of the man's name was enough to send her into a panic.

Cecil Bartrell.

Wealthy, ancient, obnoxious Cecil Bartrell.

She rested her hands on the back of a nearby chair and fiddled with the fringe. "You know how I feel about him."

"Feelings are nothing more than silly feminine whims. He is the only man of worth to show interest in you since Goodacre, and fortunately Bartrell doesn't care about the scandal surrounding our family name. Mark my words: Bartrell is your only—and last—chance to marry. If you rely on your heart and the fickle feelings found there, you will end up worse off than you already are."

How she wished she could speak the words poised on her tongue, ready to lash forward. But she knew better.

Thomas reached for the cotton tailcoat on the back of his chair and punched his arms through the sleeves. "We are having company tonight. I suggest you leave the workers alone to see to their tasks so they can depart by the time our guests arrive."

"Guests?" Annabelle jerked her head up. "This is the first I have heard of guests."

"Friends from south of here—Treadwell and McAlister. They are to attend the ball with us tonight, and they will spend the next few days here."

She recognized the names. They had both been frequent guests. Wilhurst House might be but a shell of its former glory, but at least the bedrooms were still intact, and her brother did most of his entertaining in the billiards room or the library, just as their papa had before him. The guests would likely never even see the parlor and the pitiful lack of furnishings.

But it was still a shame. At one time she would have relished a home full of friends and activity, but recent events had made it necessary to retreat from such entertainment. Besides, now that her brother had married, she was not even the hosting mistress—just the lamentable spinster sister.

"You'd best start preparing for the evening." His words snapped her back to the present. "Wear the green gown."

Annabelle crossed her arms over her chest and pivoted on her heel to leave the study. Several unanswered questions might exist in her life at present, but one thing she knew for certain: she would *not* be wearing the green gown to the Baldwins' ball.

Chapter Two ———————————

*H*ow I dread this ball tonight." Annabelle squinted in the bright early afternoon sunlight and groaned as she adjusted the red feather on her straw bonnet to keep it from bouncing against her face with each step.

Crosley, Annabelle's lady's maid, shifted the brown package in her arms and lengthened her stride to match her mistress's. "Do not fret, miss. Tomorrow this time it will just be a memory. 'Twill be over soon enough."

"That's just it." Annabelle lifted her lace handkerchief to her nose to avoid the unpleasant, pungent scents as they passed two vagabonds near an alley. "I don't think it will be over anytime soon. Thomas is determined that I should marry Mr. Bartrell, and he'll not soon forget it. I am determined that I should *not* marry him. You can see the predicament."

"It will work out in the end, I am sure of it."

Crosley's confident tone did little to squelch the escalating apprehension building within Annabelle. "You are always optimistic."

The lady's maid shrugged. "It can always be worse, miss. Always. As long as you remember that, anything is bearable."

Annabelle raised her voice to be heard above the clatter of a passing carriage and horses' hooves. "I suppose you are right. But in the meantime, if I must attend this ball, it would be more tolerable if I had a new gown to wear. Everyone will be there, and I have attended ever so many events in the yellow silk."

Crosley nodded at the package she was carrying. "I'll sew a lace overlay on the bodice, and these new gloves will breathe new life into it. Just wait and see."

Annabelle opened her mouth to respond, but a sudden, sharp tug on her right wrist jerked her entire body. Someone—or something—pulled the silk reticule looped on her gloved wrist, the force of the action nearly wrenching her from her feet.

The ribbon securing the small bag gave way, and her reticule snapped free. A cry escaped her lips, and she whirled her head around to assess the source.

A haggard beggar woman clad in a frayed, dingy gown with wild auburn hair clutched Annabelle's reticule to her chest and turned to run, but the man next to her captured Annabelle's attention. He must have witnessed the act of thievery, for within seconds he had a firm grip on the woman's arm. His much larger size easily prevented her escape.

Annabelle's heart raced as the scene unfolded before her. The woman thrashed and kicked in an attempt to free herself. The man remained steady. Onlookers paused to watch the spectacle, but no one intervened.

The man's broad back was to Annabelle. Their positions shifted, and the man seized the reticule from the woman with his available hand. After several minutes the woman ceased her squirming, and once he could free his hand, he extended the bag to Annabelle. "I believe this belongs to you."

She stared at the reticule in his hand with hesitation, as if it were a snake that might strike. She reached out and accepted it. "Yes, it does. Thank you."

The man casually adjusted the wide-brimmed slouch hat that had nearly fallen from his head in the skirmish. "Shall I call the magistrate?"

Annabelle shifted her attention to the woman who had tried

to rob her. A spark of recognition flashed. It burned slowly at first and then flamed.

Annabelle was looking at none other than Miss Henrietta Stillworth.

Clearly Miss Stillworth recognized her too, for tears pooled in her cornflower-blue eyes—lovely eyes that had been the envy of every young woman and the object of desire for every young man not but two years prior.

Shock stole Annabelle's speech. She'd heard rumors that Miss Stillworth had fallen into ruin after her parents died, but was it possible she had been reduced to such disdainful circumstances?

The man's deep words jerked her back to the present. "Would you like me to call the magistrate?"

Annabelle gave her head a little shake, as if doing so would dislodge the confusion settling in her mind. The idea of summoning a constable for a lady of Miss Stillworth's station and upbringing was preposterous. Annabelle cleared her throat. "Um, no . . . no. That will not be necessary."

Her heart ached as a tear slipped down the lady's flushed cheek. A million questions balanced on the tip of Annabelle's tongue, ready to spill forth, but another glance at the man, a stranger, silenced her.

"Very well." The man released his hold on Miss Stillworth's arm. "You are free to go."

Miss Stillworth rubbed her arm where her captor's hand had been and turned to leave.

"Wait." Afraid Miss Stillworth might leave before she had a chance to address her, Annabelle stepped closer. She opened her reticule, scooped out all of the coins in her gloved hand, and extended them to the woman, who at one time she had considered a friend. "Take these."

Initially Annabelle thought Miss Stillworth was going to reject the gift. She made no motion. But after several seconds, her chin trembled and fresh moisture filled her eyes. She accepted the coins, took two slow steps backward, whirled around, and disappeared into the swarming crowd.

Annabelle did not look away from Miss Stillworth's retreating form until the tiny woman had been swallowed by the street's business and her bright titian hair was no longer visible.

Annabelle did not understand. How had someone who had been as prominent as Henrietta Stillworth found herself in such a deplorable situation?

She turned her attention to the man who had rescued her reticule. He, too, was staring after Miss Stillworth.

The man had a strong, handsome profile, with a fine, straight nose and square jaw. He was a full head taller than Annabelle, and he carried himself well, yet his fawn buckskin breeches were smeared with dried mud, and it must have been ages since his riding boots last saw the polishing cloth. Despite this lack of refinement, he boasted a commanding figure—just the sort of man who would rescue a lady in distress.

It surprised her that a stranger would rush to her aid. Pickpockets carried blades, or so she had been warned. He could have been stabbed.

She did not realize she was staring until he spoke.

He set dark eyes on her, gave a little chuckle, and shook his head. "I don't think I've ever seen anyone do anything like that before."

Annabelle frowned, a little shocked at the stranger's response. "Are you laughing? I cannot say I find anything amusing about this encounter."

He adjusted his felt hat, and his expression sobered. "I find no amusement in it either. Far from it. I only meant that it was an unusual gesture. You gave the woman the object she attempted to rob you of. Most people would be eager to see an action like that punished."

"She apparently needs the money more than I." Annabelle handed the damaged reticule to Crosley as nonchalantly as if it were nothing more than a handkerchief. "But regardless of the outcome, it was kind of you to intervene."

The directness of his gaze unnerved her. "Think nothing of it."

Determined to fully regain her composure, Annabelle straightened her posture and lifted her chin. "I would gladly compensate you for your trouble, but I gave all of my money to the lady."

The man shook his head. "I require no reward, miss."

"Of course you do. I am certain my brother would be more than happy to repay you for your service."

"Again, it is not necessary. You must be eager to be on your way. I'll take my leave."

He bowed, and now that the fog of confusion had cleared, Annabelle's interest in her rescuer grew. A breeze unsettled his curly black hair, and the sunlight brightened his chestnut eyes.

It was highly improper for her, a lady, to speak with a strange man on the street, regardless of the service he provided. But she had to at least know something about him. "Please, if you would be so kind, to whom do I owe this debt of gratitude?"

"My name is Owen Locke, from Fellsworth in Surrey." The corner of his mouth lifted in a smile. "At your service."

Chapter Three

*O*wen had never witnessed anything like it. He turned to glance at the beautiful lady with the red feather in her bonnet walking in the opposite direction, the skirt of her gown swaying with each step in the muggy dampness. Her somberly clad servant followed close behind.

He shook his head. The lady had fallen victim to a pickpocket, and in a surprising turn of events, she gifted the thief all the coins in her possession. Astonishing.

Perhaps it did not pain the wealthy to part with such a sum, but the action was rare. What was even more curious, the lady had not seemed frightened by the incident. If anything, she seemed to pity the criminal as one would pity a wounded animal or a frightened child.

Owen paused a moment to allow a donkey cart to jostle past him on the dusty street. He'd been on his way to the Lion's Cross Pub when he encountered the robbery and stopped to intervene. From where he walked now he could see his employer, Mr. Stephen Treadwell, waiting for him just outside the pub's main entrance.

As Owen drew closer, Treadwell moved to meet him halfway. "What took you so long?" Treadwell called, straightening his waistcoat. "And why are you so dirty?"

Owen assessed the dust and straw clinging to his boots and buckskin breeches. He brushed at his linen coat. "I've been busy. Got the horses and dogs settled at the stable. Not all of us can spend the day lounging about the public house, looking pretty in our new frock coat and fancy trousers."

Most gamekeepers would never dare speak to their estate masters with such informality, much less poke fun at their attire or daily habits. But in truth, the week would not be complete without Owen remarking about the garish fussiness of Treadwell's dandy garb. The dynamics of their employment relationship did not fit a standard mold. They had shared a friendly rapport since their youth, and that bond deepened as they grew to adulthood. Now they performed very different roles, but their camaraderie remained.

Treadwell stretched his arms out in front of him, admiring the smooth green broadcloth of the sleeves. "It is a smart coat, to be sure. I'm impressed you noticed. As for you, I would think you would take better care of your appearance when speaking to a lady. What was that game you were playing?"

Owen scratched the back of his head and diverted his gaze. "Saw that, did you?"

"I did. It was not quite the manner in which I would suggest introducing yourself to Miss Annabelle Thorley, but I suppose to each his own."

Owen snapped his gaze to Treadwell. "Who?"

"Ah, the stunning Miss Annabelle Thorley." A grin slid over Treadwell's narrow face. "The lady with the bonny red feather in her elegant bonnet."

"Not Thorley, as in a relation to Mr. Thomas Thorley?"

Treadwell nodded. "The very one. Miss Thorley is Thomas's younger sister. And it seems you have made quite an impression. What sort of impression remains to be seen, but an impression nonetheless, my friend."

Owen spun around, but Miss Thorley was nowhere in sight. He filled his lungs and then released the air in a huff. Of all the people he could have encountered, he never expected the very mistress of Wilhurst House, the home where Treadwell—and not to mention he—would be a guest. Of course, as a gamekeeper he would bunk in the servants' quarters and not the family home, but the coincidence was still an odd one.

Treadwell waved a gloved hand dismissively. "I would not give it a second thought. I doubt your paths will cross again, and I shan't bring it up when I see her. Anyway, what was that dance you were doing with that beggar woman?"

Owen removed his wide-brimmed hat and wiped his brow with his forearm. "That beggar woman, as you refer to her, was attempting to steal Miss Thorley's bag. I put a stop to it."

Treadwell grinned. "Of course you did. I would expect no less. Easy to offer assistance to such a rare beauty, isn't it?" Treadwell adjusted his tall beaver hat atop his light hair. "Fortunately for her, she looks nothing like her brother."

Owen recalled Miss Thorley's smooth, pale skin and golden eyes fringed in black eyelashes. His intentions might have been to assist, but he could not deny his notice of her feminine charms.

Treadwell snickered at his own joke. "She's always been the crown jewel of the family, for as long as I have been acquainted with them anyway. At one point she caught my eye, but at the time she was engaged to another man. Goodwin was his name, I think, or perhaps Goodman. It no longer matters, for I understand that engagement is now broken."

What would cause any man to break an engagement with such an enchanting creature? But who was he to comprehend the intricate dealings of the upper classes? Owen admittedly did not always understand their ways, and the rules of courtship and matrimony were especially elaborate.

Treadwell continued with a chuckle, "'Tis a shame she has no fortune, otherwise I might consider her as a match for myself now. The rumor is that she hasn't a farthing to her name, and we both know that would never do for me."

Owen was surprised to hear that Miss Thorley had no fortune, especially considering how quickly she had handed over the few coins. "None?"

"I don't think so. Thorley tries to put on a brave face, but I've heard he is facing ruin. 'Tis a shame that her beauty has not been enough to protect her from the scandal surrounding her family."

Owen frowned. Normally he paid little attention to the gossip that fascinated Treadwell so, but he had endured scandal in his own life and he would not wish such a fate on anyone. But Miss Thorley's unusual actions had piqued his interest. "What scandal?"

"Her father, who died nearly two years ago, was one of the most prominent bankers in London. An interesting story, really. The man was born a pauper and was one of those few men who managed to not only amass great wealth but infiltrate London society. But he was a proud, impulsive man, one thing led to another, and eventually an embezzling rumor plunged the entire family into humiliation.

"It was never proven, of course, but sometimes the mere suggestion of a scandal is enough to make it so. He died before his name could be cleared. As a result, his business failed. In the last two years the family has lost almost everything. Fortunately, Thorley married well prior to the rumors, but now I fear he's finished in London. He's growing desperate, and desperate people make me nervous."

"Then why did you accept his invitation?" Owen fell into step next to him as they headed in the same direction Miss Thorley had gone.

Treadwell tapped his walking stick against the ground with each step. "He may make me nervous, but I still count him among my friends. Plus he is one of the most amusing chaps I know. Always good for a laugh."

Once a person entered Treadwell's inner circle, he was not easily ousted, even if his character was questionable.

Treadwell popped open his pocket watch and checked the time. "It does amaze me how you manage to find adventure wherever you go, and I was bored to death talking with old Farley all afternoon while you played the hero."

The mention of Farley seized Owen's interest. After all, Farley was the very reason Owen opted to remain in London instead of returning to Fellsworth after their trip to the north. He would never choose to be away from his work and his daughter unnecessarily, but Treadwell's meeting with the old landowner had been too important.

Owen lowered his hat to guard his eyes against the oppressive afternoon sun. "How did the conversation go?"

Treadwell swiped a piece of wood out of his path with his walking stick. "Oh, you know Farley. He doesn't care for me and never has. In fact, I'm probably the last person with whom he would want to discuss such a matter. But these are trying times for a lot of people, and Farley's no exception. I did mention to him that you were interested in purchasing Kirtley Meadow. He said he'd never sell, but what else would he say? He will be at the Baldwins' ball tonight. I'll talk to him then."

Owen clenched his jaw. He had wanted to approach Farley himself. He did not like relying on another for anything, even a trusted friend like Treadwell. But this was the world he was in. A man in Farley's position would not conduct business with a gamekeeper, let alone keep company with him. Their stations were too disparate. No, Farley was the sort of man who would only deal with another landowner.

"Don't worry, Locke. He will come around. I'll see to it." Treadwell slapped a heavy hand on Owen's shoulder. "He'll sell you the land, and then you can live out your dreams and hunt on your very own property until your heart is content. You just can't leave my estate without a gamekeeper. That is my one stipulation."

Treadwell's confidence should have encouraged Owen, but he was far too suspicious to share Treadwell's optimism. Whereas Treadwell was accustomed to getting his way, Owen had worked diligently for everything in his possession, and he would continue to do so until he was certain he was providing the very best he could for his daughter. Becoming a landowner in his own right was part of that plan, and he would not rest until he did just that.

Chapter Four ⸺

"There. It's finished." Crosley propped her hands on her hips, tilted her head, and studied Annabelle's reflection in the looking glass. "Are you pleased?"

Annabelle fixed her gaze on her likeness and pivoted to her right, then to her left. Crosley had been correct yet again.

Night was falling and darkness shrouded the room, but even in the dimness the newly added Belgian lace overlay on the buttery-yellow silk gown enhanced her shape, and the length of gold cord sewn along the hemline added a dramatic flair.

Annabelle ran her fingers along the new scalloped satin piping adorning the neckline. "Thank you, Crosley. It is much improved. I only hope that no one will notice it is the same gown I wore to the Dennison dinner last month."

"That's not likely." Crosley pushed a lock of blonde hair from her face and scurried around the chamber to gather the discarded scraps of ribbon and lace. "If I had more time I would have added a netting overlay to the skirt as well, but perhaps next time."

Next time.

There had been a time when wearing a gown to an event twice was an unforgivable misstep, and now she was planning for it.

As if sensing Annabelle's hesitation, Crosley frowned. "I can always sew the lace to the green silk instead, if you prefer."

Annabelle tensed. The mere mention of the green gown she had worn the night of her engagement to Samuel Goodacre soured her mood. She would never wear the dress again.

"Oh no," she stuttered. "The yellow will do."

Crosley stepped closer to her, concern darkening her fair features. "Are you well, miss? I could fetch some tea—"

"I am well," Annabelle snipped. How could she admit that she was thinking about Samuel? Her chest tightened at the recollection. His black hair. His mesmerizing green eyes. The touch of his hand on hers.

Annabelle smoothed her hand down the front of her gown, forcing her attention back to the task of dressing. Daydreaming and wishing for a different reality would not make it so, nor would it lessen the pain. Hiding away was not an option, not with her brother's current demands.

She would have to make the most of the situation.

She would attend the ball in the refurbished yellow silk gown.

She would be the object of many stares and the source of much gossip.

She would likely encounter Samuel.

And through it all, she would hold her head high.

Annabelle moved to the dressing table. Crosley joined her and removed the pins from Annabelle's hair, allowing the shiny tresses to cascade over her shoulders.

Determined to ponder no more on Samuel, Annabelle allowed her thoughts to drift to the odd interaction on the street earlier that day. "I can't stop thinking about Miss Stillworth. The poor woman!"

Crosley clicked her tongue as she drew the silver brush through Annabelle's long locks. "I never would have believed it had I not seen it with my own eyes."

Annabelle reached for a strand of pearls on the dressing table and ran it between her fingers. Their upbringings had been very similar. Both had been raised in London. Both had been educated by governesses and had enjoyed an advantageous betrothal that was broken by scandal.

Was Annabelle's story to be the same? She shuddered to think that if it were not for her brother, she might be suffering the same fate.

She lifted her gaze and watched Crosley manipulate the light-brown strands. "I cannot recall the last time I saw her. How long would you say it has been? Two years? Three? It had to be before Papa died, at least."

The lady's maid pinned a curl into place. "I wouldn't know, miss."

Annabelle pressed her lips together. Of course Crosley knew the last time Miss Stillworth had been at their home. Crosley noticed everything and forgot nothing. Annabelle sighed and studied Crosley's reflection as she wove a narrow, beaded ribbon into Annabelle's hair. Crosley was slight of figure and short of stature. Her stark gray linen gown nearly swallowed her, and wisps of honey-blonde hair escaped her white cap.

"Oh, I almost forgot." Crosley lowered the excess ribbon, reached into her apron pocket, and retrieved a small pouch. She shifted her weight from one foot to the other and held the bundle at her side. "I did something, and I am not certain I behaved in the best manner."

Annabelle paused at the odd admission and faced Crosley. "What did you do?"

"When the men were clearing the room this morning, I went through the drawers of one of the side tables while they were taking a load out to the cart. I found this." Her face paled, and Crosley thrust the pouch toward Annabelle.

Annabelle took it in her hands and turned it over. She didn't recognize it.

"I did not mean to steal it, exactly, but I thought you would want me to rescue this if I could."

Annabelle untied the pouch and tipped it to the side, cupping her free hand below it to capture the contents. She gasped. In her hand was a miniature portrait. "My mother painted this! It's me, as a child. And Thomas. Where did you say you found this?"

"In the dining room in one of the drawers. I did not mean to intrude, but I saw the boorish men removing the furnishings and thought I should check for items of a personal nature."

Annabelle let out a sigh of relief. "You are forever thinking of me, and I am so grateful. I have so few of her paintings left. I'll treasure this."

Crosley nodded as she kept her attention fixed on the piece. "She had a talent. One that you share."

Annabelle placed the portrait on her dressing table and smiled at the memory of time spent with Mama. "She did try to instruct me, but I was such a flighty thing. She was so patient."

The room fell silent, and Crosley resumed dressing Annabelle's hair. After several moments the brushing slowed. Annabelle glanced up to see a frown curve Crosley's thin lips downward and her forehead crease.

It was unusual for Crosley to display any emotion at all, let alone present such a worrisome air. "Is something bothering you, Crosley?"

She did not take her gaze from Annabelle's hair, but she lowered the brush. "There is one other thing I have not yet mentioned."

Concerned by the sober tones underlying Crosley's words, Annabelle turned in her chair and waited.

Crosley exhaled, and her eyes narrowed with the intensity of one who had a secret to share. "You are aware that your brother is having guests here."

"I am."

"One of the guests is a man by the name of Mr. McAlister."

"Yes, I know him. He was a friend of my brother from their days at Cambridge."

"Mr. McAlister's valet is traveling with him, and he asked me to give you this." Crosley pulled a small, folded note from her apron pocket.

Annabelle frowned. "What is it?"

Crosley extended it toward her. "I have not read it, of course. But his valet was insistent that I present this to you and then return with a response as soon as possible."

Annabelle raised her eyebrows and received the note. "Well, I shall be the judge of whether or not a response is warranted. It's most forward of him, isn't it? I am already a target for every gossip in London. Can you imagine if word that I received notes from male guests in my home were to get out?"

Crosley stepped back to give Annabelle privacy. "Well, they shan't get the information from me."

Annabelle unfolded the letter and angled it toward the candle to catch the flickering light.

Miss Thorley,

Please forgive the presumptive nature of this missive. I am well aware of the inappropriateness, so please forgive me for intruding on your privacy.

I will be forthcoming. Miss Thorley, your brother is in danger, and I must beg your assistance in this matter before the danger intensifies. Your brother is a great friend, and it is because of the depth of this friendship that I write this letter. We must speak. Please send word where we can converse privately, and when.

I am yours, respectfully,
Mr. William McAlister

Crosley's words broke her contemplation. "I hope it's nothing too vexing."

"Oh, Crosley." As soon as the words escaped, Annabelle snapped her mouth shut. She had been warned her entire life to watch what she said around the servants—even the ones who tended her personally.

"They are not equals. They will steal from you. Deceive you. A trusted servant is a rare thing indeed. One of affluence must always be on guard."

How often had Papa spoken those words of caution?

Crosley, too, understood the intricate dance around the narrow line between mistress and servant. She had honed the fine art of saying just enough to build trust without being intrusive. Displaying enough interest to earn confidentiality without becoming too involved.

But lately the two had spent more time together. And Annabelle had a fondness for Crosley.

But Crosley was her lady's maid.

A servant—not a friend.

It would never do to confuse the two.

But what did she have to lose? Her family was crumbling. Her status had fallen. Her friendships had dissolved. Sharing the letter would snap the thin wall separating mistress from servant.

She extended the missive with a sigh. "You may read it if you like. There is nothing to hide."

Crosley took the note, and the women sat in silence as Crosley read it.

Annabelle rubbed her forehead. "I've known he is in trouble. How could I not? He has changed so much since Papa's death. So bitter and angry. We have never been overly close, but now he is as a stranger. I don't think there is any way I can help him."

"Every person is on a journey. You. Me. Mr. Thorley. Miss Stillworth. Every single one of us." Crosley lowered the letter. "Some of us will learn and grow, and some will struggle and fail. I know I certainly could not judge another. All we can do is be there for the ones who have been put into our lives."

Annabelle stood and paced the small space between the

dressing table and the bed. "I do not care for this new side of him. Not one bit."

"Your family has experienced a great deal of pain, miss. No one can predict how he will respond to tragedy, and Mr. Thorley is no different. Responsibility changes people, and he has had a great deal dealt to him." Crosley returned the note to Annabelle. "Would you like me to deliver a response to Mr. McAlister's valet?"

Annabelle shook her head. "It would be a dangerous business to get into the habit of delivering notes to the men who are guests in our home. I'll just find the opportunity to speak with him at the ball tonight."

"Whatever you think is best. I will do as you bid."

Annabelle gazed at her reflection in the looking glass. The face looking back at her appeared much more confident than she felt. As she placed the portrait back in the pouch, her brother's voice echoed from the hall, demanding that she hurry.

Exasperated, Annabelle exchanged glances with Crosley, then turned to face the looking glass one last time.

She had no way of knowing what the night would bring, and her imagination began to weave possible scenarios. But even though her immediate future was unclear, she could predict with near certainty that no good could come from it.

Chapter Five ─────────────────────────

*N*ight had fallen, and warm rain had persisted all evening, infusing the atmosphere with muggy oppressiveness.

Within the walls of the Baldwin house was no different. Annabelle flicked her painted fan open and waved it before her flushed face.

Low-hanging chandeliers boasting an assemblage of flickering candles added warmth to the already stifling room, and the throng of shifting guests intensified the thick heat.

Annabelle pressed her back against the wall as she stood alone, observing the festivities from the shadowed corner. The musicians' lively strains filled the room, mingling with voices and laughter. The dancers whirled by at dizzying speeds, and the ladies' elegant skirts of silk and muslin flowed in the breezes created by their own movement.

She lifted to the tips of her toes to see above the crowd. Her friend Katherine had vowed to be in attendance, but as of yet Annabelle had not seen her.

She dropped back to her heels. Feeling faint from the overpowering stickiness, she abandoned her perch along the wall and moved toward the corridor in search of fresher air. Her steps slowed as she caught sight of someone she wished would have remained hidden.

Samuel Goodacre.

Would her heart ever cease pounding at the very sight of him, her breath cease growing faint and shallow?

It was not a surprise to see him at the Baldwins' gathering. He stood near the opposite wall, dressed in buff trousers and a crisp blue tailcoat with shiny brass buttons. The candle's yellow glow highlighted the careless, familiar manner in which his jet hair swooped over his broad forehead, and his freshly shaven jaw was a testament to his valet's attentions. He smiled—nay, laughed—at something the pretty Miss Templeton, who stood at his elbow, had said to him.

A pang of jealously struck her. Once he had paid such attention to her, praising and flattering her, but now another stood in her stead.

Bittersweet memories bombarded her. Ever since they had been children, their fathers were business acquaintances, and they made no effort to hide their plans for the future. Annabelle had been told from a very young age that one day she would be Mrs. Samuel Goodacre, and she had no reason to question it.

The plan was perfect: His family was established and flaunted impressive connections. Her father was wealthy but lacked the benefit of an esteemed family name. When the two families united, their power would be great.

Or so she had thought.

They had been betrothed for a year when the first hint of her father's scandal surfaced, and within mere weeks Samuel broke their engagement. She'd believed every word of his eloquent courtship, and the sting of knowing that his praise had been for her fortune and not her merit still burned. Not only had he possessed her heart, but she had counted him her dearest friend, and to have that role removed so cruelly pained her to this day.

Her heart now ached at the absence of such a companion, and it longed for acceptance and a loving family of her own.

From her safe distance Annabelle studied the lady at his side, who was dressed in silver muslin and draped in gold. A ruby pendant glittered at her neck, paling only to the bright diamond tiara atop her golden curls.

At that singular moment of quiet contemplation, Samuel turned his green eyes toward her, silencing Annabelle's thoughts.

She had been caught staring. A lady would never be caught staring at a gentleman.

They locked gazes for several seconds, neither smiling, neither looking away. Even at this distance, a lifetime was captured in the depth of his eyes.

He knew much about her. Nay, he knew everything about her—every trial, every triumph, every flaw. At one time the adoration in his demeanor sent her heart soaring, but tonight his expression was void of all emotion, as if they were no more than indifferent strangers.

She had not even realized that a smile curved her lips until it was too late. It was such a natural response. He had garnered smiles from her since the time they had been children. And he had always returned them with equal fervor.

But today his countenance darkened and he turned back to the lady on his arm.

The obvious dismissal stole the stale air from her lungs and weakened her knees. Heat rushed to her cheeks. She looked around for an escape. Someone to talk to. Anyone. A reason to think that she had not been abandoned completely.

But all around her, people she had known most of her life were engaged in other conversations. Conversations that did not include her, and likely never would again.

A tear was about to fall when a welcome, familiar voice broke her solace. "I detest him on your behalf."

Annabelle's breath rushed from her lungs in relief as she turned toward the voice and beheld Katherine McCleod. Annabelle reached out to take her dear friend's hands as she approached. "You can't possibly know how happy I am to see you."

Katherine embraced Annabelle, patted one of Annabelle's

wayward locks into place with assumed authority, and then shook her head. She lifted her nose in the air and cast a condescending glance in Samuel's direction. "He is making a fool of himself, flirting in such an obvious manner. It is sickening."

Annabelle looped her arm through her friend's and turned her back to the seemingly happy couple. "I don't think it will ever be easy to see him, even after all this time."

"Probably not, especially after the shock and suddenness of his betrayal. And might I add that I don't care much for the lady, either." Katherine fluttered her fan in front of her face and cut her dark eyes toward the woman they were discussing.

The long-stored tension in Annabelle's shoulders dissipated. "You are rescuing me, you know." She laughed, touching her glove to her forehead to absorb the moisture gathering there. "This is a wretched state in which to be. I feel like I am in exile—as if everyone is staring at me, wondering why I am here."

"You are here because you were invited."

"I am here because *my brother* was invited, and I had no choice but to attend. My chamber seems a much safer place."

"Society as a whole is fickle." Katherine shook her head at the perceived injustice. "We are all just one misstep away from scandal. I am quite sick of it. I am eager for the season to draw to a close so we can return to the country and find some peace at last."

Annabelle lifted her fan to her face to cover her smile at her friend's lie. In truth, Katherine lived and breathed for society's endless cascade of chatter, the more shocking and outrageous the gossip, the better. But despite her propensity for spectacles, her companionship was welcome and, for a bit, put Annabelle at ease.

"Where are your brother and sister-in-law? I cannot believe they would leave you alone like this."

Annabelle tilted her head. "I presume Thomas is in the billiards room. I have not seen Eleanor since dinner."

Katherine snapped her painted fan open. "It is a pity that you and Mrs. Thorley are not closer."

Annabelle would have liked to enjoy a more sisterly affection with Thomas's wife, but Eleanor had never warmed to her. And since the demise of the family fortune and the public embarrassment of Annabelle's broken engagement, their strained relationship grew colder by the day.

Katherine drew nearer, her scent of lavender and vanilla sickly sweet in the already stifling space. "I have heard reports that a Mr. Treadwell is to be a guest in your home. Is this true?"

"I understand he is to be, although I have not seen him myself."

"I just encountered him in the parlor. I have been introduced to him on a prior occasion, but it has been several years since I last saw him. What a handsome gentleman he is. Never have I seen such brilliant blue eyes on a gentleman or lady." Katherine's eyes grew wide and her voice grew nasally, as it did anytime she had news to share or gossip to uncover. "I could not help but wonder if your brother invited him to encourage a relationship between the gentleman and yourself."

Annabelle's stomach dropped. At one time news of a handsome stranger would have breathed fresh life into her girlish dreams and fancies, but her brother's insistent instructions regarding Mr. Bartrell could not be ignored. Mr. Treadwell might be amusing, but Mr. Bartrell was wealthy—an attribute that always trumped any other. Annabelle fussed with the lacy hem of her glove. "I am aware of no such plan."

Katherine lowered her painted fan. "I'm relieved to hear it. Mr. Treadwell is dashing, yes, but such a dubious reputation precedes him. Just this evening I overheard two ladies discussing him and his questionable relationship with a young lady in Brighton."

Annabelle offered a smile. "I think I am quite safe from Mr. Treadwell and his dubious reputation, or so you call it."

Obnoxious masculine laughter rang out, and Annabelle lifted her gaze to look past Katherine. A shiver of dread pulsed through her. Thomas and Mr. Bartrell walked in her direction. She scanned the crowd, looking to see if Mr. McAlister accompanied them, but he was nowhere to be seen.

She swallowed the lump of discomfort welling within her. Mr. McAlister's written words hung heavy in her mind, and she had hoped to gain more clarification before encountering her brother.

Katherine, too, turned to identify the source and then whipped her head back around, nearly disrupting the jewel-encrusted comb holding her chestnut hair in place. She said nothing—a feat that, in and of itself, spoke volumes.

The men drew closer, and the deplorable manner in which Mr. Bartrell assessed Annabelle from the top of her head to the hem of her gown brought an uncomfortable flush to her cheeks.

His slovenly physique suggested frequent overindulgences of food and drink. Despite the impeccable cut of his emerald wool coat, it still managed to hang askew on his awkward frame. A limp marred his gait, and a bruise beneath his left eye suggested a recent skirmish.

Mr. Bartrell approached her boldly, the scent of brandy and perspiration clinging to his person. His voice boomed, rising above even the resounding clamor of the music and crowd. "If it isn't the beautiful Miss Thorley."

He reached out, grabbed her gloved hand with his bulky one, and pulled it toward him in rough ignorance. He leaned forward to press a kiss to the top of it.

The thought of his lips on her hand—even her gloved hand—mortified Annabelle, and in a precipitous moment of panic she jerked her hand from his clutch.

She froze, realizing what she had done. His action had been rude, yes. But so had hers. She could feel her brother's weighty gaze on her.

Annabelle found her voice and squeaked an introduction in an eager attempt to cover her breach of etiquette. "Mr. Bartrell, you are acquainted with Miss McCleod, are you not?"

At the introduction Katherine curtsied stiffly.

He gave a wobbly bow. "It is always a pleasure to meet one of Miss Thorley's charming friends."

Katherine's eyebrow arched, and she smiled coolly in response but said nothing. Her silent expression of shock at Mr. Bartrell's uncouth behavior validated Annabelle's rejection.

He seemed unaware of his impropriety. In fact, he flashed a broad smile, revealing two missing teeth, and rubbed his hands together in front of him. "My daughters were thrilled to have met you last week, Miss Thorley. They have spoken of nothing else since your visit."

Annabelle cringed inside at the memory of meeting his three children. They had been moody young ladies, and the eldest was only six years her junior. The thought of filling the role as mother to such girls jolted her. She grasped for something to say. Anything. She nearly choked on the dry words. "They are lovely girls."

"Lovely, yes. But such headstrong natures! Even the little one." A sly grin crossed his face. "I've no idea where they would encounter such a nature, would you, Miss Thorley?"

Annabelle could not make herself smile at his lackluster joke. "I do not."

A new melody started, and Mr. Bartrell extended his hand to her. "May I have the pleasure?"

Annabelle hesitated. She could think of no quick excuse.

Katherine reached out for Annabelle's arm, halting the conversation. She flashed a practiced, flirtatious smile she often employed to get her way and directed her words to Mr. Bartrell. "I do have to beg your forgiveness, sir, but I must have just one more moment of Miss Thorley's time. We are in the midst of a particular project, and you know how we ladies are. I know I can count on you to excuse her, can I not?"

Irritation blazed in his ruddy face, and his demeanor darkened in an instant. He cut his eyes toward Thomas, but then, as if knowing there was no way to cordially refuse Katherine's request, he cocked his head to the side and bowed.

Grateful for the separation, Annabelle allowed Katherine to guide her away. But Thomas's long, determined stride soon overtook the ladies' smaller ones. He muttered an excuse to Katherine and then gripped Annabelle's arm, pulling her away from her friend.

"How could you be so rude to Bartrell?" He directed her through the crowd.

Annabelle attempted to pull her arm free while she tried to match his pace. "How could *I* be rude? How could you be so rude as to interrupt my conversation with Katherine in such a boorish manner? She's the only person in attendance at this miserable ball who is willing to even speak with me, but now I'm fortunate she even acknowledges me at all."

"I could care less about Miss Katherine McCleod," Thomas hissed.

Annabelle refused to walk another step. "Take your hand off me immediately."

Thomas gripped her arm tighter and finally stopped walking. He turned to face her. "Have you taken leave of your senses? No man wants to be married to a woman as cold as you were."

"Married?" she hurled back, her eyes widening. "Let me be perfectly clear. I've no desire to be married to Mr. Bartrell. In fact, I very much doubt that any woman would desire to be married to him, regardless of her situation and circumstance."

"You speak like an ignorant fool." Thomas leaned in and lowered his voice. "It's time you realized your position in this world. A position, I might add, that is in great jeopardy. I saw you earlier, mourning after Goodacre like a pitiful child. He is no longer a part of your future, and if you are not mindful of your actions, your future will be grim indeed."

Rage filled her mind and ruled her tongue. "How dare you presume to speak so callously about my 'position,' as you call it? If it weren't for you and your reckless actions, I might be married to Mr. Goodacre at this very moment."

"*My* reckless actions? Consider where you would be without all I provide for you. Think with your head, not with your feminine heart, Sister, or mark my words, you will end up worse off than you could ever imagine."

Thomas's gaze roamed around the room to make sure no one was watching their exchange and straightened his coat with a sharp jerk. Without another word he turned on his heel, and Annabelle stared at his back as he strode away.

Her gaze shifted to Eleanor. Her sister-in-law had apparently been watching them, but her countenance was void of any sisterly sympathy. Void of condemnation or judgment. Pitiful acceptance.

Was that what lay before her?

To marry someone as vile as Mr. Bartrell and lose all sense of self?

Panicked, she looked around for her safe friend, but Katherine was nowhere to be found. And who could blame her?

Perhaps Thomas was right. Annabelle was living in a fantasy, in the false belief that her life was going to be joyous and at ease. Time had changed her circumstances, and she needed to change with them.

What would it be like to be free of the cares of society? To leave her home at Wilhurst House and never look back at London, with its pretentious parties, dizzying social scenes, dirty streets, and soot-filled air? What would it be like to begin again in a different town, like a freshly stretched canvas hungry for new art?

The elegant dancers blurred in and out of her vision, and she swiped a tear from her cheek. She no longer belonged in this world.

Oh, if she could only run away.

The idea was ridiculous, really. But as ridiculous as it was, it blossomed in her mind.

She *could* leave, she supposed, but she would need somewhere to go.

Her options were limited, for to whom could she turn? Katherine was helpful, but her propensity toward gossip made Annabelle nervous. Her former governess would likely accept her without question, but she now resided in Scotland. The journey would be arduous and far. Her childhood friend Lydia lived in the north, but she was now married and would be a mother soon. Annabelle could not possibly impose.

She ran her finger over the lace overlay on her bodice—a desperate attempt to fit into a world that no longer accepted her. Fear that this lonely, cold life was her destiny settled in her chest, and she could not dislodge the unpleasant thought from her mind. She glanced around the room at the familiar faces and glittering displays of wealth. Yes, it was lovely to think of escaping these constraints once and for all, but it was not to be. It was a daydream and would remain just that—a dream.

Chapter Six

Would the evening's mortification never end?

Annabelle's cheeks flamed and tears of humiliation blurred her vision as she tugged the hood of her cape lower over her eyes with her left hand and looped her right through the crook of her sister-in-law's arm. The cape's heat was stifling, but it protected her from the rain and the stares of onlookers. She kept her voice low. "Keep walking."

Behind them, Thomas's slurred speech rose above the clatter of departing carriages, and the crude laughter of his comrades muffled the gentle patter of rain and demanded the attention of the other departing guests.

The walk from the Baldwins' front entrance lasted only a few seconds, but for Annabelle it was as if time were standing still, freezing her in eternal degradation. At the carriage door, the footman lifted his gloved hand to help her enter. She glanced over her shoulder as her slipper landed on the step. A gathering of fashionable ladies huddled beneath a canopy, their eyes fixed on the boisterous spectacle. As if the scandalous rumor surrounding her family did not draw enough condemnation, her brother's lewd behavior ensured they would never be accepted in polite society again. If there was any question about restoring their family to a respectable station, Thomas's conduct tonight shattered it.

She plopped in the seat and leaned her head back on the tufted cushion. Next to her, Eleanor sniffed. Annabelle turned to her just in time to see a tear drop from her sister-in-law's eye and roll down the curve of her round chin. Empathy filled Annabelle, and she reached over and squeezed Eleanor's gloved hand.

Annabelle had never felt frightened of Thomas. Not really. But as the group of drunken men invaded the small, dark carriage, a thin cord of fear wound its way around her and began to tighten.

The entire carriage lurched as the men tumbled into the vehicle. Three of them—Thomas, Mr. Treadwell, and Mr. McAlister crammed onto the seat opposite her. Disappointment nipped. Even Mr. McAlister was under the influence. The meaning of his letter would have to wait. She inched closer to Eleanor, but to her horror, Mr. Bartrell wedged himself between Annabelle and the carriage wall.

He was too close. His strong scent of rum and port overwhelmed her, and she lifted her glove to her face to block the smell. Her pulse pounded and her head felt light as the carriage door swung closed and latched, trapping the nauseating scent of spirits and heat in the small space. There was no escaping. Not until the door opened once again.

She attempted to inch nearer to Eleanor, but her gown held her captive. Annabelle cleared her throat. "Mr. Bartrell, you are sitting on my gown."

He did not respond. Instead, his head was thrown back in raucous laughter.

Annabelle spoke louder to be heard above the commotion. "Mr. Bartrell, you are on my gown. Will you please move?"

She gave her skirt a little tug, and he turned his attention toward her.

Annabelle sank back against the seat, immediately regretting addressing him. He glared at her, the torchlight outside the window illuminating the perspiration on his full face and the intoxicated redness surrounding his dark eyes.

Annabelle's stomach clenched.

He leaned closer.

She shifted uncomfortably beneath the weight of his attention.

His words slurred and saliva sprayed from his mouth with each word. "Why are you so sour tonight, Miss Thorley?"

She grimaced as his hot breath grazed her face. The spirits had loosened his tongue—and his manners. Annabelle yanked her skirt free, and the delicate silk overlay ripped.

One of her last decent gowns. Ruined. She narrowed her eyes at him.

Mr. Bartrell slid his thick arm along the back of the bench, scraping the back of her cloak.

Every muscle in her body tensed. She glared at Thomas as best she could in the carriage's darkness, hoping he would notice Mr. Bartrell's assumptive behavior and put a stop to it. But her brother— her protector, her guardian—was engaged in conversation and paid no attention to the indecent display right in front of him.

Annabelle's fingers ached from the tight grip she maintained clutching her cloak close, as if by doing so she could protect her person from the reprehensible behavior around her.

Fortunately, the ride to Wilhurst House was a short one. Instead of delivering the passengers to the main entrance, the driver directed the carriage back toward the mews, no doubt to protect the family from any nocturnal onlookers who might behold the men in their intoxicated state.

The men did not seem to notice the change in protocol, and when the carriage finally drew to a stop, Mr. Bartrell stumbled from the carriage and turned. He bowed low and offered his hand to assist her down from the vehicle.

Annabelle blatantly refused the offer. It was rude to reject such assistance, but the thought of placing her hand in his, even for such a simple gesture, sickened her.

She thought his intoxication would prevent his notice of the offense, but as her foot touched the ground, Mr. Bartrell gripped her hand and pulled her to him, the suddenness of it causing Annabelle to lose her balance.

"How dare you!" she breathed, simultaneously attempting to steady herself and free her hand. "Let go of me this instant!"

His eyes narrowed to threatening slits, and he hissed in her ear, "You're being very mean, Miss Thorley. I don't care for it."

"And I don't care to be handled in such a fashion."

The torchlight slid across his face. Darkness lurked in his eyes, and a sinister expression took hold. "If you know what is good for you, you'll rethink the manner in which you address me."

She lifted her face. "I'll do no such thing."

"You're a bit too high and mighty for your station, aren't you? Mark my words, Miss Thorley. Once we are married, I will not tolerate such behavior. A woman like you must remember her place."

She jerked her arm free, sending the inebriated man stumbling backward. "I will never marry you."

"We'll see what your brother has to say about that." He laughed and leaned close, his rheumy eyes locked on her with unnerving self-confidence. "Do not doubt it, my pet. I will possess you."

Concerned her terror would write itself on her face, Annabelle clutched her cloak and whirled around, caring not that the wind had caught her hood and blown it back over her shoulders. The rain pummeled her hair, dripped down the sides of her face, and blurred her vision, but she was determined to put as much distance between Mr. Bartrell and herself as possible. She quickened her steps over the cobbled street and fixed her gaze on the door, but then something caught her eye.

A man was seated just outside the mews, his attention focused on her. It was unusual for a strange man to be present at this time of night.

She slowed her steps. The flickering lanterns illuminated the familiar wide-brimmed hat, and his dark, wild hair hung just below the hat's brim. His broad shoulders and strong jawline were unmistakable. He was the man who had saved her reticule from Miss Stillworth.

Anger flared. What right did men have to regard her this way? Was she really just a token to be treated like an object, a thing to be controlled? First, her brother demeaned her, then Mr. Bartrell treated her vilely, and now this strange man had followed her and stared at her as if she were on display at a fair.

It was not proper.

It was not to be tolerated.

Her social standing might be shifting, but she was still a lady. And she *would* be treated as such.

Despite the incessant rain and the menace of the night wind, she pivoted and approached the man boldly. Her humor had turned. Humiliation had worn her down, and the sense that life was spinning beyond her control consumed her.

"You are the man I met on the street today." Her words rang out like an accusation.

The man stood when she spoke. He had told her his name, but in her state she could not bring it to mind. He was taller than she remembered, and much more intimidating now that she was so near to him. Stubble shadowed his chin, and he appeared quite different in the night's darkness. It was then she noticed a dog at his feet, which had stood along with its master. She took a step back from the animal.

"I am, Miss Thorley."

She drew a sharp breath at the mention of her name. "I do not recall telling you my name, nor where I live."

"No, you did not."

Frustration mounting, Annabelle crossed her arms over her chest. "Then how do you know it? What are you doing here? Did you follow me?"

Her words did not rattle him. He remained exasperatingly calm. "I did not follow you. I am a guest here. That is, my master is a guest here. I am staying in the rooms above the mews."

Annabelle frowned. Was he speaking in riddles? She looked back at the unruly bunch behind her. "Who?"

He nodded toward the group. "Mr. Stephen Treadwell. I am the gamekeeper on his estate. We are traveling back to Fellsworth, and Mr. Treadwell had business with Mr. Thorley."

Annabelle's stomach clenched. He had not followed her. Nor had he behaved in an indecorous manner. She wanted to sink into the ground or turn and run for the sanctity of her chamber. Now she was the one behaving abhorrently. She had been wrong about this man who not only had come to her assistance earlier in the day, but did not deserve the harshness of her tone.

She swallowed the lump of pride. "Please accept my apologies, Mr. . . ."

"Locke. My name is Owen Locke."

"That's right. Mr. Locke."

"Yes, miss."

"Very well, then, Mr. Locke. I am sorry. I fear the lateness of the evening has affected my manners."

She turned to leave, but his words stopped her. "I overstep my bounds, I know, but is that gentleman troubling you?"

She followed the direction of his nod, and Mr. Bartrell came into view. The very fact that Mr. Locke had noticed the impropriety of Mr. Bartrell's behavior both unnerved her and stirred her. "No."

He pressed his lips together and stepped back. "Forgive the intrusion."

She stared at him for a moment, transfixed. She did not know this man, and yet he spoke as if he had some sort of authority over her, some reason to protect her.

"Belle!" Thomas's sharp call echoed in the night mist. "Come here. What are you doing, lurking about like that?"

She had no desire to rejoin the detestable party and needed to avoid her brother. Without another word she gathered her skirts and headed to the door, but just as she drew closer to it, Thomas closed the space between them and grabbed her wrist.

"Belle! Come join us here."

"Thank you, no."

Her brother refused to let her pass. "The night is young, and we have guests to entertain."

"It is *not* young. And *you* have guests to entertain, not I."

"Mr. Bartrell would like to better make your acquaintance. It would be rude for you to retire when your presence has been requested."

Her heart thudded and she looked around for an escape. At the door was the butler, who would be of no help, but just beyond him stood Crosley. Dear, helpful Crosley.

The situation was getting entirely out of hand. Annabelle wrenched her wrist free.

"Belle, wait!"

But she did not listen.

Her brother's footsteps rang heavily, if sloppily, behind her, but when she arrived at the door, Crosley held it open.

Annabelle stepped inside and locked the door behind her before her brother could reach her.

Owen clenched his fists at his sides as he watched the scene unfold. It was not right.

The night's weather carried away the words, but the actions he witnessed spoke volumes. In a span of mere minutes, he had seen not just one, but two instances of ill treatment toward Miss Thorley.

It did not matter if the woman was the finest lady or the beggar he had met on the street earlier that day. No woman deserved to be treated with such appalling disrespect.

He was poised, ready to intervene, when Thomas Thorley finally released his sister's wrist and she disappeared into the house.

Yes, Miss Thorley had been rude to him, but it had been the expression in her hazel eyes and not her words that affected him—for it was fear, not condescension, that radiated from her.

Owen recalled seeing the same expression once before: on his late wife's face. It had been in the days leading up to her death, but he had not recognized the significance of it until it was too late. He swore he would never suffer another human to feel fear if he could prevent it. And he had not—until this night.

"Locke."

Owen turned as Treadwell approached from the carriage. He'd been paying such close attention to Miss Thorley that he'd almost forgotten why he was waiting outside in the first place. "How was the ball?"

Treadwell chuckled and scratched the back of his head, then stared up at the black sky, as if contemplating his answer. "Amusing."

Disappointment stabbed at Owen, for Treadwell's eyes were red. His sloppy gait confirmed Owen's suspicion: Treadwell was intoxicated.

Owen frowned. He knew all too well that even men who were gentlemen by day could become quite altered under the influence. Promises would be forgotten; priorities would shift. He knew the answer to his question before even asking it. "Did you speak with Farley?"

Treadwell smacked his forehead in an exuberant display, twisting his face as if physically pained. "I forgot."

Owen heaved a sigh. In Treadwell's current state, perhaps it was for the best. "Another time, then."

"Definitely. You know I'll do everything in my power to help you. You're like a brother to me." Treadwell became everyone's brother with a pint of brandy, and his overly affectionate words slid against each other as the man swayed from side to side. "These things take time, and Farley is an old goat."

Even in Treadwell's altered state, he spoke the truth. It was a waiting game. But patience was not a virtue Owen could boast. He detested relying on others, and he was involved in a game of class now. Farley would never sell his land to a mere gamekeeper. It did not matter to Farley that Locke blood and sweat had transformed the thickets and groves for centuries and that Owen's ancestors were buried beneath its boughs. Legal ownership of the land would never change that fact. For now Owen had to be content to know that the wheels were being set into motion.

He looked back at the door through which Miss Thorley had disappeared. Mr. Thorley was pounding on it, demanding admittance while a male servant fiddled with the lock.

Concern for the young woman buzzed through Owen, and the most frustrating part was there was little he could do. She was inside the great house, and he was bunking in a room above the stables. Their paths would not cross again.

This world was one he did not care for. The groves and elms of Linton Forest were calling to him, even in the midst of the midnight hours, and his heart ached to return home to his daughter. The cruel treatment of Miss Thorley had awakened memories that would be best left forgotten, and once again, he was powerless to do anything about it.

Chapter Seven ——————————————————

*A*nnabelle stormed into her bedchamber and whipped her damp cape from her trembling shoulders. She tossed the garment on a nearby settee with a huff.

A cheery fire flamed merrily in the grate, as if attempting to soothe her rumpled spirit, but the voices downstairs prevailed.

Crosley followed behind her, retrieved the cape from the settee, and shook it out.

"I will not marry that man. I won't do it." Annabelle paced the small space. She yanked her long glove off her hand, finger by finger, and then dropped it onto a cushioned chair next to the blazing fire. "I would prefer to be an old spinster living on the streets than marry a man so arrogant, so condescending, so unkind."

Crosley pressed her lips together as she calmly waited to take the discarded gloves.

"And my brother!" Annabelle peeled her jeweled bracelet from her wrist. "How dare he. How dare he! He cannot force me to marry anyone, especially someone so revolting. You agree with me, do you not, Crosley?"

When she did not respond, Annabelle ceased her pacing and looked at the lady's maid. "Crosley?"

Crosley looked down at the floral carpet, as if deliberately avoiding Annabelle's eyes. "I don't know, miss."

Annabelle dropped her hand and turned. "What do you mean you don't know?"

Crosley shrugged and draped the glove over her arm. "Mr.

Bartrell is established and, from my limited knowledge, is generally well accepted in society. He is wealthy and can offer you security. You would have an elegant home. Nice possessions. There could be a worse husband, miss."

Annabelle shook her head in adamant protest. "But such things do not matter. Not when the gentleman in question—and I use the term *gentleman* loosely—would treat me with such discourtesy. Did you witness the display by the carriage?"

"I did." Crosley's voice was soft as she placed the gloves by the fire to dry.

Annabelle moved to the dressing table, dropped to the tufted bench with a huff, and yanked the woven ribbons from her hair. Perhaps she had been wrong to share her feelings with Crosley. She'd been foolish to think the woman could understand her situation. "Would you tolerate such treatment?"

Crosley unclasped the necklace from around Annabelle's neck and returned it to the jewelry cabinet. "Mr. Bartrell is a fine match and—"

"He's dreadful."

Crosley shrugged. "Many women would find a match like him fortunate."

Annabelle reached out and grabbed Crosley's hand. "But would *you* tolerate such treatment?"

At Crosley's hesitation Annabelle returned her hands to her lap and fixed her gaze on the lady's maid. "Please tell me. I really would like to know your opinion."

It was an odd request, Annabelle knew. Crosley's role was to care for Annabelle's gowns and dress her hair, not share her opinions on her mistress's personal life. But Annabelle was growing desperate. She had no family members to offer counsel. And the lines between mistress and servant were blurring at a rapid pace. There were times she and Crosley laughed together. They had even cried together.

In fact, if their situations were not so different, they might even be considered friends.

With a sigh Crosley sat on the settee next to the dressing table and fixed her light-blue eyes on Annabelle. "I know your heart is set on Mr. Goodacre, and Mr. Bartrell is certainly not as handsome or charming as he, but you must face reality."

Annabelle swallowed her objection. After all, she had asked for the opinion.

"I have great respect for the Thorleys, but your family's situation is precarious. Given your brother's decisions and your father's past actions, it might be difficult for you to make a more suitable match than Mr. Bartrell."

Annabelle felt as if she had been struck. "Are you suggesting that another man would not marry me?"

Crosley shook her head. "No, I am not saying that. But consider Miss Stillworth. I'd wager she never expected to find herself in the situation she is in. We never know what lies ahead of us, Miss Thorley, or what the consequences of our actions might be. Perhaps prudence and practicality would serve you better than the satisfaction of realizing your heart's desires."

Miss Stillworth's story was a sobering reminder of the world's harsh realities, especially for a woman. Annabelle pulled a pin from her hair. "I would not wish Miss Stillworth's circumstances on anyone, but I refuse to accept this as my only option. Something is underhanded about Mr. Bartrell. His nature is not trustworthy, and that I cannot abide. Perhaps I seem stubborn, but I will not marry that man. I refuse to become like Eleanor and be so frightened of my husband that I lock myself away. No. There has to be another way."

Crosley offered a reassuring smile. "I hope I did not speak too freely, and I am honored that you would ask my opinion. It is only that—an opinion. You'll figure this out, I've no doubt. Perhaps a good night's sleep. Things always seem brighter by the light of day."

Save for the fire's crackling, the women sat in silence as Crosley brushed Annabelle's hair. But instead of growing calmer, Annabelle's thoughts twisted tighter when the occasional shout or burst of laughter echoed from below.

Stroke after stroke Crosley brushed, and Annabelle attempted to make sense of the feelings churning within her.

Her world as she knew it was over. And yet, as she studied her face in the looking glass, she looked the same. Same light-brown hair. Same hazel eyes. Same oval face. Her features showed no sign of the scars on her heart.

She'd heard the tales of women who fell from society for this reason or the other. Never did she dream that she would count herself among them. Crosley was right. No more marriage proposals would come. No more flirting. No more girlish exploits. Her future lay before her, bleak and desolate. Her choices were clear: marry the obnoxious Mr. Bartrell or risk becoming like Miss Stillworth.

"There, all done." As Crosley lowered the brush to the dressing table, a shout made her freeze in midmotion and turn toward the door.

"Belle! Belle!" Thomas's voice grew closer with each repetition of the word.

Annabelle looked to Crosley's reflection in the looking glass, and the women locked gazes.

Thomas's footsteps clomped outside of Annabelle's bedchamber. "Belle!"

Panic—no, fear—seized Annabelle at the sound. He had been intoxicated, and by now would be more so. No good could come of a conversation with him.

Annabelle leapt up from her seat and lunged toward the door. Pulse racing, she turned the key and stepped back, staring at the wooden entry.

Her brother's heavy fist pounded on the door, causing both

Annabelle and Crosley to jump. He shook the brass handle from the other side, and when it would not open, he rapped on the door once more. "Open this door!"

Annabelle pressed her finger to her lips to tell Crosley to be quiet. She motioned for the lady's maid to go through her dressing room and lock the other entrance.

She turned back to face the door. Thomas hammered again, shaking the door in its frame so that Annabelle feared he might knock it in.

"Bartrell told me about your behavior by the carriage. How dare you!" Each strike pummeled her with fresh fear. "Need I remind you that you, too, are a guest in this home? You are here because *I* allow it. I provide for you, take care of you, and this is how you repay me? *Belle, open this door!*"

Chapter Eight

"*You are here because I allow it.*" Thomas's words echoed in Annabelle's mind as the mantel clock struck the second hour. She glanced at the clock's face and then resumed her pacing.

After an eternity of persistent pounding, her brother had ceased his efforts and returned to the party. His absence should have brought her a sense of peace. But no—panic took up residence in her heart.

Annabelle pushed her long locks away from her face and looked down at her trembling hands. She clamped them together in front her.

Wilhurst House could no longer be her home.

She had to leave. If she remained, she would become Mrs. Cecil Bartrell.

Crosley reentered the chamber from Annabelle's dressing room carrying a nightdress. "Are you ready to dress for bed?"

Tears sprang to Annabelle's eyes. "I can't stay here."

Crosley drew closer, her brow creasing. "What do you mean? In the morning things might seem—"

"Nothing will be fine. You know that as well as I do. There is no need to pretend."

Crosley lowered the linen nightdress. "But where would you go?"

Annabelle bit her nail as she considered her options. As far as she could determine, there was but one option. She turned to face Crosley as an idea, fresh and frightening, formed. It started as a glimmer, then her mind raced to keep pace with the onslaught of thought.

Fellsworth.

She might not have considered it except the gamekeeper mentioned it and by doing so revived the dormant memory.

Her uncle and aunt were her only other living relatives, but there had been no communication for years. Even if her brother did want to find her after she left, he would never think of looking for her there.

With renewed energy she hurried to her jewelry chest and pushed open the lid. She sorted through a handful of trinkets until she found what she sought: the carved hunting dog Uncle Edmund had given her all those years ago.

He had been eager to help her mother. Would Uncle Edmund help Annabelle now?

There was no way to know until she spoke with them. She just needed a way to get to Surrey. She had little actual money, but she held up jewel after jewel. These valuables could be sold.

She was not without options—not yet.

Annabelle glanced around the room. The elegance. The opulence. Once, such material advantages would have kept her firmly planted where she was, fearful of what it would be like to live without such luxuries. But day by day the world she knew was folding in on itself.

Shouts once again met her ears. They were almost like a warning. Then a different sound rang out. A sound so unwelcome, so out of place, Annabelle winced.

Crosley jumped up. "Was that a gunshot?" She ran to the door, flipped the lock, poked her head into the hall, looked to the right and left, and then straightened before she closed the door once again.

The two women exchanged glances.

Wilhurst House was growing dangerous. This was no longer the same home of her youth. Fear for her brother pricked, and Mr. McAlister's letter of warning flashed in Annabelle's mind. She did not doubt her brother was in trouble—he was far from innocent—but Thomas was beyond saving, at least by anything Annabelle could do.

Her path was unmistakable, and she knew just what she needed to do. It was time to leave.

Owen sat on the bench outside of the mews entrance. The storm had subsided, and now a gentle rain floated down from the moonless sky. A torch nearby crackled, and its light cast reflections on the wet cobbled street. He pulled his hat lower to guard his face from the rain.

Even during the early morning hours, soot and smoke thickened the muggy London air. How Owen longed to fill his lungs with Linton Forest's fresh air and earthy perfume. A fortnight had elapsed since he was last home and with his daughter, the longest they had been separated since his wife died nine years prior. He did not belong here, and the fact grew in veracity with each passing minute.

The sound of a gunshot had pulled him—and a handful of the Wilhurst House staff—from bed and urged him out into the night once again. As a gamekeeper he was no stranger to the monstrous blast of a rifle's fire. He associated the sound with field and forest, not a town like London.

Even now his pulse raced at the unexpectedness of it. The servants had made a thorough inspection of the property and declared the shot must have come from a neighboring house or a skirmish on the street, yet Owen remained uneasy. He'd witnessed the inebriated state of the men upon their return from the Baldwin dinner. No good could come of it.

The shot's sharp crack had thrust his best bird dog, Drake, into a frenzied state, and now, after several minutes of silence, the giant brown dog finally sat and leaned against his leg, panting heavily. On more than one occasion Drake's keen nose and sharp instinct had warned him of trouble, and Owen perceived the dog's uneasiness. He surveyed the narrow alley with a trained eye and placed his hand on Drake's head. "It's all right, boy."

He was about to return to the tiny chamber above the stables when movement by the servants' entrance drew his attention. He squinted to see through the misting rain and shifting darkness.

The door opened wider, and a figure clad in a dark cloak emerged into the narrow courtyard. He'd expected to see a footman or another male servant, yet a slight feminine frame stood shrouded in the shadows.

He straightened. What would a woman be doing out at this hour?

Drake jumped to his feet and barked, and the woman jerked around and looked in his direction.

"Sit," Owen ordered.

The figure paused. Then shifted. Then headed in his direction.

Unsure of what to expect, Owen stood and took hold of his dog's collar.

"Mr. Locke?"

The woman's voice was soft and low, so much so he almost wondered if it was the whistle of the wind or his ears playing tricks on him. He cocked his head to the side. "I'm Owen Locke."

The figure finished crossing the courtyard and stepped near the mews wall, out of the torch's light. She pushed her hood back to expose her face.

Miss Annabelle Thorley.

It would have been one thing if the woman had been a servant, but she was one of the ladies of the house.

Unaccompanied.

In the predawn hours.

Alone in his presence.

Owen was far from an expert on the subject of proper behavior for a lady, but he was certain this wasn't it.

The wind picked a few wayward strands of her hair and danced with them about her face. She cut her eyes to the left and then looked over her shoulder. "I must speak with you."

Drake pranced around Owen's feet, and Miss Thorley's eyebrows arched as she stepped back from the animal.

"He'll not harm you. What can I do for you?"

She fixed her gaze on him. "Can I count on your discretion?"

"Discretion?" he echoed, surprised at the odd request.

"Yes. I need assistance, Mr. Locke, but I must request that what we discuss remains between us."

Earnestness burned brightly in her eyes, but alarm coursed through his veins. Nothing good could come of such an agreement with a lady. He knew nothing of her. And she knew nothing of him.

What assistance could he possibly offer her?

The memory of Mr. Bartrell's rough grip on her compelled him. He'd failed to protect his own wife from another man's violent hand, and the fact would haunt him until the day he drew his last breath.

Was Miss Thorley in some sort of danger? Whatever her reason, he was quite certain that if he did not help her, or at least hear her request, and some peril were to befall her, he would never forgive himself.

He gave a nod. "It will."

"You said you were from Fellsworth, is that correct?"

"It is."

"My uncle lives in Fellsworth, and I need to travel there immediately."

Fellsworth was not a large village. Surely he would know her uncle. "Who is he?"

"Mr. Edmund Langsby. He is, or at least was, the superintendent at Fellsworth School."

"Langsby?" he repeated, making sure he had heard the name correctly.

"Yes." Her eyes widened. "Are you acquainted with him?"

"I know him well." In truth Owen had known Langsby his entire life. But he had never heard the older man mention family, let alone a niece.

"I was hoping you could arrange transportation—a carriage—to convey me there as soon as possible. This morning, in fact."

Owen frowned. "That is very sudden."

"I would not ask, but it is imperative I leave London immediately."

Something was amiss. There was a carriage here in the mews. If there was need of a carriage, did she not have one at her disposal?

The entire night was not adding up. The violence. The drunken display of vulgar behavior. The gunshot. And now this.

He needed to make sense of it all. "Is Langsby expecting you?"

She hesitated. It was the first time she broke eye contact. She toyed with the hem of her cape. "Not exactly. But he will accept me. I would hire a carriage on my own, but I admit I am not really certain how to go about doing so. You were so helpful in the street earlier today, I thought you might . . ." She looked to the ground, and the torch's light splayed the shadow from her eyelashes on her smooth cheeks.

Owen would like to think he could pride himself on rationality, but her demure beauty and vulnerability affected him. Did she know how convincing she was? Was the innocence in her face authentic? Or had she perfected such an affectation to get her way? He'd known women who had mastered the art of doing just that. Yet he was in danger of succumbing nonetheless.

Her shoulders slumped slightly. "I can see that you are suspicious of me."

He shook his head. "No, not suspicious. But is there not someone at Wilhurst House who can assist you? Surely your brother would arrange for your travel during daylight hours."

She lifted her chin, as if his interest in her situation reenergized her. "This travel is of a personal nature."

He shifted his weight. "In other words, you don't want anyone to know you have gone."

She held his gaze for several moments. "No. I do not."

He folded his arms across his chest. Never had he been asked to do such a thing. Drake turned a circle and then stretched out his nose to sniff her hand.

Miss Thorley hesitantly reached out a slender hand and patted the dog's head, then tucked it back in her cape. "I would, of course, compensate you for your trouble."

It was the second time now that she had mentioned paying for his service. She clearly saw him as a hired hand—a servant to do her bidding.

Prudent thought screamed that he should decline to help her. What if she was leaving unwisely—to elope with a rogue or some other unsuitable reason? But then again, what if such an action was her last resort?

Miss Thorley winced as a crash and shouts sounded from somewhere in the house. She turned wide, expectant eyes to him and bit her lower lip. In that moment she seemed very fragile. Her brave facade was beginning to crumble.

He recognized the sounds of drunken debauchery, and he recognized the look of fear. As fond as he was of Treadwell, his employer did have a certain reputation, and he suspected the men in his company possessed a similar nature. He could not, in good conscience, deny her.

If he refused to assist her, she would undoubtedly find a way to proceed on her own. But he doubted she understood the danger of a young lady engaging in such an undertaking. She could end up in a more dangerous situation.

Another shriek echoed from the house. A fight of some sort was ensuing.

Her full lower lip trembled as she opened her mouth to speak. "I—I can see I am troubling you. Good night, Mr. L—"

"Be at the corner where I first met you. A carriage will be waiting for you at dawn's light."

She expelled her breath, and for the first time since he had met her, she smiled. "Thank you, Mr. Locke. I will be there."

Chapter Nine

"Crosley! Where are you?" Annabelle flung open her chamber door and burst inside. "Quickly! We must hurry."

Crosley entered the sleeping chamber from the attached dressing room. Her brow furrowed as she assessed her mistress. "You're all wet! Did you go out of doors?"

"I did, but that isn't important." Annabelle wiped rain from her cheek. "I need your assistance." Energized by her conversation with Mr. Locke, she tossed her cape from her shoulders, scurried to her wardrobe, pulled the heavy oak doors open, and sifted through the gowns inside. "Where is my pink gown? The one with the silver flowers embroidered on it?"

Crosley scampered behind her to retrieve the damp cloak. "What do you need that for? It is time to retire. Perhaps later in the morning—"

"No, this cannot wait until later." Annabelle finally stopped her search and whirled around to face Crosley.

"Why not?"

"Because I won't be here in the morning."

Crosley froze. A frown darkened her expression. "I don't understand."

Annabelle resumed her search, found the gown in question, and folded it over her arm. "I can't stay here, Crosley. I simply can't. I am leaving at dawn to travel to Fellsworth. And you must come with me."

Crosley dropped the cape on the settee. "Fellsworth? Where is Fellsworth? You aren't making any sense. You can't just leave!"

"I can," muttered Annabelle as she reached down in the bottom of the wardrobe and retrieved a pair of kid half boots. "And I will."

"How will you get out of London, let alone to another town? And what will you do for money?"

A rogue sense of adventure surged through Annabelle and ignored Crosley's concerns. "This is my opportunity for a fresh beginning, free of this nonsensical behavior, and I'm going to seize it."

"But you've hardly even been outside of London. How will you get there?"

Annabelle tossed the boots on her bed, lifted the candle from her dressing table to light her way, and stepped closer to Crosley. "Do you remember Mr. Locke? The man we met when we encountered Miss Stillworth on the street earlier?"

Crosley nodded and pushed a stray lock of blonde hair from her face.

"He is the gamekeeper on Mr. Treadwell's estate and is traveling with him now. In fact, he is staying in rooms above the mews while Mr. Treadwell is a guest here."

Crosley propped her hand on her hip. "Is that where you went? How do you—?"

"He has agreed to arrange a carriage to transport me to Fellsworth." Annabelle handed the candle to Crosley, moved to the chest at the foot of her bed, and knelt before it. "My uncle is a school superintendent there."

Crosley held the candle up high to give Annabelle plenty of light. "I've never heard you mention an uncle before."

Annabelle pushed open the trunk's lid. "He's my mother's brother. I only met him once when I was a child. Thomas has never met him and I daresay he may not even know of Uncle Langsby's existence. Thomas would never think to look for me there. I can disappear."

"How do you know you can trust this man, this Mr. Locke? He is a stranger. He could be a criminal. Or worse. He could be a murderer."

Crosley's point was a valid one. 'Twas no secret, impulsiveness was a trap that often snared Annabelle. Despite this flaw, she had always been able to rise above any truly negative outcomes. But never had she even dreamed of any action this brazen and reckless. But was she any safer here than with a man she did not know?

She spoke quickly, as if to convince Crosley as well as herself. "I am willing to take my chances. Besides, Mr. Locke will not be traveling with us. He's only making carriage arrangements. We will be quite safe."

"That's even worse. It is not safe for a woman to travel alone." Crosley shook her head, and in a rare moment of displayed affection, she rested her hand on Annabelle's shoulder. "I implore you to act prudently. You've rarely traveled outside of London, and you've never traveled alone."

Annabelle jumped to her feet, abandoning her search of the trunk, and grabbed Crosley's hands. "That is exactly why you need to come with me."

The women locked gazes for several moments, and then Crosley drew a deep breath. "Please help me understand. Your brother is my employer. Will you be retaining my service in Fellsworth? Will I still be your lady's maid? And if I don't go with you, what of my position here?"

Annabelle dropped Crosley's hands. The first shadow of discouragement fell on her since she had left Mr. Locke. She had not considered the fact that Crosley might not accompany her. But she was right. Annabelle did not pay Crosley's wages. Her brother did.

Annabelle yanked the valise from the trunk and stood. "You are *my* lady's maid. So without me, I fear there will be no position here for you."

Crosley swallowed and looked to the ground.

Annabelle hated to see her uncomfortable, so she forced a cheery tone to her voice. "You can return to London and find another position after I am in Fellsworth. Or, consider that my uncle runs a school there, or at least he did. He might know of a position for you. Either way, I will write you a glowing recommendation. Please."

Annabelle chewed her lip. Time was not on her side, and her confidence wavered.

A final idea popped into her mind. She hurried to her bureau and lifted her jewelry box. She retrieved a gold necklace with a small ruby pendant. Her father had given it to her when she was just a girl. She would hate to part with it, but right now, fear lanced her sense of sentimentality.

She clenched her fingers around the piece and squeezed. Now was not the time to worry about such details.

"Accompany me to my uncle's house and this is yours. I don't care what you do with it. Keep it or sell it, but consider this payment for a service."

Crosley's blue eyes grew wide.

It was a generous offer, and perhaps a foolish one on Annabelle's part, for the necklace was easily worth at least a year's wages for a lady's maid. But she was not so obtuse that she did not see the truth in Crosley's warning. Annabelle was acting rashly. She needed Crosley with her to be a voice of reason. And traveling would be much safer with a companion.

Crosley closed the space between them and clutched the piece in her work-worn hands. "Are you certain?"

Annabelle nodded. "Indeed I am."

"Very well. I'll go with you."

Annabelle smiled and hugged Crosley. "Wonderful! As long as we are together we shall be fine."

Crosley did not return the embrace. "You will write me a letter of recommendation, though? Once we are in Fellsworth?"

"Of course. It will be the first thing I do." Annabelle reached out once again and squeezed Crosley's hand. "I am in your debt. Thank you."

A slow grin slid across Crosley's face and dimpled her cheek.

"Now, now. Enough of that. What are the arrangements you made with Mr. Locke?"

Annabelle propped open the valise and pushed a wayward lock from her face with the back of her hand. "We are to meet him at dawn at the corner where we encountered Miss Stillworth. A carriage will be waiting."

"Well, if you trust him, then I must too. We'll only be able to take what we can carry. What will you take with you?"

"I can get my own things. You go pack what you need and meet me here."

Crosley turned to leave, but Annabelle stopped her. "Wait. I can't take all of these gowns with me. Please. Take what you want."

Crosley stopped, and her mouth fell open. "I can't."

"Of course you can. If anyone can alter them, you can. After all, you made several of them. I insist."

Crosley stepped toward the wardrobe as if she were looking at the gowns for the first time, when in truth she saw them every day. "I wouldn't know, miss."

"Here, we must hurry." Annabelle reached into the wardrobe and retrieved several gowns—one of pale-blue sprigged muslin, another of cream-colored lustring embroidered with lilac flowers, a third winter gown of printed broadcloth, and a final one of hand-painted silk with intricate Vandyke points decorating the hem. She snatched a dark-green spencer, a shawl of white Indian lace, and several pairs of thin kid slippers and extended all the items toward Crosley. "Take these, and enjoy them."

Crosley's eyes grew wide. "But this is too much, surely."

"I will never step foot in this chamber again, and they all won't fit in my valise. Now go pack your things."

With a small skip in her step, Crosley turned and fled the room.

Annabelle's heart thudded as she propped her hands on her hips and assessed her belongings. She needed to hurry. She gathered four gowns of varying weights and styles, chemises and petticoats, and other necessary garments that could be rolled small enough to fit in her valise. She exchanged her satin dancing slippers for a sturdier pair of beige kid boots. She gathered her brush to clean her teeth. Her comb. Her rosewater. She hurried to her jewelry box and gathered what she could sell.

She opened the chest's smaller drawers to ensure she did not miss anything important and gathered a few other treasures: a letter from her governess, several of her smaller paintings, and the toy dog Uncle Edmund had given her. She hesitated. Her watercolor box sat on the table. It would be awkward to carry, but she could not leave it behind.

She scurried to the small table next to her bed and retrieved the journal that had been her mother's. She flipped over the leather cover and thumbed through the stiff pages. Verses and prayers written by her mother's hand graced each page, and tiny notes were written along the sides.

Annabelle rarely opened this book, for the words inside stirred precious memories and brought more pain than comfort. These pages held a glimpse inside the heart of the woman who had endeavored to raise a lady of faith. As she turned the pages, she saw prayer after prayer written on behalf of her children—for happiness and security.

Annabelle snapped the book shut.

Her mother's prayers must have gone unheard.

Once she was certain she had retrieved all her valuables, she moved to her writing desk. Despite her desire to disappear without a trace, it was necessary to leave some sort of letter so Thomas would not assume she was kidnapped and try to find her.

The contents of Mr. McAlister's letter caught her off guard. Her brother was in trouble, she was sure of it. The last thing she wanted was for that trouble to follow her to Fellsworth.

She opened her drawer to grab a piece of paper but spied something she had not touched in months: the stack of letters Samuel had written to her during their courtship.

She lifted the bound bundle. Dozens of memories rushed her at the sight. She should leave these. For what did they mean to her now? They were part of a life she would never again reclaim. But something within her could not bear the thought of parting with these keepsakes. They were a symbol to her, gleaming in a world that, at the moment, loomed dark and dangerous.

Without another thought she tucked the prayer journal, along with the letters, in her valise. She could burn them later if she wanted. But chances were, once she fled she would never return to London.

Her fingers trembled as she applied pressure to the quill. Gone was the beautiful penmanship her governess had spent months helping her perfect. The activity in her brain seemed to slow yet race at the same time. She was not sad to leave London; quite the opposite was true. But the magnitude of the journey before her overwhelmed her senses.

The ink was splotchy as her quivering hand attempted to keep the quill's point smoothly on the paper:

Thomas,

I am grateful to you and Eleanor for your kind hospitality, but the time has come for me to leave London. Perhaps one day our paths will cross again, perhaps not. In the meantime, I wish you both well.

Your sister,
Annabelle

She folded the letter and propped it against the candlestick on her desk. Once this letter was read, there would be no turning back.

Chapter Ten

"We don't have to proceed." Crosley poked her head out of Annabelle's chamber and peered down the darkened corridor. "There is still time to change your mind."

Annabelle tightened her grip on her valise. Excited energy had given way to anxious trepidation as she stood cloaked and prepared to leave the only home she had ever known. "I'm certain this is the right course."

"Very well, then. Let's go down the back stairwell," Crosley whispered. "There's less chance that we will be discovered."

The servants' stairs were awkwardly narrow. With no candle to guide their way, Anabelle struggled to maintain her balance on the uneven steps. Her valise bumped against the close stone wall, and her foot slipped on the worn wood.

As they descended to Wilhurst House's main level, Annabelle held her forefinger to her lips to signal Crosley's silence.

Tense male voices echoed from the billiards room. "Did you hear something?"

Another responded, "I didn't hear anything."

"Yes, I heard something. I'm certain of it. Coming from the hall."

Annabelle stood perfectly still and clutched her watercolor box to her chest. She was so close to escaping the home's confines. She would not falter now.

For several moments all was silent, but then heavy footsteps resounded from the polished floor. Before the women could retreat back to the stairwell, Thomas appeared in the wide doorway. Yellow firelight glowed behind him, illuminating his disheveled dark hair and his clenched jaw. He was still dressed in his formal attire, though his coat had been discarded, but it was his eyes that caught her attention. They were wide and wild, not unlike Miss Stillworth's had been. Annabelle lowered her gaze to his waistcoat. Dark splotches marred the patterned fabric.

Was that blood?

Her heart thudded and panic squeezed the air from her lungs.

The night's odd events slid into place, like a puzzle being completed.

The shouts.

The gunshot.

The blood clearly was not his.

But whose was it?

The siblings stared at each other for several moments, and then he nodded toward the valise in her hand. "What are you doing?"

Everything she needed—or wanted—to say was in the letter. She attempted to push past him, but he flung out his arm.

As she forced her way forward he smacked her across the face to stop her, the impact slinging white stars across her vision. Disoriented and confused, she struggled to keep her footing.

While Annabelle regained her composure, tiny Crosley lunged forward, shoved Thomas's chest, and lurched his inebriated form backward.

Crosley grabbed Annabelle's hand and pulled on it. "Run!"

Had Miss Thorley changed her mind?

Owen hopped down from the carriage, his boots landing in a puddle formed by the midnight rain.

He glanced to the right, then to the left, and squinted to see in the low-lying, shifting fog, the thickness of which would rival that of any forest or grove.

No sign of the lady.

The coachman called down from his seat, his gravelly voice gruff with annoyance. "I thought you said we were to meet someone here at dawn. Where are they?"

Owen strained to see in the purple mist. "Just a few more minutes."

Dawn was arriving, and with it the early morning activity swarmed. Owen stepped aside to allow a woman carrying a basket of white flowers to pass, and a cart transporting crates of chickens rattled by. Somewhere a boisterous laugh pealed in the still air, and in the distance a bawdy drinking song cackled in dissonant tones. With every passing moment the day's light gained strength and intensity. He shifted uncomfortably. Maybe she had changed her mind.

While he watched a man struggle to control a young horse, he heard footsteps running toward him, and a breathless voice called out, "Mr. Locke."

He turned to see Miss Thorley, shrouded in a cloak of gray wool. As she approached she let down the hood, and he narrowed his eyes. A fresh blue blemish marred her pallid cheek.

He sucked in a sharp breath and expelled it slowly. The notion that any man could do this to a woman infuriated him, and the sight bolstered his conviction: he was right to assist her.

He reached for the wooden box she toted under her arm. "I was beginning to think you decided not to come."

Miss Thorley gave her head a sharp shake, determination dominating her expression. "No, sir. I will not stay at Wilhurst House."

As she spoke, a petite woman scurried around the corner, struggling under a satchel's weight. She drew to a stop next to Miss

Thorley. She rested her hand on her hip and leaned over, trying to catch her breath. "I had no idea you could run so fast, Miss Thorley."

The woman's speech was not as refined as Miss Thorley's, nor was her cape cut nearly so fine. The top of her blonde head barely came up to Miss Thorley's shoulder, but her light eyes sparkled and her cheeks reddened.

This woman had been with Miss Thorley when they encountered the thief.

Miss Thorley pushed her hair from her face. "Mr. Locke, allow me to present Miss Margaret Crosley. My . . . companion. Miss Crosley will be accompanying me on my journey."

He raised his eyebrows. He'd assumed she'd be traveling alone. He was uncomfortable enough with arranging such travel for one lady . . . but two?

He bowed toward Miss Crosley, and she dipped her head in response.

Miss Thorley looked to the carriage. "I trust this is the conveyance we are to take?"

"It is. Allow me." He reached out to take Miss Thorley's valise.

She handed the bag to him. "Thank you for making the arrangements. I trust the driver needs payment for his service."

"I have taken care of it."

She fished in her belongings and withdrew a small purse. "Will you kindly give this to him? It should cover the costs."

Owen crossed his arms over his chest. "As I said, I have taken care of it."

She held up her hand in refusal. "Then please, you must keep it for your trouble."

Growing annoyed with her incessant attempts to pay him, he gently pushed it toward her. "I don't know what your plans consist of, but you may need that more than I do."

To end the conversation, Owen took Miss Crosley's bag and put it and Annabelle's valise in the carriage. "Are we ready?"

"We?" Miss Thorley blinked and looked toward her companion. "Miss Crosley and I are ready, if that is what you mean."

"No, I mean *we*." Owen pulled open the carriage door. "I intend to accompany you to Fellsworth."

Miss Thorley's eyes grew wide. "That is not what we agreed upon."

"It is dangerous for women to travel alone, and I will not have your fate—whatever it may be—on my conscience."

Miss Thorley clenched her jaw, and red blotches appeared on her neck. "Surely you have duties to tend to. We have no wish to keep you from your responsibilities."

"Edmund Langsby is a friend of mine. He would not permit a woman to travel unaccompanied, and neither will I. Now, either I accompany you, or I will send the driver on his way. Your choice."

After several tense seconds, the blonde chimed in. "Oh, it won't be so bad, Miss Thorley. How long can the ride take? The sooner we are on our way, the better."

An entire silent conversation transpired as the women locked gazes at length. Miss Thorley sighed. "Very well, Mr. Locke. We should be grateful for your company."

Owen opened the door wider and offered his hand first to Miss Thorley and then to Miss Crosley.

He waited until the women were settled before he joined them in the carriage. He had no idea what the next few hours would hold, but he did know one thing for certain: there was no turning back now.

Chapter Eleven

*A*nnabelle settled into the plain rented carriage and glanced through the window. The sun was rising in the morning sky, and London's dirty landscape had given way to the gentle beauty of pastoral fields and verdant meadows.

She rested her gloved hand on the carriage's hard bench. With the simple black leather seats and stark brown walls, the vehicle was not as fashionable as her family's. She recalled the luxurious blue velvet trimming and lush carpets at her feet.

None of that mattered anymore. All that mattered now was getting safely out of London.

She lifted her palm to her cheek. How it burned. Had Thomas's hand left a mark? Try as she might, she could not erase the memory of the fury in his countenance after he struck her. A shiver cascaded through her.

Next to her, Crosley had fallen asleep. Her former lady's maid had removed both her bonnet and her cape and now used the cape as a blanket. Her head rested on the carriage wall, and long locks of hair hung over her face. The night had been a long, sleepless one for both of them, and now would be the ideal time to rest. Annabelle would need her energy and her wits about her to plead her case to her aunt and uncle. Whereas Crosley had little trouble finding peace, Annabelle's heart raced with uncertainty.

She wished Crosley would awaken. In Annabelle's normal world, the impropriety of being alone with a man in a carriage was unforgivable, and Crosley had served as a chaperone on numerous occasions. But Annabelle had broken with propriety the moment she decided to leave London. There would be no recapturing it. The moment her foot touched the carriage step, she traded the life she knew for another one yet unknown.

Annabelle took advantage of the silent moment to assess the man who had offered her so much assistance. Across from her, Mr. Locke's arms were folded over his chest, and his lips were pressed in a firm line. She could not tell if he was angry, annoyed, or merely tired. She had always prided herself on being a decent judge of another's emotion, but Mr. Locke was hard to read, for his austere expression displayed none.

He was a handsome man, she decided. His hair was dark—almost black. It was not short, nor was it long enough to be gathered in a queue. It hung about his face, wild and untamed, in thick curls. Dark stubble accented a strong jaw and cleft in his chin, and his tanned coloring stood as a testament to a profession that kept him out of doors. He was not necessarily dressed as a gentleman, but he dressed well nonetheless.

She had never met a gamekeeper prior to Mr. Locke, but he did not look the part of a servant. Fawn buckskin breeches hugged muscular legs, and his well-cut coat of sturdy dark-blue wool emphasized broad shoulders. His light-gray linen waistcoat was buttoned high on his chest, and his neckcloth had come slightly loose.

He looked uncomfortable, like an animal trapped in a cage much too small for it. Thick, black lashes framed his chocolate-colored eyes, which were fixed on the landscape flashing by, unaware of her assessment.

How much she owed this man. Had their paths not crossed unexpectedly, she doubted she would have had the courage to set a plan into motion.

Why had he helped her? He had not needed to, and more than

once he declined her offer of compensation. She had even been rude to him. Could he really just be kind? She had never known anyone willing to do something for another without the promise of a return.

He looked over and caught her staring.

She was far too tired to reprimand herself or even to think of anything clever to say. The entire night passed without sleep, and her cheek ached from where she had been struck.

He was seeing her at her worst.

"Your friend must be weary." She was grateful when he spoke and shattered the uncomfortable silence.

Annabelle glanced over at Crosley, who had curled in farther toward the carriage wall. With every breath a little snore escaped her nose. "It is amazing that she can sleep with all this movement. But it has been a long night."

"I'll wager it has. You'll be at Langsby's house before you know it. Your aunt will see you are well taken care of."

His confident words were like a balm. "How long have you known my aunt and uncle?"

"Let me think." He ran his large hand down his face. "I've known Langsby all my life. He and my father were friends. I thought I knew him well. That is why it was such a surprise to meet you."

"I am not surprised he never mentioned me," Annabelle said matter-of-factly before pausing to choose her words. "Every family has a story, Mr. Locke. Mine is no different. Mr. Langsby is my mother's brother. He and my father were at odds. After my mother died, the relationship ceased completely. I have not heard his name mentioned in our house for at least a decade."

"So you've not had contact with him?"

Annabelle shook her head. "Not since my mother's death. It is hardly proper to arrive unannounced, but surely my uncle will understand, given the—"

When she realized what she was saying, she stopped short.

76

She did not want Mr. Locke—or anyone else—knowing too much about her.

He returned his attention to the landscape. The white morning light slid through the opening, highlighting the straightness of his nose. "Langsby is a reasonable man. Strict, disciplined, but sensible. He will be happy to see you. Have you ever been to Fellsworth?"

She nodded. "Once, many years ago when I was a child."

Mr. Locke shifted on the bench. "I usually see Langsby a couple of times a week. My daughter attends Fellsworth School, and I visit her there often."

Annabelle did not know why it should surprise her to hear that Mr. Locke had a daughter. His demeanor seemed more suited to that of an outdoorsman than of a family man. It stood to reason that if he had a daughter, he had a wife. But she would not be so impolite as to inquire about such personal details. So Annabelle remained silent. She'd experienced more than enough impropriety for one day, and she had no wish to open herself up to more.

"How is your cheek?"

Annabelle lifted her head, and her hand flew to her face. "Oh dear, I have not seen it. Does it look bad?"

He clicked his tongue and gave his head a sharp shake. "It looks like it hurts."

She slumped back against the seat. "I hoped it would not leave a mark. I can only imagine what my uncle will think."

Mr. Locke leaned forward and rested his elbows on his knees. "I don't pretend to know what you have been through or how you have gotten that mark on your cheek. All I know is what I have seen with my own eyes. 'Tis not my place to say, but I think you made a brave—and wise—decision to leave. Your uncle will not turn you away. Nor will I. You just need ask and I will serve how I can."

He stared into her eyes for several moments, as if to convey his sincerity. His kindness sparked something in her—a sense of connectedness and safety—that she had not felt in a very long time. The sensation frightened her, but at the same time the tension in her shoulders eased. Her heart wanted to rest in the security of his confidence, but her mind cautioned her against misplacing her trust.

She reached into her cloak pocket and wrapped her fingers around the dog carving. In her hasty packing, the trinket had found its way into her pocket instead of her valise. She clutched the tiny toy and pulled it free.

Memories from her visit to her uncle's came to her in snippets: A faded, autumnal garden behind the superintendent's cottage. The overpowering floral aroma of her aunt's rosewater. The mess of dusty books cluttered on the shelves in her uncle's library.

"What do you have there?" Mr. Locke's words interrupted her thoughts. "May I?" He held out his hand.

"Of course." She placed the carving in his work-worn palm.

He gave a little chuckle. "A spaniel."

"It was my mother's when she was a girl. Uncle Edmund gave it to me when I was in Fellsworth. I suppose it is silly that I still have it."

"No, not silly." He handed it back to her. "I purchased a dog very like that the other day."

"You did? I never really imagined anyone buying a dog before."

"Mr. Treadwell and I traveled to Cambridge to visit a renowned breeder. We buy at least one or two puppies a year to train as hunting dogs. The spaniel I referred to is just a puppy, of course, and she is as wild as the day is long. But with the right training, she will make a good bird dog one day."

"Where is the puppy now?"

"She's still in London, at the kennel in a local stable where we board the animals while Mr. Treadwell is a guest at Wilhurst House. We'll transport the dogs home when Mr. Treadwell is ready to return to Bancroft Park."

"I'm afraid I know little about hunting dogs, or even animals in general. I have rarely traveled outside of London. My father and brother used to attend hunting parties, but that was long ago, and I never accompanied them."

"Yes, I have met your brother before."

Annabelle snapped her head up. "You have?"

"On several occasions. He is a regular guest at Bancroft Park during the shooting season."

Annabelle drew a deliberate, slow breath. She would not ask Mr. Locke about his opinion of Thomas, but apprehension pulsed through her. If Mr. Locke knew of her brother, who else in Fellsworth did as well? She wanted to escape her brother's influence, not land somewhere he frequented.

Their conversation fell quiet for several minutes. After a while Annabelle thought he might have drifted off to sleep.

"You knew her, didn't you?"

After their silence, his question startled her. She drew her eyebrows together in question.

"The woman on the street."

Annabelle stared down at her hands. "I did. That is to say, I do." Conversation with Mr. Locke was becoming easier, and she felt as if some sort of explanation was necessary. "Her name is Henrietta Stillworth. She was a friend of mine at one time. We lost contact years ago. I had heard that her family had encountered financial hardships, but I never would have suspected such an outcome."

"It was kind not to report her. Many would not have been so gracious."

Annabelle gave a little shrug. "I only wish I could do more for her. It is a sad reality for women, Mr. Locke. She was raised with every advantage, but it is shocking to see how quickly it can dissolve into nothing. I must be careful; otherwise I could very well find myself in the same predicament."

"Nonsense. You have family. Langsby will come through for you."

"I hope you are right, Mr. Locke." She smiled at him.

The carriage's wheel hit a rut, and the entire conveyance shifted and leaned before setting right again. Annabelle pressed her hand against the wall to steady herself, and Crosley twisted in her seat, but not before muttering indecipherable words and giving an un-ladylike snore.

Despite the pain in her face and the somberness of her situation, Annabelle could not help but laugh at the display. Mr. Locke also chuckled, and then he fixed his attention on her. "All will be well, Miss Thorley. You shall see."

Chapter Twelve

"We've arrived at last!" Crosley shielded her eyes from the afternoon's brightness as she stepped down from the carriage. "Are you prepared to see your aunt and uncle?"

Annabelle evaluated the modest cottage in front of her. "I don't know how anyone can be prepared for something like this."

The structure appeared as Annabelle remembered it: a slate roof, weathered stone walls, and several latticed windows peering over the walled grounds.

Annabelle adjusted her footing on the rocky path beneath her feet. She and her mother had walked, hand in hand, along this very walkway all those years ago.

"Listen to me, Annabelle. Your surroundings will not be what you are accustomed to, so refrain from staring. Speak when spoken to, and stand up straight! You are a privileged young lady, and I expect you to behave as such."

What instruction would her mama give Annabelle now as she stood on the cusp of such a precarious situation?

She slung her cloak over her arm and wiped her forehead. The heavy garment seemed unnecessary this time of year, but she could not leave it behind. She would need it in the winter months ahead. The stifling summer heat pressed in on her, and the canopy of ominous gray clouds trapped the heat against the earth. An unusual scent met her, and she lifted her gaze to see a wall of climbing pink roses not far from where she stood.

Transfixed by their simple beauty, she stared. Such flowers were rare in London, and even if they were present, the town's pungent scents would mask their sweetness. She inhaled, taking a moment to appreciate the freshness of it. No smoke. No soot. Only the gentle aroma of earth and flower.

Mr. Locke stepped behind her with her valise in one hand, her watercolor box in the other, and Crosley's satchel hoisted over his shoulder. As he passed her, he offered a lopsided smile and motioned for her to follow him. "It's now or never, Miss Thorley."

Annabelle returned his smile and straightened her shoulders. Mr. Locke was right. Now was not the time to dissolve into a puddle of uncertainty.

She fell in step behind him as he blazed the stone path to the front entrance. She glanced down at her gown and gave an inward groan. She was still dressed in the thin attire she wore to the Baldwins' the night before—a ridiculously ornate gown for travel and inappropriately cut for day wear. It was splattered with dried mud from running in the London streets and wrinkled from hours of sitting in the carriage. Her bare arms and neck felt sticky. Dirty. She would require a bath this night, and Crosley would need to wash her hair.

But Crosley was not her lady's maid.

She flicked dried mud from her arm. She would have to make do on her own.

She waited as Mr. Locke knocked on the door.

A maid, whose dull expression was far too somber for her youthful age, appeared, dressed in a gown of drab gray covered by a crisp white linen apron. She stepped aside to allow the travelers to enter, led them to her uncle's study, and announced Mr. Locke.

The sights within the cottage, even the scent of it, breathed fresh life into the memories that time had faded. It was the smell that Annabelle recognized first when she stepped near the study. The aroma of dusty books mingled with the overpowering perfume of freshly cut roses and flowers. The chamber appeared exactly the same, although the room, which had felt so large when she was a child, was cramped. Books still haphazardly lined the shelves. Framed paintings still cluttered the plaster walls.

Mr. Locke entered the study first, but Annabelle glimpsed the older man over the gamekeeper's shoulder. He was the same man who had scolded her for eavesdropping all those years ago, but his white hair was thinner, and his lanky frame was even leaner.

"Locke." Uncle Edmund stood and extended his hand. "Thought you were traveling north. We didn't expect you back for quite some time."

"I just arrived from London." Mr. Locke shook her uncle's hand. "I've a delivery for you."

Uncle Edmund frowned, his gaze lifting over Mr. Locke's shoulder and landing on Annabelle and Crosley. His bushy eyebrows drew together. He stepped past Mr. Locke and fixed his pale eyes on Annabelle. "As I live and breathe," he muttered. "Annabelle? Is that you?"

She sighed in relief when he recognized her. A smile crept over her face. "Hello, Uncle."

But he did not return her smile. Instead, his weathered face wrinkled, and he stepped toward her and put his finger under her chin to angle her eye toward the window's light. "Child, what has happened to you? Have you been injured?"

"Do not be alarmed, Uncle." She allowed him to take her by the elbow and lead her farther into the crowded space. "It looks worse than it is, I fear."

"Of course I am alarmed. My sister's only daughter appears on my doorstep, bruised and battered, and I am not to be alarmed?" He snapped his attention to Crosley, as if suddenly aware of her presence. "And who is this?"

"Uncle, allow me to present Miss Margaret Crosley. Miss Crosley is my . . . companion."

"Miss Crosley, you are welcome here." He looked back over his shoulder to the maid. "Summon Mrs. Langsby at once, and then bring tea."

Uncle Edmund turned his attention toward Mr. Locke. "You come in too, Locke. If you've just traveled from London, you need sustenance, and I suspect you have a story to tell me on how you came to encounter these two ladies."

Her uncle offered Annabelle a chair, and she sat in the very high-backed, worn chair her mother had occupied when Annabelle had been caught eavesdropping. A sudden pang of melancholy struck her. How different life would have been for her and her mother had they heeded her uncle's warnings all those years ago.

They were about to get settled when Aunt Lydia bustled into the room, and Annabelle rose.

The woman, who was more portly than Annabelle recalled, brought vivacious energy to the chamber. Her faded copper hair bounced around her flushed face with each step. She pulled off her gloves and straw bonnet and discarded them haphazardly on the settee next to the door.

"Where is she? Where is she?" Aunt Lydia whirled around. As her focus landed on Annabelle, dismay reddened her already-ruddy face. "Oh, my dear!" She rushed toward Annabelle and folded her in an embrace.

Annabelle stiffened in its tightness. Not even her own mother had shown her such open physical affection. Aunt Lydia released her, then narrowed her blue eyes on Annabelle's bruise.

Annabelle shifted uncomfortably under the scrutiny.

"This is unbelievable. Simply unbelievable. I am thrilled to have you in my home, dearest. Of course I am! But I do wish this cloud of mistreatment were not hanging over us." She pivoted to face Mr. Locke, wringing her hands in front of her. "I do hope you have an explanation of some kind, Mr. Locke, as to why you are delivering our niece to us in such a state."

Annabelle shook her head. "Mr. Locke has been nothing but kind to my companion and myself, Aunt. In fact, he has performed us a great service."

"Then how is it you are here, and with an injury?"

"I have found myself in a difficult situation. When I was here last, I overheard Uncle Edmund tell my mother that your home would always be open to her or her children should we have need, and I was hoping the offer was still an option."

Annabelle could see the questions written in her aunt's expression. "There is no question you are welcome here, is there, Mr. Langsby? I imagine there is more to this story, but it can wait for another time. First things first, let's get both of you out of those dirty things, poor dears. Time will sort all out, will it not? In the meantime, clean clothes, a good freshening up, and tea will make all the difference."

Annabelle expelled a sigh. At least they were accepting her and Crosley, for now.

She glanced back at Mr. Locke, who now held his hat in his hand. It was the first time she had seen him without it, and his hair was thicker and curlier than she had thought. "Will you be here when we return, Mr. Locke?"

He shook his head. "I am not sure."

He had been such a vital part of her journey to Fellsworth that she felt oddly uncomfortable at the thought of him departing. Perhaps it was that he was her last tie to London. Whatever the reason, she found herself sorry to leave. "I appreciate all that you have done for Miss Crosley and me. Your kindness will not be forgotten."

Mr. Locke bowed and Annabelle curtsied. With unexpected reluctance she turned to follow her aunt from the room.

Owen's gaze did not leave Miss Thorley until her form vanished through the threshold.

Even with her mud-caked gown and disheveled hair, her beauty and strength of spirit captured his attention.

Langsby pushed the door closed behind them once their footsteps faded. "Those ladies look weary."

Owen squared his shoulders toward Langsby. "I can't blame them. I doubt they slept last night, and the ride from London was grueling. The roads were rutted and twice a horse threw a shoe."

"Sit down, Locke." Langsby waved a bony hand toward the chair. "Tell me how you came to deliver my niece from London—a niece, I might add, whom I haven't had any contact with in more than a decade."

Owen sat, then leaned forward and propped his elbows on his knees. He knew an explanation was necessary, but he was not sure where to begin.

He cleared his throat. "On our way back to Bancroft Park, Mr. Treadwell decided to travel through London at the invitation of Mr. Thomas Thorley."

Langsby lowered himself into the chair opposite Owen. "I know my nephew by name only. I have never met the lad."

"Mr. Thorley and Treadwell attended Cambridge together, and their paths cross every now and again." Owen stretched out his booted foot. "Last night, Mr. Treadwell and the Thorleys attended a ball or something of the sort. I was present when the carriage returned, and I witnessed Miss Thorley being treated poorly."

Langsby's narrow face sobered. "What do you mean?"

"The gentlemen in the party overindulged. One man, I don't know his name, jerked Miss Thorley by her arm. And I saw Mr. Thorley himself grab her roughly when she tried to enter the residence."

"That is abominable." Langsby rose to his feet. "And what do you know of the bruise on her face?"

"I'm not sure how that happened, but something was not right in that house." Owen hesitated, not sure how much to reveal. After all, most of what he had heard was speculation. "During the early morning hours, after the party returned, a gunshot woke the staff."

"My word, a gunshot?"

Owen nodded. "I don't think anyone was injured, but it was enough to unsettle the house."

Langsby returned to his chair. "How is it that you are the person traveling with her?"

"Upon learning that I was from Fellsworth, Miss Thorley told me she was your niece. She later asked me to hire her a carriage. After what I saw, I could not in good conscience refuse her, nor could I risk the possibility of her trusting someone whose intentions may not be honorable. Had I not genuinely believed her to be in danger, I never would have intervened."

Langsby adjusted his spectacles. "I suppose I should be thanking you, then."

"Not at all. I was surprised to learn you have family. I've never heard you mention them."

"Annabelle's mother, my sister, was a headstrong, willful thing. She made poor decisions—decisions for which she paid dearly. Let us hope her daughter does not follow in her footsteps."

"Is your sister living?"

"No, she succumbed to winter fever more than ten years ago. It's not shocking to hear my nephew would be in trouble of some sort. If he is anything like his father, there is truth in what you've heard."

Owen stiffened at Edmund's harsh words. "I have encountered Mr. Thorley on several different hunting parties at Bancroft Park. I've no wish to cast judgment on a man I do not know, but his behavior was always eccentric. Last night was no different. I can see why Miss Thorley thought herself in danger, especially under his guardianship."

"And what of the woman accompanying Annabelle? What do you know of her?"

"Very little, other than she is Miss Thorley's companion."

Langsby stood and moved to the window, and Owen stood and fidgeted with his hat. He had done what he promised and eased his conscience: he delivered the women to a place of safety. But unrest plagued his innermost thoughts. For what was to come of Miss Thorley?

The floorboard above him groaned, and the muffled sound of feminine footsteps crossed the space. He glanced up at the ceiling. A part of him wanted to remain and make certain all was well, but another matter called to him. "They are safe, then. I should like to see Hannah before I leave."

"Of course. I have work to tend to in my study at the school, so I shall walk you there myself."

Owen followed Langsby down the narrow corridor and back out into the hot sunshine. He savored a deep breath of beloved country air and exhaled. Normally, seeing his daughter was the bright moment of his day. But his chest felt unusually tight and his heart thumped.

Even though he knew Miss Thorley was safe with Langsby, his mind's eye could not erase the sight of her bruised cheek. It called to mind another horrific act of violence against a woman—one he had been unable to prevent and that resulted in his wife's death.

It had not been his fault, but he would carry the guilt until his dying day.

Miss Thorley's injury also had not been his fault, but he would never forgive himself until he saw that she was, without any question, safe.

Chapter Thirteen ──────────────

*T*he cloudy looking glass did not lie. Annabelle touched her fingertips to her cheek as she assessed her reflection.

Mr. Locke had been right. Her face was bruised and her cheek swollen. It was no wonder that her skin throbbed and her head ached. She straightened her posture. Anger at her brother raged afresh.

Never again.

Never again would she allow herself to be in a situation where she could be treated as such. It may have taken giving up everything she knew, but at least for today she was safe.

Aunt Lydia had ushered them up a narrow, uneven wooden staircase to a room where the maid had already placed their things. It was the same room she and her mother had occupied when they were guests here, and everything was just as she remembered it: a single narrow bed with a wooden frame pushed against the papered wall and a painted rocking chair next to the room's only window. A tall chest of drawers stood opposite the bed, and a washbasin was tucked in the corner.

Her plain surroundings were a stark reminder of the price she was paying for her newfound freedom.

Aunt Lydia pushed open the window, and instantly a cooling breeze swirled into the small chamber. "This room has not been used since my sister visited us last spring." She fussed with the rough linen curtains at the window. "You two can share this room until other arrangements can be made."

Annabelle turned away from the mirror. She was too tired to consider what the "other arrangements" might be. "It is very kind of you to make space in your home for us on such short notice."

"Think nothing of it." Aunt Lydia propped her hand on her plump hip. "It has always pained my husband that he lost touch with your family."

Annabelle sighed. "It has been a long time, hasn't it?"

The older woman stepped from the window and took Annabelle's hands in her own warm ones. "It has been far too long. Such a beautiful woman you've become. You look so much like your mother did at your age, with the exception of your hair, of course. She had the blondest hair I'd ever seen."

Her aunt's words of family probed at a section of her soul Annabelle kept carefully guarded. Not since Samuel had someone called her beautiful. And the references to her mother made her homesick for a life she had years ago.

Refusing to allow her emotions to rule her thoughts, Annabelle gave a little sniff. She reached out and looped her arm through Crosley's and forced a smile. "Aunt Lydia, I have not yet had the opportunity to properly introduce you to Miss Margaret Crosley."

Crosley dipped a curtsy.

"You are welcome in our home, Miss Crosley. Any friend of Annabelle's is accepted under our roof."

Annabelle removed her arm. She was hesitant about sharing too much about her relationship with Crosley, and at this point, it was best for everyone to think of her as Annabelle's friend. "I have known Miss Crosley for many years, and she has been kind enough to travel with me so I wouldn't have to brave traveling alone."

"Indeed. I was quite interested to learn that Mr. Locke had accompanied you from London, but not surprised. He is a thoughtful man. How extraordinary that you should know one another."

Annabelle studied the woven rug beneath her feet. How could

she ever explain that she had approached a strange man and so boldly asked him such a personal favor? Perhaps Mr. Locke wouldn't expose her faults. She had made so many reckless decisions over the past day that the magnitude of them threatened to overwhelm her.

If Aunt Lydia noticed any hesitation in Annabelle, she gave no indication of such. "Mr. Locke is a favorite around Fellsworth, and a friend of the school particularly. His talents as a gamekeeper and his knowledge of the outdoor world are quite well known. In fact, for the past several years he has been good enough to teach the older boys the foundation of trapping and hunting. He is quite indispensable."

Annabelle's interest was piqued. "He did not mention his connection to the school, but he said that his daughter was a student."

Aunt Lydia nodded, her blue eyes wide. "Hannah is her name. Such a sweet little girl, even if a bit of a handful. And she is the very likeness of her dear mother, God rest her soul."

Annabelle lifted her head at the mention of the child's mother's demise. It would not be proper to inquire about what happened to the wife of a man she barely knew.

Aunt Lydia waved her hand. "I'm eager to catch up on all of your news, but I'll wager that you want some rest after the journey. Traveling always makes one so weary."

Just the mere mention of rest brought a yawn, and Annabelle held her hand to her mouth to hide the discourteous action. "I do believe I am in need of a little sleep."

Aunt Lydia stepped close to Annabelle and rubbed her arm with motherly affection. "It does my soul good to see you, child. I wish you were here under happier circumstances, but whatever the reason, your presence brings joy to both your uncle and me."

With that, Aunt Lydia quit the room. Neither Annabelle nor Crosley moved until the sound of her retreating footsteps faded. Crosley hurried to the window and looked to the grounds below. "I can't believe I'm here. I have never been outside of London before. It is so beautiful! Look at all the trees."

Annabelle looked past her companion to see the school, a giant U-shaped limestone structure with paned windows and a slate roof. Several smaller buildings were positioned around it, and a web of paths and walkways connected them all. The scene was alive with activity: somberly clad children played in a grassy area across from the main building, and a carriage pulled to a stop outside one of the entrances.

Crosley whirled from the window, stifled a yawn, and dropped to the bed. "I can't wait to explore the grounds, but it will have to wait. I want to sleep for hours and hours."

Annabelle wished she could share the other woman's enthusiasm, but uncertainty still plagued her. Undoubtedly a nice rest would help her see the situation more clearly. She had not slept since the previous night, and her eyes cried for rest. Before she could nap, however, she needed to remove her gown. She could sleep in her chemise, but she would be much more comfortable once she was free from her gown and stays.

Annabelle turned toward Crosley. "Can you help me with these buttons?"

Crosley rolled to her side and propped herself up. Normally, Annabelle would not even have to ask the question. Crosley stared at her for several moments before she pushed up to a standing position.

Even though they had left London mere hours ago, the dynamic was already starting to shift. Crosley's actions were making it clear that she was not acting as lady's maid anymore. Crosley wordlessly helped Annabelle disrobe, and Annabelle moved to the fresh basin of water. She washed her arms and hands, then took great care as she pressed the linen towel to her face so as not to agitate the bruising.

She glanced back at Crosley, who had freed herself from her

own gown and already dressed in a chemise. Her hair was loose about her shoulders. Come to think of it, Annabelle had never seen Crosley with her hair down or in any other attire besides the gray gown she wore nearly every day.

"You seem happy," said Annabelle.

"I am." Crosley shook out her dress and hung it on a hook next to the door. "I have never in my life been a guest anywhere, and now I am in a room suited for important guests and someone else will bring me tea. Can you imagine?"

Annabelle could only stare. She was struggling to convince herself that she could function in a world without servants, while Crosley was embarking on an entirely new, exciting journey.

"Do you need help, then, getting that sleeping gown on?" Crosley asked, almost as an afterthought.

"No, thank you." She could manage this garment, although her other intricate gowns were not so simple and would require assistance. The thought vexed her.

Annabelle tugged it over her head and smoothed the lace along the neckline, pausing to watch Crosley as she retrieved a hairbrush and brushed her own hair.

With a sigh, Annabelle lifted her soiled gown. She probably would not have many opportunities to wear it anymore, but she could not leave it as it was. Had they still been in London, Crosley would have removed every speck and stain from the delicate silk fabric and returned her evening gown to a pristine state.

But they were no longer in London.

Not entirely sure what to do, Annabelle dipped the cloth in the washbasin and dabbed at the dried mud.

"What are you doing?" Crosley called across the room.

Annabelle thought it was apparent. "Cleaning my gown."

"Not like that. If you rub it, you will set the stain. See? Look how it is smearing."

Frustrated with her own incompetence, Annabelle let her hands drop to her side. "Then what am I to do?"

"Rubbing it with salt should do the trick." Crosley closed the space between them and snatched the garment from Annabelle's hand. "I'll see to it."

"Perhaps you can show me then. I will need to learn these things for myself."

Crosley gave a little laugh and shook her head. "Oh, Miss Thorley, you are going to have a great many things that are more important to learn than cleaning a gown. I fear you are in for quite a shock."

Chapter Fourteen

*O*wen waited on the bench outside the study of Mrs. Brathay, the headmistress. The daylight hours were ticking by, and he needed to return to London before Treadwell noticed his absence, but he could not quit Fellsworth without seeing Hannah.

He was one of the fortunate parents. He saw his child at least every week. Most of the children who attended Fellsworth School had no relatives in the county. Many of them had gone months or even years without seeing their families. Hannah was one of the few local students who could return home when the need arose.

As grateful as he was for all the school offered Hannah, he was torn. In a perfect world, his wife would be raising their daughter in their home, teaching her and instilling in her faith and discipline.

After his wife's death he did his best to raise Hannah on his own, but when Mr. Langsby offered to make an exception to allow her to attend school at a younger age than generally accepted, Owen had to agree. What did he know about teaching and raising a girl? If only he could give his daughter another mother, another woman who would invest in her.

The beautiful Miss Thorley crossed his mind. For just a moment he allowed his thoughts to linger on the brightness of her eyes and the soft curve of her cheek. But it would only be that—a fleeting thought. He had learned his lesson about setting his sights on a woman beyond his social status, and he had paid a dear price for doing so. He was a gamekeeper. His life was spent in the outdoors, not with courting. And with the shocking circumstances surrounding his wife's death, what woman would willingly step into the gamekeeper's cottage?

"Papa!"

Owen jerked his head up as his daughter's cheery voice echoed in the paneled corridor. He smiled. The sight of his daughter running toward him made the trip to Fellsworth worth it.

He stood and extended his arms, and the child jumped toward him. "You're home!"

He lifted her from the ground and squeezed her in a tight embrace before he placed her back on the ground. "There now, poppet. Let me have a look at you."

She giggled and gave a little curtsy. Hannah was clothed in the black gown she wore to school every day. A white cap covered most of her fair hair. Her rosy cheeks boasted a healthy glow, and her bright-blue eyes danced with mirth.

"Have you grown taller?" he teased and held his hand out in front of him as if making a measurement. "When I left, you were but this high, and now look at you."

"Papa, you are being silly." Hannah giggled again. "People don't grow that fast."

"Then how do you explain it?"

"Well, maybe I am bigger. Did you get any new puppies on your journey? Please say that you did!"

Owen nodded. "We will have two new puppies in the kennel, a black one and a brown one, and I think they're going to be quite a handful. I've never seen such wiggly dogs in all my life."

"Boys or girls?"

"Two girls."

"Where are they? Did you bring them with you?"

"No. They are still in London. I'll go back for them, but then I should be home for good in a couple of days."

A pout turned Hannah's lips. "But you are home now! Why do you need to leave again?"

She leaned in toward him, and he put his arm around her narrow shoulders. She was tiny for nine, and even though at times she seemed quite grown up, other times she seemed so young and vulnerable.

"It cannot be helped, but do not be sad. I won't be gone nearly so long this time. So now tell me. How have you been?"

She gave a little shrug. "Fine, I suppose."

"You suppose? Don't you know?"

She didn't respond. She only shrugged again.

He motioned for her to sit on the bench next to him. "What are you learning in your studies?"

She did so, then leaned her head against his shoulder. "Miss Tendall is teaching us new arithmetic. I don't like it one bit."

"But it's important for you to know these things. How will you help me keep track of the hunting logs if you don't know your sums?"

"I know." She swung her legs and then stretched the toes of her boots to touch the wooden floor. She suddenly whirled to face him. "When you get back, can I go fishing with you?"

"Of course you can. You and me."

"And Drake." She smiled.

"We would never go without him."

She seemed satisfied with his answer for several seconds. "Henrietta says that fishing is for the boys and that we girls should work on our sewing instead."

Owen feigned shock. "What? And who says that?"

"Henrietta Smith. One of the other girls here. She laughed at my sewing and said that if I spent more time doing things like all the other girls did, my embroidery would not be so dreadful."

"Does she know what an excellent fisherwoman you are?"

Hannah hung her head. "Nobody cares about that, though."

"I care about it. Doesn't my opinion matter?"

She smiled under his praise. "My embroidery isn't very pretty."

"I am sure your embroidery is not nearly as bad as you think it is."

She nodded her blonde head.

"And in the meantime, you work hard on that arithmetic and embroidery. You'll master both, mark my words. Now, you'd best rejoin your classmates. We don't want Mrs. Brathay getting upset with me for keeping you from your studies."

Hannah jumped to her feet, kissed him on his cheek, and trotted back down the hall. She paused at the end, looked back in his direction, and raised her hand in farewell. Her smile faded, and her eyes lingered on him a bit longer than usual.

He frowned as she disappeared around the corner. Her cheery greeting had warmed him, but the somber undertones of her words concerned him. He left Fellsworth with the happiness and safety of two ladies weighing heavily on his mind.

By the time Owen arrived back to Wilhurst House via a mail coach, London's evening mists had returned, and ominous fog shrouded all.

He had spent a large part of the ride thinking of a way to explain his absence. He did not want to betray Miss Thorley's trust, but he would never mislead his friend by lying, either. But when he arrived at the mews, Treadwell was nowhere to be found. A cluster of servants had gathered in the courtyard at the back of the house near the servants' entrance.

He recognized one of the men as Randall, who had driven the carriage home from the Baldwin ball. Two of the men held torches to bring brightness to the day's fading light, and the heated tones and sharp words piqued Owen's interest.

His steps echoed in the courtyard, and the group turned as he approached. Randall broke away and approached Owen. "Welcome back."

Owen nodded and looked past the driver to the cluster of men. "Thanks."

"The boys were just wondering where you'd gotten to. We noticed your dog was still in the kennel, and we were afraid you'd left him behind."

"No. I will be here until Mr. Treadwell departs." He was reluctant to share too much information. "I had business to tend to."

Randall lowered his voice and angled his body toward Owen, as if taking him into his confidence. "You left before the discovery was made, then."

Owen cocked his head. "What discovery?"

The driver's broad face sobered. "There's been a murder."

"Murder?" Owen had not seen Treadwell, and concern for his friend raced through him. "Who?"

"That fellow who came home with the master last night. McAlister. He was found dead just in the next alley. The servants here were likely the last people to see him alive."

Nausea rolled over Owen—not only because a human had died, but because the man had been one of Treadwell's associates. "How did he die?"

Randall scratched his chin and lowered his voice even more. "Shot in the stomach."

Owen's chest tightened.

The gunshot.

They'd all heard it. And they'd all believed it had been harmless.

The two had to be connected.

"Who shot him, does anyone know?"

Randall flipped his collar up and lowered his voice. "That's the greater mystery, isn't it? We may never know who is responsible for such evil. 'Tis a shame he was a guest in this house. This family has come under enough scandal as it is. They may never recover from this."

Owen was surprised at the readiness with which the carriage driver shared such personal information. In some houses the family matters were private, and the staff would never dare to speak of such details with an outsider. But if the staff of Wilhurst House was anything like Mr. Treadwell's staff at Bancroft Park, the news would be all over the countryside as fast as one could travel.

Owen needed to find Treadwell to determine what he knew. He prepared to bid the man good night, but Mr. Randall's next words stopped him in his tracks.

"As if his death wasn't mysterious enough, we've another interesting matter on our hands. Mr. Thorley's sister left the house during the night with nothing more than a note bidding her brother and the mistress a farewell. Her maid is gone too."

Owen remained stoic at the words, but he could not walk away without more information. "Are the two connected?"

Randall shrugged. "I doubt it. Miss Thorley is a peaceful thing, always has been. But that maid of hers can be a bit of a handful. Her brother's the tall footman over there on the right—the blond-headed lad. If anyone would be riled up, he would, but he doesn't seem too concerned. Says his sister is a scrappy thing who can take care of herself. Things are not adding up, if you ask me."

Owen stifled a groan. He had no idea that Wilhurst House employed Miss Crosley's brother. He had been so focused on getting Miss Thorley to safety that he had not considered the impact Miss Crosley's absence would have. Perhaps he had been too zealous in his decision.

He would have to abide by what he had done, come what may. Owen only hoped he would not regret his actions.

Chapter Fifteen ─────────────────────────────

*A*nnabelle stood outside her uncle's study—just as she had all those years ago. But instead of clutching her paintbrushes and straining to hear an adult conversation, she gathered every ounce of courage she could muster.

Both she and Crosley had slept through dinner the previous day and did not wake until the rooster crowed to signal this day's break. They then spent the day in solitude while both her aunt and uncle tended to their duties at the school. The long hours had passed in fretful silence, and now that her uncle was home, Annabelle had been summoned to the study.

The forthcoming discussion with Uncle Edmund regarding her future could not be avoided. She had been so preoccupied with leaving London that she had not considered what would transpire once she succeeded.

Annabelle paced to the right, then the left in the narrow corridor. Desperation descended upon her, and she lifted her gaze to the low, beamed ceiling as if an answer would appear on the plaster surface.

She had invaded her uncle's home and now she could only guess his reaction. He could send her away, offer her a home, help her find employment, or assist her in selling her jewels and find her suitable lodgings.

She could bargain with him. She could beg. She could plead.

But she could not go back to London.

Annabelle wished she had someone to turn to for guidance,

but she had only herself on whom to rely. Her father would have told her money would buy her way with anything. Her mother had been a woman of strong faith—a faith that Annabelle had never really understood—but she knew what her mother would have told her to do: pray for guidance.

Annabelle bit her lip before pivoting to face the door standing ajar. She smoothed a lock of light-brown hair back into place and drew a cleansing breath. Be it money, prayer, or both, she needed a miracle.

Not wanting to keep her uncle waiting, she knocked on the rough door.

"Enter."

She stepped into the chamber, her dainty slippers soft on the worn carpet. Outside, thick clouds blocked much of the daylight, and the room seemed much darker than the previous afternoon. The staccato pops of rain on the study's paned window blurred the view outside to a sea of green and gray. Uncle Edmund was seated behind his desk, and Aunt Lydia, dressed in a gown of slate muslin, was seated in the chair by the fireplace.

"Annabelle." Uncle Edmund stood when she stepped through the door. "Come in, child."

Her aunt turned in her chair to face Annabelle. "I am sorry we were not here to greet you when you awoke. I trust you slept well?"

"I did. Thank you." Annabelle knitted her fingers together in front of her. "I apologize for sleeping through dinner last night. It was a thoughtless thing to do. I am afraid the journey took a toll on me."

"Of course it did. That road from London is an abomination." Her aunt shook her head. "It is a wonder that any carriage makes it here in one piece with all the wheels intact. You are entitled to rest after all you have been through."

Yes, she had been through quite an ordeal, but the phrase

sounded so lamentable, as if she were a victim of some great tragedy. Annabelle did not wish to appear weak. After all, she had made a decision to leave; she was not forced. And the last thing she wanted was to be pitied.

She jutted her chin out and straightened her shoulders. "Everyone faces trials, Aunt. 'Tis a sad reality, but I have just chosen to change mine, and I am optimistic about the future."

"But to be struck in such a manner is unforgivable!" Her aunt shuddered.

Annabelle arched her eyebrow. It *was* unforgivable. But it was the catalyst that pushed her forward.

Uncle Edmund cleared his throat. "It was a brave choice, Annabelle. Perhaps a dangerous one, but I daresay you made the best decision with the information you had at hand, and no one can fault you for that. Just as your mother was, you are always welcome under my roof, and I am glad you came to me when you needed help."

"Please sit down." Aunt Lydia motioned to the chair next to her. "We must discuss this situation and decide what is to be done about it."

Annabelle's heart raced. Ideally her aunt and uncle would open their doors to her indefinitely, allow her to stay in the tiny bed-chamber as long as she needed to sort things out. But her muscles contracted as she prepared for the worst. "Of course."

"Tell me a little bit about your situation." Uncle Edmund folded his arms across his chest. "I have not seen you in so long. I know your mother died, but what of your father? Is he still living?"

"My father died two years ago of apoplexy. Thomas inherited everything—Papa's business, Wilhurst House, all his possessions. I have been living with my brother and sister-in-law since then, at my father's request."

"I am sorry to hear he died." Her aunt frowned. "You must miss him very much."

Annabelle nodded. "Life changed dramatically with his death."

"I fear my questions are of a personal nature, but I do hope you'll forgive me. I must understand your reasons for leaving your brother's house." Uncle Edmund lowered his voice. "Were you physically harmed in the home?"

Given the state of her cheek, it would be easy to assume that her environment had been an abusive one. But that was not the case—not initially, anyway. "Yesterday was the first time my brother has ever struck me."

"Is that what prompted your departure?" Sincerity laced her aunt's words.

Annabelle shook her head. "I had decided to leave prior to this instance."

Her aunt continued. "But why, my dear? That is such a drastic measure."

"My brother desires me to marry a man whom I regard as unsuitable." Annabelle shifted in her chair. "Please believe me, I'm not one of those silly girls who won't marry a man for his appearance or lack of wealth. My opposition isn't based on superficiality. His character possesses a sinister nature. He made me uneasy, and to be quite frank, he frightened me. Thomas made it clear that my options were limited. Either marry the gentleman in question or be without a home. I chose the latter."

"But you are such a lovely lady. How could your options possibly be limited? Are the men in London daft?" Her aunt toyed with the hem of her lacy shawl. "I would imagine that the young men would be forming a line at your doorstep."

"You are very kind, Aunt, to say such a thing." Annabelle hesitated, weighing how much to divulge. "I was engaged at one point, but the gentleman changed his mind."

Aunt Lydia's hand flew to her chest. "Why?"

Annabelle sighed. There was no reason to hide the nature of her disgrace. It was not a secret, really. "Shortly before my father died, he was accused of participating in an embezzlement scandal. Even though guilt was never proven, my fiancé broke the betrothal, citing my family's sullied reputation."

Uncle Edmund stood and turned to look out the window. "Does Thomas know that you have come to Fellsworth?"

"I left a note informing him I was departing, but I did not tell him my destination. I did see him as I was leaving, however."

"And he did not ask where you were going or try to stop you?"

"He did, but he was inebriated at the time, and that is when this happened." She touched the bruise on her cheek.

Uncle Edmund ran his hand over his pointed chin. "I must admit that I feel uncomfortable about you being here without Thomas's knowledge, but based on your account, I certainly understand. I also understand from Mr. Locke that other questionable efforts were in play. Therefore, I invite you to stay here at Fellsworth, with my blessing."

Relief raced through her, tingling in her hands and pushing her heart to beat faster. "Oh, thank you, Uncle. I promise you, I will do my very best to move things forward and start a new life."

Uncle Edmund exchanged glances with his wife, and he straightened his waistcoat. "You are most welcome, Annabelle, but unfortunately the invitation is not without a condition."

Realizing her lapse in etiquette, she clasped her hands in her lap. "Oh. I see."

"You are welcome to stay here not as a guest, but as a junior teacher at the school."

Annabelle's mouth fell open, and she quickly snapped it shut. She swallowed the instinctive protest welling up within her. She could not be a teacher. She had never even been around children. She managed to squeak out, "A teacher?"

"Yes. At our school a junior teacher is basically a teacher in training. Think of it as an apprenticeship. You will not be a lead instructor, but we are always in need of adults to work with the children. If I knew my sister, you most likely had the very best governess, so I do not doubt your ability."

"Yes, I had a wonderful governess, but I—"

"Good. Then it is settled." He brushed his hands together. She thought his actions signaled he was done with the discussion, but he continued. "There is one more thing that must be said."

Annabelle suspended her breath, afraid that at any moment he might change his mind.

"I have been the superintendent of Fellsworth School for more years than you have been alive. I have dedicated my life, as has your aunt, to its care and its running. The students here have been like our children. Those employed here are our family."

Annabelle held his gaze.

"I cannot, in good faith, allow for any arrangement that would jeopardize their safety or comfort, and I understand from Mr. Locke that your brother has a bit of a violent temper."

A violent temper. What else had Mr. Locke said about her family to her uncle?

Uncle Edmund continued. "Who knows that you have come here?"

"Only Miss Crosley. And Mr. Locke, of course."

"Then I think anonymity is best. I would advise you to keep the details of your private life to yourself. This town is small and word travels fast. The last thing we want is trouble. You shall stay here in this house until your bruising heals to prevent any gossip, but then we shall get you acclimated to Fellsworth life. And as for Miss Crosley, what can you tell us of her?"

Annabelle sighed. It was no use to keep Crosley's identity a secret. "Crosley was my lady's maid. I can no longer afford to compensate her for her service, but I was eager to leave and I didn't want to travel alone. I paid her to accompany me, but now that we are here, I'm not sure what her future plans entail."

"And do you recommend her? Has she a sterling character?"

The letter of recommendation she promised to write flashed in her mind. "Yes. I'd recommend her for anything. She has been nothing but a faithful servant to me."

"Then I am prepared to offer her a position in the kitchen. Mrs. Langsby oversees all such additions, so she will work out the details with Miss Crosley personally."

Annabelle had survived the first leg of her journey to freedom, and now it looked like both she and Crosley would have a fighting chance. "Thank you, Uncle. I know she will be very grateful for the opportunity."

"You must understand. I believe in hard work. I know your life has been, well, different from the lives here. We cannot support you in the lifestyle to which you have been accustomed, but I have found, in almost every instance, that hard work and responsibility only strengthen a person. Welcome to Fellsworth School, Annabelle."

Chapter Sixteen

*H*ome. He was home again.

Owen filled his lungs with the earthy perfume of trees and forest, thicket and vale. The ever-present carpet of leaves crushing beneath his boots sang a lullaby as he led his horse through the dense growth, and the distant popping of a woodpecker was a sweet strain to his ears.

"Give me the scents of bark and leaves over those of London any day," Owen said more to himself than to James Whitten.

Whitten guffawed. "You go away for a couple of weeks and return a poet. I've never seen the like."

Owen chuckled and adjusted his rifle against his arm as he glanced over at Bancroft Park's older under-keeper. "You know me better than that. Did you get the horses settled?"

"I did. The stablemaster said he was only expecting one, but I know you told him two. He will figure it out, though. I am a bit concerned about the bay. She's not taking her grain."

"I'll stop in and talk with the stablemaster later today."

Owen had just arrived home earlier that day from London. Only three days had passed since he delivered Miss Thorley and Miss Crosley to the superintendent's cottage and bid farewell to Hannah, but it felt much longer. London was dirty and loud, and the distressing news of the murder had not left his mind. He never did connect with Treadwell once back in London. The spontaneous man left word that he was traveling to Bath and would return to Bancroft Park within the fortnight. While in London Owen purchased another horse, attended a hound auction, and ordered several new rifles in anticipation of the next hunting season.

He was glad to be back amongst what was familiar, and his responsibilities had piled up while he'd been away. He would get to them all in due time, but one duty in particular weighed on him.

Poaching had always been an issue on the estate, and over the past year he had seen an increase in activity—footsteps in the morning grass, the occasional discarded arrow or length of copper wire, and traps that did not belong to him. Activity had increased tenfold when a local mine shut down, and Owen and his under-keepers patrolled the area in the midnight hours. On more than one occasion he had chased shady characters from the land he had vowed to protect.

"Who handled the night patrols while I was gone?"

"I did them myself, every night. Had some of the footmen stand guard as well."

"And?"

"Thursday last I chased two fellows from the east meadow. Fired a warning shot and they went running. The day before that, I came across trampled grass and a few lengths of rope. I followed the trail but it disappeared at Foster's Pond."

Owen clenched his jaw. "Show me the site later, will you?"

"'Course." Whitten kicked a stick out of the way on the forest path, then adjusted the weapon on his shoulder. "Heard you came back from London the other day with an interesting delivery."

Owen winced at the reference. No need to ask Whitten to explain his statement. Nothing occurred in Fellsworth without it quickly becoming public knowledge. He had hoped word would not spread, especially since he had not had a chance to discuss his actions with Mr. Treadwell, but like it or not, his spontaneous decision to help Miss Thorley had repercussions.

Wilhurst House's driver's words of the murder stood fresh in

Owen's mind. Surely the timing of Miss Thorley's departure and the murder was mere coincidence. Miss Crosley also had left at that time. He knew even less about her. But regardless, he had made the decision to help them both, and he needed to be willing to accept any consequences.

"You would have done the same thing. Trust me on that."

Whitten laughed. "Probably not. But I have heard that the lady in question is quite a beauty. My Martha delivered hares to the school just the other day and met her when she called on Mrs. Langsby at the cottage. Said the newcomer was the loveliest person she ever did see, and you know that is high praise from my wife."

Owen could not deny the truth in Mrs. Whitten's words. He had thought of Miss Thorley several times since leaving her in Langsby's care. Something lurking in her hazel eyes had intrigued him, and mystery swirled around her—a mystery he would like to solve.

Whitten kicked another stick from his path. "She also said you were a fool for taking her to the Langsbys' instead of persuading her to become mistress of Bancroft's gamekeeper cottage."

It was one thing to comment on her beauty, but another thing entirely to suggest a commitment. "If you are referring to matrimony, you know I have no interest in marrying again. Miss Thorley needed assistance, that is all."

Whitten threw his head back in laughter so raucous that the swallows fled the canopy of leaves above them. "When it comes to pretty women, a man is always thinking matrimony. Gamekeeping is a lonely endeavor, Locke. It would do you good, if you ask me. Doesn't do for a man to spend all of his time in the woods and none with a lady."

Owen adjusted his satchel. "You know my history and the history of this place. It isn't fair to ask a woman to take on those ghosts."

Whitten's tone sobered. "But enough time has passed. It is time you thought of your own future again. I tell you this as a friend."

The corner of the stone cottage's thatched roof came into view, and a dog's barking pierced through the cacophony of the wind through the leaves and the birdcalls. The chimney's familiar scent of smoke welcomed Owen home and puffed gray-and-white vapors into the sky.

It had been his father's home before him. Even though Owen was born in the gamekeeper's lodge in Kirtley Meadow, he spent his early life in this ancient structure surrounded by his mother and sister. His family had never known want, but his mother emphasized faith over fortune, and his father preached that a man's wealth was pride in a job well done and not the number of his possessions. It was the place where he sat with his father and learned to clean his firearm, train dogs, and trap hares. His mother and father were dead now, and his sister lived several counties away, but he did not live alone.

His housekeeper, Mrs. Pike, had been his wife's maid before they were married, and after his wife's death, she stayed on. Years passed, and what started out as a temporary arrangement became permanent.

Mrs. Pike was in the front garden, working in the house's shadow. As usual, her unruly, graying hair hung in a single braid down her back. Long strands of silver had pulled free from the tether and wisped about her face and shoulders, and it was this wildness and her odd, unconventional ways that contributed to the chatter that had swirled about her the day she first set foot in Fellsworth.

"Mrs. Pike," Owen called out.

She straightened from her gardening, brushed the leaves from her soiled apron, and propped her fist on her thin waist. "There now. You're home."

"Can't believe you haven't ousted the woman from your house yet," Whitten muttered from the side of his mouth as they approached.

"She's harmless."

"Harmless or not, that woman is as odd as they come." Whitten eyed her.

"She may view the world differently than most, but she helped me with Hannah when I had no idea what to do. I'm in her debt." Owen chuckled as they stepped into the courtyard. "Besides, if it weren't for her, who knows when I'd get a decent meal."

Bancroft Park was ripe with rumors, and after his wife's death, he was the subject of every wagging tongue, especially given the tragic and odd events leading up to it. Mrs. Pike was accused of aiding the murderer, of sorcery, and of every other manner of foul play. People expected him to throw her from the land, but he never believed the chatter. Mrs. Pike was opinionated, but she had been a loyal servant. He could not knowingly send her to the poorhouse—and sleep with a clear conscience.

Mrs. Pike gathered her work-worn skirts and stepped over her rows of herbs toward them. Trouble was written in the furrow of her brow. Owen doubted he would have to wait long to hear what it was.

"While you were gone a limb fell over my chamomile. Do you think that Mr. Whitten moved it?" She fixed narrowed eyes on Owen and waved in Whitten's direction. "No, he would not. And what kind o' man couldn't be bothered to help a woman with such a task? No decent man, t'be sure."

The wiry woman and gruff under-keeper locked gazes in a wordless battle of obstinacy. It appeared the long-standing feud between the two was as spirited as ever it had been since the day Whitten criticized Mrs. Pike's care of the hounds well over four years prior.

Owen ignored her grumbling and tied his horse to a tree trunk. "Where's this limb?"

She jerked her finger toward a small herb garden boasting mounds of small white and yellow flowers. Across it lay a branch about the size of a man's leg. Not heavy, but likely too cumbersome for the older woman.

Owen looked to Whitten, doing little to hide his annoyance. "You wouldn't move that?"

Whitten sniffed and ran his thumb over his whiskered chin and glared in Mrs. Pike's direction. "I don't take kindly to orders. Ask a body to do something, not order him about as if you was a duchess."

Owen reached over, lifted the limb with one hand, and sent it soaring toward the woodpile.

Mrs. Pike's eyebrows rose. "There now, Mr. Whitten, see what a good man can do when he sets 'is mind to it? 'Tis not that difficult to act the gentleman."

"Bah." Whitten grimaced and turned back to Owen. "Give a shout when you want to go to the path by Foster's Pond. Until then, I've got real work to do."

Mrs. Pike crossed her thin arms across her chest and lifted her chin in triumph as she watched the old under-keeper stomp through the underbrush toward the main road. "Never met 'is like, that sour old goat. Serves 'im right, after what I heard of 'im."

Owen brushed the debris from his hands. He could always count on Mrs. Pike to relay the latest gossip. "And what did you hear of him?"

"Not fitting for a lady to say." She sniffed. "But the next time he comes around, lookin' for some rosemary for his toothache, he can keep walkin'. I'll not be sharing any o' my rosemary with the likes o' 'im."

Owen ran his hand down his face. "Well, if you won't tell me what he's done, I'll be off to see to my evening rounds."

"Will ye be back for dinner, then? I'll not keep the stew on all day. Makes the meat shrivel up to next to nothin' and the potatoes as dry as I don't know what. I'll not spend all day on fare just to have ye waste it."

Owen rolled his eyes and returned to his horse. "I'll be back in a few hours."

"See that you are, else it's to be bread and cheese for your supper." She picked up the rake and returned to her duties.

Owen whistled for Drake. "Good day to you, then, Mrs. Pike."

The early afternoon sun slanted across Fellsworth School's meticulously manicured lawn. Annabelle lowered her paintbrush and drew in the lush scent of summer roses and sweet honeysuckle. Would her amazement over such beauty and vibrancy ever cease?

Crosley was already settled at the school and working in its kitchen, but for the past several days, Annabelle had spent her mornings and afternoons painting in her aunt and uncle's private garden amid the entrancing foxglove and fragrant lavender while the bruising on her face subsided.

No wonder her mother had always spoken so fondly of her childhood in the country. Mama had always said that one day they would leave London for good. Now Annabelle understood her desire. But even if her mother had survived the winter fever, her father would have forbidden such a venture.

She shrugged the sobering thought from her mind. Annabelle was tired of feeling sad, fretting about the future, and mourning the past. She had resigned herself to her new role, and now that her strength was returning, so was her determination.

So now she sat in the lush space, paintbrush in hand, small canvas propped on the easel with the sun blanketing her shoulders with warmth.

An unfamiliar male voice broke her reverie. "Pardon me, miss. I've no wish to intrude."

Annabelle glanced up from her watercolors. A stranger—a

handsome one, with dark eyebrows and light eyes—stood at the gate. How long had he been there, observing her?

"I do not wish to disturb your solitude." His friendly voice boasted confidence. "I am here to call on Mr. Langsby."

She straightened her shoulders. "He is not here, I am afraid. He is at the school."

A half smile quirked up one side of his mouth, then he swept his straw summer hat from his head, revealing thick light-brown hair. "Forgive me, but I do not believe we have met."

"No, sir, we have not." Annabelle lowered her paintbrush to her side and glanced back at the home's back door, hoping, praying, that anyone, even the maid, would appear. This was not how her introduction to the people of Fellsworth was supposed to occur. She was to wait until after her face healed.

She waited for him to excuse himself and go back to wherever he had come from, but he continued to stand at the gate.

Speaking with a strange man, especially alone, was an unforgivable breach of the rules of etiquette. But how could she escape without extraordinary rudeness?

"Pardon my boldness, but are you Mr. Langsby's niece?"

She could find no way to avoid such a direct question. "Yes, sir. I am."

He stepped farther into the garden, as if they were great friends instead of strangers. "Well, how fortuitous for me to have come, then. Miss Thorley, isn't it?"

She stiffened. "You know my name."

"Yes, your uncle shared the news with the headmistress that you would be joining our ranks in a few days, and, well, nothing stays secret for long at Fellsworth School."

She frowned at the familiarity with which he addressed her. "Forgive me, but how are you connected with the school?"

"Simon Bryant, at your service." He bowed. "I teach the young men at the school. I will pay a call to his study. You know Mr. Langsby—if he is not at home, he is at the school. He is one of the most dedicated men I know."

Annabelle used her hand to shield her eyes from the sun, which after being warm and inviting, was now oppressive.

His gaze narrowed and lowered from her eyes. "What a beautiful pendant. Is that an amethyst?"

Flustered that he was so intimately studying the jewel about her neck, she grabbed the piece to cover her bare skin. "It is."

His smile remained unchanged. Unflinching. "A very beautiful jewel for a very beautiful lady."

He turned to leave, then stopped. "Oh, wait. I wanted to ask you something. With your permission, of course."

Her stomach sank at the directness of his gaze and the confidence of his countenance. She was walking a fine line of propriety. "You may."

"Are you any relation to Mr. Thomas Thorley? The name is an unusual one. I wondered if by chance there was a connection."

Annabelle's heart stuttered. She had hoped for complete anonymity. She had only been here a couple of days, and already she was losing control.

He stood there calmly, his gaze on her expectantly.

"I am."

When she did not offer to expand, he drew closer to her. "I have known Mr. Thorley for several years now. He travels here every winter for the hunting over at Bancroft Park. The man enjoys a good hunt." He looked at her as if he knew a secret.

Gooseflesh pebbled her arms, yet her temperature seemed to rise. Thomas could *not* find out where she was. He just couldn't.

After several moments of awkward silence, his animation returned. "Well then, I'd best let you get back to your task, and the midday meal will soon be concluded, which means my classes will resume. It was a pleasure to make your acquaintance, Miss Thorley. I am sure I will see more of you in the coming weeks."

She said nothing, only dipped her head in a parting curtsy. She did not take her gaze from him until he disappeared through the gate.

She rubbed her arms in an attempt to shake off the awkward interaction. She lifted her brush to the canvas, but her hand trembled so the stroke of pink paint wobbled out of line. She drew her hand back and looked to the empty space where Mr. Bryant had been.

Perhaps the visit was innocent enough. Perhaps it was not. But the sneaky suspicion that Fellsworth was not as safe as she thought it would be had taken root, and she feared that suspicion would not be easily shaken.

Chapter Seventeen

*T*he late-afternoon sunlight cast long shadows over Foster's Pond. Owen glanced down at the grass along the waterline. Whitten had been right: The grass was trampled and the reeds broken. The path was too broad to have been made by a deer or fox. Only an inexperienced poacher would leave such incriminating evidence.

Whitten had already returned to tend the hounds, and Owen needed to be on his way to Fellsworth to deliver game to the kitchen, but as he turned to the tree line, something shiny glimmered on the ground. He dismounted, removed his leather glove, and knelt in the flattened grass. A small length of copper wire, just the sort a poacher would use for catching carp.

Owen pursed his lips in frustration, stuffed the wire in his pocket, and stood. He had dedicated his life to this land and the living creatures on it. He refused to stand idly by while someone treated it with such disrespect.

Owen mounted once more, and his horse settled into a comfortable walk through the east meadow. Owen checked the hares tied to the back of his saddle and tightened the rope securing them. If he hurried, he could have the game to the school and see Hannah before the children retired for the night.

He surveyed the property. The feathery undergrowth brushed along his boots as they cut a path through the waving sea of grass. Drake trotted along beside them, the top of his brown head barely visible in the meadow's thick growth.

The trilling of a group of starlings overhead captured Owen's attention, and he glanced left to see two deer nibbling leaves at the forest line. He guided his horse away from the rabbits playing in the underbrush.

He closed his eyes and breathed the thick summer air. He loved this land. He loved the scents. The animals. The freedom of existing in nature. Being away from it for a couple of weeks had renewed his gratitude for the life he had built for himself. But still, a single thread of restlessness pulled through him. His unusual conversation with Miss Thorley had disquieted his normal contentment.

Their interactions, fleeting as they were, had awakened something in him—a desire that had not abated since he left her at her uncle's home. Something in Miss Thorley's actions—a fearless desperation for something new, something different—called to him.

It represented a truth that brought to light the gaping hole he'd so earnestly tried to fill with the business of everyday activities.

Ever since Diana died, loneliness lurked in his heart's shadows. Its dulling pain had become his unwelcome companion. The endless winter nights and the repetitive summer days had reinforced the sensation. He'd been successful at suppressing it. Or so he'd thought. But now dissatisfaction churned.

He surveyed the land. Through death and trial, heartbreak and solitude, it had been his one constant. But it was not his land. And it never would be.

It belonged to Treadwell.

Owen's thoughts turned for the hundredth time to Kirtley Meadow. The older Hannah grew, the more he wanted something substantial for her. Owning Kirtley Meadow would provide for her and secure her tie to the land that was her legacy.

The east meadow stretched nearly an acre past Foster's Pond, and beyond that, statuesque elms and wispy ash trees rose majestically toward the serene sky. He let the reins slacken and gave his horse his head. Before long autumn would be at their doorstep, and hunting parties and fox hunts would demand his attention, but for now he could enjoy the slow pace.

He adjusted his rifle at his side and prepared to turn the horse toward the road to Fellsworth School when Drake stopped suddenly and pointed his nose toward the pond.

"We're not hunting now, boy." Owen adjusted the dog whistle hanging at his neck. "Let's save it for another day."

Normally at Owen's voice Drake would release his lock on the animal at bay. Instead, his tail ceased wagging. His focus intensified. He pranced nervously alongside the horse. He snipped a low bark.

Owen squinted to see in the distance. "What do you see there?"

The dog's tail wagged once more, and he turned a circle.

Owen dismounted, planted his feet on the soft ground, and adjusted his rifle. "Show me."

The dog whirled and burst through the grass, creating a wave on the green sea. Owen gripped the horse's reins as he followed in Drake's direction. A rabbit, or perhaps a ferret, had caught his dog's eye.

But as he drew closer, he saw what the dog had heard—a person hiding in the grass.

He narrowed his gaze. The dog was not tracking an animal.

Drake was tracking a person.

The hairs on Owen's neck prickled. Rarely did poachers conduct their business during the daylight hours, but a nearby mine's recent closing and flooding in the north fields made poachers more desperate . . . and braver.

He gripped his weapon tightly. Poachers were never unarmed—and always dangerous.

Owen squinted to see in the slanting sunlight and saw beige rough linen, as if he was looking at someone's back.

Owen cocked the hammer on his rifle, preparing himself for

what might meet him. "You are on Bancroft Park property. Show yourself."

The person did not move.

Owen called louder. "You are trespassing."

Drake barked and inched toward the body.

At the sound a flash of black and gray bounced. To Owen's surprise it was not a man. A boy's thin frame sprinted through the grasses.

Owen ran after the boy and with his long gait quickly overtook him. He grabbed the boy's collar.

"Let go of me!" The youth jerked, squirming to free his coat from Owen's grasp. "Let go!"

Owen held his coat firm. "Be still, boy."

The trespasser continued thrashing. "I haven't done anything wrong!"

"I said be still! I'm not going to hurt you. I am just going to talk to you."

The boy eventually stopped his flailing. Perspiration plastered his dark hair to his pale forehead, and his small chest heaved with the wild exertion. He refused to look in Owen's direction.

Owen recognized the boy. John Winter was a student at Fellsworth School. Once a week Owen took a group of boys out in the forest to teach them about hunting and survival, and Winter had been a part of the most recent group. The goal of such outings was to help prepare the young men for life beyond Fellsworth School. Not to encourage poaching.

It was the very thing that had been Owen's concern since he first started the program: the more he armed the boys with knowledge of fowl, fish, and animals, the more comfortable they became in the element. He was teaching them the very skills they would need to indulge in illegal activity, but he thought Langsby was teaching them enough about character to alleviate that threat.

But this boy's actions confirmed Owen's fear.

He nodded at the child's hands. "What do you have in your hands there?"

John tucked his hands behind his back, hiding the contents.

Owen tightened his grip on the boy's collar. "I'm not letting you go until you show me what you have."

John lowered his ruddy face and moved his hand just enough to present a length of rope.

"And just what were you planning to do with that?"

"Nothing."

"Nothing? With a rope in the forest? Perhaps you thought you would set a snare?"

The boy's dark eyes grew wide. "No, no, I didn't! I promise!"

"How about you and I take a walk, hmm? I think Mr. Langsby would like to know why you were in my forest instead of tending to your studies." Owen stretched out his hand, and the boy handed over the rope.

He released the boy's collar and gave his shoulder a nudge to get him walking. Owen kept pace next to him, just in case he decided to run.

Chapter Eighteen

"What do you think of the school now that you have had a chance to explore it for yourself?" Uncle Edmund fell into step with Annabelle as they crossed Fellsworth School's main courtyard.

Annabelle looked to the top of the bell tower as it chimed the hour. For the past two hours her uncle had taken her on a tour of the school grounds, helping her become acquainted with the space that was to become her home. "It is impressive, Uncle. Really it is."

"I know I shared a great deal of information with you, but in time you will become better acquainted with our way of life." Uncle Edmund adjusted his hat as he and Annabelle walked down the narrow brick lane from the brew house to the main school building. "The school, as an institution, is really quite self-sufficient. Anything we do not make or grow ourselves is brought in, and we have little need to go into the village for supplies."

Annabelle wrinkled her nose as the unfamiliar scent of yeast and grain tickled it, and the unpleasant scent of manure and animals traveled on the morning breeze from the nearby pastures. She had been at Fellsworth for over a week now, and this was her first venture out of the superintendent's cottage.

He'd given her a tour of the outer stables and the kitchen gardens, the chapel, the blacksmith, and the conservatory. Large structures of brick and limestone rivaled some of the buildings she saw when she and her mother had traveled north. The school even boasted a working coal yard to provide for the winter warmth and a cow house and slaughterhouse to provide enough meat to feed such a large group of people.

Her uncle's chest swelled with affection and pride as he pointed out the cobbler shop and bake house. Annabelle's mind swam with all she had learned and seen, and she feared she would not remember it all or perhaps lose her way.

"I cannot believe how large the grounds are." She quickened her gait to match her uncle's brisk pace. "Why, it is a village in and of itself!"

"That is the idea. Complete self-sufficiency. These children need to become acquainted with the ways of the world. Their parents have sent them to us to care for them, and for most children, they will not return home for years on end. 'Tis a harsh world in which we live, a cruel one, and the children must realize that they must use the tools they have and work toward the greater good."

Annabelle stiffened at the term *self-sufficiency*. She had never been self-sufficient. Up until a few days ago she had not even dressed herself without the assistance of a maid. A pang of shame swept over her.

As if sensing her silent concern, her uncle added, "I do need to remind you, however, that these children may be at a boarding school, but this is not the sort of school that you or your brother would have attended. These children are not from wealthy families. Quite the opposite is true. Many of their parents have sacrificed relationships with their children for an education that will equip them for their lives ahead. The children here work hard to learn trades.

"Some of the older students work in the slaughterhouse, and others work in the bake house and brew house, and it is expected that they work to help earn their keep. Students are involved in the running of every part of the school, from tending the kitchen gardens to managing the laundry. Each child has at least one daily chore, and it is our job to see that they appreciate the value of a job well done. Our students leave here ready to go into service or an apprenticeship, and we do not want them overwhelmed and bewildered when they do."

Annabelle thought of her own education—of Latin and French, painting, dance, harp, and singing. A single governess had dedicated years solely to Annabelle and had been charged with the task of preparing her to enter genteel society and make an advantageous match.

And where had that gotten her?

She knew nothing of the skills her uncle described, and thinking about the tasks ahead unnerved her.

"The girls' school and the boys' school are about equal in size, 150 students in each, but the two schools never interact, except for chapel on Sundays."

He pivoted to face the school's main entrance. "The main building there houses the library, my study, and other shared rooms. Then off the main hall to the left are the boys' school and dormitories and to the right the girls' classrooms and dormitories. That is where you will, understandably, spend most of your time."

Despite her trepidation, a little thrill surged through Annabelle. She'd been mourning for so long that the idea of a new purpose appealed to her.

Her uncle was about to show her the library when he stopped and looked down the path. Annabelle pivoted to see what he was staring at.

Mr. Locke was walking down the school's main drive.

He was a welcome sight—a familiar face after spending several days in relative isolation. He did not smile as he approached; instead, his expression seemed almost sullen. But despite that, he truly was a handsome man—handsome in a way to which she was unaccustomed. In London the men she encountered were polished and pristine, but Mr. Locke possessed a rugged air.

His hair was wild and unkempt, even from below his wide-brimmed felt hat, so unlike the fashionable style many young men wore. It was blown by the wind and curled according to its own will. A coat of rough brown linen highlighted the broadness of his shoulders, and tan buckskin breeches tucked into tall riding boots bore testament to his profession.

He was on foot and led his horse with one hand, and the other hand he had firmly on a boy's shoulder. Drake trotted alongside him, his tail wagging with each step.

It was impossible for her to guess the boy's age. Ten? Eleven? Despite the afternoon's heat, the boy's round face was pale, and his dark eyes were wide. He was dressed in the school uniform of gray trousers and a black coat, but he wore no hat, and his ebony hair clung in damp clumps to his face. His small chest rose and fell with each breath. Apprehension twisted his young face.

Annabelle frowned in pity. Her uncle's disposition changed as well. His steps slowed, and his demeanor tightened to one much more intimidating.

Mr. Locke gave a slight bow. "Miss Thorley. Mr. Langsby."

"Mr. Locke." Her uncle's voice was low and dauntingly soft. He crossed his arms over his chest and focused his attention on the boy. "Mr. Winter. Should you not be about your studies?"

The boy shifted but remained silent.

"I encountered Mr. Winter in Bancroft Park's east meadow." Mr. Locke extended a small ball of rope. "He was in possession of this."

Her uncle took the bundle and tapped it against his hand. Annabelle was not sure what was going on, nor what the significance of the rope was, but based on the men's sober expressions and the look of fear in the boy's eyes, the situation was a serious one.

Her uncle stepped closer to the boy. "I am sure you have a good explanation as to why you were on Bancroft Park property."

The boy gulped and looked to the ground. "I haven't, sir."

"I see." Langsby pushed his spectacles up on his nose. "You would not have been using this rope for any sort of hunting now, would you?"

The boy did not look up.

"Mr. Locke, I am in your debt. Thank you for bringing him to me and leaving the magistrate out of it."

Mr. Locke nodded. "I know you will take care of the situation."

"This matter will be dealt with swiftly and appropriately, I can assure you. And it will not happen again." Her uncle stepped back to allow the boy room to walk around the horse. "I am sorry to have burdened you. I am sure you had much more important things to do with your time than to escort Mr. Winter home."

"Don't give it another thought. It is important that Mr. Winter here knows that there are very serious penalties for trespassing, and if he had intended to use that rope in an act of poaching, the consequences would be very dire. He would be wise to steer clear of Bancroft Park property completely."

Owen watched uncomfortably as a tear escaped the boy's eye and plopped down his freckled cheek.

He felt bad the boy was frightened, but it was much better for him to face Mr. Langsby than the magistrate, especially on the significant charge of poaching.

Langsby clamped his hand on the boy's shoulder. "I think it is time we go have a talk with the headmaster, don't you?"

The boy did not respond but kept his head lowered.

Owen glanced up to assess Miss Thorley's take on the situation. Her usually full lips were pressed into a narrow line. A straw bonnet covered her hair, but even with the brim's shadow he noticed that the bruising on her cheek was fading. She looked relaxed. Rested. Pretty.

The sight of her reminded him that he'd been carrying the

news about Mr. McAlister's murder for days, but he had not had the opportunity to inform her of the happenings of a guest in her home.

As Langsby turned to guide the boy down the path, Owen spoke. "I have some news for Miss Thorley from London. Might I detain her for a moment?"

Miss Thorley lifted her head at the mention of London, and Langsby looked to his niece. "Of course she may remain if she wishes. This situation may take a while to deal with. Annabelle, would you be so kind as to tell your aunt I might be late returning for the evening meal?"

She nodded. "Of course, Uncle."

"Good." Langsby turned back to the boy. "Come with me, lad."

When Langsby was out of earshot, Owen adjusted the horse's reins in his hand and gave Drake the command to sit at his feet. "I hope you do not mind my asking to speak with you."

"Not at all, Mr. Locke." She smiled, and at the sweetness of it, he felt his shoulders relax. "It is pleasant to see a familiar face after so many days in the cottage."

He was not gifted at making polite conversation. He did not want to blurt out the uncomfortable news, and her presence made his mind feel sluggish. "How are you getting along here at Fellsworth?"

"Very well." She stilled her bonnet's silky pink ribbon as a breeze swept in from the north. "My aunt and uncle have been kind and attentive."

"I'm not surprised. Your injury appears to be much improved."

"Oh." She gave a little laugh and touched her cheek. "It is healing well, thank you."

"Now that you are here, do you plan to remain in Fellsworth?"

She nodded and raised her eyebrows. "Indeed. My uncle has been kind enough to allow me to stay on as a teacher."

"A teacher!" His effort to hide his surprise failed.

"Well, a junior teacher to be more exact." Her voice trembled slightly, and she fidgeted with her sleeve. "Starting this night I will take up residence in the ladies' apartments."

How would a woman used to the luxuries of London fare in a simple attic chamber? "I imagine that'll be quite a change for you."

"It is. But I can hardly complain. At least here I am safe. And free."

He wanted to ask her more details, but propriety prevented it. "And Miss Crosley? Has she returned to London?"

"Actually, she will be remaining in Fellsworth for the time being as well. Obviously I no longer require a lady's maid, but my aunt saw fit to offer her employment in the kitchen. I have not spoken with her, but Crosley, that is, *Miss* Crosley, is one of the most adaptable people I know."

Her face darkened, and she turned back to watch her uncle and the boy, who were still walking across the expansive lawn to the school. "The child seems terribly frightened."

Owen adjusted his coat's collar and tugged his neckcloth. "He's in a great deal of trouble, I'm afraid."

She frowned. "That doesn't seem right. Are you sure he was trespassing and did not lose his way? He looked surprisingly upset for such a small offense."

"If I suspected that the boy had only become lost, I would've sent him on his way without another thought. The truth is, I suspect he was involved in—or at least contemplating—poaching."

"But why would you suspect that? I don't think he would have need for food. And he is just a boy."

"No, he wouldn't be hungry while a student at Fellsworth. More likely he would be doing it to sell the game."

She shook her head. "But that doesn't make any sense."

"It happens quite often. Seasoned poachers know the risks of hunting on a private estate. They could hang for such an offense. It is not unusual for them to pay boys like Mr. Winter to poach for them."

"That is terrible!"

"I've no doubt that Mr. Winter knows it is wrong, but I suspect someone has promised him a fortune, or at least some sort of reward that makes it worth the risk. If the boy is caught, the man who was paying him gets off free while the boy suffers the consequences."

She watched her uncle and the boy disappear into the boys' wing. "What would happen to him if you went to the magistrate?"

"It would depend mostly on whether or not Mr. Treadwell chose to push the matter. I've had the sad experience of seeing a boy his age hang for being caught in the act of killing an animal. It hasn't happened on land that I have been responsible for, but it does happen."

Miss Thorley lowered her gaze.

"Fortunately, Mr. Winter has your uncle, the boys' headmaster, and the rest of the staff here at the school. They'll set him right and place him on a more productive path."

Her eyebrows drew together. "Will you inform Mr. Treadwell of this incident?"

"It's my duty to inform him of everything that happens on his property. But don't worry. If it turns out that someone was paying the boy to poach on his behalf, I will find out."

Owen shifted. As much as he would like to stay and talk with Miss Thorley about anything, the news of the McAlister murder weighed on him. Really, it was not his place to get involved, and yet, he felt a strange sense of obligation to her.

He cleared his throat and checked to make sure no one was within earshot. "As you know, I returned to London after leaving you with your aunt and uncle."

"Yes. Of course." She fretted with the hem of her lacy shawl. "Now that I am here, London seems like it might as well be a million miles away."

He adjusted the horse's reins in his hands, uncertain of how best to proceed. "When I was there I had an interesting conversation with the driver at Wilhurst House. Are you acquainted with Mr. McAlister?"

Her gaze did not waver. "Yes, I know him."

"Did you know him well?"

A flush rushed to her cheeks, and she brushed her hair from her face. "I have been acquainted with Mr. McAlister for several years. He was a friend of Thomas's. But no, I did not know him well."

The name had some effect on her. But what was it? Sadness? Melancholy? "Do you remember hearing a gunshot the night you decided to leave?"

Her eyes narrowed, as if she were cautious to speak on the topic. "I do."

"Apparently your butler made a full investigation of the property and found nothing amiss, but the next morning Mr. McAlister was found dead in a nearby alley. He had been shot in the stomach."

The color drained from her face. "Shot? As in . . . ?"

He nodded as her voice trailed off, and he gave her a moment to comprehend the gravity of his news. "He died of the injury."

Moisture pooled in her eyes. Her lip trembled. "Is it known who is responsible?"

"They don't know. When I left, a private man had been hired to learn what he could. I can see the news distresses you, but seeing that it was your home, I thought you should know."

She looked to the side, toward the Fellsworth tree line, as if focusing intently on some distant object.

One of the most important skills Owen's father had taught him was how to read people, but he did not know her well enough to be able to gauge her response. Many women he knew were prone to dramatics, but Miss Thorley seemed quite still on the matter. Her expression gave up little emotion, but the creeping red blotches on her neck and chest and the flushing of her cheeks expressed more than her words ever would.

She shook her head slowly. "I just cannot seem to comprehend this."

"I did not mean to upset you, but I thought you needed to know."

Her brow furrowed and she turned. "Thank you. If you hear of any developments, will you inform me?"

"Of course."

He patted his horse's neck. "At least you are safe here, come what may."

She smiled as she looked to the forest. The breeze lifted a loose lock of hair and fluttered it over her face, and she lifted her delicate white hand to still the strands. She opened her mouth to speak but then closed it again. When she looked back at him, her usually bright eyes were framed with redness. He wished he had a handkerchief to give her.

He leaned lower. "I know you have been through an ordeal, Miss Thorley. I do not wish to overstep my bounds, but if there is something you need to talk about or any questions you might have, I hope you know that you have a friend in me, should ever you need one."

She gave a little sniff, shook her head, and looked to the ground. "What you must think of me, Mr. Locke."

"I think you have been in a difficult situation. And you have handled it as well as any lady could."

Knitting her fingers together, she looked back at him, and her thin eyebrows drew together. "There was something odd that happened just the other day."

He sobered. He had not really expected her to confide in him. He had only hoped to lay the foundation for a friendship. But the tension in her expression and the moisture in her eyes made it clear something bothered her. "What was it?"

"I was in my uncle's garden the other afternoon, alone, and a gentleman called."

Owen frowned. Everyone in Fellsworth knew that if you needed to speak with one of the Langsbys, they were always at the school and rarely at home, especially during the afternoon hours. He remained silent.

"He said he is a teacher at the school, a Mr. Bryant. He asked after my uncle. I told him he wasn't home, but it was very odd. He knew my name, and then he asked me if I was related to Thomas."

Owen's horse nudged at him, and he shifted the animal's muzzle away. "I know Bryant. He grew up around here and used to be Treadwell's frequent guest at Bancroft Park, so it wouldn't surprise me if he had met your brother on a hunting party or card game or something of the sort. But do not let it distress you. Bryant is generally harmless."

"I suppose it was just a surprise, that's all."

"If he gives you any trouble at all, let me know. I've no problem having a conversation with him. I am here most days in one capacity or the other. I am at your service."

"Thank you, Mr. Locke. You have already done so much for me." She gave another little sniff. "At one time I thought I knew exactly what my future held. Now, I haven't the slightest notion."

"Unfortunately, Miss Thorley, none of us knows what our future holds. A fortnight ago you had no idea you would be here in Fellsworth, and I bet this morning young Mr. Winter had no idea he would be sitting in the headmaster's study trying to justify his actions."

She responded with a forced smile as a group of children crossed the yard, and Drake stood up and circled around Owen's legs.

He did not want to leave Miss Thorley, but from the corner of his eye he saw a group of teachers watching them. He knew how gossip could travel, and the kindest thing he could do for her at the moment was to let her get about her business.

"I have some hares for the kitchen. I'd best deliver them before the hour grows late." He bowed. "Good day, Miss Thorley."

She smiled and dipped her head.

He gave the horse's reins a tug and whistled for Drake and then headed toward the kitchen's back entrance.

As he walked away from her, he immediately felt her absence. He cast a glance back in her direction. Her white skirt swayed with each step she took, her bonnet's ribbons whipping in the breeze.

It had been many years since he had allowed himself to invest in a woman. Not since Diana. But seemingly out of nowhere Miss Thorley appeared, and somehow he felt responsible for not only her safety, but her happiness as well. His own contentment now seemed intertwined with hers, and he had the sensation that his journey with Miss Thorley was just beginning.

Chapter Nineteen

*E*very action Annabelle had taken in the last week culminated in this moment. She stepped into the small room, valise in hand, and assessed the tiny attic chamber that was to be her new home.

Twilight was falling. The final meals of the day had been served, and outside the room's two narrow windows, brilliant hues of pinks and oranges painted the fading sky.

Ever since her discussion with her aunt and uncle, she'd known this day was coming. Her bruising, although not gone entirely, had subsided, and now it was time to move out from the protection of her uncle's home.

Her shoulders sagged in a momentary lapse of decorum as she shifted her eyes from the rough planked floor to the row of four narrow beds separated by small chests. She groaned. She had never shared a chamber with anyone. Ever.

She closed her eyes, as if by doing so she could erase the sight of the dowdy room from her memory. She forced her mind's eye to conjure her chamber in Wilhurst House—a room of lush, vibrant satin fabrics in shades of pinks and greens and ornate gilded wallpaper boasting a tranquil country scene. A space with warm candlelight, a crackling fire, and inviting overstuffed chairs.

She opened her eyes and exhaled. No amount of wishing, dreaming, or imagining could transport her to such a place. This was her space now. Bare. Cold. Uninviting.

She had two choices—be miserable or try to make the most of the situation.

She was not sure which bed was to be hers, so she rested her valise on the floor next to the washbasin and stepped to the open window. A cool night breeze puffed inside and danced against the thin linen curtains. She adjusted the fabric to survey her new domain. She could see the kitchen gardens and the back wall of the school stables. If she arched her neck, she could see the gray thatching of her aunt and uncle's cottage, and beyond that lay the village of Fellsworth. A church spire jutted into the sky, and a dirt road snaked amid the brown stone buildings. A late-summer haze hung damply over the ground below.

It was so calm, so peaceful compared to the view outside her London window, where shouts and smoke floated through the thick, soot-filled air. But here the air was thin and light, and scents of earth and forest laced every breeze.

A few children scampered in the yard, playfully dancing in the twilight, and two kitchen workers labored in the garden, their heads covered with white caps. She lifted her gaze toward the cottage where she had spent the past several days, and something—or rather someone—caught her eye.

Mr. Locke was speaking with someone she did not recognize. There was no mistaking his broad shoulders or his notable height, even in the day's fading light. A broad-brimmed hat covered his dark hair, and a light-brown coat hugged his muscular torso. In one hand he held a giant black horse's reins, and Drake sat at his feet.

Comfortable in the knowledge that she would not be caught staring from such a distance, Annabelle allowed her gaze to linger on Mr. Locke. While they were traveling together, she had failed to notice a great deal about him. But in the quiet moments over the past few days, the memory of him would sneak into her thoughts.

"What are you looking at?"

Annabelle jumped at the suddenness of the voice and whirled from the spot.

Crosley stood in the doorway, her blonde head tilted to the side.

In one hand she held a candle, and her other hand was propped on the hip of her new black dress. A knowing smile played on her thin lips.

Annabelle dropped the curtain and clasped her hands behind her back. "Nothing."

"Nothing, hmm?" Crosley smirked and with purposeful steps strode next to Annabelle and lifted the curtain's corner. After a glance to the ground below, she let the curtain slip from her fingers. "He is handsome, is he not?"

Heat crept to Annabelle's face. "I don't know what you're talking about."

Crosley laughed. "Oh, I know you far too well. Why, you have been looking at Mr. Locke, am I right? Please don't pretend you didn't notice him, for I will not believe you."

Annabelle's mouth opened, and she promptly snapped it shut. Never would Crosley have dared to address her with such familiarity, at least, not in their traditional roles.

Annabelle crossed the room and picked up her valise. "I was doing nothing of the sort. Besides, you should not speak of men in such a manner. It is not decent."

"Not decent?" Crosley huffed. "Why not?"

"It . . . it just isn't proper." Annabelle adjusted the valise in her arms.

"Proper? What do I care about what is proper?" Crosley's voice rose. "We are not in London anymore."

Annabelle looked away to hide the emotion on her face. She had not seen Crosley in several days, and she seemed like a different person entirely. Crosley had always been so disciplined. Her words had always been pristine and gentle, but now she was speaking in a manner Annabelle never would have expected.

Crosley continued. "Besides, you and I are not necessarily guided by the same philosophies. I prefer to speak my own mind and not be persuaded by someone else telling me what to say or do."

"I am not persuaded by others," defended Annabelle. "I should think my decision to leave London would stand in testimony to that fact."

"Oh, do you now?" Crosley's smirk dripped with sarcasm.

Annabelle weighed her words before she allowed them to slip from her mouth. She lowered her voice and cooled her tone. "I find you quite changed, Crosley."

Crosley flung her arms out, like an estate master surveying his land. "Good. I am glad. For why should I not be different? I am no longer a lady's maid in the fine house, bound by the constraints of obedience and decorum. I am a kitchen girl in a school. As long as I do my work, nobody cares if I speak my mind or not. It is not a lofty position, no, but one not limited by a mistress and it's free of the expectations of others."

Annabelle could not be more shocked at Crosley's cheekiness. She brushed her hair from her face. She did not want to argue—not when Crosley was the only familiar face in a sea of the unknown. "If that is your feeling on the matter, then I am happy you are confident in your new role."

"Oh, I am happy." A laugh escaped. "Are you not happy? How could you not be? Isn't this what you wanted? To be free?"

Annabelle pressed her lips together, grateful for the room's gathering darkness. To be honest, she didn't want any of it.

She had not wanted to be forced to make a decision to leave her home in the black of night.

She had not wanted Samuel Goodacre to break their engagement.

She did not want to have to rely on an uncle she did not know to make provisions for her.

When Annabelle did not answer, Crosley's face fell. "Perhaps this—all of this—is for the best. After all, I have been acquainted with you for years. When was the last time you were truly happy?"

The question flamed the spark of frustration burning within

her. "I don't think that is a topic we need to discuss." Annabelle had not intended for her words to be voiced with such vehemence.

Crosley used her candle to light another one and let her opinions flow unchecked. "I do not know what will happen tomorrow, the day after that, or the week after that, but this I know for sure: you will be about as happy here as you allow yourself to be. And I, for one, intend to be very content."

Annabelle lifted her eyebrow. She was not sure how to interpret this new version of Crosley, but she would not have this conversation. She nodded toward the beds. "Which one should I use?"

Crosley pointed to the bed on the end. "Sorry, you have the bed closest to the window. The girls say it can be pretty drafty in the winter months."

Feeling more dejected than ever, Annabelle dropped her valise on the narrow bed and plopped down on it.

With arms folded across her stomach, Crosley moved back to the window and looked down at the courtyard. "My, but Mr. Locke is a handsome man."

Annabelle unfastened her valise, refusing to engage.

Crosley dropped the curtain and sat on the edge of Annabelle's bed. "The female staff were all aflutter when they noticed him on the property. They melted into silly schoolgirls, no more mature than the students that walk these grounds."

Annabelle pulled a gown from her valise and shook out the wrinkles. She may be in a new situation, but she would not bend so low as to discuss such an improper topic so crassly.

Crosley leaned forward, as if preparing to share a very great secret. "They seem quite worried about you too. They said he never speaks to any of the female staff. Ever. And just today he spoke with you on the lawn ever so long."

Nervous warmth spread over Annabelle at the thought. She liked Mr. Locke. She enjoyed his company and felt respected in his presence. And she liked that he was comfortable talking with her. But she had thought their conversation on the lawn to be a friendly exchange. To know it was the source of gossip pained her. She did not want to alienate herself from the other women before she had even made their acquaintance.

Crosley toyed with her cuff. "They have told me a bit about his past. It is tragic and romantic."

When Annabelle did not cease her unpacking, Crosley straightened. "Do you not want to know about it?"

Annabelle picked up a pair of slippers from her valise and moved them to the chest. "I don't think that it is—"

"I know, I know, you do not think it proper. But wait until you hear." Crosley reached across the bed and grabbed Annabelle's hand to cease her movement. "His wife was murdered. Murdered! Can you imagine?"

At the shocking word, Annabelle stilled and snapped her gaze to meet Crosley's wide-eyed stare. "What?"

"Yes. She was murdered in their own home when their daughter was just a baby."

A sinking sensation tugged at Annabelle. Mr. Locke had seemed so stoic and composed. She never would have imagined that he suffered such a loss.

The poor man.

The poor child.

Annabelle said nothing, but she resumed her task and removed a gown from the valise. Now that she had heard the first bit of the story, there was no denying that she needed to hear the rest.

The candle's light reflected on the soft angles of Crosley's long face. "According to Louise, a woman who shares this very chamber, Mrs. Locke had a beau before she met and married Mr. Locke. The beau was presumed dead in war, but when he returned he found Mrs. Locke married to another. A forbidden, scandalous romance ensued. After quite some time, the man killed her in a rage when she refused to run away with him, and then he was so distraught that he took his own life."

At this, Annabelle's heart ached in her chest.

"You have heard that Mr. Locke's child attends the school here."

Annabelle nodded, unable to pretend that the story did not touch her. "I have."

"Well, there is question as to whether or not the child is even Mr. Locke's natural daughter. The rumor that she is the child of the mysterious soldier follows her wherever she goes."

Annabelle needed to stop the gossip. Crosley had crossed a line. "How can you speak of such things of a man we barely know?"

"It doesn't matter now," snipped Crosley. She stood from the bed and placed the candle on the stand next to the washbasin. "If you did not hear it from me, it would only be a matter of time before someone else told you. I've been here well over a week now, and I have learned that gossip and stories travel faster than they did through the staff at Wilhurst House."

Annabelle stiffened. Did rumors like this fly through her old home? If so, she had been oblivious, but her family definitely would have given the servants much about which to engage in tittle-tattle.

Her father's warning about not trusting servants leapt through her mind. No, Crosley was not the woman she had believed her to be. The truth of it struck Annabelle's heart more than she cared to admit.

She propped her hands on her hips and looked up at the wide, dark beams crossing the ceiling. A whole new world was opening up before her—a world she was not sure she understood or even wanted to understand. But like it or not, it spread before her, wide open and scary.

Chapter Twenty

"Don't move a muscle."

Annabelle stiffened her arm and stood perfectly still as Crosley pinned the sleeve at her wrist. Crosley stood back and flicked her gaze from the length of one sleeve, to the other, and then back again.

Annabelle looked down at the faded, coarse gown with a sigh.

The awkwardness of her odd conversation with Crosley had dissipated, and night had fallen. The light from two candles lit the space, and now the former lady's maid was altering the school gown to fit Annabelle's form.

Annabelle held her breath as Crosley finished her pinning. She was not sure why Crosley offered to help her with the gown, for she seemed to take pleasure in the fact that Annabelle was clearly out of her element. But whether it was to gain the upper hand or to prove Annabelle's insufficiencies, Annabelle was grateful just the same, for she would have no idea how to begin the task.

Crosley knelt on the floor as she pinned the hem. The chamber had no long looking glass in which Annabelle could check her reflection, and she shifted uncomfortably in the garment. The sleeves hung long over her hands, and the bodice drooped.

She pressed her lips together. She would not be upset over a gown. At least she was free here. She would not have to marry Mr. Bartrell. But that did not mean she had to *like* the gown.

Crosley stood from her work and stepped back, propping her hands on her hips as she assessed the length. "Fortunately the woman who wore this before you was much taller. This hem can be adjusted to the right length. Are you going to wear the boots with this or the slippers?"

At Wilhurst House her entire dressing room had been filled with slippers and boots of every color and material. And now the thought of wearing the same shoes day after day was just another reminder of the sacrifices she was making.

Annabelle tilted her head. "I suppose the boots are most practical."

"It's difficult to believe that this might be the last gown I fit for you." Crosley motioned for Annabelle to lift her arms and pinched the fabric along Annabelle's side to see how much would need to be taken in.

As Crosley pinned the fabric, the door opened. Two women bustled into the room—one was dressed in a gown like the one Annabelle now wore, and one was dressed in a gown like Crosley's. Their steps slowed and their expressions changed with interest as they noticed Annabelle.

Crosley straightened. "There you are. Here is the woman I was telling you about. Annabelle Thorley. This is Louise Stiles and Jane Henton."

Miss Stiles's hair was neither brown nor blonde, but the hue lingered somewhere in between. Her thin lips quirked downward and her brow furrowed.

Annabelle forced a smile. "How do you do, Miss Stiles."

"Miss Stiles?" The plain woman chortled as she eyed Annabelle from head to toe. "We don't rely on protocol here. Call me Louise. So you are old Langsby's niece, are you? Heard you was coming. Didn't know we'd be sharing a sleeping place, though."

Annabelle had hoped to keep the fact that she was the superintendent's niece quiet. She did not want to be treated differently.

Before she had a chance to answer, Miss Stiles blurted, "What happened to your face?"

Annabelle's hand instinctively flew to her cheek. She had thought it looked better, but apparently traces of faded blue and subtle yellow were still visible. "An accident, I am afraid."

"An accident? You must be a clumsy one then. You'd be wise to give a care in the future. Fellsworth School has little time for those who do not pay attention to their surroundings."

Annabelle's mouth fell open. Never had she been talked to in such a disrespectful manner by a kitchen maid. Never.

The coarse woman latched her gaze on Annabelle and did not look away, almost as if issuing a silent challenge.

Annabelle swallowed her instinct to scold the woman, as she would have done had the woman been a servant in her house. But she no longer had servants—nor was she a mistress of a house. If anything, other people had power over her.

Annabelle lifted her chin. She would not stoop to unbecoming behavior, regardless of her situation. "Thank you, Miss Stiles. I shall remember that in the future."

Miss Stiles raised her eyebrows. "Oh, will you now?"

"Leave her alone, Louise." The other woman with softer features and a kinder smile draped a shawl over one of the far beds and walked toward Annabelle. "Like Margaret said, I am Mrs. Jane Henton. Welcome to our chamber, Miss Thorley."

Annabelle paused for a moment. She had called Margaret by her surname for so long it would take her a while to get used to hearing her former lady's maid referred to by her Christian name.

Mrs. Henton looked around the space. "I know these quarters are probably not what you expected, but I am told it takes a little time for the chambers to be arranged."

"Oh no, this is, uh—perfectly adequate." Annabelle pivoted to give Crosley access to the back of the gown.

"Adequate, is it? Not good enough for the likes of you?" Miss Stiles tilted her head.

Annabelle was already tired, and she did not feel like a battle, especially with a woman she did not know. "As I said,"—she fixed her gaze on the ruddy-faced woman—"it will do."

Jane lowered her voice. "Do not pay any heed to Louise, Miss Thorley. She is overly blunt, I am afraid. Our introductions have not started on the best note, and I am sorry for it. I do hope you will call me Jane. Everyone does."

Annabelle nodded.

Crosley motioned for Annabelle to turn and step out of the gown.

Annabelle complied. She reached for her wrapper and secured it around her waist before moving back to her bed.

Jane followed her. "I hope you are feeling better."

"Hmm?"

"Margaret told us you were not feeling well and that is why you were staying with your aunt and uncle instead of coming to the school right away. I hope your affliction has passed."

"I am very well. Thank you." Annabelle glanced at Crosley from the corner of her eye. What else had the woman disclosed about her and the reasons they were in Fellsworth?

"My, but your things are pretty." Jane propped her hands on her hips and looked at the pile of Annabelle's gowns, underdresses, and chemises on the bed. "Is that Belgian lace?"

Annabelle straightened, surprised—and pleased—to find that the woman knew of such things. "Yes, you are familiar with it?"

"I am. Before I came here I was an assistant to a dressmaker in Bath, and I have always been fond of such lace as a trim. And this shawl! Beautiful. Unfortunately you will not have a great deal of opportunity to wear such lovely things here, but they are pretty to look at nonetheless. Where is it you come from?"

Annabelle considered her response. She could certainly name her town without giving too many details of her previous life. "London."

"Your possessions are certainly the finest of any teacher here." Jane's gaze lingered on the peach netted gown.

"She had the best situation of us all prior to Fellsworth," added Crosley, a playful grin on her face. "She was a companion to a young woman who got quite fat and could not fit into her gowns anymore. So she gave ever so many things to Annabelle. More's the pity, right?"

Annabelle's eyes widened. Crosley had just referred to her by her Christian name. She just nodded, supposing she should be grateful for Crosley's interjection.

She had not given much thought to what she would tell others when they inquired about her past. And Crosley was right—it was no secret that both lady's maids and companions were often the recipients of the mistress's castoffs. Such an explanation would account for Annabelle's possessions. She was uncomfortable with lying, but the less that was known about her past, the better.

The other girls began preparations for bed. There was little talk. Louise read. Jane wrote a letter at the room's only desk. Crosley had gone down to sew the dress by light from the kitchen's fire. Eventually, Louise and Jane both extinguished their candles and went to bed. Annabelle knew she should sleep also, but she felt too ill at ease.

She pulled up a chair between her bed and the wall, next to her small wooden chest that would house all of her belongings. The low, sloping ceiling made her feel caged in, and sitting as opposed to standing seemed more comfortable. She leaned forward and lifted the iron latch and pushed the lid open, wincing as its hinges creaked.

She glanced over her shoulder to make sure the noise had not woken her roommates. Her candle's light slanted on their sleeping forms. Neither of them moved a muscle. In fact, the steady rhythms of their breath seemed loud in the small space. It was a wonder any of them could sleep at all given the noise of it.

Annabelle gave a little shiver. With night, coolness fell over the room, and she rubbed her hands together in front of her. How they trembled. She rubbed them together again.

Annabelle needed to finish unpacking, but she found concentrating on the task at hand difficult. Her mind wandered to the news Mr. Locke had shared regarding Mr. McAlister's murder. The thought of any person losing their life in such a violent manner made her ill. She thought of the missive he'd sent her. Now she would never know what he wanted to tell her. Another shiver traversed her spine. Perhaps if she had known, she could have helped prevent his death in some way.

But the most troubling recollection was that of the blood on her brother's attire. He couldn't have been involved, could he? But why else would there have been blood?

Her brother had always been fond of boxing. Perhaps they were behaving like boys and had a bit of a brawl. Or perhaps he had tripped and fallen and cut himself. As much as she tried to convince herself of possible scenarios, she could not persuade herself of his innocence.

She glanced back at the sleeping women before she lifted the stack of Samuel's letters from her valise. They were still bound in a blue ribbon. A part of her wanted to indulge in the memories and read the letters one by one, allowing them to transport her to another time and place. But she resisted. It was getting harder and harder to find solace in his words. Now they were so long ago, they seemed more like a fairy tale than anything else.

She placed the letters in the bottom of her chest and reached for her watercolor box sitting next to her valise. She opened the lid and shifted the mixing tile back in place. She flipped down the clip on the bottom of the lid. A few of her favorite private projects were still pinned there, just as she had placed them in London. One by one she lifted them from their place. A portrait of her childhood dog. A portrait of her father. A portrait she had painted of her mother.

She swallowed a lump of grief at the sight of her mother's likeness. It was not a very good likeness. She had painted it from memory. Annabelle had been only twelve at the time, and her watercolor technique was unrefined. The strokes were unsteady and their weight was uneven, but she had managed to capture her mother's straight nose, blonde hair, and hazel eyes.

Would her mother approve of the choices she had made?

She returned the painting to the watercolor box and lifted her father's portrait. It, too, had been painted many years ago, but the likeness was there, complete with dark hair and stern black eyes. No smile. She lowered the painting. Try as she might, she could barely recall her father's smile, so rare was the action.

With a sigh Annabelle returned the contents to the watercolor box and tucked the entire box into the chest and then pulled out the pouch of jewelry. She poured some of the contents of the bag onto her lap. A garnet-and-diamond ring. A sapphire brooch. Her amethyst pendant. A string of pearls from the East Indies. The beauty in these fine pieces sparkled, but it was their exquisiteness that she valued. These were her security.

Should she ever find herself alone again, she could sell these and live quite comfortably. Perhaps it would be wise to try to sell one in town, as soon as she could steal away.

She cast a glance back at the sleeping forms. The only person who knew she possessed them was Crosley, but even she did not know exactly what Annabelle had brought. Her confidence in the former maid to keep her secrets wavered. Annabelle's only concern now was keeping her jewels safe and out of sight.

She divided the pieces up as best she could, worried that keeping them all in one place could jeopardize their safety. She tucked a ring in her watercolor box. Tucked a necklace in the toe of one of her slippers. She tore a small hole in her mattress and stuffed a trinket inside.

Annabelle pushed her hair from her face. She hoped she would not need to sell them soon. She and her uncle had not even discussed if she would be compensated for her work as a teacher. She had no idea how much it would cost to live, what she would need to buy, or anything else along those lines. She'd never had to worry about those things . . . until now.

She was about to close her valise when she spied her mother's prayer journal at the bottom. The other items she had unpacked had brought her some sort of comfort, but the sight of the leather journal unnerved her. She lifted the smooth tome and turned it over in her hands.

Annabelle had been unaware that her mother kept a journal until after her death. She had been going through her mother's things when she found the book tucked in one of her trunks. Once she realized that the volume contained her mother's private thoughts, she did not even tell her father of her discovery. Instead, she hid it away, keeping it as a secret, although painful, memory. In fact, she had never even read it in its entirety.

She flipped open the cover and angled it toward the candle's flickering light. On the pages were drawings, stories, and prayers. Her name flashed on one of the pages, and Annabelle stopped.

PRAYER FOR ANNABELLE

Let her know love, and let her know the peace that comes with forgiveness. Keep her safe from those who wish to harm her, and give her strength as she faces life's challenges. Give her grace to walk through shadows, wisdom to make decisions, and discernment in where to place her trust. Let her life be a happy one, marked with laughter, and give her health so she may live long and continue to spread the joy that she has brought to my life. But most of all, let her always feel loved and wanted, for she is the light in my darkness.

She pressed her eyes closed to squeeze the moisture from them, closed the book, and tucked it in the bottom of her trunk.

Her breath came in shuddery gasps. She did not want to cry. For she had been strong. She had been resilient. But now, her mother's whispers, written more than a decade ago, threatened to undo her.

She wished she could have her mother's faith and believe that a prayer could bring her safety and happiness, but perhaps she was too far down her own path for God to hear or respond to her. God had not answered her mother's prayers, and she doubted He would answer hers.

Feeling almost desperate for consolation, she snatched up the book again and found the page. It had been so long since she prayed on her own, but she read the words once more. Perhaps God would listen to her, perhaps He wouldn't. But at least, for a moment, the words brought her comfort.

Chapter Twenty-One

Owen rapped his knuckles on the thick oak door to Langsby's study before he pushed it fully open. "Have a moment?"

Langsby looked up from the paper in his hand and pushed his spectacles up on his nose with his forefinger. "Locke, come in. Just the man I need to speak with. Sit down."

The study was dark, and in fact, Owen was surprised that Langsby had not yet returned to the superintendent's cottage for the night. A small fire blazed in the grate, and two candles were aflame on Langsby's desk.

Owen had remained at the school longer than he anticipated. After delivering the hares to the kitchen, he had been asked to stop by the stables to take a look at one of the ill horses. Because of his knowledge of animals, he was often asked to help when they fell ill at the school, and by the time he was certain the horse was out of danger, the hour had grown quite late.

He sat across from Langsby. It took a moment for his eyes to adjust to the darkness.

Langsby leaned back in his chair and folded his arms over his chest. "I spoke with young Winter."

"And?"

"I asked what he was doing in the meadow, and at first he said merely exploring. I kept after him for an explanation, and he eventually shared the truth."

Locke leaned forward. "And what did he say?"

"He admitted that he was paid to go onto Bancroft property to catch rabbits, but he refused to name any names."

Owen slapped his knee. "I knew it."

"We will keep working on it." Langsby pushed the stack of letters to the side. "He has been suspended until he agrees to give me names, and he is currently being kept apart from the rest of the students."

"I hate that it has come to this." Owen leaned back in his chair. "It is not the first time I have dealt with poachers who have paid children to do their work, but it has always been children from either the miners or the gypsies, never a boy in Winter's position."

"I expect more out of my students, Mr. Locke. I've said it a dozen times, and I will say it until the last day I draw breath: developing character and conscience will always trump an academic education, and I see this as one of our biggest challenges yet. I will not rest until I am certain that no other boys are involved in this scheme. I have already added two more night watchmen and have informed the instructors that they will take turns monitoring the boys' dormitories to make sure no one leaves during the night hours."

"I know you'll see to the matter, Langsby."

"Thank you again for not taking this to the magistrate. A charge like this could ruin a boy's chance at a decent future. We will get to the bottom of it." Langsby folded his hands on the desk's leather inlay, as if to signal the end of his train of thought. "I trust you had a pleasant conversation with my niece."

Owen nodded. He did not know why he should feel uncomfortable discussing her. "Yes, I did. I had news from London to share."

Langsby eyed him suspiciously, as if poised to ask for more details.

Owen quickly changed the subject. "She told me she is to be a teacher. That is quite a change for her."

Langsby nodded. "It would have been easier for all parties, perhaps, to allow her to stay on as a guest at the cottage, but what lesson would be learned there? If she is serious about leaving the life she knew, she will need to become more acquainted with life outside of London. This is one way of doing it."

"What will she teach?"

"That is up to Mrs. Brathay. I only hope that Annabelle finds value in the experience. I must say, knowing her mother, I fully expected Annabelle to abandon her plan after a day or so of our quiet life here in Fellsworth. But she has surprised me. I've not heard one complaint from her."

"Miss Thorley may have had a life of privilege, but I can attest to the fact that her environment was anything but peaceful. I saw only a snippet, but what I did see was enough to convince me that she should no longer be in that situation."

The bell atop the chapel chimed, reminding Owen of the hour. "I am to meet Whitten for the night watch." He stood and returned his hat to his head. "I will be by tomorrow. Send word if Winter shares any more details, will you?"

Owen quit the study, exited the building, and stepped out into the cool night.

The day's heat had broken, and a calm breeze lifted the flaps of his coat and tousled his hair. He turned to look at the upper windows as he departed. Flickering candles danced in a handful of the paned windows, but for the most part, all was silent and still.

As he turned back to the gate, he noticed two women watching him from behind a distant wall. He slowed his steps, and when they realized he noticed them, they retreated into the night's shadows.

Normally, such spying would have no effect on him. He was not one to concern himself with the opinions of others. The village and school could not resist a good story, and no doubt poaching was not enough fodder for gossip.

To be truthful, he had grown used to the stares over the past several years. The whispers. The rumors.

Diana's murder had stunned their small village. Not only did it shake the very foundation of his life, but it had cast a long shadow on the village as well.

He had loved Diana. But her betrayal had killed bits of his soul and forever altered his ability to trust. And what was worse, the sting of her unfaithfulness lanced afresh every time someone whispered the rumors about his daughter's paternity.

True, Hannah was a fair, tiny little thing who bore no resemblance to him, but he would never betray the child. He may not have been able to protect Diana from another man's evil, but he would give his very life to protect Hannah from the cruelties of society and prejudice.

In his heart he was ready to love again. Loneliness was a bitter foe, and it was becoming more and more difficult to see the forest's solitude as a place of reprieve.

As he walked toward the school's main gate, movement near the stable shed caught his eye. He slowed his gait. No one, other than perhaps the groundskeeper, should be out on the property this far from the main buildings this time of night.

Concerned for the school's general well-being, he narrowed his gaze. It was dark, but he could determine that the figure was a woman with light hair.

Could it be Miss Crosley?

He would have noticed if another woman had such light hair. It was down around her shoulders, and even though he was not an expert on the requirements for the women at the school, he had never seen one of the teachers with her hair untethered in such a fashion.

He noticed more movement, and a male figure joined her, tall and lanky, shrouded in the night's shadows.

Owen fixed his gaze on the gate ahead. It was not his business if a Fellsworth School staff member was involved in a romantic interlude. That was Langsby's jurisdiction, not his. But as Owen cast a sideways glance at the couple, he was certain. It was Miss Crosley.

Within moments, the couple disappeared into the shadows, and Owen fixed his attention back on the gate. Something was amiss at Fellsworth, but he could not concern himself with such details. He had his own battles to fight, and fight them he would.

Chapter Twenty-Two

*A*nnabelle had never been so frightened in her life. She had heard gunshots. She had been struck by a man. She had even run away from her home in the middle of the night.

But never had she faced so many little faces.

About twenty young girls gathered in the room. Mrs. Brathay, the headmistress, had assigned Annabelle to assist Mrs. Tomlinson, the teacher who taught the youngest girls reading and grammar.

Annabelle stood silently in the corner, observing the session.

The girls sat at the two tables, quietly and primly, their eyes fixed firmly on their instructor. All of them wore the same black frock and white cap atop their heads.

Annabelle did not know how old they were, and she was too embarrassed to ask—for what sort of teacher could not judge a child's age? But she watched with interest as the girls took turns reading aloud from a book that was passed along the line.

From where she stood she could glimpse the clock tower. Time crawled by.

She probably should be paying more attention to what the children were reading, but instead, she was watching their faces. So many girls. So many different stories. Her uncle had said many of these children came from poor families and had been sent here for a chance to better themselves.

After what seemed like an eternity, the clock struck the hour, and Mrs. Tomlinson dismissed the girls and approached Annabelle.

"They are going out to their free hour in the girls' garden, but I would like you to stay behind and help this young lady review today's lesson."

Annabelle held her breath as she looked at the little blonde child still seated at the table. She was staring down at a closed book.

Mrs. Tomlinson continued. "All you need to do is listen to her read and help her with any words that are giving her trouble."

Annabelle nodded.

"I will be in the garden. Let me know if you need any assistance, but I think you can handle this."

Wishing she shared Mrs. Tomlinson's confidence, Annabelle bobbed a curtsy. Bolstering her confidence, she crossed the room, the tapping of her boots painfully loud on the polished wood floor, and sat next to the child.

The girl glanced at her and then returned her attention to her book.

Annabelle wasn't sure what to say first. "I am Miss Thorley."

"How do you do, Miss Thorley?" The girl's voice was soft and sweet. "I am Hannah Locke."

Annabelle tilted her head. "Are you Mr. Owen Locke's daughter?"

A little smile curved the child's lips at last. Whereas Mr. Locke's hair was dark and curly, the child's hair was so blonde that it appeared nearly white at her temples. A white cap covered her head, but long, straight strands escaped its confines. She was a lovely child, with a fair complexion, rosy cheeks, and round face.

The rumor Crosley shared with her flamed in Annabelle's mind. It was true. The child bore no resemblance to her father.

"Are you ready to read?" Annabelle needed to tend to the task at hand. "I am eager to hear the story."

A frown darkened Hannah's face as she lifted the book, and her light eyebrows drew together in stubborn resistance. Annabelle sensed she should correct the child's attitude, but her confidence was lacking. She had never given a child instruction. Never.

She decided on a different approach. "Tell me. What do you like to do when you are not reading?"

The little girl shrugged and looked out the window. "I don't know."

"I don't believe that. Surely there is something you like to do. Sing? Draw?"

Hannah wiped a loose lock of hair from her face and stared at the table's polished surface, her expression void of emotion. "I like to fish."

"Fish?" Annabelle frowned. She was not sure she heard the child correctly. Never had she heard a young lady say that she enjoyed fishing. "As in fishing in a pond?"

Hannah's shoulders seemed to relax. "Yes. My papa takes me fishing sometimes."

"Ah. I have met your papa, you know."

Hannah's pale eyes brightened and she smiled, revealing a missing tooth. "You have?"

"Yes." Annabelle felt a little measure of success that she had gotten the child to smile. "He is the gamekeeper at Bancroft Park, is he not?"

Hannah nodded.

"He was very nice to me. You should be very proud to have such a kind father."

Hannah twisted in her seat to face Annabelle, her interest in the activity out the window abandoned. "He is the bestest papa."

Amused by the girl's sweet lapse in grammar, Annabelle leaned close. "You mean, he is the *best* papa."

"Yes." Hannah scrunched her face. "That is what I said, isn't it?"

Annabelle hid a smile. "He does not live far from here, does he?"

"No. Our cottage is on the other side of the trees, just past the pond. Sometimes when there are no leaves you can see the chimney smoke from the edge of the school garden. Papa made a path through there, and sometimes we hike home that way. But only sometimes."

"You are fortunate, then. I understand that most of the children do not get to see their families very often."

"My papa comes almost every day. The forest on the other side of the garden is part of Bancroft Park, so he is working in there a lot." A fresh pout darkened her countenance. "I wish I could live there with him."

"I am sure he has a good reason for you to live here."

"Papa is gone a lot during the night, and he says it is safer for me if I live here. Plus he says I will learn more things here—things he can't teach me."

"I am sure your father knows best what you need." The bitter memory of her own father stole across Annabelle's memory. They had lived under the same roof, yet he was rarely available. She could not help but wonder how life would have been different with a more loving father.

"You are not like the other teachers."

A little surge of panic rushed through Annabelle. Her secret would be found out, surely. "Oh, how so?"

The little girl shrugged. "You aren't so mean."

Annabelle resisted the urge to smile. "I don't think the other teachers are mean. Not really."

Hannah lowered her voice, as if taking Annabelle into great confidence. "They get mad at me when I don't know the words."

"Maybe they are just trying to encourage you."

Hannah shook her head in emphatic disagreement. "My papa says that as long as I try my best I am doing good enough, but that is not what the teachers say."

"Well, I happen to think your papa is right."

Hannah cocked her golden head thoughtfully. "Did you have teachers when you were little?"

"I had only one teacher, but I did not attend a school like this. I had a governess."

"Did you like her?"

Annabelle relaxed. It was nice to think of happy memories, and she was enjoying the banter with Hannah—more than she thought she would. There was an honesty to the child, a lack of pretense, which, after such a difficult week, Annabelle found refreshing.

"I liked her very much. Her name was Miss Bornhill. She is Welsh and at times had a very strong accent, but she would always have peppermint comfits in her reticule."

"I have never had a peppermint comfit before."

"You haven't?" Annabelle found it odd the child had never tasted the confection. But then, Fellsworth was not the same as London. "We will have to find you some to try."

"Was she nice? As a teacher, I mean?"

"She was, and she was very patient. But I am afraid I was not always the best student."

"Did you get in trouble when you were little?"

She got in trouble not only when she was little, but as an adolescent. And even as an adult. "I did."

"What did you like to do when you were a girl? Did you like to go fishing, like I do?"

"I have never been fishing," confessed Annabelle.

Hannah's mouth dropped open. "Not ever?"

"No. There are not many ponds in London." Annabelle failed to mention that she never would have been allowed to participate in such an unladylike pursuit. "But I had plenty to do to fill my time."

"Then what did you like to do?"

"I liked to paint."

Rustling sounded at the door. Annabelle turned to see Mrs.

Tomlinson in the threshold. She could feel the silent reprimand. She was supposed to be reading with the child, not reliving her own childhood memories.

Annabelle swallowed. "You know, reading may be hard, but the more you try, the better you will become. Like fishing. I bet it took you quite a while to learn how to do it properly."

At the mention of reading, a scowl returned to Hannah's face.

"I will make you a promise." Annabelle picked up the book and extended it to Hannah. "You study these words really hard, and tomorrow I will bring you some drawing supplies and I will teach you how to draw something. How about that?"

The little girl smiled and nodded emphatically. "Really?"

"But you must promise me that you will try hard. Oh, and you probably shouldn't tell the other girls because I'm not sure what the other teachers will think. It will be our secret."

A genuine giggle bubbled from Hannah, and she took the book in her hands.

Annabelle smiled. It was nice to think she had made at least one little friend at the school.

Later that afternoon, Annabelle hurried down the path to Fellsworth School's main gate. She had exactly one hour before she was due back to her duties.

She looked over her shoulder to make sure no one witnessed her escape. When she was certain she was not being observed, she hurried through the gate and made her way down the lane to the Fellsworth town square.

A little thrill surged through her. She tightened her clutch on her reticule that contained a strand of pearls—a strand that she hoped to sell today at one of the shops. A month prior she never would have dreamed of doing such a thing, but she had little choice. At the moment she was settled and comfortable at the school, but she had little money.

She could not help but remember how Miss Stillworth tried to steal her reticule that day. Even after all these weeks it still troubled her to think that one day she could end up in a very similar situation to her unfortunate friend. Nothing was certain, and it scared her to think that nothing may ever be certain again.

She'd had so many new experiences as of late, and her emotions swung wildly from one sensation to another. Fear of her brother. Disgust about Mr. Bartrell. Relief that her uncle allowed her to stay at Fellsworth. Uncertainty over her new environment. Feelings of inadequacy in her new role.

But there were positive ones as well. Her aunt and uncle made her feel like a part of a family. She warmed under the memory of the conversations she had with Mr. Locke. In the midst of her weakness, a glimmer of strength and self-sufficiency broke through.

Finding the village's town square was not difficult. A cluster of shops and carts were positioned neatly around a cheery fountain. Wooden signs hanging outside of the shops indicated what they were: butcher, grocer, apothecary, milliner, tailor. She did not see a jeweler sign. She paused when she saw a sign labeled "Dressmaker."

Uncertainty pulsed through her as she pushed open the door. A small bell atop the door chimed as she entered. The shop was much simpler than the elegant modiste shops she frequented in London. Normally when she would come into a shop, Crosley accompanied her, and usually a footman or two came along to carry her purchases. This shop was very different. Only two simply cut gowns were on display. Several bolts of fabric lined the walls, and ribbons hung from the low, dark ceiling. The scent of firewood overwhelmed the stuffy space, and smoke from a nearby fire teased her nose.

A woman stood behind the counter, engrossed in a ledger, but as

Annabelle approached her, a floorboard squeaked under her weight and the shopkeeper looked up. She eyed Annabelle suspiciously. "May I help you, miss?"

"Yes. That is, I hope so." Annabelle forced a smile.

The dressmaker's demeanor remained firm. "I take it you are from the school."

"I am."

"I've not seen you before." The dressmaker stepped from behind the counter and tilted her head to the side. "Are you new?"

Annabelle nodded, cautious not to reveal too much about herself. The less said regarding her situation, the better. "I have a necklace I would like to sell."

The woman shook her head in immediate dismissal. "We do not buy jewelry, miss."

"I understand, but I was hoping you would take a look anyway."

The woman put her hands on her hips and opened her mouth to protest, but Annabelle retrieved the pearls and extended them before the shopkeeper could respond.

The woman accepted the necklace and lifted it toward the light from the window. Her expression changed as she examined the piece. "This is beautiful."

"It has been in my family for generations," Annabelle quickly informed her.

The dressmaker eyed her, and Annabelle pressed her lips shut. If she didn't want to answer more questions, she should be silent.

"It is very pretty, but I cannot buy it." The dressmaker gave her head a sharp shake and extended the necklace back toward Annabelle.

Frustration mounted. Annabelle had assumed the shopkeeper would be so enamored with the necklace's beauty that she would offer a tidy sum to have it in her shop. Her instinct was to try to persuade the woman, but movement outside the window distracted her.

Mr. Bryant stood just on the other side of the window, his light eyes fixed on her.

A sliver of panic raced through her. She was not supposed to leave the school grounds—not without permission. She had been caught.

But what was Mr. Bryant doing outside the dressmaker's shop?

She turned her attention back to the counter, trying to pretend she had not seen him looking at her. But she flicked her gaze back to the window. Mr. Bryant was definitely staring at her. The sly, knowing gleam in his eyes unnerved her to her very core. Had he followed her?

It was almost as if he wanted her to see him.

The same anger that pulsed through her that last night in London raced through her. She would not allow herself to be frightened. The only course of action was to approach him directly and ask his intention.

The task at hand almost forgotten, she bid the shopkeeper a hasty farewell and tucked the trinket back into her reticule. She scurried out from the modest shop and into the bright afternoon sunshine, prepared to confront the pretentious Mr. Bryant. But as she turned to her right to face the spot where he had been standing, Mr. Bryant was not there.

She frowned. She looked to the left and back to the right. But he was nowhere to be seen.

Despite the sun's intense heat, her blood ran cold.

Mr. Bryant was playing a game with her.

Frustrated and a little unnerved, she headed back down the village's main lane toward the school's entrance. Her heart was even heavier than when she left. She had failed to sell her pearls, and what was worse, Mr. Bryant had witnessed the ordeal. But she suspected that Mr. Bryant's interest in her went far beyond mere jewelry, and that frightened her most of all.

Chapter Twenty-Three

*I*t's been far too long since I have been out in the forest." Treadwell fell into step with Owen as they walked through the backwoods of Linton Forest the following week. The sunlight flitted through the emerald canopy, and swallows swooped in the branches overhead. "It is so peaceful out here. I envy you, Locke, passing your days here."

Owen glanced up as a group of ducks flocked overhead toward Foster's Pond. "Autumn will be here soon. Before you know it you'll be out with the hunting parties every week."

"Are the pheasants ready for the season?" Treadwell squinted toward the trees. "I haven't seen any about."

"Oh, they're here, but they've enough sense to keep away from the man with a firearm." Owen winced at the volume of Treadwell's voice. They'd catch nothing today if the man continued speaking so loudly.

"Good." Treadwell shouldered his weapon, oblivious of Owen's annoyance. "You know how these hunting parties go. Guests can get so grumpy when they can't find birds. Whether or not they can shoot them is another matter entirely. Do you remember when we were boys how your father would take us ferreting?"

"I do. And do you recall the time you were setting the fish trap at Foster's Pond and fell in? I thought your father was going to have an apoplexy when my father took you back to the main house."

Treadwell laughed and shook his head, then sobered. "Father

could not see the humor or the adventure in such an activity. I often envied you, you know."

"What? Me?"

"Yes. Did you never wonder why I was always around and asking your father for shooting lessons? Your father invested in you and taught you. My father provided a tremendous living for me, but that was the extent of it. When he died, I knew him no better than I knew the butler or my tutor."

Owen stiffened. He and Treadwell were friends, but their discussions rarely took such a personal turn. His own father's death left the single biggest hole in him—even more than the loss of his mother and Diana. Owen's entire childhood was spent at his father's side, learning about the fowl of the air and the beasts of the fields. He'd begrudged the hard work of the gamekeeping life as a boy, but now he saw the value and purpose in it. He may have envied Treadwell's pampered upbringing, but looking back he would not trade his experience for anything.

The soft sound of rustling leaves made Owen start. He put his arm out to stop Treadwell, then put his finger to his lips. Within seconds he had his target in sight, the weapon's stock against his shoulder, and pulled the trigger.

"Amazing," breathed Treadwell as Drake ran ahead to retrieve their game. "I didn't even see it."

Owen shrugged his game bag from his shoulder. "Just instinct now. See that bunch of undergrowth there? The rabbits like to gather there, especially at this time of day."

Treadwell shook his head and waited for Owen to bag the game. "I came along today because I wanted to speak with you about something."

Owen raised his eyebrow as he knelt and fastened the bag. "And?"

"I spoke with Farley yesterday about Kirtley Meadow."

Owen stopped, rested his elbow on his knee, and fixed his eyes on Treadwell. "We've been walking all morning and you just now bring up this news?"

Treadwell smirked and pulled a slip of paper from his emerald waistcoat. "I paid him a little visit the other day and we had a chat. I told him I would give you this."

Owen's heart raced as he looked at the folded missive. "What's that?"

"Go ahead." He extended the letter to Owen. "Read it."

Owen stood and took the letter. He stared at it as if it were either magic or poison.

At one time Kirtley Meadow had been part of Bancroft Park, but Treadwell's father had gambled and lost the land in question to Farley's father when Owen was just a lad. The original Bancroft Park gamekeeper's cottage stood in Kirtley Meadow—the very cottage had housed generations of the Locke family. There was nothing remarkable about the land itself. It was beautiful, of course, with lush elm groves and sparkling ponds, but it would be of little interest to most. But to Owen it held a symbol of his family's past. His ancestors were buried under its willows. While the property he sought to purchase would never be a great estate like Bancroft Park, it would be enough for him to make a living and to honor his family's legacy.

As Owen hesitated, Treadwell rolled his head to the side in exasperation. "Will you just read it? For a gamekeeper you are unusually dramatic."

Owen drew a breath and opened the letter. He scanned it quickly, hungry to comprehend the letter's meaning without wasting time in the details. His heart clenched as the meaning of the words sank in. "He is willing to sell the land. But there are conditions."

"What sort of conditions?"

Owen handed the letter to Treadwell. "You can read it for yourself."

The letter, which initially he had hoped would give him the answers he so desired, only frustrated him further.

Treadwell's voice increased an octave as he perused the missive. "What? This amount is twice what the land is worth. How can Farley think that anyone would pay this?"

"First of all, keep your voice down. We'll catch nothing if you carry on like that," growled Owen. "Besides, it doesn't matter that it is twice what it's worth. It is twice what I have, so the topic is closed."

Treadwell's voice lowered. "That's it? You are just going to walk away? This is the beginning of a negotiation. Or I can loan you the money. I have told you that before."

Owen shook his head. "I'll not be in debt to any man, for any reason."

"You sound like your father. You Lockes and your wretched principles. Your life would be much easier if you would hold yourself to a more realistic standard."

"It is not only the money. Finish reading the letter." Owen pointed his gloved thumb at the paper. "The sale of the land is contingent on the fact that I help him solve his poaching issues. Seems he is dealing with a particularly stubborn band, and he isn't having any luck with the magistrate."

Treadwell chuckled. "What? You think you couldn't do it?"

Owen resumed walking. "'Course I could do it. But I am employed by Bancroft Park, not Walmsly Hall."

Treadwell handed him back the letter. "He also asks for you to visit him at Walmsly Hall to discuss the matter. It can't hurt to just hear the man out."

"I suppose you are right." Owen turned his attention to the row of hedges lining the path where rabbits liked to nest. Perhaps he would figure something out, as Treadwell suggested. Or perhaps he would remain only a gamekeeper. Time would tell.

But it was another thought, equally as invasive, that had been on his mind since their hunt began, even more so than Kirtley Meadow. Owen could not shake the odd circumstances surrounding the McAlister murder.

He was not sure how he had expected Miss Thorley to react at the news of the murder when he told her. She had been visibly bothered about it. Her neck had grown blotchy, a reaction, he was beginning to notice, that occurred whenever she was alarmed or frightened.

Miss Thorley's unnerved behavior in some way reminded him of Diana. She had become increasingly odd in the weeks leading up to her murder. At the time he attributed her erratic behavior to loneliness. It had been autumn, and Treadwell's father was still alive. The elder Mr. Treadwell was an avid hunter and hosted back-to-back parties where Owen would be gone from home for days. His and Diana's new marriage was a tense one—a union of two personalities that were far too different.

He would never cease blaming himself for her death. He should have noticed the signs—she had been fidgety, she looked unwell, and she said she had not been sleeping much. But when the truth of what had happened came to light, she was already gone. He would never know if the man had been threatening to expose the relationship or trying to persuade her to leave Owen. Regardless, the experience made him more observant in general, and Miss Thorley's response to McAlister's death had been too apparent to ignore.

It was not his business, he knew. But Treadwell could keep no secrets and was an endless source of information.

Owen tucked the letter in his pocket. "I didn't get a chance to speak with you before you left London for Bath."

"Where were you, by the way, the day after we arrived? I went to the mews looking for you and they said you were gone."

Owen was not in the habit of lying, but he also did not want to incriminate Miss Thorley. "An errand, 'tis all. But it seems I missed all of the excitement."

Fortunately the answer pacified Treadwell. "Yes, the decision to depart for Bath was sudden. But after the discovery of McAlister's body, and the fact that Miss Thorley left in such a hurry, the family was distraught. Thorley's wife fainted more than once. You know me. I am not one to abandon an interesting scene, so I traveled with them."

"What exactly happened to McAlister?"

Treadwell drew a deep breath and expelled it forcefully, as if it were difficult to recount the specifics of the night. "I don't know. Surely you saw how the party was shaping up. It was a bit too raucous, even for me. When we returned to the house, we went to the billiards room. Thorley and Bartrell began to argue. Bartrell wanted—nay, demanded to marry Thorley's sister, the lady you met on the street that day in London. It was quite uncomfortable for McAlister and myself, being forced to witness such a personal argument. Apparently Miss Thorley refused him quite severely. Not that I blame her, for he is a pompous, pretentious man who grated on my nerves terribly. His only redeeming quality is that he is a terrible hand at cards so I made a tidy little sum. But as the night wore on, he became quite dark and sullen, so I retired to bed."

"Did you hear the gunshot?"

"Did you?"

Owen nodded. "I heard one gunshot. According to the driver I spoke with, it might have been the shot responsible for McAlister's death."

Treadwell shook his head. "I heard nothing. After a bit too much brandy, I was dead to the world. When I awoke, a magistrate was at the breakfast table and Mrs. Thorley had a case of the vapors."

Owen tucked the bit of information he did receive in the back of his mind: Miss Thorley was escaping an unwanted marriage—a fate she deemed worse than teaching at a poor school.

But still something seemed off.

And he determined to find out what it was.

Chapter Twenty-Four

$\mathscr{A}$nnabelle was late.

Again.

She forced her hand through the black linen gown's sleeve and muttered under her breath as her finger caught in the hem.

Normally Jane would wake her, but this morning Jane had breakfast duty and had to oversee the youngest girls as they set the breakfast tables. Annabelle had awoken when she left but had fallen back asleep.

Would it ever be easy to wake up in the morning at an early hour? For her entire life she had been used to sleeping as late as she liked, and never did she have to wake herself.

She fumbled with the tie at the back of her neck and reached for her boots. Perhaps one day she would master the art, but for now, waking up before the sun was definitely one of the most difficult aspects of her new life.

Once her boots were secure, she grabbed a hairpin. She twisted her hair into place before scurrying through the door. Her footsteps echoed on the wooden floor as she flew down the empty hall and main staircase toward the girls' classrooms.

She stopped outside the door of the chamber she was supposed to be in. She waited for her pulse to slow and normal breathing to resume before she pushed open the heavy oak door. Annabelle winced as it squeaked on its hinges, drawing even more attention to the fact that she was nearly a half hour late for her class.

Mrs. Tomlinson turned and lifted her chin to look down her

pointed nose at Annabelle. Her sharp, dark eyes flashed. "Ah. Miss Thorley. So good of you to join us."

Behind her, a chorus of girlish giggles filled the high-ceilinged chamber. Mrs. Tomlinson whirled around, silencing the snickers with her glare. She then turned back to Annabelle. "I've other classes to tend to. Your tardiness has put me behind schedule. Can I trust you to hear the girls' reading so I can get the other classes under way?"

Annabelle froze under the intensity of Mrs. Tomlinson's directness. "Of course, Mrs. Tomlinson. I mean, I will see to the reading."

Mrs. Tomlinson pressed her lips into a firm line and held Annabelle in her gaze for several seconds. Annabelle wanted to shrink into the ground and was suddenly mindful of how untidy her hair must be.

"Very well." Mrs. Tomlinson broke her focus and gathered a small stack of books on the table next to her. "Ladies, mind Miss Thorley. I expect a good report."

And with that, the older teacher left the room.

The deafening silence weakened Annabelle's resolve as she stepped to the front of the room and retrieved the book Mrs. Tomlinson had left behind. Her hand trembled as she picked up the reader and turned to face the twenty-one sets of eyes watching her every move.

She swallowed to moisten her dry throat. "Uh, can someone please tell me what you were reading?"

Nobody moved.

Panic welled within her. Annabelle fixed her eyes on a plump, dark-headed girl in the front row. "Miss Cranden, can you please tell me what you were reading?"

The girl looked to her neighbor before she responded. "We were just about to start reading the story that begins on page 29."

Annabelle expelled a sigh. "Can you start the reading for us?"

Miss Cranden stood up and began reading, her voice clear and strong in the room's stillness. Annabelle fixed her eyes on the back wall. It was going to be a long morning.

"I am so glad that is over." Annabelle hurried down the path leading from the girls' dormitory to the garden.

Jane lengthened her gait to match Annabelle's hurried one. "I was sorry to hear that you overslept. I should have made sure you were awake."

"It is not your responsibility to make sure I am up." Annabelle purposely slowed her steps. "Please tell me this gets easier."

"Do you mean waking up on time?"

Annabelle smiled. "No. Teaching. I have been here for weeks now, and I seem to be no better at it than I was the first day I arrived."

Jane looped her arm through Annabelle's. "Don't fret. It really does take time. Besides, you are doing better than you think. The children can be a handful, especially the little ones, and whether you think so or not, they seem to be fond of you."

"Then why do they not listen to me?"

"They will. Earn their trust and respect." Jane gave a little laugh. "They gave me quite a fit when I first started teaching, especially the older ones, but they have come around."

It was the noon hour, and the children had broken their studies for the midday meal. Instead of eating in the tiny room set aside for the teachers, Annabelle and Jane had opted for a stroll in the garden. After several days of intense summer heat, an overnight storm had sliced the oppressiveness, and today a gentle, cool breeze was just what Annabelle needed to find peace after a trying morning.

They walked in the shadow of the willow trees. Annabelle drew in the soft aroma of bark and pasture. As strange as it was to admit, with the exception of the early hours she was growing accustomed to the change of pace. Slowly the pains associated with her old life were subsiding, and the repetitive rhythm of Fellsworth School was becoming her norm. She found unexpected comfort in the strict routine and purpose in the discipline, even though adherence was difficult at times. She had even come to accept the new manner of dress and found it freeing not to change her gown several times a day.

"How long have you been here?" Annabelle was curious to learn more about the woman who was quickly becoming her friend. They shared a chamber, but they didn't have much time to spend in conversation. "You appear so comfortable here."

"Oh, bless you. I came here four months back. After my husband died I had no family left in Bath, so I was eager to accept the position here. Louise Stiles and I actually arrived on the same day."

"Did you know each other prior to your arrival?"

"No, it was purely by chance. She is quite a character, though. I am grateful you and Margaret have arrived." Jane sobered. "The rumor is that you have never taught before."

Annabelle turned her head to face the other woman. "Is it that obvious?"

"No, not obvious, I did not mean that. But there has been talk that you received the position because of your uncle, and for no other reason. I tell you this not in gossip or to make you feel uncomfortable, but the staff here can be difficult to navigate. It is quite difficult to obtain a position as a junior teacher, and I only wanted you to be aware."

The first dry leaves of the season crunched under Annabelle's boots as she walked along the path. "I suppose the rumors are true. I needed somewhere to stay, and my uncle was kind enough to provide this living. And I am grateful."

Jane smiled. "Well, I have grown quite fond of you, if that is of any consequence, and I am glad you are here. You are a far more pleasant chamber mate than Louise, that is certain, and in time I think you will prove your merit."

"I hope so."

Annabelle enjoyed Jane's company. Other members of the staff treated her with suspicion and coldness, and her odd encounters with Mr. Bryant made her uncomfortable, but Jane treated her as an equal. Perhaps Jane might be able to shine a little light on the subject for her.

"May I ask you a question?" Annabelle tugged at the ribbons of her bonnet.

"Of course."

"Do you know Mr. Simon Bryant?"

"Yes, he is one of the boys' teachers. Why?"

"Nothing really. I have not met any of the boys' teachers yet, but I did encounter him at my uncle's cottage a few weeks back."

"Did he behave inappropriately?"

"No, nothing of the sort. It was just a feeling, that is all."

"Well, I am not surprised you have not met any of the male teachers. Mrs. Brathay is quite insistent that we have as little inter-action with them as possible. The rule is quite strict. Our schedules are set so we only see them in church on Sunday. On more than one occasion I can think of, a female staff member has been relieved from her duties for being too familiar with the male staff."

Jane adjusted her hat and looked sideways at Annabelle. "Oh, and we also will be able to interact with them at the Autumn Festival. Has anyone mentioned that to you yet?"

Annabelle tilted her head. "No, I don't think so."

Jane's face brightened. "Oh my, I can hardly wait for it to arrive! It is still a couple of weeks away, but I have heard ever so many wonderful stories about it. Dancing and music and merriment. It is the one time of the year the townspeople are invited to the school grounds to celebrate the harvests from our agricultural efforts and mingle with the staff."

Annabelle's interest was piqued. "That does sound exciting."

"And what is even more exciting is that it is the one time we are allowed to dress in attire other than these horrid black dresses, to hearken back to the school's earliest days before a uniform was enforced."

Annabelle was glad to hear of it. She was about to ask more questions about it, but as they walked along the garden's low wall toward the school's main gate, she heard a giggle.

"Did you hear that?" Jane stopped and turned. "The children should all be taking their meals."

Annabelle frowned. Something was oddly familiar about the voice. "I did hear it. From where do you suppose it came?" She stepped away from Jane and around the garden's wall where she thought the sound originated.

And what she saw horrified her.

For there, in the distance, stood Crosley.

With a man.

Obviously unaware that she was being observed, Crosley threw back her head in laughter. Her blonde uncovered hair caught the few bright rays of sunlight that managed to squeeze through the shifting gray clouds. She reached out and touched the coat sleeve of the laughing man, who lifted his finger to her lips to tell her to be quiet.

Jane approached, and her steps slowed as she took in the intimate sight. "Oh my."

The man's finger lingered on Crosley's lips, and instead of resisting his touch, she leaned in closer. He wrapped his arm around her waist and pulled her tight.

Annabelle could handle the silence no more. She tore her gaze away from the scene. "We should leave."

But Jane stood firm. "It's Mr. Hemstead."

"Who's Mr. Hemstead?"

Jane did not take her gaze off the pair. "He is one of the boys' schoolteachers. A handsome man, but a dangerous one as far as a pretty female is concerned. Miss Crosley would do well to avoid him."

Concern pulsed through Annabelle. Even though there had been several odd, tense moments between Crosley and her, she wanted to protect her former lady's maid if she could. "Why?"

Jane kept her voice low. "I have not made his acquaintance personally, but apparently he fancies himself quite the catch. I do not know why your uncle allows him to continue here, for if the rumors are true, he has put more than one young woman in a compromising situation. His father is on the school's advisory board and provides substantial financial support. That is the only reason I can think of."

The chiming bell atop the chapel marked the end of the meal hour. Crosley turned to leave, but the man reached out his hand to playfully stop her.

Jane pulled back from the gate and straightened. "I must go, but since you are her friend, it might be wise to advise her to guard the company she keeps."

Jane's warning burned in Annabelle's ears as the other woman headed back down the path. Annabelle waited for Mr. Hemstead to leave Crosley's side, and then as Crosley took the path back to the school, she hurried to catch up with her former lady's maid.

"Crosley, have you gone mad?" Annabelle hissed as she jogged to fall into step next to the shorter woman.

Crosley did not slow her pace and fixed her eyes on something in the distance. "What do you mean?"

"You were with a man. Alone! What were you thinking? Anyone could have seen you." Annabelle righted her bonnet, which had tilted to the side with her hasty action. "You know full well behavior like that could result in your termination."

"You fret far too much. Besides, Mr. Hemstead is kind. I think he likes me very much."

"Therein lies the problem, Crosley." Annabelle lifted the hem of her gown and struggled to keep up. "According to Jane he has quite the rake's reputation."

"That sort of thing might concern you, but it does not concern me." Crosley increased her pace.

"Well, it should. Men like that can be dangerous."

Crosley came to an abrupt halt and faced Annabelle. "And you know of such things? Of 'men like that'?"

Annabelle lifted her hand to still the hair flittering about her face. "We have both heard stories of how women—seemingly good, wholesome women—have fallen prey to a handsome man. It is just a warning, Crosley. I mean, Margaret. From a friend."

"A friend?" Crosley crossed her arms over her chest. "Why, is it because you care so much for my future?"

Annabelle finally made eye contact. "As a matter of fact, I do."

Crosley's light eyes narrowed. "We should probably come to terms on one fact. You and I came here together, but we are not family. We are not friends. I worked for you, waited on you. Primped you. Dressed you. Kept your secrets. Brought you tea and coffee whenever your heart desired. That does not make me beholden to you for anything, nor does it give you the right to comment on my personal affairs."

Annabelle winced at the words, surprised by their sting. She opened her mouth to speak, but Crosley had not finished speaking her mind. "You might be willing to throw away marriage proposals like they were rubbish, but some of us can't afford such luxuries. I, for one, do not want to end my life as a spinster."

Annabelle clenched her jaw to prevent harsh words from spilling forth and then took a deep breath. "If you are insinuating that *I* threw away a marriage proposal, I—"

"You can interpret my words however you like, but I am not going to pass up the opportunity to marry and be settled. Mr. Hemstead may be that man or he may not be. But that is my decision to make, not yours. You'll not be able to tell me what to do anymore."

Frustration welled within Annabelle. Never had Crosley spoken to her that way. "I only meant that—"

"And while we are on the subject, you would be wise to heed your own advice."

Annabelle winced at the sharp tone. "I don't understand."

"I think it's terribly ironic that you warn me of such things, when you yourself had an open conversation with a man right in the middle of the courtyard for all to see."

"Who?" Annabelle demanded, her defenses rising.

"Mr. Locke."

She huffed. "What does he have to do with this conversation?"

"Perhaps you have the same idea as I. You just do not want to admit it."

Annabelle's head swam at the myriad insinuations flying at her. She was not in a position to scold Crosley, as Crosley was well aware. In fact, Crosley could spoil Annabelle's entire situation with one slip of the tongue. How could Annabelle have been so foolish as to get herself so indebted to another?

She lowered her voice. "I've no desire to argue with you. I'm only suggesting that it would be sensible to guard your character and heed what others are saying."

"I could care less what others say about me." Crosley leaned closer. "Perhaps you should stop pretending to know me and my character. Let me be clear: we may have lived together, but we were not friends, and I've no desire to be so."

Chapter Twenty-Five

*A*fter the odd encounter with Crosley, Annabelle longed for solitude.

She looked up to the sky and watched a cluster of birds fly by. She did not want to return to school, and she did not have another class for an hour.

Annabelle had not realized how sheltered her old way of life was. She'd grown comfortable in her bubble of isolation, and she felt unsure of how to handle the constant presence of other people. She had thought the lack of luxury would be the hardest part of this transition, but that assumption was far from the truth.

She glanced back to see Crosley's small form stomping toward the kitchen garden. Their conversation had left her feeling weak and foolish. How naive she had been for assuming Crosley's sincerity all those years.

There was little she could do about that now, and she did not want to give Crosley the satisfaction of knowing how sharply her words had cut. The mention of Mr. Locke and the following accusations had struck a chord, for in reality Annabelle did want the security a husband would offer. She wanted a home of her own and the knowledge that she belonged somewhere of her own merit. And right now, she was far from either.

Annabelle stepped through the garden gate that led outside of Fellsworth School property. Doubt choked her. Perhaps she had made a mistake in coming here. But what good would it do to second-guess her decision now? There could be no going back.

Step after step took her deeper into the forest. It was much cooler beneath the canopy of green boughs, and the soothing birdcalls and gentle twinkling of sunlight streaming through the emerald leaves made it seem like a fairyland. She closed her eyes in the forest's calming stillness and took several deep breaths.

She did not need Crosley's friendship. But what did she really need? Rest? Security?

Her body was tired, but it was more than that—her mind was tired. Tired of change. Tired of not meeting the expectations of those around her. Tired of feeling like a leaf in a pond, bouncing and swaying with the water's will.

A sudden voice pulled her from her reflection.

"Miss Thorley. What are you doing here?"

Annabelle turned around to see Mr. Locke, straight and tall upon his brown horse, a rifle across his lap. Drake trotted next to his master, but he did not stop with the horse. Instead, the brown dog scampered toward her, tail wagging. He came quite close and sniffed her hand.

She smiled at the animal's affection and then looked up. "I was just taking a stroll."

"Do you know that this is Bancroft property?" His eyes were shadowed by the brim of his hat, hiding his eyes and any expression held within.

She drew her eyebrows together. "I did not mean to trespass."

"I did not say it to make you feel like you were trespassing." He dismounted from his horse, the keys at his waist jingling as he did so. "There are traps along this area over here. I caution you to be careful, 'tis all."

"Thank you for the words of caution." She rubbed her arm. "I lost track of how far I had walked. It is beautiful here. I never realized spaces like this existed. There was certainly nothing to match it in London."

Owen tipped his hat back and took several seconds to observe his surroundings, almost as if seeing them for the first time. "I would take the solace of a forest over the hustle of London's streets any day. Just listen to the silence. My father always said that if the mind is too cluttered, you will never hear your soul's whispers."

Annabelle never would have expected such a rugged man to reveal such a tender sentiment. He looked up at the leaves once more. Appreciation was evident in his tanned face as he surveyed the space. He clearly saw more than trees. More than a forest. He was in his home.

It really was good to see Mr. Locke. He removed his hat, and slivers of sunlight played in the wild, curly black locks. He shook his head to brush them out of his face.

As much as she didn't want it to be true, the conversation they had on Fellsworth property the other day had been weighing heavily on her mind. "I am glad to have encountered you, for I wondered if you have received any more news of my brother."

He flipped the horse's reins over the animal's head and looped them around a low-hanging branch. "Unfortunately I know nothing new, other than your brother and sister-in-law have relocated to Bath. That is all Mr. Treadwell shared with me."

"How odd." She stilled her bonnet's windblown ribbons. "My sister-in-law does not care to leave London."

"From what Treadwell said, I think the situation was so dire that she wanted to be free of it."

Annabelle could not blame Eleanor, and pity for her sister-in-law's situation threaded around her. Their family had already been the source of scandal. News of the murder of a guest in the Thorley home would spread quickly. It would be impossible for any member of the family to show their face without whispers and stares. Even if the murderer was never found, the scandal would follow their family wherever they went.

A bird chirped overhead, and she squinted to see it in the branches above. "May I tell you something, Mr. Locke?"

"You may tell me anything you wish."

Annabelle's chest tightened. "It concerns Mr. McAlister."

His eyes narrowed on her, and for a moment she regretted bringing the topic to light. But the memory of that night had been pressing on her, and who else could she speak to about it? "That night, before we left for the ball at the Baldwins', Crosley brought me a missive from Mr. McAlister."

She watched him, waiting for some sort of shock at learning she had received a note from a man, but no such response came. "In it he told me that my brother was in dire trouble and he asked me to meet with him privately to discuss it."

His expression remained stoic. "And did you speak with him?"

She shook her head and looked down at the leafy carpet beneath her feet. "I could not risk the scandal of responding in a letter, and I had hoped to talk with him at the ball, but that never happened. And now . . ." Her words faded.

He shifted his weight from one foot to the other. "Do you have any idea what he was referring to?"

Annabelle gave a little laugh and tucked a wayward strand of hair behind her ear. "My brother is always in some sort of predicament, Mr. Locke. I probably should have been more concerned when I received the note, but my brother had made it perfectly plain that I had no business interfering with his dealings. I can't help but wonder if Mr. McAlister's message had something to do with what transpired that night. Furthermore, I wonder if in some way I could have prevented what happened."

"You cannot take such an act upon yourself, Miss Thorley. It is a horrible act, but it is not yours."

Her gaze landed on the weapon now resting against Mr. Locke's shoulder. She knew nothing about weapons or firearms. But her brother kept smaller versions of them in Wilhurst House. And something like it had taken Mr. McAlister's life.

He nodded at the rifle in his arms. "Is this making you nervous?"

Embarrassed she had been caught staring, she managed a thin laugh. "I am just not used to seeing those carried about so casually."

"There is nothing casual about them. In fact, I keep it completely out of sight when Hannah is around. She is nervous around them too. Here, I'll put it down if it makes you more comfortable."

His action indicated that he intended to stay in her presence for a bit longer. A strange, girlish flutter stirred within her. She was glad. She did not want him to leave.

A bird swooped from the branches and landed on a nearby shrub, the suddenness of it taking Annabelle by surprise. "What sort of bird is that? I never saw it before I came to Fellsworth."

"That?" He pointed at the bird and raised his eyebrows. "That's a warbler."

"She is a pretty little thing, and I have seen several of them since I came to Fellsworth. I didn't see many birds like that in London."

"Well, *she* is actually a *he*. You can tell by the black cap on his head." Mr. Locke stepped toward the bird, and it took flight and disappeared into the waving leaves. "Meddlesome creature, really. But harmless."

She was not used to feeling so unknowledgeable. In the London drawing rooms she was well versed in the topic of literature or the fashion of the day. She found it refreshing, if not humbling, to explore a new topic. "You must think it odd that I know so little of these things."

"Not really. You are from a town. I have been here a lifetime. My earliest memories took place in these very woods, and I have not wandered far. I know these woods like the back of my hand. Take this warbler, for instance. You've not seen him in London because it is not safe for him there. No food. Too dangerous. But get him in the right environment and he will thrive, just like people do."

Annabelle liked Mr. Locke. Something about his nature made her feel as if she had known him all her life. Maybe it was because he had already seen her at her worst, or maybe it was because she felt as if she had no more to lose.

She allowed her perfect posture to slacken ever so slightly. "I suppose I don't know where I belong anymore."

"Yes you do." His response was swift. "Otherwise you would not be here in Fellsworth."

She gave a little laugh. "Are you always so confident?"

"Confident? I wouldn't say confident. But I do believe that we have God-given instincts. We are not just placed on this earth haphazardly. Each of us has a path. Each of us has a purpose. It is part of life to find that path and follow it."

She was quickly realizing that Mr. Locke was not guided by societal convention. He was direct and self-assured. His words sounded like those her uncle would say, or even her mother. "You mentioned God-given instincts. Are you a man of faith, Mr. Locke?"

"I've seen far too much to be otherwise, Miss Thorley."

Was she a woman of faith? She did not know. She thought of the prayer her mother had written for her. The prayer she read, attempting to make it her own. Had God even heard it?

An awkward silence hovered, and she felt as if she needed to say more. She sat on the log behind her. "I attended church with my mother as a child, but after her death my family never went again. And my governess used to make me memorize Scripture. At one point, I would guess I could have recited several verses. But now I fear it has faded from memory. I just don't know anymore."

He surprised her by crossing the small clearing and sitting on the log next to her. She could feel his warmth as he neared. He rested his elbows on his knees, just like he did in the carriage ride from London. He looked down at the ground for several seconds and then focused his attention somewhere off in the distance.

"Things happen in life we cannot understand. We can only do our best and seek God's guidance and move forward the best we are able." He turned to look at her directly. "All will work out well in the end, Miss Thorley. You'll see."

How could a man whose wife had been murdered view the world so optimistically? She had experienced pain, but so had he. And he seemed to handle it much better than she. "I envy you, Mr. Locke."

He chuckled. "And why would that be?"

"You seem to be at peace with the world."

He looked off into the forest again. His expression darkened. "I don't know if I would go that far."

She could not help but stare at him. He was unlike anyone she had ever met. She quickly considered the men who had been in her life before coming to Fellsworth. Her father. Her brother. Samuel Goodacre. Cecil Bartrell. Their primary focus had been on improving their social and financial standings by any means necessary. As a group they were never content, never at peace.

Mr. Locke seemed to be the opposite of these men in so many ways. Could he really be as genuine as he seemed?

A gentle silence balanced between them. She was grateful for his presence, but then, as quickly as that realization glimmered, Crosley's harsh words echoed.

She was alone.

With a man.

Just as she had cautioned Crosley about.

And even though she was not flirting, she could recognize the double standard. She stood from the log and wiped bits of debris from her hands. "I suppose I should return to my duties."

He stood as well.

She felt hesitant to leave. He, at the very least, was becoming a friend. "In fact, I will be spending time with Hannah later today."

His face brightened. "My daughter tells me you have been teaching her to paint."

Annabelle laughed. "Yes. She is working on it."

"I hung her painting of a cat in the cottage." A smile crossed his lips. "Very pretty."

Annabelle smiled at the memory of the childish painting. "She will improve, with time and practice."

"I appreciate you taking her under your wing. She can be so shy, and sometimes I wonder if she is truly happy at Fellsworth. I am grateful to you for showing such interest in her." He gathered his horse's reins once again. "Do you paint often?"

"A little. That is, I used to. I am not sure I will have much time moving forward, but as you said, paths and purposes change."

He stepped closer. "For what it's worth, Miss Thorley, I admire the decision you have made. I know it was not an easy one, but a brave one, and I commend you."

Her cheeks warmed under his praise.

"I do not wish to make you uncomfortable, but nor do I wish to have discussions about you without your knowledge. Treadwell mentioned that you were being pressured into a matrimony."

What else had Mr. Treadwell divulged about her past? "Do not apologize, Mr. Locke. It was hardly a secret. Likely every person in London was aware."

"No man has the right to force a woman to marry against her will."

"I don't know if I would go so far as to say 'forced.' 'Strongly, emphatically encouraged' may be more accurate."

"Do you miss your family?" He lifted his gun back to his shoulder.

She tilted her head. She was glad to be free of her brother. It would be a lie to say that she missed him. And as for her sister-in-law, she did not really know her. Not well, anyway. "I suppose the most accurate statement would be to say that I miss the way my life used to be."

Chapter Twenty-Six

Miss Thorley should not have been in Linton Forest. And yet he had encountered her, and Owen could not help but smile at the recollection.

He ducked his head to miss a low-hanging branch as he reluctantly rode back toward the east meadow. Drake trotted alongside, his furry head barely visible in the tall grass, and his horse tossed his head in the afternoon air.

He could have easily passed the day in her presence. She had seemed well, if not a little distracted. With each interaction he learned something new about her, and his attraction to her intensified. The newness of her presence in Fellsworth had to wear off eventually, but now, in the forest's quiet, it was easy to allow his unguarded mind to open to possibilities of a different future.

After Diana's death he had accepted the fact that his romantic days were behind him. His inability to protect her affected him profoundly, and to this day, complete forgiveness was unattainable. That failure pushed him harder. He prided himself on protecting what was around him—the land. The animals. His daughter.

It was for that reason Miss Thorley was dangerous.

He already felt the budding need to protect her from those who wished her harm. The stronger his feeling of regard for her grew, the stronger that need became. But he knew the bitterness of failure—and the crippling consequences that accompanied it.

Miss Thorley, in many ways, reminded him of Diana. Both were from London. Both were the daughter of a gentleman. Both were born far beyond his station. Both women had chosen to leave their lives behind and start anew, and he would be wise to heed history's lessons.

But he could not deny the incessant whisper echoing within him. What would it be like to have a family? To be welcomed home into the arms of a woman who was eager for his return?

It was yet another reason he needed Kirtley Meadow. Even though the Bancroft Park gamekeeper's lodge was his home, it was haunted by the horrific memory of what happened there all those years ago. The walls trapped him with the ghosts of the past. For years he had considered it his punishment, but now he was beginning to wonder if a fresh start—and self-forgiveness—was possible.

By the time he arrived back at the Bancroft Park stables, the afternoon was starting to fade. Treadwell met him in the courtyard.

"Locke. There you are. Been looking everywhere for you."

"What can I do for you?"

"I received confirmation that we will be having guests for a pheasant hunt—the first hunt of the season."

Owen nodded. Treadwell was not one for planning in advance. "When?"

"Next week. You're sure the pheasants will be out?"

Owen dismounted. "They're out there. The dry spring and summer may have been difficult on the crops, but the nesting birds flourished."

"Good. I will confirm the plans." Treadwell slapped his riding crop across the palm of his hand. "The guests will be here for a week. No doubt we will shoot every day."

"How many, and will they require mounts?"

"I am expecting five. And yes, they will all need horses."

"Do you want me to prepare the arms, or will they be bringing their own?"

"I would assume they would bring firearms, but you never know with this party."

Owen frowned. Many of Treadwell's friends were well versed in the hunt and preferred their own weapons. In fact, the same hunting parties gathered in the forest each year. The Danhaven clan during grouse season. The Grentons during fox season. Time had taught him which guests needed his assistance and which were experienced enough to give them their lead. "Who will be joining you?"

"Thorley and Bartrell. You remember them, of course."

"Thorley?" Owen snapped his head up at the name.

"The very one. You remember him, right? They are interesting characters, and pretty much invited themselves. Not that I mind—I'm always up for a good hunt. Three of their colleagues will also be joining us, although I don't know them as well. They've been dejected ever since the terrible happenings in London when we were there last. I suspect they're seeking a diversion. But it should be a good time. I can always count on Thorley to keep things interesting."

Alarm pricked Owen's senses. Miss Thorley's earlier words regarding Mr. McAlister's note flashed before him. He had little doubt that Thorley was in trouble, and Miss Thorley had traveled so far to be away from him. He did not want the man anywhere near her. "Pheasants can be tricky, even for experienced shooters. Are you sure that it is the right hunt for them?"

Treadwell shrugged. "He said he wanted to hunt, and I am sure they have hunted the animal before. We'll just get Whitten and Geoffrey to come along to help. The way those boys like their brandy, the chances of them actually getting out of their beds to brave the morning chill are unlikely. But I should like to be prepared just the same. I trust you'll arrange things appropriately?"

Owen's chest tightened. "Of course."

"Oh, and did you decide what to do about Farley's offer?"

"I am to visit him tomorrow. I should know more then."

Annabelle sat with Hannah in the middle library.

Hannah beamed with pride as she closed the book. "I did it, didn't I?"

Annabelle patted Hannah's arm with pride. "See? When you put your mind to it and try your very best, you can do it."

Hannah leaned her blonde head forward to look past Annabelle at the watercolor box. "Now can we paint?"

"I think you deserve it." Annabelle pulled the box toward herself. "What should our subject be?"

Hannah bounced in her chair. "Let's try something besides a rabbit. My last one didn't turn out very well."

"Your rabbit turned out perfectly." Annabelle hugged the box to herself. "How about we paint something small? The day is fine. Shall we take the box outside and find our subject?"

Hannah nodded eagerly.

They stepped from the library into the school's courtyard, which was next to the girls' garden. It was free time for the girls, and they were clustered in groups. Hannah stole glimpses of the girls as they passed.

"If you would rather go play with the other girls, we can paint another time."

Hannah pressed her lips together and shook her head. "No, thank you."

Annabelle held her hand above her eyes to guard against the bright sunlight as she assessed the other students. They were laughing. Playing. A handful of them had their small rackets poised for battledore and shuttlecock. Others were engaged with their cup-and-ball, while the older girls held their sticks and ribbon-clad hoops for a game of the flying circle. The children who were normally so reserved in the classroom now seemed happy and carefree.

Annabelle did not have a lot of experience with childhood friendships. With the exception of her brother, she rarely had other children to play with. She returned her sights to Hannah. She did not watch the girls. Instead, her gaze was fixed on the toe of her boot. Was it sadness? Shyness? Annabelle couldn't tell.

She adjusted the box in her hands. "Well then, if you are certain, where would you like to go? The flower garden or the orchard?"

Hannah's demeanor brightened. "The orchard."

"Wonderful idea. Lead the way, Miss Locke."

They found a spot in the south orchard near the garden wall, where Hannah's beloved forests were evident just beyond. Annabelle set up the box and propped up the small easel. They sat in the orchard's long grass and Annabelle placed a fresh piece of paper and set out the water pot. "Do you want to paint a peach?" she asked.

Hannah nodded eagerly.

Annabelle stood, plucked a ripe peach from the tree, placed it on a nearby stump, and returned to the grass. "Take the brush like this, get it wet, touch it to the color, and that is all you do."

Eyes wide, Hannah took the brush and pressed the tip against the paper. She smiled as she swirled the brush on the paper, observing how it left a trail of color in its wake. "This is fun!"

"If you want to add a little shading, like a shadow, you can make it darker here. See how nice that looks?" Annabelle smiled as she watched the child's enthusiasm. "It is good to see you smile. When I notice you around the school, sometimes you seem so solemn."

The child's paintbrush slowed, and she did not respond.

Annabelle tilted her head. "Are you happy at school, Hannah?"

The girl nestled in the grass. She dipped the brush in more paint and did not look away from the paper.

"You don't seem very enthusiastic about it."

Hannah shrugged and studied the brushstroke she had created. "I don't think the other girls like me very much."

The admission surprised Annabelle. "Why do you say that?"

"One of the girls said I have white hair and it makes me look like an old woman. And another one said I was not very smart. They are not very nice sometimes."

"Oh, I understand." Annabelle scooted closer to Hannah and tucked her legs beneath her.

"How could you understand? I thought you said you didn't go to school with other girls."

Annabelle nodded. The child had a point. But she did know what it was like to be on the outside looking in. For the past two years she had fought to prove her merit. The memory of the night of the Baldwin dinner flashed before her. But nothing she'd done had made a difference.

A breeze danced through the orchard, carrying on it the scent of peaches at their prime. Annabelle hugged her knees to her. "Well, I don't think your hair makes you look like an old lady. Quite the opposite. It is the purest blonde, and I happen to know for a fact that the girls tease you because they are jealous."

Hannah squinted in the sun. "Really?"

"And as far as you being smart, well, I just sat with you in the library and listened to you read dozens of words that you have not read before, and I think that proves how intelligent you are."

Hannah's shoulders relaxed, and she tilted her head and pressed the brush to the paper.

As Hannah explored the paints, Annabelle's own memories of painting as a child surfaced. Her mother used to watch Annabelle paint, just as she was watching Hannah. Mama had been so proud of her accomplishments. She had praised her, encouraged her. But what good would those accomplishments do her now?

Sadness tugged at Annabelle. If Annabelle had married Samuel, it was very probable she would have been a mother by now. It had always been a hope of hers. A dream. She always wanted a daughter and to have a relationship like the one she'd had with her own mother. In her current situation, Annabelle's prospects were bleak. Who would want to marry a poor teacher?

She thought of Mr. Locke's words from earlier in the forest. *"We are not just placed on this earth haphazardly. Each of us has a path. Each of us has a purpose. It is part of life to find that path and follow it."*

She had thought she knew her purpose, thought she had figured out the intricacies of life, but it was not meant to be. Where would her path lead?

Chapter Twenty-Seven

$\mathcal{T}$he day Owen had both anticipated and dreaded had finally arrived. He tapped the heel of his boot against the marble floor as he waited in Walmsly Hall's vestibule.

Farley's home was certainly not as fine as Bancroft Park. The building itself was every bit as old, but whereas Bancroft Park had been meticulously maintained, the demise of the Farley fortune was evident in Walmsly Hall's current state.

Owen turned as the butler approached.

"Mr. Farley will see you now."

Owen followed the wiry, hunched man through the great hall, the sound of his boots heavy on the stone floor, to the library's entrance.

Mr. Farley was a quiet man who did not appear in public often. The fact that he had been in London when Owen and Treadwell were was a peculiar coincidence. It was odd that Treadwell and Mr. Farley would speak to each other while they were in another city but would rarely cross the bridge to speak to each other as neighbors.

The hefty man sat in a large chair, a thick book in his hand. He appeared much older than Owen remembered. His dusty-brown hair had whitened, and the lines around his eyes and mouth were etched much deeper than at their previous meeting. Mr. Farley grunted. "I take it you received my letter."

Owen adjusted his hat in his hand but did not look away from Mr. Farley's direct stare. "I did."

"Sit, Locke." Mr. Farley snapped his book closed and tossed it on the desk. The *thud* echoed loudly in the tidy room.

Owen sat on a straight-backed wooden chair, but he was far from comfortable.

"Can I offer you refreshment?" The offer sounded less than genuine.

Owen was not here for any other reason than to discuss Kirtley Meadow. "No, thank you."

"Let's get to it." Mr. Farley rubbed his hands together. "I spoke with Treadwell. He says you are interested in purchasing some of my land."

"I am."

"And what would a gamekeeper like you want with it?"

Owen adjusted his hat on his knee. "My family used to live on that land. I was born there, my father was born there, and his father before him. My family members are buried there. Surely you can understand the attachment."

Mr. Farley shook his head. "A weak sentiment, boy."

Owen ignored the patronizing tone and the condescending use of the word *boy*. It mattered not to him what Mr. Farley thought about his reasons for wanting the land.

When Owen did not respond, Mr. Farley sat back in his chair. "I've worked hard over the years to expand the estate and make it profitable. What makes you think I am willing to sell?"

Walmsly Hall was in financial trouble. Everyone knew it, but Owen thought it best to avoid the topic. The man who had occupied the former gamekeeper lodge at Kirtley Meadow died a few years ago, and it had been sitting empty ever since. "With the tenant's death, I thought it would be an ideal time."

"An ideal time for you or for me?"

Owen only returned the man's pointed stare.

Mr. Farley broke the silence. "I'm growing too old for games, and I can see you are in no humor for idle conversation, so I will be blunt. Normally I would never consider such a suggestion that I am in need of assistance. Just as I am too old for games, I am too set in my ways to go tramping across forest and vale, and from what I am told, you are the man most capable of helping me. I've not had a gamekeeper on my land since Landem died two years ago, and we are facing the same issues you are facing at Bancroft Park."

"Poachers," Owen supplied. "All the wooded lands in the area are. With last year's flooding and the closing of the Wickford mine, people are growing desperate."

"I have heard reports of gamekeepers south of here taking money to turn a blind eye to the deeds of the less fortunate. What do you think of that?"

Owen narrowed his gaze. "If that is your way of asking my opinion on the behavior of some of my colleagues, then I would respond that gamekeeping is not a hobby I play at, sir. This is my profession. I have dedicated my life to it, and I know no other way."

"I meant no offense." Farley stood and limped to the window and stared out for several moments. "I like you, Locke. I think you are a man of your word, and my instincts are rarely wrong on such things. I am losing more and more game by the day. I went hunting the other day, for my own amusement, and did not come across a single animal worth shooting. I have reports daily from the groundskeepers that they sight strangers on my land. I do not have the manpower to take care of the situation on my own. Help me with the poachers, and I will sell you the land you want. I am willing to come down on my requested sum if you can find the parties responsible."

Farley reached for a piece of paper and his quill. He drew his gray eyebrows together and dipped the quill in the inkwell. He wrote on the paper and then passed it over the desk to Owen. "Go on. Take it."

Owen stood from his chair and accepted the paper. The ink was still wet as he read the number. He blinked. This number he could afford.

Owen was careful to show no reaction, for his enthusiasm at the prospect was tempered by reality. His spare time was limited, and what he did have was dedicated to Hannah. Farley was asking a great deal of him to rid the land of poachers. He was unsure how he would find the time to meet the man's request.

Owen shifted his stance. "I am employed by Bancroft Park and my time is spent there."

"I do not see this as a contest, Locke. Like I said, I am not interested in games. My only interest here is preserving the self-sufficiency of my estate as a whole and ensuring there will be enough game to support future generations without having to reintroduce animals into the space. If I must part with land at a lower price than I think it is worth, so be it. Take me up on this offer. I will only make it once. Rid Walmsly Hall land of poachers, pay the requested sum, and Kirtley Meadow will be yours."

Chapter Twenty-Eight

*O*wen had not been at liberty to set foot on Kirtley Meadow since he was a boy—not and avoid trespassing. But now, with Mr. Farley's permission, he stepped eagerly over the mossy earth and was free to explore the space once more.

In his mind's eye, he could still see his father ahead of him to point out any traps that might have been left. Even today he carried a stick to tap the ground, just in case a wayward trap remained.

Kirtley Meadow was a beautiful bit of earth, especially at this time of day, when the sun was just beginning its ascent to the heavens. It had mossy knolls and valleys lush with emerald undergrowth. A wide creek bubbled through the grassy lowland, tumbling over smooth gray stones that had likely been in the same place since before Walmsly Hall was even constructed.

Farley had been right about one thing—the area held few signs of wildlife. No rabbit nests dotted the low-lying brush. No indented fox trails led down to the water. What he did find were numerous signs of human activity. Something near his boot caught his eye, and he knelt to pick up several frayed rope fibers. To most they would have blended in seamlessly with the long grass. But he had seen this before.

He needed to be on his way if he would be joining Hannah for church on the school grounds. He rarely hunted on Sundays and restricted any work to merely tending the animals in his care, for he devoted the afternoons to Hannah. He squeezed the rope in his hand. If he was to find the source of the poaching on Walmsly Hall grounds, as well as at Bancroft Park, he needed to act whenever possible.

He walked along the creek bed, which fed into a fishing pond. At this time of day, the fish should be close to the surface, but even though the pond was relatively clear, he saw none. He began to circle the pond, where the mud was soft. He should be able to see signs of life at this pond—hoofprints from deer drinking from the water, paw prints of the curious fox—but he saw mothing. Instead, boot prints caught his eye.

He knelt next to them. They were smaller than his, like those of a youth. His mind went to young Mr. Winter. But these boots prints were too small, even for him.

Owen continued his path around the pond. Several more boot impressions marked the water's edge. He reversed his route around the pond, disguising his own boot markings as best he could. He decided it would be best to return at night.

As he turned to go back through the forest, something caught his eye. A flash of black. A color he would not normally see in the forest. He stepped backward, retreating into the long morning shadows.

And then he saw it again.

He did not have his rifle, but his pistol was tucked in his coat. He knew better than to enter the woods without any protection, not because of the animals, but for this very reason. He wrapped his fingers around the handle and pulled it free.

He stepped toward the sight. And then, the figure whipped around. Owen stiffened.

It was a boy. In a black coat. A black Fellsworth School coat.

Owen lowered his weapon. He'd not shoot a boy. The boy sped across the woodland and disappeared into the thick forest. And then another boy popped up and followed close behind.

Something was going on with the boys at Fellsworth School.

Someone—undoubtedly an experienced poacher—was influencing them at the school, and it spread beyond young Mr. Winter. There could be no question—it was far too coincidental to encounter not one but three boys.

He had a hunch that if he could track down the man responsible for this, then he would take a significant step forward in reducing the poaching activity not only at Bancroft Park, but at Walmsly Hall as well.

Later that morning, Owen met Hannah just outside of the Fellsworth main hall for church.

The student body was too large for the church in the village, and as a result both the boys' school and the girls' school gathered together once a week for service in the school's chapel. The service was the one part of school life that was open to the villagers.

Sunday morning was usually Owen's favorite time of the week. It was a special time with Hannah, and then they would go back to the lodge. But today, his heart was heavy.

Once seated next to Hannah on the bench they sat on every week, he looked out over the crowd assembled. Almost three hundred children attended the school—half of whom were boys. And someone was attempting to sway some of those boys to try their hand at poaching.

Hannah opened her prayer book and retrieved a piece of paper. She extended it toward him. "Look what I did, Papa."

He unfolded the paper, and on it was an orange circle with green leaves. Her face beamed, and he put his arm around her. "Did you paint this?"

"I did. Miss Thorley helped me. Do you know what it is?"

Owen looked at the picture. Surely he should know what it was, but he could not figure it out. "Of course I do, but why don't you tell me and see if I am correct."

"It is a peach."

Owen nodded. "Exactly what I thought, poppet."

He plopped a kiss on the top of her cap and turned his attention to the other happenings in the room.

Even with the windows open, the high-ceilinged room caged the early autumn warmth, and despite the discomfort, the room was quiet. It was amazing, really. Row after row of children sat motionless, clad in heavy, black clothing. And they were so well behaved.

Owen could remember being a boy and looking over the gate at the Fellsworth children in the yards tending to the school's orchards and animals. It was one of the reasons he was so insistent that his daughter participate. He wanted her to learn to think for herself. Read. Write. But most importantly, he wanted her to know that her value lay not in making a successful match as an adult, but in developing her character now.

Hannah sat next to him quietly, primly, her small hands folded in her lap. Her hair was covered with a white cap, and only tiny white-gold strands hinted to the color. The caps made all the girls look alike. Modest and proper.

The teachers sat in a long row of chairs lining the stone wall. The male teachers lined the east wall, the female teachers the west. The light streaming in from the windows landed on the female teachers. They, too, appeared uncomfortable under the heat. The formal teachers were at the front, and the junior teachers to the back. They all were dressed in high-necked gowns of black, and white caps covered each head. But in the row of women, Miss Thorley sat the straightest. She radiated elegance. Perhaps it was her nature. Perhaps it was the way she was taught. He liked the thought of Miss Thorley influencing his daughter and teaching her. He would be proud if Hannah grew to exhibit such strength and grace.

The rest of the staff was along the back row. He spotted Miss Crosley right away. She leaned back in her chair against the wall. He could not help but think of when he saw her with the man. He had no wish to judge, but he was surprised that she would risk her position in such a way.

He completed his scan of the room, looking down the row of male teachers. It was presumptive to assume that one of the men was aware of, or perhaps promoting, poaching among the male students. The boys all had humble beginnings. With the school's help they would have brighter futures, but if they continued down the poaching path, their futures would be bleak indeed.

He knew, at least by sight, the male teachers—Mr. Hemstead, Mr. Miller, Mr. Bryant, Mr. Ashworth, and a handful of others. Some of them had come through the school system, and others had traveled far to assume their current roles.

He lifted his gaze to the workers seated at the back of the room. Attending Sunday service was a requirement for everyone who worked on the school grounds, and in the back sat the brewmaster, the blacksmith, the stable hands. Any one of them—or none of them—could be involved in the poaching. And Owen would not rest until he found out the truth.

Chapter Twenty-Nine

*H*e'd been watching her. Direct stares. Subtle grins.

Annabelle exited the church as quickly as she could. Despite the morning's stifling heat, her blood ran cold. Not since the night her brother struck her had her nerves felt so frayed.

She hurried across the school grounds, slowing only once to cast a glance over her shoulder to make sure she was not being followed. From a distance, she saw him through the swarm of people, standing on the edge of the church grounds, speaking with a man she could not identify. Even now, his gaze was on her.

Mr. Bryant.

Perhaps her imagination was getting the best of her. Maybe he wasn't looking at her, but only in her direction. It would not be the first time she'd fretted unnecessarily since arriving at Fellsworth.

But this felt different. Mr. Bryant was different. He knew her brother. He'd followed her into the village and watched her as she attempted to sell her jewelry. Perhaps his attention was innocent enough, but the unwanted focus revived the fear associated with her decision to leave London. Those facts alone made Annabelle want to put as much distance as possible between the two of them.

Before long she was at the girls' building, and she dashed up to the attic chamber. She was the first one back, and she bustled into the tidy, stark room, pulling her cap from her head as she did so. She hurried toward the window to look at the grounds below.

Mr. Bryant was nowhere to be seen.

She heaved a sigh and sank down on her bed. Every other Sunday afternoon she would be relieved of her duties at the school, and today was her day. She needed to free her mind from the dis-comfort Mr. Bryant had caused her if she was to enjoy the afternoon.

Crosley entered the room just behind her and dropped her reti-cule on her bed. "What are you doing?"

"I've been invited to dine at my aunt and uncle's." Annabelle reached behind her back to unfasten her gown.

Crosley raised her light eyebrows. "When are you leaving?"

"Presently." Annabelle struggled to untie the strings closing her gown. "I want to change attire. I can hardly wait to be in something besides this black one."

Jane, who arrived after Crosley and was also going to enjoy a free afternoon, noticed Annabelle's struggle with the tie and approached her. "I will help you."

With a grateful smile Annabelle pivoted and allowed Jane to untie her gown. Then she shrugged it from her shoulders. She quickly changed her petticoats to one of lighter muslin and relished the sensation of the refined fabric. With Jane's help she donned a white underdress and a pale-blue netted overdress—one that she had not even touched in weeks.

Crosley eyed Annabelle's selection. Annabelle thought for a moment she was going to disapprove. But then Crosley wordlessly changed into the gown of cream sateen Annabelle had given her the night she left London. Alterations had been made. In addition to the lilac flowers, pink ones had been embroidered along the hem-line, and lace trim had been added to the sleeves. Crosley shook down her blonde tresses and masterfully braided several lengths, looped them, and pinned them to the top of her head.

"I'm going for a walk." Crosley straightened from the looking glass and snatched her reticule from the bed.

Miss Stiles walked into the room, face still flushed from the morning's warmth. "Would you like company? I need to go back down to the kitchen garden. I'll walk with you."

Crosley turned around. "Thank you, no. Some time alone is just what I need." But the hastiness of her tone told another story.

They watched as she left the room. Jane shook her head with a *tsk*. "I'll bet a month's wages that she is going to meet with Mr. Hemstead. And oh, I wish she wouldn't."

Annabelle bit her lip. She shouldn't comment on Crosley's actions. Ever since their harsh conversation in the garden, the gap in their relationship had widened. Crosley had grown more secretive and quiet.

"It is a good thing Mrs. Brathay has not learned of her behavior." Jane turned to allow Annabelle to help her with the buttons on the back of her gown. "Girls have been dismissed for less. But then again, Miss Crosley has become somewhat of a golden child, hasn't she?"

Annabelle dropped her hands, confused by Jane's words. "What do you mean?"

Jane's eyes widened. "Surely you have seen how she sews, have you not?"

Annabelle fixed her eyes on the buttons in front of her. "I have."

"Margaret mended one of the girl's dresses, and Mrs. Brathay took notice of her work and was quite surprised to learn that a girl who had served as an elegant lady's maid was working in the kitchen. The rumor is that she will be promoted to teacher."

Annabelle whirled around. "A teacher of what?"

"Sewing and domestic arts. Mrs. Brathay thinks she could be beneficial to the girls who will be going into service or seeking employment for dressmaking."

A strange emotion pricked Annabelle. She liked to think that she wanted the best for Crosley, but now she wasn't even sure she really knew who Crosley was.

Annabelle's stomach sank at the thought of her own shortcomings as a teacher. The sad reality disturbed her: Crosley was excelling in her skills regardless of her odd behavior, and the only reason Annabelle was retaining her position here was because of her uncle.

After Jane was free from her gown, she dug in her chest for a fresh one. "You still have never said how you and Crosley knew each other prior to coming here. One may suspect there is something to hide."

Annabelle hesitated and fussed with a bonnet. She had managed to avoid the question thus far, but she had not been asked the question directly. "We knew each other in London, and she decided to travel with me to Fellsworth for a new beginning. Other than that there really isn't much to tell."

"But you are so different from each other. In fact, there are days when it would be hard to know the two of you were even acquainted at all."

"Relationships change over time, I suppose." Annabelle donned her bonnet. The conversation was becoming too personal. "Enjoy the day, Jane. I will see you later this evening." She left their small attic room, her watercolor box in hand, and rushed down the paneled staircase, the ancient steps groaning under the weight of each footfall.

At the landing she stopped to take several deep, steadying breaths and allowed her pulse to slow. She wanted to put the awkwardness behind her and focus on enjoying her few hours of precious freedom. She stroked her hand down her gown, smoothing the fabric that still bore a few wrinkles from being folded in her trunk.

Uncle Edmund was waiting for her in the main vestibule. After the service he had returned to his study to retrieve a handful of books, and now he stood at the edge of the stairs, waiting for her. As she approached, he looked at the box in her hands. "What's this?"

"My watercolors. I hope you don't mind. I thought it might be nice to do some painting this afternoon."

"Here, I will trade you." He reached out to take the watercolor box from her. "These books are a bit lighter than that box."

Together they crossed the grounds as they walked to the cottage. Annabelle had come to Fellsworth expecting her uncle to be as she remembered him: strict and severe. But the harsh man she remembered from her childhood was really more quiet and thoughtful. Over the last several weeks she had grown to see a softer side of him—a side that cared deeply for those around him.

The sun splayed on the manicured lawn. Its warmth felt comforting on her arms and seeped through the bonnet atop her head. They passed through the girls' playground and garden where the girls were spending their free time.

"It is good to see the children run, isn't it?" Her uncle's love for his life's work was evident. "Such activity is healthy for them."

Annabelle focused on a group of girls skipping rope. What would it have been like to have such a childhood? "Did you and Mama play like that?"

"Your mother was forever in trouble for climbing trees. One time she got stuck on a branch and our father had to climb up after her." He chuckled. "Our mother was beside herself with attempting to make Mary more ladylike."

Annabelle smiled. She liked hearing stories of her mother. "I often wonder what life would be like if she were still living. I do miss her."

"As do I." He squinted in the bright sun and furrowed his bushy brows. "I harbor regrets when it comes to Mary. I often wish I would have done more to encourage our relationship after she married your father. But she was so headstrong."

"Of all the words I could think of to describe Mama, headstrong would not be one of them. Determined? Perhaps. But not headstrong."

The cottage's iron gate squeaked on its hinges as Uncle Edmund pushed it open. "As much as I hate to admit it, your father and I did not agree on much of anything, and I think it embarrassed your mother. But you are here now, and our family can be complete once again."

Our family.

How long had her heart yearned to belong somewhere? His words indicated that she was a welcome addition to their home, and her spirit warmed.

Later that afternoon after the meal, Annabelle joined her aunt and uncle in the cottage's modest parlor. Sunshine flooded the quaint room through two large paned windows. Three thick wooden beams ran the length of the white plaster ceiling, and two faded sofas stood perpendicular to the massive hearth. No fire blazed in the space because of the late summer heat, but the scent of years of wood smoke lingered.

Her uncle had placed her watercolor box on a small side table just inside the door. As her aunt sewed and her uncle read, Annabelle stepped over to the box, popped it open, let down the compartment on the underside of the lid, and retrieved a stack of paintings. She flipped through the thick papers, reliving flashes of memories with each one.

She had never shown her work to anyone besides her mother, governess, or painting master. No one else would have been interested. Even Samuel had shown little interest in her creative endeavors, and he referred to painting as a trivial occupation that ladies played at to pass their time.

But after speaking with her uncle about her mother, she thought he might appreciate seeing her likeness, even if it was only a mediocre resemblance.

Painting in hand, Annabelle turned and approached her aunt and uncle. "I thought you might like to see this. I painted it after Mama died, but it's the last likeness I have of her."

Uncle Edmund lowered his book, looked up, and removed his spectacles. He discarded the book on the chair's arm and stood, his attention fixed on the painting. His words were slow, as if greatly awed by what he was seeing. "Oh, Annabelle, my dear, look at how you have captured her likeness."

She felt sheepish under the praise. "I tried. I was young when I painted this. It was done after she died. But I thought you might enjoy it, if for no other reason than the memory."

Aunt Lydia stood and stepped behind her husband. "Why, it looks just like her!"

Annabelle picked up another small portrait. "I know you have never met Thomas, but I painted this one of him. I could not persuade him to sit very long to have his portrait painted, but it is a pretty close likeness."

Uncle Edmund lowered the picture of her mother and took the one of Thomas. He studied it for several moments. "I see your father when I look at this. So many years have passed since I saw him last, but I recognize him just the same."

She wanted to ask so many questions but held her tongue. She was not sure if it was appropriate. Her papa was a strict man, but regardless everyone seemed to be fond of him. Everyone except for Uncle Edmund.

After several moments of silence, she asked, "Why did you dislike my father so?"

"It isn't that I disliked your father exactly." Uncle Edmund lowered the painting and returned his spectacles to his face. He pressed his lips together, as if contemplating his words. "Mary and I lost our father when I was ten years of age, and it was very difficult on all of us. With no other man in the house, I always felt fiercely protective of Mary, even though she was three years my senior. Our father's death significantly altered our financial status. When Mary met your father, she believed him to offer her the security we had been without and to be the answer to her problems."

Annabelle sank into the chair next to the table. Her own

situation was in some ways similar to her mother's. She had never heard another person speak about her parents' relationship, and she sensed she was about to get the answers to the questions her uncle had put into her head all those years ago.

"I was concerned with his nature from the very beginning. He was too spontaneous, too impudent. But Mary saw none of what I saw. She saw a handsome, brazen, daring young man who was rapidly rising in society. I believe she allowed her fear of an unknown future to cloud her judgment. By the time the truth of his nature was revealed, she was already married."

Sensing her aunt's gaze, Annabelle looked to see her aunt smiling at her, as if eager to change the subject to a more pleasant one. Her aunt's blue eyes lit, and her faded copper curls bounced. "I've a brilliant idea. You should paint your uncle!"

Annabelle raised her eyebrow. "It has been a long while since I painted a portrait. I am sure it would disappoint."

"But how do you know if you do not try? Oh, please do. It would mean ever so much to me. I have no likeness of him, and I can't recall the last time we had a painter at Fellsworth."

Annabelle looked at the earnest sincerity in her aunt's expression. She and her uncle had done so much for her—how could Annabelle deny her?

"If you promise to extend grace," she offered.

Her aunt clasped her hands together. Uncle Edmund cracked a rare smile. "I've never been painted before."

"We can get started right now if you like." Annabelle stood from her chair. "Be seated in the chair next to the window so we have the light." She arranged her things around her, asked for some water, and set up her box.

Annabelle looped her painting smock over her head and tied it behind her back. "After my mother died, my governess insisted that I study under a painting master to develop the skill. I fear I had no talent for music or dancing, and I suspect she feared this would be my only ladylike endeavor. I suppose all of those hours have proven to be in vain now. For what good is such a talent now?"

Aunt Lydia tilted her head. "What do you mean? Do you not enjoy it?"

"Of course I enjoy it." Annabelle smoothed her paintbrush's bristles. "But it does little to help me at the school. I fear I am dreadfully behind the other teachers in what we are to be sharing with the girls. Of course, reading and arithmetic are one thing. But I can hardly teach sewing or any of the domestic arts."

Aunt Lydia stepped closer. "But just because it is not helpful at the moment does not make it invaluable."

Uncle Edmund shifted his position. "Please do not make the mistake of thinking that just because you do not use the talent on a daily basis, the time and effort are wasted. It is true of any skill, is it not? The dedication and discipline required to develop any talent are what is important. The task at hand is not nearly as meaningful as the shaping of the character and the mind. Your work, and the time it took, is evident. And that is where the pride should lie."

Never had anyone spoken such words to her. Her papa acted as if painting was a waste of time, but her uncle seemed to understand the importance of it, and that sentiment alone endeared him to her all the more.

The afternoon light slid across the room as they remained for quite a while in silence. Uncle Edmund sat in his chair, still and straight. Aunt Lydia sewed. Annabelle painted. And for a time she felt as if all was normal at last.

The clock on the mantel struck the four o'clock hour, and her uncle looked to the timepiece. "I expect Mr. Locke to visit today. I should have thought he would be here by now."

Annabelle's brush slowed at the mention of Mr. Locke's name.

Ever since their private interlude in the forest, he had occupied her mind. At the very thought of him, her heart fluttered within her.

"He is an interesting person, isn't he?" she said, not taking her gaze from her work.

"There isn't a finer man in the area. I knew his father well, and I am pleased to say that he is the very likeness of the man."

Annabelle bit her lip as she tapped her brush in the color. If she was to learn the truth about him, there would be no better person to ask than Uncle Edmund. "I have heard rumors about him."

"Rumors?"

"Yes." Annabelle lifted her eyebrow playfully. "I am sure it is no surprise that the teachers have a story about everyone."

Aunt Lydia clucked her tongue. "I'd not doubt that. Those women will take a story and run with it. What tales have they been spinning?"

Annabelle lowered her brush. "I heard his wife was murdered. Surely there is some mistake."

"Sadly, no." Uncle Edmund exchanged glances with his wife. "It's been several years now, but the story is still as sad as it was the day it occurred. It was a black mark on our village."

"But what happened? It is hard to believe that something so violent could happen here."

"It is a tragic tale, really." Her uncle removed his spectacles yet again and pinched the bridge of his nose. "Locke's wife was a gentleman's daughter, flighty and high-strung. Diana Wilcox was her name. They married quickly. I remember thinking how odd it was that a man as sensible as Mr. Locke would make such a hasty decision. But the decision was made, and he brought her to the gamekeeper's cottage at Bancroft Park. They did not attend the church on the school grounds but one in the village, so we did not see her very often, but there was always something about her that did not quite fit in."

Annabelle felt an immediate tie with the young woman. Did she herself not feel like an outsider? "How so?"

"She was an unpredictable thing if I remember, but lovely. Very lovely. It was easy to see why a man would be taken by her beauty. But she had another side—a history. As the story goes she was betrothed to a man before Locke, a soldier in the infantry who was believed to be killed in battle. Only after she married Mr. Locke did her soldier return without so much as a scratch.

"Unbeknownst to Mr. Locke she renewed her acquaintance with the soldier. No one knows with certainty what happened, and probably nobody ever will fully know, but Mr. Locke and one of the under-keepers returned from a hunt to find them both dead, and with Miss Hannah asleep in her cradle, blessed child. To learn of the death of a loved one and a betrayal at the same time, why, it was enough to crumble any man. The Wilcox family asked to take the child, but Mr. Locke refused to part with her."

The story sickened Annabelle. "Poor Mr. Locke."

"Of course, scandal and rumors ensued. It has been all these years and still people whisper when he passes. For the first several years he was quite a changed man—dark and angry and sullen—but more recently there has been a glimmer of the old man returning."

Annabelle slumped her shoulders. Hearing the story from her uncle, a reliable source, seemed to make it that much worse. "Such a horrific story."

"He is dedicated to his work and his daughter, as he should be." Aunt Lydia fixed her pointed gaze on Annabelle. "But what he needs is the love of a good lady."

Annabelle refused to meet Aunt Lydia's stare. Heat crept up her neck. Such a comment.

"Oh, look." Aunt Lydia stood from her chair, looking out the front window. "There is Mr. Locke now."

Chapter Thirty —————————————————————

*O*wen knew in an instant that he was in danger of losing his heart.

He'd stopped by the superintendent's cottage as planned after spending the day with Hannah to inform Langsby about seeing the boys in Kirtley Meadow. But when he arrived, the unexpected sight of Miss Thorley slowed his steps and his breath. For a moment he saw nothing but the brightness of her hazel eyes and the luster in her light-brown hair.

She wore a gown of light blue. The soft fabric rested delicately on her shoulders and exposed graceful white arms. Not since London had he seen her in anything besides the black Fellsworth gown with a high neckline and long sleeves.

She was beautiful.

And she was looking at him.

For a moment he forgot why he was here.

"Mr. Locke." Langsby looked up from his chair. "I would rise to greet you, but my niece is painting my likeness. I do not wish to disrupt her."

"I wouldn't dream of disrupting you." Owen found his voice, bowed toward Miss Thorley and her aunt, and gestured toward the painting. "May I?"

"By all means." Miss Thorley leaned back so he could see the work. "I am almost done."

Mrs. Langsby lowered her sewing. "She has been working at it all afternoon. Is it not a work of art?"

Miss Thorley continued her painting. It was amazing, really.

Delicate strokes spoke to a keen eye for detail. She captured the older man's essence, from the wrinkling around his eyes to his thin lips to the spectacles balanced on his nose. She had turned simple colors and abstract strokes into something captivating.

He had never watched anyone paint before. It was a mesmerizing process, how she could take the medium and turn it into something completely different.

"It's beautiful." Owen chuckled. "Well, as beautiful as Langsby can be."

She laughed at his joke, brushed her hair from her face with the back of her hand, and tilted her head as she studied her work in silence for several seconds. "I think my uncle has a noble brow."

"Noble brow indeed." Langsby huffed and then cleared his throat before he turned his attention to Owen. "What did you want to speak with me about?"

Owen fidgeted with his hat in his hands, acutely aware of Miss Thorley's presence. "You have company. I've no wish to intrude. I can come back at a later time."

"Nonsense." Langsby waved his hand dismissively. "Anything we discuss in front of my wife and niece will stay here. Sit, Locke."

Owen knew how gossip traveled in the school, so if Langsby was willing to discuss matters in front of Miss Thorley, she must have his trust. Owen did as bid and sat next to Miss Thorley, the only remaining free chair in the room.

He sharpened his focus. "I have been asked by Mr. Farley of Walmsly Hall to look into poaching activity on his land."

Mr. Langsby sobered. "Farley? That is odd. I was under the impression that the relationship between Walmsly Hall and Bancroft Park was quite strained."

"It is. At least between Mr. Farley and the Treadwell family. But this is a private matter, one that does not have to do with Bancroft Park."

"How interesting." Langsby shifted toward him slightly. "Go on."

Owen was keenly aware of how Miss Thorley was watching him from the corner of her eye. He was hesitant to say too much, but what did he have to hide from Mr. Langsby, Miss Thorley, or anyone for that matter? "I am interested in purchasing Kirtley Meadow from Mr. Farley. Up until now Mr. Farley has refused to part with the land, but he has relented. The stipulation is that I help him rectify the poaching issue on his land."

"Kirtley Meadow. That is where the old gamekeeper cottage is, right?"

Owen nodded. "It is. But that's not why I am here. I was at the property this morning, and I encountered two more Fellsworth boys."

Langsby's expression darkened, and he nearly jumped from his chair. "Fellsworth boys? Who were they?"

"I did not get a good look at their faces, but I recognized their attire." He glanced at Mrs. Langsby, whose worried eyes were fixed on her husband. Her lips had turned down into a frown. "I know you have taken steps to address the issue, but I am growing increasingly concerned the issue is bigger than we thought."

Langsby drew a deep breath and rubbed his bony hand across his forehead. "I had hoped that business would be past us by now."

Owen continued. "Maybe we are missing someone obvious. Perhaps one of the blacksmiths or maybe one of the brewers? In my experience the most successful poachers are the least likely candidates. They appear to be hardworking, upstanding citizens, which is the perfect cover for their work. They hide in plain daylight, which is why they're so difficult to apprehend."

Langsby sat back in his chair and looked toward the beams crossing the planked ceiling. "Let me think. The staff here is a large one. But my wife, the headmaster, the headmistress, or I have handpicked each one. It would be a shocking revelation if it came to be."

"Keep a watch. I do not wish to be an alarmist, nor do I wish to see a boy enter a life of crime. I would like to have your permission to speak with members of your staff to see if I can learn anything."

"You have my permission to speak with anyone you like regarding this matter. I shall speak with the staff as an entirety and reiterate the seriousness of such a situation. Thank you for bringing this to our attention. We will do whatever necessary to put an end to this."

"The sooner the better," added Owen. "Hunting season begins in just days, and the forests and fields could become quite dangerous with the hunting parties Mr. Treadwell has planned."

"Can the hunting season really be upon us again?" Mrs. Langsby fanned her face. "Merciful heavens, this summer has flown by."

Owen smiled at the woman. How she hated to see her husband upset—an endearing quality. She possessed a gift for steering conversations, and he recognized her desire to shift the conversation now. "It has. Autumn's colors are already presenting themselves."

Mrs. Langsby's face brightened. "And, of course, the Autumn Festival will be here before we know it."

Miss Thorley lifted her head. "I have heard about this festival. Jane told me about it."

"Oh, you will adore it, my dear. It is the largest celebration in Fellsworth! An entire evening of dancing and eating, laughing and merriment. People come from far and wide to join in the merriment." Mrs. Langsby looked at Owen. "You will be attending, will you not?"

"I would not miss it."

Mrs. Langsby stood. "Will you join us for dinner, Mr. Locke? Cook made a special meal for us in anticipation of Annabelle joining us, despite the fact that it is Sunday."

Owen adjusted his grip on his hat. "This is a family dinner. I could not impose."

"When is a friend an imposition?" exclaimed Mrs. Langsby.

He had to admit, dinner and time with friends, including the lovely Miss Thorley, was definitely an improvement over his plans for the evening. "If you are sure, I would be happy to join you."

Dinner passed with easy conversation. In fact, happiness welled within Annabelle at the simple event. This feeling, this sensation, was what her heart had longed for. Her uncle teased her with playfulness. Her aunt fussed over her with motherly love. And not since Samuel had Annabelle's heart leapt at a simple smile or question from a man as it did with Mr. Locke.

Outside the window the sun was setting, shooting brilliant strokes of pinks and oranges across the fading blue sky. Tomorrow would signal the start of another week's tasks. She was sad as the evening was drawing to a close. The thought of returning to the tiny attic room and the loneliness lingering there dimmed her spirit. Even her aunt and uncle's tiny attic room seemed preferable to the one she shared with Jane, Louise, and Crosley.

But despite her disappointment at the day's ending, Annabelle's heart swelled—could this be what her heart was seeking? A home with her aunt and uncle? The attention of a gamekeeper? Simple dinners and genuine conversation?

At dinner's end Uncle Edmund was called to the school on a matter of urgent business, and Aunt Lydia escorted Annabelle and Mr. Locke back to the parlor where Annabelle needed to pack her painting supplies.

Aunt Lydia was about to be seated when a twinkle sparkled in her eye. In an abrupt motion she reached out and took Mr. Locke by the arm. "Oh, I've a brilliant idea. While you are waiting for your uncle to return to escort you home, Annabelle dear, you must paint Mr. Locke."

Sarah E. Ladd

Shyness rushed in a flush to Annabelle's cheeks. Her emotions concerning Mr. Locke were changing and growing at such a rapid pace that the idea of studying him so intently unnerved her.

Owen's laugh relieved her. "Miss Thorley's talents would be put to much better use painting someone else. Yourself, perhaps?"

"La, what do I need with a painting of myself?" Aunt Lydia waved her hand in the air. "But you, Mr. Locke, how Hannah would treasure such a gift."

He smiled. In fact, he was smiling more and more. When she first met him, he had seemed somber. Serious. But tonight his behavior seemed relaxed. He was in the company of his friends, and his comments were unguarded. His countenance was quite changed.

He turned dark, smiling eyes on her. "What do you think, Miss Thorley? Mrs. Langsby seems to think you can paint me. Do you?"

His direct attentions incited a flutter in her heart. She could not deny that the thought of spending more time with him appealed to her. In fact, a renewed energy flowed through her. She grinned. "For Hannah, I will try. Sit there, by the fire. We don't have much light."

He straightened his coat and sat on the chair.

Her aunt clasped her hands before her. "I've got to write instructions for the cook, so I will be just in the kitchen. I trust you will let me know if you need anything?"

Annabelle could not prevent her eyes from widening.

Her aunt was leaving her.

Alone.

With Mr. Locke.

In London this never would happen. Time and time again she was learning that the rules of etiquette and decorum were slackened in Fellsworth.

Annabelle muttered a response to her aunt's question. "Uh, I can't think of anything I need."

Mr. Locke gave a little shrug. If the idea of spending time alone with her unnerved him, he gave no indication of such. "You are kind to offer, but I am quite content."

He pushed his fingers through his curly black locks. "Shall we get started, Miss Thorley?"

Aunt Lydia propped her hands on her hips. "Well then, I shall be back shortly. And when I return, I expect to see a lovely portrait of our Mr. Locke."

She scurried from the room, and as her footsteps quieted, the crackling of the fire—and the heat radiating from it—intensified.

Annabelle drew a deep breath. Her aunt's intentions were obvious. A flush of excitement warmed her face. Aunt Lydia had clearly decided that Mr. Locke was an appropriate beau for her. She had made the comment before he arrived that day, and several suggestive comments and knowing glances during the course of the dinner confirmed Annabelle's suspicions.

Now she felt strangely nervous as she assessed him. The fire's glow flickered on the angles of his face, and she set about arranging her painting materials in preparation. "Have you ever had your portrait painted before?"

He gave a good-natured laugh. "Actually, it might surprise you to learn that I have."

She raised her eyebrow. "Oh? Recently?"

"Well, actually it was not a portrait exactly. It was a silhouette." He rubbed his hand over his chin, his tone sobered, and he looked down at his hands in his lap. "My wife created it for me, at her home in London before we were married. She was quite talented."

The mention of his wife surprised her. With Mr. Locke's reserve it was a personal topic she did not expect to arise. But since he seemed so comfortable with it, she felt brave. She cleaned her brush in the water pot and blotted it on her towel. "My uncle tells me she was a gentleman's daughter."

"Which probably makes you wonder what she was doing with me?"

She snapped her head up, afraid he was offended, but a smile crossed his lips—the same smile he had used with his friends at dinner.

The tension in her shoulders eased. "Well, you have said yourself that you do not care for London and you much prefer life in the country."

"You are right, Miss Thorley. Very perceptive. But I did not meet Diana in London. I met her in Bath."

"Bath?" The elegant town was a winter favorite for many of her London acquaintances. "I have never been there myself but have heard it is intoxicating."

"Well, I am not sure if intoxicating is the word I would use to describe it. Busy, hot, and pompous seem more accurate descriptions. I was accompanying Treadwell to the north to a breeder and he broke his journey in Bath. That is why I was there."

"Oh. I see." She straightened the paper before her. She cast another glance at his straight nose, full lips, and the cleft in his chin. It felt almost indecent to be studying him so intently. A tremor shook her hand as she poised her brush over the paper. "But now you have piqued my curiosity, Mr. Locke. That does not explain how you made your wife's acquaintance."

A smile dimpled his cheek, and he looked to the wall behind her, as if reliving a happy memory. "I was very young at the time, mind you, and was much more likely to throw caution to the wind than at present. Treadwell was invited to a masquerade ball and he invited me to attend."

"A masquerade ball!" She laughed, giving her head a shake and pressing her brush against the paper. "You surprise me. I must say that is the last thing I would have expected to hear from you."

"It does sound odd, doesn't it? At the time Treadwell and I had been having a great number of discussions about life in the city versus life in the country. He dared me to attend to see what I thought of his sort of entertainment, behind the anonymity of a mask, no doubt, so I complied."

Candlelight illuminated her space as her paintbrush outlined his square jaw. "And what did you think of the event?"

"For the most part it was tedious. But if it weren't for the ball, I never would have met Diana. I never meant to attempt to elevate my social standing by attending. Far from it. I meant to observe, nothing more. But I encountered Diana quite by accident, and with my identity hidden, I thought nothing of passing the evening in conversation with such a charming lady. One thing led to another, and the next thing I knew, we were married and she was leaving her life of privilege to move to Fellsworth."

She motioned for him to angle his face toward the light. "That is quite a story."

"In hindsight I realize I was probably wrong for taking her away from the only life she had known. But at the time, she was so unhappy that I allowed myself to think she needed me to save her from an unpleasant situation."

Annabelle remained silent at his story. Had he not saved her from an unpleasant situation as well?

She wanted to know more, but instead of offering more details on the topic, he fell quiet.

The conversation shifted and flowed easily as she painted his torso. His broad shoulders. Muscular arms. Dark eyebrows. Intense eyes. He shared a little more about his childhood—about long summer afternoons helping his father in the meadows. She told him about how she spent her childhood afternoons painting with her mother. The conversation was warm, unguarded. It was different than her conversations had been with Samuel.

Thinking back, she realized her interactions with her former beau had been more about impressing him and improving her status than deepening the bond between them. She'd been so careful not to say anything embarrassing or that would cause him to think of her in a different light. Perhaps it was because she was a little older or she had experienced much more, but she felt no need to alter her opinions or cast a shadow on the truth as she talked with Mr. Locke.

The door rattled open, and her uncle appeared in the threshold. Annabelle lifted her gaze to the mantel clock, unaware of how much time had passed.

Uncle Edmund's return ended their solitude. "What are you up to? More painting?"

"Yes, Aunt suggested that I paint Mr. Locke." She leaned back so her uncle could see her work.

He adjusted the spectacles on his nose as he assessed the painting. "Well now. That is quite impressive. And quite an improvement on the original subject."

She laughed at his joke. "I am not finished yet, clearly, but I think I have enough of a start that I can finish it in the coming days."

"I hate to hurry you along, dear, but I need to escort you back to your hall by curfew."

"Yes, I should be returning to my duties as well." Mr. Locke stood before he turned to Annabelle. "Thank you, Miss Thorley. I look forward to seeing the finished piece. Please pass along my gratitude to Mrs. Langsby for an enjoyable evening."

Mr. Locke bid farewell to Uncle Edmund, and within seconds he was gone.

Annabelle felt his absence immediately as he exited the parlor. Mr. Locke took with him the energy in the room, and her heart was already longing for the time she would see him again.

She smiled up at her uncle, who was looking down at her with fatherly affection. "He is a kind man."

"A kind man, yes. An honorable one. And he seems quite taken with you, my dear."

Heat rushed to her face, but her heart leapt also. Annabelle started to clean her brush. She looked to the empty space where Mr. Locke had been.

Perhaps her uncle was right. Perhaps Mr. Locke was smitten with her. She allowed herself to remain in the optimistic joy of such a sentiment for a few seconds before forcing her mind back to more practical matters. He was vastly different from Samuel, but had she not also believed Samuel to be different than he actually was?

She would do well to guard her heart, for as charming as Mr. Locke could be, she knew the pain of betrayal, and she needed to protect herself from it, whatever the cost.

Chapter Thirty-One

"She's gone!"

Annabelle jerked her head up and paused in her task of gathering readers. Mrs. Tomlinson rounded the corner of the middle library, her eyes wide, her cheeks flushed. "Mrs. Tomlinson, is something the matter?"

"Goodness, yes. I just need to catch my breath." The older woman held one hand to her chest and the other in the air. "Miss Locke is missing."

"Hannah Locke?" Annabelle whirled around and lowered the books. "Missing?"

"Yes. She is nowhere to be found." Alarm shrilled and quickened the woman's voice. "We are all on the search for her and cannot locate her anywhere. Have you seen her today?"

Annabelle shook her head. "No. Did you check her chamber?"

"Of course we did. She is not there."

"And you asked the other girls if they have seen her?"

"Yes." Her voice rose an octave. The older teacher fanned her flushed face with her hand. "No one has seen her since the midday meal. Oh dear, this is not good."

Annabelle tensed. She had enjoyed getting to know Hannah over the past several weeks, and it was not like the girl to defy the rules, let alone disappear. Something had to be wrong. "Have you notified Mrs. Brathay?"

Mrs. Tomlinson gave her head a sharp nod. "The kitchen staff is out searching the grounds now, but with all this rain they are having trouble."

Annabelle looked to the window and to the forest's edge and the pewter sky above it. A steady, cool rain pelted the wavy glass and settled a chill over the grounds. "Do you think she would have gone to Bancroft Park? To her father?"

"One of the blacksmiths was going to ride out to the gamekeeper's lodge, but I am concerned. It is unlikely Mr. Locke will be home this time of day."

Annabelle chewed her lip and moved to lookout the window. Two men jogged through the courtyard. They had to be in search of Hannah.

Genuine concern coursed through her. Annabelle would hate to hear of any child lost or missing, but she had developed a fond attachment to the wide-eyed, friendly child.

Mrs. Tomlinson knit her fingers together in front of her. "Please keep a lookout for her, and if you think of any place she might be, please do not hesitate to let me know." With the parting words, the flustered woman quit the library.

Annabelle looked at the sky again. When Hannah had talked of wanting to go home, she mentioned the path through the forest near the garden wall. Would anyone else know about the path to which Hannah had referred?

As a clap of thunder grumbled low far in the distance, Annabelle made up her mind. She would go find the path herself.

She hurried out into the early afternoon. The rain had already started to muddy the paths, and Annabelle wished she had thought to grab her shawl. She made her way to the school garden and headed for the stone wall that separated it from the forest.

Once she arrived she stared into the path's dark depths, trying to decide what to do. It looked so different than it did the day she had encountered Mr. Locke. His warnings of traps and animals rushed to mind. Even though Hannah was a gamekeeper's daughter, did she understand the danger that lurked between her and her home?

"Hannah!" she called out. A flock of birds suddenly flew from nearby branches, causing Annabelle's heart to leap in her chest. She cupped her hands around her mouth and called again.

She waited for a response, but none came.

Annabelle hurried along the path that bordered the forest. Hannah had told her that the cottage was visible when the trees were bare, so it couldn't be that far.

As the distance between her and the school increased, she looked back toward the buildings. People scurried out, no doubt seeking the child, but no one seemed to look toward the forest. Did it not make sense that if Hannah did not want to be at the school she would go home?

She lifted her skirts and stepped off the path into the woods. Hannah had also said her home was on the other side of the pond. With the pond in sight, Annabelle inched forward, keeping an eye out for traps.

She walked deeper. Carefully. Watchfully. She rounded the pond's swampy bank, taking great caution not to slip. Looking behind her, she could no longer see the school. In fact, greenery and branches swallowed any trace of the path she had traversed.

She swallowed a lump of trepidation as she gazed in the other direction. There was no sight of a cottage, as Hannah had claimed.

Annabelle turned a full circle, trying to get her bearings, but with the constant movement of wind whistling through the branches and the rain's disorienting rhythm, she was, herself, becoming quite lost.

The forest was much noisier than she imagined it would be. Even in the rain the birds fluttered among the branches and called to one another. The wind whistled through the leaves and roared past her. It was as if the forest had its own language—one she did not understand. Annabelle called the child's name several times, then strained to hear any response.

But none came.

"Hannah!" Annabelle wiped the moisture from her face and stepped farther into the green. She ducked to avoid hitting her head on a low-hanging branch, and she lifted her heavy skirts to keep them free from the overgrown underbrush. "Hannah, where are you?"

She was not sure exactly how long she searched the forest, but a sound rose above that of the wind and rain—a sound she had not yet heard in the forest.

Sobbing.

Annabelle's heart lurched, and she hurried her pace. "Hannah!" She cried out again, louder and stronger.

Finally, a response. Sobs choked the soft and weak words, but they were audible. "I'm here!"

"Keep talking so I can find you." Annabelle followed the voice and ran in that direction.

She found the girl huddled in the damp underbrush. Her cap was missing and her blonde hair clung to her face in wet clumps. Muck and mud covered her black dress, and her red-rimmed eyes were glossy with tears. Sobs shook her tiny shoulders, and she was gripping her ankle with both hands.

"I-I stepped on this, and now my foot is stuck, and I—I—"

Annabelle gasped as Hannah moved her hands from her ankle. Bright-red blood soaked the white stocking. Upon closer inspection she saw it was . . . a metal trap clamped around her foot.

Fighting the urge to panic, Annabelle dropped to her knees to assess the trap. She had never seen one before. It was small—it would have been easy for anyone to overlook, especially in the forest's thick undergrowth.

"Surely there is a way to get this off of you." Annabelle pushed her wet hair from her eyes, blinked away the moisture, and gritted her teeth as she fumbled with the sharp trap until she found a small lever to unlock it. The trap clicked open far enough to remove it from the girl's foot.

Hannah cried afresh as the trap fell free.

Annabelle sat back on her heels. Hannah would not be able to walk. It was out of the question. Annabelle was going to have to carry her. But to where?

"I have no idea where we are." Annabelle assessed the location. "Do you?"

Hannah moaned. "My home is there, through those trees."

"Here, let me help you." Annabelle tried to put the girl's arm around her shoulder, but the disparity in their heights was too great. Annabelle lifted the weeping girl and carried her as best she could.

Annabelle smelled wood smoke's sharp scent before she saw any structures, but soon the cottage came into view. It was a tall building of stone and timber framing, with small windows and a thatched roof. Gray smoke puffed from the chimney and mingled with the cool, foggy rain. A dog yipped somewhere in the distance. Puddles formed in the courtyard, and two chickens wandered in the space.

Struggling under the child's weight, Annabelle called across the yard, "Help, please!"

No response. Annabelle made it to the door and kicked it with the toe of her boot. Moments later, the wooden and iron door squeaked open.

She had been expecting Mr. Locke, but an old woman with long, silver hair in a single plait opened the door. Her face blanched. "Hannah! What's this?"

Fearing that she might drop Hannah, Annabelle pushed past the woman, her breath coming in huffs. "She got her foot caught in a trap. She's bleeding. Where should I put her?"

The older woman snapped into action. "Here, on the sofa."

Annabelle rushed to the long sofa and lowered Hannah to the fur coverlet slung across the back, careful not to jostle her foot.

"Quick, we need to get this boot and stocking off," instructed the woman, speaking loud to be heard over Hannah's crying, which had begun afresh when they entered the house. "The bleedin' must stop."

Annabelle stepped back to allow the tiny woman room to work. "How can I help?"

"Quick." The woman motioned to a rough table in the corner. "Fetch me the scissors there."

Annabelle hurried to the table referenced in a corner of the kitchen. Jars and vials cluttered the otherwise tidy work space, and bunches of dried flowers and herbs hung from the ceiling. "I don't see them."

"In the jar there. Look again. And bring me the candle too."

Frustrated, Annabelle searched the small space. She finally located the tool, grabbed it in one hand, took the candle in the other, and delivered them to the older woman.

It was dark in the cottage. The thick clouds outdoors prevented light from entering the small windows, and the fire in the grate had burned low. Despite the heat of exertion, the wetness of her gown and hair sent a shiver coursing through Annabelle. She stoked the fire for more light before she returned to Hannah's side.

"It hurts!" wailed Hannah, her small chest rising and falling with each breath, her bright-blue eyes fixed on the wound.

The woman peeled back the stocking from the wound and shifted her position to get a better view. "Nasty gash, that is. I know your papa's warned ye about the traps before. Ye shouldn't 'ave been there. What were ye doin' in the forest, anyway?"

Annabelle stiffened at the curtness in the woman's tone.

Hannah sniffed. "I just wanted to come home, that's all."

Annabelle stole another look at the woman she had heard the other teachers talk about—Mrs. Pike—on the rare occasions Mr. Locke had come up in conversation. She was rumored to have a temper, but she was also famed for her ability to aid in healing. With her untidy hair and simple tan gown, she did not look like what Annabelle had imagined.

"Your ankle will be fine, but we must get some salve on it. Stay put, girl."

Annabelle nestled on the sofa and cradled Hannah's shoulders, whispering words of encouragement to the crying child.

Mrs. Pike gathered several different jars and bottles in her arms, a bowl, a piece of cloth, and other items, then spread them out on another table and mixed a few ingredients together in a wooden bowl. She reached for a flask and poured liquid into the mug. She balanced the mug and the bowl in one arm, shooed Annabelle out of the way, and sat next to Hannah.

"Drink this. It'll dull the pain." Mrs. Pike lifted the mug to Hannah's mouth.

Hannah sputtered the drink and wiped her sleeve over her lips. "That's terrible!"

"No more terrible than the pain." Mrs. Pike ignored her protest and smoothed the earthy-smelling paste over the gash with her bony fingers and then bound it with a strip of linen. "Yarrow will help. We need to get ye out of these wet things or you'll catch your death."

By the time Hannah's foot was bandaged and her clothing changed, she had fallen into a quiet slumber. Annabelle was not sure what the older woman had given the child to drink, but it had taken effect.

Mrs. Pike put her hands on her hips and looked down at the child. "There, she'll sleep now. Best thing for 'er, what with a pain like that." She wiped her hands on her apron and turned to Annabelle. "Now, how about ye start by telling me who ye are and how ye came to be carryin' Miss Locke in such a state?"

Annabelle bit her lip. She had meant to be helpful, but it seemed that this woman almost blamed her for Hannah's injury.

"I am Annabelle Thorley, a teacher at Fellsworth School."

Mrs. Pike sniffed. "I've never seen ye there before."

"I've only been there a couple of months."

"Oh yes, I heard o' ye." Mrs. Pike raised her eyebrow at the recollection. "You're ol' Langsby's niece, if I'm not mistaken. Well, Miss Thorley, I repeat, how did the child come to be in such a state?"

Annabelle resisted the urge to shrink back against the wall. She would be lying if she said the woman's direct stare and commanding manner were not intimidating. "Hannah went missing from the school, and I found her in the forest with her foot caught in a trap."

"So you just 'appened to be in the forest and just 'appened to find her there?"

Annabelle shifted at the insinuation in the older woman's voice. The room was growing warm with the stoked fire, and she squirmed uncomfortably in the damp clothes. "No. Hannah told me about the shortcut to the cottage, and I thought I might find her there. I—I thought the school sent a rider out here to see if she was here."

"If they did, I didn't see 'im. Mr. Locke is in the north forest today, and I've been back in the shed tendin' the hounds." Mrs. Pike nodded toward Annabelle. "Ye should get out o' those wet things too, lest ye fall ill yourself."

"Oh, oh no. I'll go back to the school. They will be wondering how Hannah is."

"Ye can't go now. Do ye not hear the storm?"

Annabelle's heart sank. She rubbed her arms as she walked to the window. The rain fell in sheets now, even harder than when they arrived. The puddles in the yard had grown to cover most of the small courtyard.

"Besides, 'tis not likely ye will find your way back to the school on your own. I've lived here for years and still get turned around in the forest on a fine day, let alone a day like this." The woman left the room, and after several minutes she returned with a bundle. "Here.

Ye can put this on while your things are drying. Ye can change in there. If ye need help, let me know."

Annabelle eyed the clothes, surprised that the woman presented a garment of such elegant brown silk. She was hesitant to take the items, but Mrs. Pike was right. She had no idea how long she would be here, and she did not wish to remain in a wet gown much longer. She accepted the bundle, held the items away from her to prevent them from getting wet, and went into the adjoining room. She closed the door behind her and turned to assess the chamber.

It was a simple room. A bed covered in a faded, patched quilt was pushed against the far plaster wall, and a single window covered with a dark-blue curtain permitted a sliver of light. Beside the bed stood a chest of drawers, and a trunk faced it on the opposite wall.

She crossed the room and placed the items on the bed. For the most part she had mastered the art of dressing and undressing without Crosley's help, but she barely managed to shed the wet garment and petticoat. Before long she donned the simple, if not old-fashioned, gown with long sleeves and a high neck. She let down her hair, shook her locks to dry them, used her fingers to release a few tangles, and left it long down her back.

She returned to the sitting room with her wet things.

"Just put those next to the fire to dry," Mrs. Pike called over her shoulder as she scurried about the room.

Annabelle did as she was bid, and when she turned, Mrs. Pike had a cup of tea waiting for her.

"Drink this," she encouraged, moving it even closer.

Annabelle took the warm cup in her hands. The liquid had a strong scent. "I've not smelled tea like this before, I don't think. What is it?"

"It's me own blend. One that will keep ye from falling ill from spendin' so long in the rain."

Annabelle could not deny the allure of the steaming liquid, but still she was hesitant. The stories of Mrs. Pike and her fondness for herbs and remedies rang loudly in her mind, and she had borne witness to the effect the drink had on Hannah. She lifted it to her lips with both hands.

"Sit 'ere, by the fire."

Annabelle obeyed the instruction and sat in a chair opposite Hannah, who still slumbered on the sofa. She took another sip of tea in an attempt to relax her tightening nerves and looked around the room, trying to imagine Mr. Locke here.

It was a dark room, yes, but she found it to be quaint. Two sofas—one on which Hannah was sleeping—were perpendicular to the fire, and two overstuffed wing-backed chairs flanked the mantel. A heavy fur blanket was over the back of the empty sofa, a shelf of books lined the wall next to the fireplace, and several firearms and powder horns hung near the door. On the mantel above the hearth ticked a small clock, and next to it sat a pipe, a small wooden box, and a carved statue of a deer. A large, bright rug covered the rough planked floor, and off to the side was the table where she had found the scissors for Mrs. Pike. Three large, dark beams ran the length of the low ceiling, and several candles winked from around the room.

And then she saw it.

On the wall opposite hung a silhouette.

She did not see how she could have missed it. The black outline was stark against the white background, but Mrs. Locke's regard was evident in the care she took with the portrait. She had captured his curly hair, his straight nose, his strong chin. It was a handsome piece.

Being in Mr. Locke's house with his daughter, his housekeeper, and the very real memory of his wife made Annabelle's chest tighten. She had invited him to step into her world on a number of occasions, but with the exception of their meeting in the forest, she had not stepped into his. Until now. Now that she was here, Annabelle worried what his reaction would be.

With a heavy sigh Mrs. Pike sat in the chair like the one Annabelle was in. She picked up a linen shirt that undoubtedly belonged to Mr. Locke, lifted the seam, and took her needle to the rough fabric.

"How long have you lived in Fellsworth, Mrs. Pike?"

Mrs. Pike paused. "I came several years ago when Mrs. Locke married Mr. Locke. I had been her servant for years, so she asked me to stay on with 'er. I can tell ye this place was quite a change from what we were used to."

Annabelle recalled the murder rumor she had heard. It was not her place to ask questions, but being in Mrs. Locke's home made her curiosity too much to bear. She started with a question to which she already knew the answer. "Where did you and Mrs. Locke live before coming here?"

"London mostly, but we traveled a great deal." Mrs. Pike took a sip of tea. "They were happy years, Miss Thorley, but oh, so long ago."

Annabelle was surprised by the older woman's wistfulness. She had clearly been attached to her mistress. "I am impressed that you decided to stay on here after her death."

Mrs. Pike nodded. "It's not an elegant space, to be sure, what with the dogs 'n' ferrets in the kennels out back. But Mr. Locke was in such a state after Mrs. Locke died. I stayed on to help with the babe, even though I never cared for a wee one in all my days, and it gradually changed into how we are today."

Mrs. Pike lowered her sewing. "She was a beautiful person. Hannah here is the spitting image of 'er. Acts just like 'er too. Feisty. Headstrong. I'd like to think that the girl would have enough common sense to stay out o' the forest in the rain, but ye see how things turned out."

Annabelle looked over to the sleeping child with fondness.

They fell into a comfortable silence—partly because Mrs. Pike was so focused on her task and partly because Annabelle was growing drowsy. The excitement and physical exertion had taken a toll on her, and the steady rhythm of falling rain mingled with the crackling of the warm fire was a mystical sort of lullaby.

She leaned her head against the back of the chair and let her eyes fall closed . . . for just a minute.

Chapter Thirty-Two

Evening's long shadows were falling as Owen strode down the narrow path through Linton Forest to the gamekeeper's cottage, just as he had thousands of times before. The stone home was so familiar, it should have been a place of solace. But every time he approached, he could never—and would never—be able to shake the memory of what happened there.

The memory of that day was burned into the plaster walls and etched into every surrounding tree. A part of him would always grieve for Diana. But another part of him never wanted to see this place again.

His resolve was never stronger: he would find the men responsible for the rise in poaching. He had no choice if he ever wanted to start fresh in the Kirtley Meadow cottage.

The scents of the damp forest were alive around him, causing him to pause and fill his lungs with their cool, natural goodness. Autumn was falling, and even in the failing light he noticed the first glimpse of orange-tipped leaves overhead. His boots splashed through the rainy puddles along the path, and he adjusted the hares he had caught over his shoulder. As soon as the rain ceased, he would take them to the cook for the week's meals.

As they drew closer, Drake ran ahead of him, splashing mud with each pounding paw. Owen kicked the dirt from his boots and sat on a bench outside of the lodge to remove them. He slid his coat from his shoulders and draped it over his arm before opening the door.

Mrs. Pike appeared as soon as he entered. "At last. Thought ye'd never get 'ere."

"Why?"

"There's been an accident," she said low. "Don't worry, Hannah will be fine, but—"

"Hannah?" he blurted, alarm coursing through him. "What's wrong with Hannah?"

"She stepped on a trap. She—"

"A trap?" Why would Hannah be anywhere near a trap? His gaze searched the dark room. "Where is she?"

"There."

Within seconds he crossed the small room. His chest squeezed as he beheld his tiny daughter lying on the sofa, a blanket pulled to her chin, her light hair splayed over the pillow. Her mouth was open as she slept, and her chest rose and fell with each breath. She looked so still.

"Is she all right?" he demanded.

"Yes. She will be. She has a nasty gash on 'er ankle though, and it likely bruised the bone. I gave 'er something for the pain, and so she will be asleep for a while."

Mrs. Pike's words eased him a little. Her skill at healing was phenomenal. She had bound his own various wounds a time or two.

His sweet, precious daughter, marred by the very traps he'd placed. His mind leapt to the worst. He had seen what traps could do to animals, but he never imagined one would affect his own daughter.

How many times had he warned her? If she was at the cottage, the reminders were constant. He had thought her safe from the danger when she was at school—it was one of the reasons he insisted that she attend.

He flipped up the cover and assessed the wound as gently as he could. A bright spot of red had seeped through the bandaging. "How did this happen?"

"She was walkin' home through the forest."

"What was she doing walking home through the forest?"

He lifted his gaze and noticed a figure covered with a blanket, curled up in the chair next to the fire. He did not wait for Mrs. Pike's response. "Who's that?"

"Miss Thorley. She's the one who found Hannah and brought 'er here."

How, of all people, would Miss Thorley find his daughter in the forest?

He never would have dreamed that this woman would be in his home. And yet, here she was, wrapped in a blanket, slumbering, as if she belonged here all along.

"Miss Thorley. Miss Thorley! Wake up!"

A childlike voice roused Annabelle from a dreamless sleep.

"Hmm?" she muttered, not fully awake.

"Miss Thorley, you must wake up. Mrs. Pike says our supper is ready, and Papa is here."

Confused as to why someone was waking her, Annabelle rubbed her face, arched her head to straighten the crick in her neck, and opened her eyes.

The sight that met her snapped her awake.

Across from her sat Mr. Locke, as calmly as if he was quite accustomed to having a young woman napping in his sitting room.

"Oh my," she muttered as she straightened in the chair, startled to see a man so close to her. She touched loose strands of untethered hair behind her ear, and memories rushed back. Hannah's foot. The storm. Her dress.

"I am so sorry." She gave a little laugh and diverted her gaze from Mr. Locke. "How is your foot, Hannah? Feeling any better?"

Hannah pouted. "It hurts."

"I imagine it does."

Annabelle's heart pounded painfully fast. She had to address the awkwardness of the situation right away. She met his gaze fully. "I did not intend to take such liberties in your house, Mr. Locke. Please accept my apologies for falling asleep like this."

He lowered his paper, then his head in a bow. "No apology needed, Miss Thorley. I understand you rescued my daughter from the trap. I am in your debt."

She shifted uncomfortably under the praise. "You are not in my debt, but I should return to Fellsworth. The others will be wondering about Hannah."

"But it's still raining, Miss Thorley." Hannah's eyes grew wide. "And thundering and lightning. You will get wet all over again."

"No need to rush, Miss Thorley." Owen placed the paper on the floor next to him and leaned forward. "I have sent Whitten to Fellsworth with the message that you are both here and you would return when the rain stops."

"You must at least eat with us, Miss Thorley," pleaded Hannah. "It is such fun to have you in our house. We never have guests. Well, we never have guests besides Mr. and Mrs. Whitten. It will be merry. You must stay."

Annabelle blinked away the drowsiness and looked around the room. The stew did smell delicious. She had not eaten since the morning meal.

But it was more than that. She was surprised that despite the awkwardness of the moment, she enjoyed the company. Mrs. Pike could be heard singing from the kitchen. The brightness in Hannah's expression was contagious. Then she met Mr. Locke's gaze.

She gave a little shrug. "If it isn't too much trouble."

Hannah's voice shrilled, "It isn't trouble! Is it, Papa? Oh, please say you will stay!"

Mr. Locke stood from his chair. The low height of the ceiling made him seem even taller. The firelight flickered against the side of him, highlighting the day's stubble on his jaw and catching on the damp strands of his hair. The rumble of his voice was oddly warming. "Of course it's no trouble. Please join us. You are more than welcome in our house, Miss Thorley."

Did he really want her here? She felt as if she was intruding.

Annabelle stood, shook the creases out of her borrowed dress, and folded the blanket that had been draped over her. She set it over the back of the chair, smoothed another wrinkle out of the linen gown, and patted her hair.

When she looked up, Mr. Locke was staring at her. His eyebrows drew together in what appeared to be confusion.

She suddenly felt self-conscious of the manner in which the bodice hugged too tight and the sleeves hung too short. Heat crept up her neck and chest.

Gone was Mr. Locke's easy personality. Instead, his expression grew quite sober. His eyes narrowed, and his lips flattened into a thin line.

"Is something wrong?" she asked.

As if suddenly aware he was staring, he gave his head a little shake. "No. I mean to say, yes, yes, I am fine."

But he wasn't fine. His brows had drawn together, and his jaw twitched. His entire demeanor had darkened.

The house that had felt warm and inviting seemed to close in around her.

Without another word he turned and disappeared through the door to the kitchen.

Even above the crackling of the fire and the steady rhythm of the rain, she heard their hushed voices. Mr. Locke's voice was first.

"Why is she in Diana's dress?"

"What, that ol' dress?"

"It was Diana's."

"Yes, it was, but she doesn't need it now, does she?" Mrs. Pike's words were clipped.

"That's not the point." His voice was strained. "She shouldn't be in it."

"Well, what would ye have me do? The girl rescued your daughter and got soakin' wet while doin' it. I couldn't just let 'er catch 'er death, now could I?"

"Shh. Keep your voice down. That doesn't matter. Surely there was something else around here."

"I would have given 'er one of mine, but it would have fallen clear off 'er. That would set gossipin' tongues waggin', now wouldn't it?"

Annabelle heard no more after that.

She was wearing his wife's gown.

His *late* wife's gown.

No wonder he looked at her with such disapproval.

She groaned and looked up at the ceiling. How foolish she felt. Why had she not realized it when she dressed in it? It made sense now. The fine fabric. The old-fashioned style. She wanted to disappear. Would nothing ever be simple? Be easy?

Mr. Locke returned and lifted Hannah in an effortless movement. "Shall we eat?"

Annabelle could feel the heat rising up her chest and neck. She glanced down at her arms. Sure enough, they were blotchy. She could only hope the darkness of the room hid her visible mark of discomfort.

Candles were spaced on the table, giving the room a soft glow. She sat at the rough table. Mrs. Pike appeared with a big black iron pot and filled the bowls with a thick beef stew. Bread and cheese sat atop the table. The scene was warm. Inviting.

Mr. Locke sat his daughter in the chair opposite Annabelle, and then he took the chair at the head of the table. After saying a prayer over the meal, he turned to Hannah. "Why were you in the forest today, poppet?"

The child's gaze shifted from her father, to Annabelle, and back to Mr. Locke.

"Well?" he prompted.

Hannah hung her blonde head. "I'm sorry, Papa."

"But why were you there?"

"I wanted to come home."

Mr. Locke cocked his head. "Why?"

"The girls were being mean." Hannah's eyes filled with tears. "I don't want to be there anymore."

Mr. Locke glanced at Annabelle, as if to gauge her opinion on the topic.

She held his gaze for several moments before he turned back to the child. "But it was raining. Why didn't you wait until I came for our visit? You know we can talk about these things then."

"It wasn't raining when I left," she said, her blue eyes wide. "But when it started raining, I couldn't see. I was close to home. Please, Papa. Don't be upset with me."

He reached out and patted Hannah's hand. "I'm not upset, dearest. Just concerned."

"How did you come to find Hannah, Miss Thorley?"

Annabelle pressed the rough napkin to her lips and lowered it to her lap and gave him the same story she gave Mrs. Pike.

Mr. Locke frowned. "It was a very reckless thing you did, Hannah. You know how dangerous the woods can be. Furthermore, Miss Thorley could have been injured while searching for you."

Hannah looked down at her stew.

His face softened, and he exchanged glances with Mrs. Pike. "But what's done is done. We will talk about this more later, but you cannot return to school with your ankle in the state it's in."

Hannah lowered her gaze. "Yes, sir."

The rest of the meal passed without ceremony. Once the topic of

Hannah's actions ceased, the conversation shifted to a more casual one, and words flowed easily. Besides the meals she shared with her aunt and uncle, this was one of the most pleasant repasts Annabelle had had in weeks.

The day's last sliver of light slanted through the window, brightening the entire room and signaling the rain's end.

Mr. Locke looked at Annabelle. "Sounds like the rain has stopped. We'd best get you back to Fellsworth. It will be dark very soon. Do you know how to ride a horse?"

She blinked at him. She had never been on horseback in her life, and the idea made her nervous. "No."

"Would you like to try? I'm afraid the carriage would have trouble on the muddy path, and walking is out of the question. The road just south of the bridge always washes out after a bout of weather like we had today."

"Well then," she said with a smile. "I shall try my best."

"Good." He pushed back from the table and stood. "I'll go get the horses and will return shortly."

After the door closed behind him, Mrs. Pike stood and began gathering the dishes. By the time he returned, she had bundled Annabelle's wet clothes and had them ready for departure.

Annabelle knelt next to Hannah and smoothed the girl's hair. "I am very glad you are safe, Hannah."

"You are not upset with me? I am afraid Papa is upset with me."

"I am not upset with you, dearest. And neither is your papa. He is just worried, I think. It is scary to think that someone you love could have been hurt. Your papa loves you very much." Annabelle smiled. It was hard not to compare the relationship between Hannah and Mr. Locke to her relationship with her own father. How would he have reacted if she had gone missing?

"When will I go back to school?" Hannah's voice was soft in the evening stillness.

"That is for your papa to decide."

Hannah turned her face to Annabelle. "Will you come and visit me?"

Annabelle smiled down at the little girl. She felt a tug of affection, one, she imagined, that was what motherly affection would feel like. "Of course. Nothing could keep me away."

Chapter Thirty-Three

O wen rode back to the cottage's courtyard, leading a small bay. The horse was an old, friendly animal he had outfitted with a lady's sidesaddle. Of all the horses in the stable, Bess would be the easiest for a new rider to handle.

He dismounted, tied the horses to the post, and headed toward the cottage. A small part of him dreaded the ride back to Fellsworth School alone with Miss Thorley. He knew all too well the tendency for gossip on school grounds, and no doubt the sight of Miss Thorley emerging from the woods alone with a man would set tongues wagging and could cast a shadow on her character.

Another part of him, however, could not deny his eagerness for a few moments alone with the young schoolteacher. He had savored time with her. Their stolen moment in the forest. The leisurely dinner at the Langsby home.

Back inside the cottage, the firelight illuminated a scene that made his chest tighten and his breath catch. Miss Thorley was kneeling beside Hannah, reading from one of the few books in the house. Hannah's genuine smile was one Owen did not see often enough.

Perhaps the girls at school had been mean, as Hannah said. Perhaps not. Had he not wanted his daughter to have a gentle feminine influence in her life? A motherly woman to guide her and offer advice? Miss Thorley and Hannah seemed to have formed a friendship, and that fact alone endeared Miss Thorley to him even more.

He cleared his throat. "Are you ready to leave?"

Miss Thorley said something to Hannah, smiled, squeezed the child's hand, and stood. Then she and Mrs. Pike met him in the courtyard.

Owen grabbed his rifle from its stand, slung it over his shoulder, and headed out to the horses. Miss Thorley approached the horse with caution, her head tilted.

"This is Bess." Owen patted the bay's muzzle and smoothed her mane. "She is the gentlest horse at Bancroft Park and is a favorite of the ladies of the house for her calm nature. I think she should suit you well."

Miss Thorley smiled, lifted her skirt to step over a puddle, and patted the horse. "How do you do, Bess?"

The horse flicked her tail.

Owen had retrieved a small stool, and Mrs. Pike helped Miss Thorley onto the sidesaddle and then handed him the bundle of damp clothes to put in his saddlebag. "Comfortable?" Owen asked.

She nodded. "Yes, thank you."

He gave her a quick instruction on how to get the horse to move and stop, and before long they were on their way to Fellsworth School.

The cool breeze was a welcome relief from the stretch of warm days that had settled on Fellsworth, and now autumn's cooler days were outnumbering the steamy ones.

He cast a glance over at the lady riding next to him. She looked only slightly uncomfortable atop the slow steed. As usual she sat tall and straight, her head held high. It amazed him that through all she had endured, she still managed to conduct herself with such poise and decorum.

The sun was setting, and the clouds were breaking. The soft pink light filtered through the forest trees. This was one of his favorite times of the day. And Miss Thorley's presence made it even lovelier.

"I can't begin to thank you enough for helping Hannah." He kept his voice low. "What was she thinking, to run off as she did? I've tried to instill in her that the forest is dangerous, especially this time of year. I'm surprised she would act so rashly."

Miss Thorley glanced over at him before she returned her gaze to the path. "I have not been around children long and I am hardly an expert on the topic, but I don't think she meant to cause any harm. She simply wanted to come home."

Miss Thorley's answer tugged at him. "Is she miserable there?"

"I don't think she is miserable. I just do not think she knows quite how to manage her feelings."

After several moments of silence, Owen spoke. "I am grateful you were there for her today."

"I am too."

"I don't mean in just a physical sense." He wanted her to know that he appreciated the kindness she showed. "Without her mother, I am afraid she has no woman to turn to."

"But what of Mrs. Pike? She seems quite attentive."

"Mrs. Pike is a good woman, but she is not the most tender of souls. I had hoped sending Hannah to the school would help round life out for her, but now I am not sure."

"Give her time, Mr. Locke. My childhood was very different than Hannah's, but I do think she will learn a great deal from this situation."

"I'm sure you're right."

They rode in silence for several moments. Pink skies were fading to deep purple, and while Owen didn't mind riding in the dark, he did not want a new rider doing so.

"I think I may owe you an apology, Mr. Locke."

He frowned. "I am not sure what for."

"I did not mean to eavesdrop, but I heard you and Mrs. Pike discussing this gown."

Inwardly, a groan pulled at him. "Please pay no mind to what I said. It was just a surprise to see the gown again, that's all."

"I imagine it was. I would hate to think that I am the cause for reminding you of a painful memory."

A painful memory.

It was more than a painful memory.

Diana's death was a turning point that shifted his entire life's course.

It shook his trust.

Made him question his faith.

Caused him to wonder if there was any good in the world.

Normally he would never bring up the topic, but he felt as if he had to. "I do not mean to assume, but surely someone has told you of my late wife's passing and how it came about."

Miss Thorley looked down at the reins in her hand. "I have heard. And I am sorry for it."

He did not feel the need to expand on the topic. He had let her in that night at the Langsbys' when he first brought up Diana. It had been an unguarded moment. He had slipped. Said too much. But now that he had already discussed Diana with Miss Thorley, it felt almost safe to continue the conversation.

By now they were almost at the school, and darkness had completely descended. The breeze was almost chilly, and clouds were gathering once again. Very little moonlight lit the narrow path through the trees, but what he saw made him pause.

"Whoa." He drew his horse to a stop and reached out to stop Bess.

"What is it?" Miss Thorley's voice was barely above a whisper.

"There. In the path." He pointed ahead of them at a trunk blocking their way. It had fallen at an angle that the horses would not be able to simply step over. "A tree has fallen. See?"

"Oh."

"Don't worry." If he had been alone and it had not been so dark, he would have jumped the trunk without a second thought. But such would not do for Miss Thorley. "We are close enough to the main road now. We can walk the rest of the way, if that is agreeable to you."

She expelled a little laugh. "I would actually much prefer it. I don't think I make a very good horsewoman."

He scanned the tree line and then looked the opposite direction toward the main road. It was still early for poachers, but he didn't like the idea of her being out here after dark.

He swung his leg over, looped the reins above his horse's head, and then turned to assist Miss Thorley. "Just lead the horse. She'll go where you direct. And then just follow me."

He cut a path around the fallen trunk and, ensuring it was safe, led Miss Thorley around.

When they were both safely on the other side, he switched the side he was leading his horse from so he could walk next to her. He slowed his gait to match her dainty one.

All around him, fog from the rain hung a misty veil on the forest's darkness. The moon flittered in and out from behind large, fast-moving clouds, and in the distance, an owl was awakening for its nocturnal activity.

The sight of Miss Thorley nearly stole his breath. Bits of moonlight highlighted the feminine slope of her nose and glistened on her long, untethered light-brown locks. He tried not to stare, but his attraction to her was growing stronger. He worried for her, laughed with her. She had been in his home, and she had earned his daughter's trust. Up until now, he had managed to explain his interest in her as a desire to help, but now he found himself wanting more.

By all accounts he should not be alone with her, walking through the depths of the forest. He was softening toward her, and the more he was in her company, the more he could imagine what a future with her could be like.

He broke the silence. "Have you finished the painting?"

A smile crept across her lips. "I have not. But I will. I promise."

"I'll not forget."

She rubbed her arms, and it dawned on him. She was cold.

Of course she would be. He was used to the weather this time of night, but her gown was thin, and the air was damp. "You're shivering."

She tilted her head toward him and smiled. "I am fine."

He unfastened his coat, shrugged it from his arms, and held it out to her.

She eyed the coat. "I couldn't."

"Of course you could. Take it."

Her smile of gratitude threatened to undo him as she accepted the garment and wrapped it around her shoulders. "I feel I am always thanking you for one thing or another, Mr. Locke. You are very kind to me."

"After today it is I who am forever in your debt. Hannah is the most precious component of my life. If something were to happen to her . . ." His voice faded as the thought of a life without his child flashed before him. "If something were to happen to her, I cannot imagine ever being happy again."

She walked in silence for several seconds. "You have a dear relationship with Hannah. It is lovely, really. I envy such a relationship. My memories of my family are not nearly as happy as the memories Hannah will have of her childhood. You are a good father, Mr. Locke."

The mention of her family catapulted a shot through him. He had almost forgotten Treadwell's news. He considered what to do with the information. He enjoyed being alone with her. The last thing he wanted to do was upset her. Yet she deserved to know. He had too much respect for the journey she had been on to withhold the information from her, as much as the thought of sharing it ripped at him.

"There is another reason I am glad we have a few minutes alone."

She looked at him, an eyebrow raised in question, but said nothing.

"I spoke with Mr. Treadwell, and he informed me there is to be a hunt on our property soon."

"Oh?"

"Yes, September is here, and the men will be eager to hunt." He was not really sure how to proceed. "This is a bit awkward to say, mostly because I know it is not my business."

"Mr. Locke." She chewed her lip. "You are making me nervous."

Owen hesitated, and then his words tumbled forth. "Mr. Treadwell has given me the names of the guests for a hunting party that will be joining us at Bancroft Park next week. Your brother and Mr. Bartrell are among them."

"My brother?" She jerked and stopped short, and her voice rose an octave.

Bess, spooked at the sudden change in her voice, skittered to the side.

Owen reached around her to grab the horse's bridle.

With the motion, his leg brushed against Miss Thorley's skirt. He was closer to her than he had ever been, and he did not want to back away. But when the horse was calm, he regained a respectable distance.

"I know it is difficult, but try not to be too alarmed. If you remain at the school and he remains on Bancroft Park property, your paths should not cross. Given your reasons for leaving London, I just thought you should be aware."

She sniffed, and in the fading light he could not make out her features. "He will be so near. All my effort to remove myself from the situation seems in vain. Perhaps it was ridiculous to think that I could transition to another world, that I could disappear. I suppose I didn't think the situation through enough."

Her shoulders slumped slightly, and for the first time, she seemed to regret her decision to leave. It dawned on him that besides Crosley and her aunt and uncle, he was the only one who knew the truth about her.

He reached out again, this time to stop Bess. He wasn't really sure why. His body acted on instinct and waited for his reasoning to catch up. All he knew was that he could not let this moment of vulnerability and uncertainty, fear and regret, pass without addressing it. He did not back away this time.

She lifted her hazel eyes to him, eyes that had the increasing ability to arrest his thoughts. He had seen so many emotions written in them since meeting her. Anger. Relief. Fear. Restraint. Despair. He wanted to erase those emotions and replace them with a new one.

She lifted her arched eyebrows, as if to ask why they had stopped.

For several seconds they stood in silence. He reached out and took her hand in his, almost as much to capture her attention as to connect with her physically.

She did not resist or pull away. Miss Thorley lifted her eyes to him, her expression ripe with expectation.

"Listen to me, Annabelle." The use of her Christian name surprised even him. He rubbed his thumb on the top of her hand as he contemplated his words. "You made the wise decision. The brave decision. No woman deserves to be treated as you were. Your brother will not harm you. Not ever again. I will make certain of that."

Moonlight slanted through the boughs of the nearby ash trees and highlighted the moisture pooling in her eyes.

"Do you believe me?" He refused to allow her to look away.

She nodded and adjusted her hand to lace her fingers through his. She nodded again and then smiled.

"Good."

In the distance, thunder growled, signaling that the rain could return.

He squeezed her hand once more, then let it fall. He could not take liberties, regardless of how his heart cried to. "We'd best get you back to the school. But I beg you, try to be at peace. Your brother's visit is only that, a visit. Nothing more. He will not be here long, and then all will return to normal."

He offered her his arm, and she rested her hand gently on it as they resumed walking. "*Peace* is an interesting word. My mama always said that peace is not dependent upon your circumstances. It is dependent upon where you place your faith."

"Wise words." He was finding that she often referred to her mother, as if trying to find truth. "And do you agree with her?"

"I thought I had peace when I was in London, before my father died. How naive I was. But the more of life I experience, the more I realize that it wasn't peace at all. However, I am trying."

"When Diana died, I was angry. I'm sure that is no surprise. Angry at God. Angry at myself. Angry at the monster who committed the crime. I felt responsible and felt I did not deserve peace. But time heals and scars form. We cling to faith because at the end of the day, what else can one really rely on? Certainly not our own strength or wisdom."

She gave a little laugh. "Why are you so kind to me, Mr. Locke?"

"Owen. Call me Owen."

"All right, then, Owen. Why? You have come to my aid time and time again. You've offered advice and guidance. I fear I have given you very little in return."

Owen stopped once again and turned to face her. He reached out and smoothed a wayward lock of hair from her forehead. He studied the curve of her cheek, the fullness of her lips. "You have given me more than you realize, Annabelle. The more I know of you, the more you give me hope for a different type of future, and for that, I am indebted to you, whatever the future may bring."

Chapter Thirty-Four

Owen's chest tightened when the door closed behind Annabelle as she entered the girls' dormitory. Mrs. Brathay and the Langsbys were waiting for them, and after a quick discussion about Hannah's condition, the parties parted ways and Owen headed home.

He went back the way they had come. It would be too dangerous to take the horses through the forest. And it would give him the opportunity to keep an eye out for any suspicious activity.

As he crossed the main courtyard, he looked back at the attic windows of the girls' wing. Candlelight winked from the paned dormer windows. He knew what kind of suspicions awaited Annabelle, and how he wished he could be there to protect her from them. No doubt today would make her the object of staff gossip.

He turned his attention to the darkened road in front. He was eager to return to Hannah. As he came to the forest line just on the other side of the school's main gate, he slowed the horses.

Did he see movement?

It could be attributed to a deer, but the shifting shadows seemed too large to be any other animal. He ducked the horses just inside the forest line to hide them from view.

Clouds floated across the sky, shifting the shadows that darkened the night. He waited patiently as the figures moved into better view.

From what he could see, a male, a female, and two youths were together.

Could this be the source of the boy poachers?

Suddenly the woman broke away from the group and climbed the stile to the school's garden.

Owen rubbed his hand over the stubble on his cheek as he watched the situation unfold. He had thought that a man inside the school might be influencing some of the youths . . . but a woman?

Bess whinnied, shattering the night's stillness. The remaining figures disappeared into the forest. He had a rifle, but with two horses he could not track them and remain unnoticed. But what he had witnessed lit a new fire beneath him.

He had a job to do, and there would be no sleep tonight.

Annabelle shook out her damp black gown and hung it from a hook on the wall. Thanks to Mrs. Pike's attentions the garment was mostly dry, and with any luck it would be completely dry by morning. She carefully removed Mrs. Locke's gown, folded it neatly, and set it atop her chest.

She could feel Louise and Jane watching her, waiting for her to explain, but she kept her mouth pressed shut, and they did not ask. Annabelle was grateful Crosley was nowhere to be found.

What a day it had been.

Annabelle had been bombarded with questions upon her arrival. Some of the teachers approached her with sympathy. Others eyed her with suspicion. Everyone knew that Hannah had been found injured, but everyone also knew that Annabelle had been the one who returned the child to the gamekeeper's cottage.

She heard the whispers as she and Mr. Locke spoke with Mrs. Brathay. She had been alone with the man, and that single fact made her seem guilty for some unknown atrocity. The whispers jumped to the most scandalous conclusion.

Even in the politest society of London the situation could have been explained. In fact, the concern would have been for her constitution after such a trying day. But nobody here seemed to think anything of the emotional effect the day had on her. Instead, all the focus was on the scandal.

Annabelle was sick of scandal. Did it follow her wherever she trod?

She removed her stays and petticoat, and once she was down to her chemise, she folded her wrapper around her and sank down onto her bed.

How her pulse raced.

Mr. Locke.

Owen.

Oh, how the thought of him made her heart light. The memory of her hand in his made her imagination take flight in a way it had not since her engagement to Samuel.

She was slipping, hard and fast, and was in perhaps her most dangerous situation yet. She had risked so much over the course of the past several weeks—her security, her future, her safety—but now she felt as if she was on the cusp of risking the most precious thing of all—her heart.

As she sat on the edge of her bed, brushing her hair, the chamber door creaked open. Jane and Louise had headed down to finish their evening duties when Crosley tiptoed in, dressed in a black cape and clutching a satchel in one hand and a candle in the other. Her hair was wild about her face, and her cheeks were flushed.

Annabelle looked over her shoulder. "I was wondering where you had gotten to."

"I have been in the kitchen sewing by the firelight." Crosley tossed her satchel on her bed and set the candle on the chest between their beds. "How is Miss Hannah?"

"She got her ankle caught in a hunting trap, but she will be fine."

Crosley sat on her bed and leaned over to remove her boots. "You spent the entire day at the gamekeeper's cottage then, didn't you?"

Annabelle chose her words carefully. "Most of it. The rain kept us inside most of the day."

"Isn't that cozy?" A coy smile spread across Crosley's face.

Annabelle didn't care for the inflection in Crosley's voice. "What are you trying to insinuate?"

Crosley raised her blonde eyebrows and shrugged. "Nothing. I just think you are very clever."

"Clever?" Annabelle returned her brush to her chest and retrieved a length of ribbon. "I don't see how."

Crosley tucked her boots under her bed and gave a little giggle. "Perhaps I misjudged your refusal of Mr. Bartrell. Maybe you are after a husband after all."

Annabelle gathered her hair to put it in one long braid and whispered between clenched teeth, "I am not after a husband. Quite the opposite. You know I have gone to great lengths to avoid just that. I did not go to the cottage by choice."

"You can understand why that is hard for everyone to believe, can't you?" Crosley took the pin out of her own hair and shook out her locks. "Even though no one comes right out and says it, it goes without saying that Mr. Locke is quite a catch."

"I have no wish to *catch* Mr. Locke, or anyone else for that matter. I should think you would set them straight on that account." Annabelle was growing agitated. She did not yet fully understand her feelings for Mr. Locke, and she certainly did not wish for them to be scrutinized.

"Oh, do not become so annoyed with me." Crosley began to brush her own hair. "I just think you should be a bit more concerned about the reputation you are forging for yourself."

Annabelle could not hold the sharpness of her own tongue. "You would do wise to follow your own advice."

"Who, me?" Crosley feigned innocence. "I don't know what you mean."

"I think you do." Annabelle pinned Crosley with her stare. "I am referring to your interludes with Mr. Hemstead."

"Oh, that." Crosley waved her hand. "You are making too much of it."

"Just as you made too much of my being at the Locke home?"

Crosley lowered her brush. "You may be shy about your intentions, but I will not be. And why should I be? I want a husband, make no mistake about that. For years I have had to take care of myself and provide for myself. I know you do not understand that, but believe me. If you spend much more time in your current role, you will perhaps grow to regret your decision to refuse Mr. Bartrell and start to see a man like Mr. Locke in a different light."

Annabelle turned away and pressed her eyes shut. She did not want to hear Crosley's words.

She did not regret her decision.

No. She was tired, that was all. And she refused to argue with Crosley.

"I am going to sleep." Annabelle pulled down her blanket and extinguished her candle before climbing into bed. She rolled over to face the wall. She could hear the former lady's maid bustling about the room, tending to the day's final activities.

Annabelle's cheeks flushed with frustration toward Crosley, but at the end of the day, was Crosley really to blame?

My mother always said that peace is not dependent upon your circumstances. It is dependent upon where you place your faith. She had not thought about her mother's words in ever so long, and it struck her as interesting that it should be a conversation with Owen that revived the memory.

What she was feeling felt nothing like peace.

Annabelle rolled onto her back and glanced over at Crosley, who was just turning down her covers. With a puff she extinguished her candle, which engulfed the room in darkness.

Annabelle could not feel comfortable with her current situation. Too much had changed, and she doubted she could ever really have true peace.

She pressed her eyes closed. Her mother's prayer flitted through her mind for the hundredth time. She had not intended to, but she had thought about the prayer so much that it had been committed to memory. At first, the thought of her mother's words made her uncomfortable, but gradually, over the course of several weeks, they started to bring comfort.

She tried to remember the words her mother had used in their nightly prayers, but the memories were fuzzy. All she could remember was her mother telling her to just say what was on her heart.

She drew a deep breath, looked to the darkness, and whispered, "I don't know what to do. I don't know what to feel. All I know is that I am scared for what my future holds."

A tear slid down her cheek. "Please help me know what to do."

Chapter Thirty-Five

$\mathcal{K}$irtley Meadow stretched before Owen. Midnight's vaporous fog hovered over majestic elms and unfamiliar undergrowth. Eerie silence loomed in a space that should have been alive with the tawny owl's cry and the scurry of badgers in the thicket. Not even the usual whistling of the wind through the dying leaves broke the ghostly stillness.

He strained to hear. Whatever the group had been up to at the edge of the school, he had to be on guard. He'd set watchmen on Bancroft Park's property and was confident they were up to the task, but it was Kirtley Meadow that needed his attention now.

Owen found a clearing near the path and tied his horse to a tree. It would be easier, not to mention safer, to explore the area on foot. He retrieved a long stick and tested the ground with each step. Even though the meadow had not been under the care of a gamekeeper for quite some time, the last thing he wanted was to trigger a trap. Hannah's experience earlier in the day reminded him just how dangerous his line of work could be.

Judging by the moon's location, he'd been in the meadow a couple of hours. He was about to head for home, but as he turned to leave, a distant flash caught his eye.

His heart thudded at the sight, and he crouched low.

After several seconds, he saw it again. It looked like moonlight reflecting off metal, perhaps a blade or a gun barrel.

He crept closer stealthily, as if tracking a rabbit or a fox. He double-checked his person to make sure he would not give away his presence. It was an intricate dance of advancing and checking for traps, all while keeping the flash in sight.

He licked his lips, and despite the cool air, perspiration began to dot his brow. He sensed that weeks of watching and waiting were about to pay off. He flexed his fingers on the stock of his rifle as he inched closer.

The hiss of whispers met his ears.

Satisfaction spread through him, hot and fast. He had done it. He'd located at least some of those trespassing on the meadow. If this were Bancroft Park property, he would have retreated and returned with Whitten. It was dangerous to confront a poacher alone. But Kirtley Meadow was his charge. He could not expect a Bancroft Park employee to help him now.

He squeezed his eyes shut and breathed a prayer for safety. A prayer for wisdom. The last thing he wanted was bloodshed of any sort.

Blood roared in his ears, and he inched closer toward the muffled voices. He pivoted. Two youths and one man huddled around something on the ground.

He took advantage of their distraction and stood to his full height.

He cocked his rifle, shouldered it, and pointed it right at the man. "Do not move."

The perpetrators jerked up their heads. The whites of their eyes shone bright.

Owen held his gun steady. "Boys, I suggest you run out now before I change my mind."

The boys hesitated and Owen spoke louder. "Get out of here. And mark my words, I had better never see you in these woods again."

Without another word, the boys looked at each other and took off running into the forest depths.

Owen fixed his stare on the man. He was not interested in

ruining the lives of two youths, who more than likely were students at the school. He was more interested in bringing to justice a man taking advantage of them.

Gun aimed, Owen stepped closer to the man. "Hands up."

The man slid his hands in the air. "'Tis not what you think."

"It's exactly what I think." Owen drew nearer, and at the man's foot was a fox, limp and lifeless. A rifle was on the ground next to him. Now that Owen was close, he recognized the man from the school. He'd never met him, and he didn't know his name, but bittersweet satisfaction coursed through him. He'd been right.

He glanced around to make sure he was alone. "Get on the ground. Facedown. Put your hands behind your back."

At first the man hesitated, and Owen steadied his rifle. "It's my job to shoot trespassers on sight. I'd take advantage of this moment of generosity."

The man dropped to the ground. Owen stepped closer, careful to avoid the poacher's arms and hands, and pressed a heavy boot on his back. Gun pointed downward, he retrieved a length of rope and quickly and skillfully bound the man's hands and then his feet, giving him just enough slack to take small steps. He jerked the man to his feet. "I think the magistrate will be very interested to meet you."

"Have you heard?"

Annabelle whirled from her post, surprised at the sudden interruption. Jane stood in the threshold, chest heaving.

Annabelle glanced back at her young charges and tightened her shawl against her shoulders to ward off the early morning chill. The girls were supposed to be in their time of quiet reflection, but every girl's eyes were fixed on their guest.

"Go about your reading, girls. I will be right back."

Annabelle stepped into the hallway. "What is it?"

"Oh my dear, everyone is aflutter. The talk is all over the school, and it is quite shocking. Mr. Hemstead, whom we believed to be involved with Margaret, has been arrested for poaching!"

Annabelle jerked her head back and closed the door to her students. "What?"

"It's true. He was apprehended by Mr. Locke last night. Apparently Mr. Locke caught him in the act. He threatened Mr. Hemstead with a gun, bound him with a rope, and took him to the village lockup, which is where he is now, waiting to meet with the magistrate. It is all so shocking! Mr. Langsby has already left for town to see if he can be of any assistance in the matter, but the situation is looking dire for Mr. Hemstead. With his father being so prominent in the area, I can only imagine what a stir this will cause."

Annabelle brushed her hair from her face as she contemplated what she had just been told.

Jane grabbed her hand as if to recapture Annabelle's attention. "All of this excitement as of late is just too much to bear! First yesterday with Hannah and now this. Poor Mr. Locke has had quite an eventful week."

Annabelle ran her fingers through her shawl's fringe. Part of her was happy for Owen's success. Another part of her worried for his safety. It sounded like dangerous business.

Jane whirled back around. "Oh, and I almost forgot this part. Mr. Hemstead was paying some of the boys here at the school to help him poach. Can you imagine? I don't know all of the details, of course, but Louise was in the main hall when the magistrate called on Mr. Langsby this morning. She said old Langsby's face turned all red and she had never seen him so angry. Apparently Mr. Locke and Mr. Langsby had suspected something of the sort, but Mr. Locke would not reveal the names of the boys involved."

Annabelle thought of the day, several weeks ago now, when Owen delivered the boy to her uncle. "At least no one got hurt," she muttered, more to herself. And then, as she thought of her friend, her shoulders sagged. "Does Cros—I mean, Margaret—know of this?"

"I don't know. I have not seen her. But I wouldn't concern yourself about it too much. If anything, this is a positive development. She will be disappointed, I am sure, but at least Mr. Hemstead's true nature was revealed before any serious damage could be done."

Annabelle nodded. "I suppose you are right."

"I must go. I will let you know if I hear anything else."

Jane withdrew, and Annabelle returned to her students. She tried to focus on the task at hand and concentrate on the girls' questions and reading, but the sounds of shouts and hurried footsteps in the hall distracted her.

The rest of the day, Annabelle kept her eye open for Crosley.

But she was nowhere to be found.

Chapter Thirty-Six

*T*hick fog hugged the grounds of Bancroft Park as evening began its descent, and a chill blanketed all. Autumn had definitely made its presence known, and Owen filled his lungs with the crisp air. He had dreaded this event since he first learned of it, for today Mr. Thorley and Mr. Bartrell arrived.

Owen stood with the rest of the staff, prepared to meet their guests and master. Normally Owen's presence was not required whenever a guest arrived, but he had a special interest in this particular event. He needed to see Bartrell and Thorley for himself.

When the carriage finally drew to a stop, Owen braced himself. Treadwell was the first to emerge from the carriage. He jumped down with the energy of a youth and directed his attention to Owen.

"My good man." He grinned and reached out to shake Owen's hand. "I hear we have a hero in our midst."

Owen was in no mood to discuss the poachers, not when Thorley and Bartrell were so close.

Treadwell slapped his other hand on Owen's shoulder. "I received a letter from the magistrate while in London. He told me you single-handedly delivered the man responsible for the poaching here in the Park, not to mention Farley's property."

Owen tried to focus on the conversation at hand, but his gaze fixed on the other two men exiting the carriage.

"You don't seem very pleased with yourself." Treadwell motioned for Owen to walk to the side where their conversation would not be overheard. "I'm told the magistrate arrested another man as a result of Hemstead's confession. He said there was evidence that the game was being sold as far away as Chichester. Chichester! My hares and rabbits, in Chichester."

Owen's jaw twitched as he watched Thorley hop down from the carriage and turn to assess the main house. "Let's hope this sends a message to any other locals thinking of stepping foot on land that does not belong to them."

"Indeed. And do you know if poaching is down at Walmsly Hall as well? Are you to get your Kirtley Meadow?"

"I met with Mr. Farley just yesterday. He intends to wait to ensure the poaching is indeed under control before he will make the sale official, so we will see. It will take quite some work to return the game stock to the levels it has been in the past, but it can be done."

"Well then, I am happy for you." Treadwell turned, as if he was preparing to rejoin the group, and then stopped. "And Hannah? How is she? I heard she suffered an injury."

Owen nodded as they walked back to the others. "She did. She stepped on a trap. But she is on the mend and has returned to school."

"Good. Ah, our guests." Treadwell extended his hand in greeting as Thorley and Bartrell stood outside the carriage, waiting for the footmen to retrieve their belongings. Treadwell turned to Owen. "Locke here will see to your weapons and ensure they are sufficiently cleaned and prepared for the hunt."

Owen's stomach clenched as he bowed in the direction of the gentlemen. He needed to remember his place. He was the gamekeeper. He was not the social equal of these two men.

Thorley tilted his head. "I know you."

Owen raised his eyebrows but said nothing. He forced his lips into a straight line.

"Yes." Thorley took a step closer and pointed his finger at Owen. "You were with Treadwell in London at Wilhurst House."

Owen nodded. "I was."

Thorley lifted his chin, as if to establish his social dominance, and paused several seconds. Then he turned back to Treadwell. "Let's move inside. I've grown quite tired of the carriage and could fancy something to drink."

Owen turned to leave, and something—or rather, someone—caught his eye. The footmen were retrieving the trunks from the carriage, but one footman he did not recognize.

He squinted to see in the fading light.

The footman quickly removed his hat, combed his fingers through a shock of thick, blond-almost-white hair, and replaced his hat before returning to his task.

It was the Wilhurst House footman the carriage driver had pointed out to him the day after McAlister's murder.

Miss Crosley's brother.

Owen muttered as he quieted the dogs. They were eager to be off, but the hunting party was late.

He was hardly surprised. He adjusted the satchel of extra ammunition and the basket of food and drink that had been sent down from the main house.

Whitten whistled at one of the dogs before he faced Owen. "What's got you so riled this morning?"

"Hmm?" Owen jerked his head up from the rifle he was checking. "Nothing."

Whitten huffed. "You're as cross as the day is long. I'd think a man who broke that stubborn ring of poachers would be in better spirits."

Owen checked his hunting knife and tied it to his saddle. "Nah. It's not sitting right with me."

"Why? The magistrate said he got a full confession from Hemstead, didn't he? Even got the name of another man he was working with."

Owen shrugged and patted his horse's neck, then stepped around the animal to get to the cart. "Don't forget who Hemstead's father is. One of the most powerful men in the county. Of course the magistrate is eager to accept his confession and not ask anything else."

Whitten ran his hand over his whiskered chin. "What is it you are suspicious of, then?"

Owen whistled to a hunting dog that had wandered from the pack. "I'm not sure the poaching is behind us. I wouldn't be surprised to learn others are involved."

"And what of the boys?"

"The magistrate has left it up to Langsby to handle their punishment."

Whitten whistled low under his breath. "That's a stroke of luck for those boys, isn't it?" He tied a pack to the back of his saddle. "So I guess you'll be buying Kirtley Meadow, then?"

Owen snapped his head around. "Where did you hear about that?"

"Bah. You know how news travels." Whitten moved to the cart and adjusted the hunting rifles. "And it's a good thing, says I. Your father was fit to be tied when old man Treadwell lost that bit of land. It would make him proud to know it was in the Locke family and out of the hands of the Farleys."

Owen ignored his friend's candor and returned to his horse. At the moment he did not find a great deal of satisfaction in apprehending Hemstead. Not even the prospect of owning Kirtley Meadow could placate him.

He'd not slept well the previous night. What frustrated him the most was not knowing if the men knew of Annabelle's presence at the school. His instinct screamed that they were aware, but he could not be sure.

When the hunting party finally arrived from the main house, rain drizzled down from the foggy heavens. In addition to Thorley and Bartrell, a group of Treadwell's friends from Guildford were also present.

Owen had avoided Thorley and Bartrell as much as possible. Just the memory of the bruising on Miss Thorley's cheek incited his anger, and he employed every ounce of self-control to keep from executing his own form of justice.

Complete avoidance was not possible, however.

It was Thorley's turn to shoot. Owen was behind him with a loaded rifle waiting to exchange the spent gun when Thorley was ready.

Thorley's words were flat and low as he sat in the brush, scanning the landscape, waiting for the pheasant to make its appearance. "You were the man who spoke with my sister after we arrived home from the Baldwin ball, are you not?"

Owen checked the lock on the rifle in his hand. "Yes, I spoke with her."

Thorley lowered his weapon, pulled a flask from his hunting jacket, and took a swig. He extended it to Owen in an offering. Owen refused, and Thorley returned it to his jacket with a shrug.

Owen was not sure what the significance of the question was. It was probably an innocent observation, but he would have thought that Thorley had been too inebriated to notice his presence.

"Tell me, are you very familiar with this area?" Thorley's eyes still scanned the horizon.

"I am."

"Then surely you have heard of Fellsworth School."

The name sent fire through Owen's veins. His daughter was there. Miss Thorley was there. His mind raced to map the implications. "I know it."

He waited in uncomfortable silence. It was as if the man was toying with him, feeding him leading questions and then pulling back. Owen glanced over at Whitten, who was assisting Bartrell with reloading his weapon.

Thorley ran his fingers through hair the same color as his sister's. "If you are familiar with the school, then perhaps you know my uncle, Edmund Langsby."

"I do."

"Is the school far from here?"

Owen tightened his grip on the stock. "Not too far."

"That's good to hear." Thorley eased back and pulled a snuffbox from his tan waistcoat. "I intend to pay a visit before I leave. I've never met him, and now that I am in such proximity, I think it only mannerly. Don't you agree?" He slid Owen a sideways glance.

Owen was not a self-conscious man. Not much made him nervous. But the younger man was sly, devious, and shifty.

Thorley took his shot—a sloppy one that failed to hit its target and alarmed the pheasant. He cursed under his breath at the bad aim and handed his gun back to Owen. "I've also heard a report that another one of my relatives is at Fellsworth School."

Owen's jaw twitched as he adjusted the dog whistle hanging at his neck.

"Perhaps you have seen her. My sister. Miss Annabelle Thorley. Do you recall her?"

Owen bit his tongue and set about reloading the weapon to help Thorley prepare for his next shot, keenly aware of Thorley's gaze on him as he completed his task.

"You surprise me by saying nothing. From what I was told, you played a tremendous role in my sister's presence here in Fellsworth."

Owen ceased his work and met Thorley's gaze fully. He would not be intimidated, especially by a man as weak as Thorley, nor would he apologize. Owen stood to his full height and extended the weapon back to Thorley. "Your sister is a strong woman who makes her own decisions."

"So you do not deny that you assisted her?" Thorley jerked the weapon away from Owen.

"I don't deny it at all." Owen picked up his own rifle. "In fact, I admire your sister's bravery and would offer my assistance again in a heartbeat."

"How noble of you. Does Treadwell know of your actions, I wonder?" A grin slid across Thorley's face, and he reached over to pat one of the hunting hounds near him. "Oh, and there is one other thing. It's quite amusing, really. I am sure it is a rumor, but you know how these things are. I've been told that you fancy yourself in love with my sister."

Owen eyed the man, waiting for Thorley's point.

"If that is the case, perhaps I should inform you that Annabelle is an engaged woman. She will marry Cecil Bartrell very soon. So if you have a care for your position here, you'd do well to remember who your employer's friends are."

Owen took aim at a pheasant in the meadow and pulled the trigger. He did not miss his mark. "Miss Thorley is free to marry whomever she chooses."

Thorley threw his head back in raucous laughter that caused nearby birds to take flight. "A woman will marry whom she is told to marry."

Owen arched his eyebrow as Drake retrieved the game. "If that's what you believe, then you misjudge your sister. And if you think you can intimidate or manipulate me, you are wrong."

Thorley's smile faded. His hazel eyes narrowed. "Stay away from my sister, Locke. I'll not repeat myself. Consider yourself warned."

It was Owen's turn to smile. "You do not frighten me, Mr. Thorley. But perhaps it is you who should consider yourself warned, for if you upset your sister in any way, I will be there to make sure she is safe."

Chapter Thirty - Seven

*T*he door to the classroom flung open. Annabelle whirled around to see her uncle, winded and wide-eyed, standing in the threshold. Alarmed at the expression on his face, she lowered her book. "Mr. Langsby. Is everything all right?"

Uncle Edmund surveyed the students sitting primly at their tables, stepped closer to Annabelle, and lowered his voice. "Miss Thorley, you have a visitor. In my study."

Annabelle blinked. In her months here she had never known her uncle to disrupt a lesson in such a manner.

He turned to face the girls. "Ladies, I am sure you can continue your studies in silence while Miss Thorley steps out for a moment, can you not?"

The girls nodded, and Annabelle frowned as she handed her book to young Kitty Miles to her right. "I will be back as soon as possible," she instructed. "Please read aloud, one page each, until I return."

Once they were in the corridor and the door closed securely behind them, Annabelle took her uncle's arm and whispered, "What is it? Is everything all right?"

"Mr. Locke will explain everything."

Her heart leapt at the sound of Owen's name, but then concern gathered when she glimpsed her uncle's darkened expression.

"You look worried."

"No, not worried. Just concerned."

She followed him down the paneled staircase, across the school's main foyer, and through the narrow corridor to his study. Outside a dreary, early autumn rain pelted the school's stone walls, and the gray, dismal light from the narrow windows ushered her into the chamber. Mr. Locke was waiting for her, just as her uncle had said.

A full week had passed since Hannah stepped on the trap.

A full week since Owen held her hand in his in the forest at dusk.

A full week since her heart had truly opened to the thought of romantic love.

As she entered, Owen turned from the window and swept his hat from his head. The day's pewter glow settled on his broad shoulders and accented his black hair. His dark eyes flashed and then softened. A gentle smile tugged at his lips but never fully formed. The sight of him weakened Annabelle, but her giddiness was tempered by the unknown circumstances surrounding his visit. She clutched her hands behind her.

His gaze flicked from Annabelle to her uncle and then back to her. "I hope I am not interrupting. I need to speak with you. It's important."

Her words were barley above a whisper. "You could never interrupt me, Mr. Locke."

Uncle Edmund cleared his throat loudly, shattering the odd formality. His voice was strong, his words clipped. "You have news to discuss, and I have business to attend to. I shall return shortly."

Owen's eyes did not leave the older man until he disappeared through the threshold. He then turned his full attention to Annabelle, and his words tumbled forth like water released from a dam. "I shared this news with your uncle, and he agreed that you needed to know."

She stiffened. "Goodness, you are making me nervous. Do you have news from London?"

He stepped closer. His scent of earth and rain encircled her. "I have no news from London, but I do have news of your brother. He is here, Annabelle. He arrived at Bancroft Park last night. I wanted to let you know earlier, but we have been hunting today and this is the first I could get away."

His words, although low and soft, struck her. She did not realize she was holding her breath until her lungs began to burn, and she drew a sharp intake of air. She should have expected it. Had Owen not warned her of the impending visit? She waited to speak until she was certain she could keep her tone level. "When did he arrive?"

He stepped even closer and ignored her polite question. "You need not pretend with me, Annabelle. I know this is distressing news."

She forced a timid laugh and clamped her hands before her to prevent them from trembling. So Thomas had found her. The room's waning fire suddenly felt too warm. She lifted her face to look him in the eyes. "I'll not pretend. Not with you."

"There's more. Bartrell is with him. They both know you're here, and your brother knows I helped you leave London."

Heat rushed into Annabelle's face and panic lanced her nerves. "But how would he know where to find me?"

Owen shook his head. "I don't know. He was traveling with a footman, who I believe is Miss Crosley's brother. Does that seem odd to you?"

Annabelle chewed her lip. "It is not unusual for my brother to travel with a footman, especially since his valet was dismissed after my father's death. That particular footman, though—Billy, I believe, is his name—is an odd choice. I am sure that Crosley, at some point, told her family of her whereabouts, and by doing so disclosed my location. I wonder if that is how Thomas learned I am here."

Owen lowered his voice, as if taking her into confidence. "I don't know. Perhaps it was Crosley, but did you not also say that Bryant claimed to know your brother? He could have informed him as well. Listen to me. Your brother told me that he intends to call on your uncle, and he will probably ask after you when he does. I've no wish to alarm you unnecessarily, but I do want you to be careful."

The warmth drained from her face. "And Uncle Edmund knows he is to call?"

"Yes." His voice was still low, but a new tenderness radiated from his expression. "And there is something that your uncle does not know."

He took another step toward her. His chocolate eyes gleamed with endearment, just as they had that night in the forest. "Someone is feeding your brother information."

The discrepancy between his words and his expression puzzled her, and his nearness bewildered her senses. "Why do you say that?"

He was close enough now that she could feel his warmth radiating in the chilliness of the room. She resisted the urge to lean into it. His gaze captured hers, refusing to allow her to look away. "Your brother told me that he knew I fancied myself to be in love with you."

She was powerless to look away. "In love?"

His hand reached for hers. His fingers curled around her own—intimately. Possessively. He shifted so he was facing her fully and brushed her hair from her face. His touch was gentle. Affectionate. "I expect nothing in return by telling you this, but I could not let another day pass without making my feelings known."

Emotions bombarded her, fast and furious. Joy, giddiness, hope—all were released at his words. Forgotten was the fear that had consumed her only moments ago. Tears rushed to her eyes, but unlike the tears of the past several months, these were tears of happiness and optimism. A smile took control of her lips as she tried to organize her thoughts.

Then the door creaked.

Owen dropped her hand and stepped backward. The distance between them widened once again, and the warmth generated cooled.

Embarrassed to have been caught in a tender moment, Annabelle fairly jumped backward. "Uncle Edmund."

"Well then, did Mr. Locke tell you his news?"

Annabelle cast a sheepish glance back to Owen, whose demeanor was once again matter-of-fact. He stood with his hands behind his back, his posture straight, as if nothing had transpired between them at all.

Still jittery from their encounter, Annabelle found her voice. "Yes, he did."

Uncle Edmund's eyebrows drew together. "And are you all right, my dear?"

"I am."

Owen retrieved his hat from her uncle's desk before directing his words toward Annabelle. "Just be sure to stay here, close to the main buildings, while they are in the area. Your brother and Mr. Bartrell should only be here a few more days. Until then, stay clear of the orchards and gardens."

Owen turned his attention to her uncle. "Keep an eye on her, Langsby. I'll let you know of any new developments from Bancroft Park. Good day to you both." He bowed low and exited the room.

Her uncle's sigh filled the space, breaking the stark silence left in Owen's wake. He scratched his head and turned to face his niece. "I know you came here for anonymity, and I am sorry that we were not able to provide that to you."

Annabelle only partly heard her uncle's words, for she had moved to the large window and was watching Owen as he departed down the main drive.

Her uncle, too, looked at the retreating form. "He is a good man."

Annabelle nodded, her eyes not leaving Owen until the rain made him impossible to see. She swallowed the lump forming in her throat, regretting the fact that she did not have the opportunity to respond to his affectionate words. She said, "He has been very kind to me."

"Kind, yes, but even a fool can see that his concern for you goes beyond neighborly regard. And do you return his favor?"

Her flush returned as she moved away from the window and closer to the fire's glow. She had been expected to marry Samuel, and her opinion on the matter had never been solicited. And now her uncle was openly asking her how she felt.

When she did not immediately respond, he continued. "It has been years since I have been to London, and I certainly do not pretend to understand the young people and their habits. I know you must think me an old man who knows far more of running a school than of romance, and on that count you would be right. But I consider myself quite an expert on the human character and reading people. Mr. Locke may not be as gallant or refined as the men I am sure you were used to in London, but no man could be more loyal."

Unwanted moisture pooled in her eyes. Normally she would hide such a personal response, but she allowed her uncle to place a sheltering arm around her shoulders.

"This I know. There is no need for you to worry or to fret. You are among friends and family now, a family who will protect you. You are safe here, Annabelle, and whatever you choose, wherever your path takes you, you will always have a home."

Chapter Thirty-Eight

Annabelle brushed a piece of dust from her painting of Owen. It was not her best likeness, but she could still make out the charming cleft in his chin and the arch of his eyebrows.

She had finished the piece several days ago in stolen moments when she was in her room alone. She had worked in solitude, for she could not risk one of the other women seeing her paint it. At the moment everyone was busy preparing for the festival, but for now, she rolled the dried painting and tied it with a blue satin ribbon.

She sat back. Her lips turned up in a smile, and her stomach fluttered. She still couldn't believe it. The memory of his voice's tender inflection as he said the words sent a tremor through her.

He loved her.

She loved him.

And she would tell him tonight at the festival.

Jane bustled in, and Annabelle tucked the painting under her bed. A pretty flush brightened Jane's cheeks. She carried a bundle of fresh flowers in her arms. "I have brought these for our hair. My, but your dress is lovely."

"Thank you." Annabelle smoothed her hand down the front of her gown of pale lavender silk. If felt good to be dressed in such a gown. She felt feminine. Girlish. Pretty. She had to admit that she was looking forward to the festival. The stretch of gloomy, rain-drenched days had given way to a milder, sunnier clime, just in time for the festivities and preparations to take place. The idea of a pleasant diversion intrigued her, and she was excited to wear one of her older gowns. Owen's warning about her brother still simmered in the back of her mind, but it had been several days since he arrived at Bancroft Park, and he had yet to make an appearance at the school. She hoped he had changed his mind and would not visit.

Annabelle was about to ask Jane to put some of the flowers in her hair when Crosley entered the room, and the conversation between Annabelle and Jane fell silent.

Annabelle watched Crosley from the corner of her eye. The former maid was dressed in Annabelle's cast-off gown of pale-blue sprigged muslin. Her blonde hair was pinned away from her face, and the long locks flowed beautifully down about her shoulders. But her face was pale. Dark shadows formed half-moons beneath her light-blue eyes. She did not utter a word.

Ever since Owen informed Annabelle that Billy Crosley was traveling with Thomas, she had been extra cautious around Crosley. She wanted to confront her about it directly and ask if she had betrayed Annabelle to her family, but she refrained. No good could come of arguing with Crosley now. Ever since Mr. Hemstead's crime had been discovered, Crosley had been unusually quiet and somber. Annabelle knew Crosley was hurting, and she could not help but feel sorry for her.

Crosley wordlessly gathered her shawl and left the room, and after the door closed behind her, Annabelle and Jane exchanged glances.

Jane resumed her dressing, and Annabelle crossed the room to check her reflection in the small looking glass. She touched her face where the bruising had been. The shadow had been gone for months, and she looked rested. Gone were the shadows beneath her own eyes. She felt attractive again. Confident again. Happy again.

She looked down at her gown. It was missing something. She dug in her trunk until she uncovered her amethyst necklace. She had not worn it since Mr. Bryant commented on it in her uncle's garden.

Mr. Bryant would undoubtedly be at the festival, but she did not feel frightened of him today. Not even the fact that her brother and Mr. Bartrell were so near could dampen her excitement. She believed Owen: he would protect her. With him by her side, no harm could befall her.

"I can't believe it is finally here!" squealed Jane, tucking one of the flowers into her hair as they left the school and stepped out onto the grounds. "It has been so long since I have been to a festival of any kind."

Annabelle looped her arm through her friend's. Twilight's purples and blues had fallen, and the rising full moon cast a magical glow on the grounds. The Autumn Festival was in full effect. Villagers and country folk had flocked to Fellsworth School, and the children bustled with excitement.

Scents of tarts and cakes mingled with the roasting pork's spicy aroma. Violins' songs danced on the crisp autumn breeze, and on the far lawn, lines of villagers jumped and clapped in their country dance. The students bobbed for apples picked fresh from the orchard. In the blacksmith's courtyard and stable areas, a boxing exhibition was set up for the men, and other contests of strength were taking place. Masculine shouts peppered the night, and children raced and played, the normal strict expectations set aside for the evening's activities. This festival was not nearly as elegant as the balls in London—the food was not as sophisticated, the music not so refined—but to her, it was an enchanting sight to behold.

"It's a wonder, isn't it?" Annabelle filled her lungs with the fresh night air.

"It is." Jane brushed a leaf from her gown. "And it is nice to see you looking relaxed. You have seemed so preoccupied of late."

"Have I? I did not mean to be."

"What does it matter if you were?" Jane lifted her face to the breeze. "Most people in your situation would be preoccupied, I would say. In fact, I daresay it will not be long before you leave Fellsworth School."

Annabelle stopped short. "Why would you say something like that?"

"Don't look so shocked!" Jane's laugh rose above the flutist's ditty. "It is no secret around the school that you and a certain handsome gamekeeper have developed quite a bond."

"Jane!" Annabelle scolded as the heat reached up her neck. "Really, you shouldn't say such things."

"But am I wrong?"

Annabelle did not answer but resumed walking.

The crowd ebbed and flowed, and yet Annabelle looked for Owen. They had not spoken privately since their interlude in her uncle's study, but he had said he would be in attendance tonight.

Then she saw him, making his way through the crowd. How her heart soared at the sight.

He wore no hat. His dark, curly hair was combed into place, in spite of the breeze attempting to free it. Instead of his hunting jacket and buckskin breeches, he wore navy breeches and a tan coat. His dark-brown waistcoat contrasted against his ivory neckcloth.

His gaze latched onto her—the simple act of which threatened to steal her breath. Attentiveness radiated in his expression, and a smile curved his mouth and dimpled his clean-shaven cheek. In him she was beginning to see a new future—one of family, of love.

He stopped in front of them. He bowed.

Annabelle and Jane curtsied, then Jane grabbed Annabelle's arm. "Oh, I have forgotten. How clumsy of me. I told Louise I would help her carry out the tarts from the kitchen. Excuse me, will you?"

Her reason for leaving was obvious. She wanted to leave them alone—as alone as they could be at the festival. But Annabelle found no embarrassment at the action. If anything, her experiences over the past months had thickened her skin and made her care even less what others thought of her.

At the moment, all that mattered was Owen.

He raised a playful eyebrow in her direction and leaned in close. "You look beautiful, Miss Thorley."

She took his extended arm. "Why, thank you, Mr. Locke." She could not wait any longer. "Thomas? Is he gone?"

Owen frowned. "No. Not yet."

"Do you know when they are leaving?"

"I do not, but I do know that at present they are immersed in a heated game of cards, so if history repeats itself, that particular party will not leave Bancroft Park until the light of day. Do not worry about them. Not tonight." He nodded toward the dancers. "Would you care to dance with me?"

Annabelle exhaled the air she had been holding. The idea of forgetting about Thomas for the night and focusing on her handsome beau greatly appealed to her. "I would indeed."

Torches and bonfires illuminated the night, with their spicy scents and dancing light adding to the evening's merriment. All around them couples danced, swirled, and sang with the music.

She leaned in closer to Owen as they prepared for their first dance. Her smile would not leave her face. Gratitude for where she was bubbled within her. She was safe here. Free to laugh as she liked. Free to dance as she chose. Free to smile at the man who set her heart ablaze.

Hannah took a break from the children's activities and danced several dances with her father before returning to her games. After an hour of dancing, the musicians broke to rest. Owen took her by the hand and led her through the crowd to the forest's edge. He stepped in between the trees and wove deeper into the woodsy fortress, and then he stopped.

The moonlight cast a swaying, lacy pattern through the tangle of branches and leaves above them. The festival music resumed, and Owen turned to her. He looked at her hair. Her eyes. Her lips.

She recalled Mr. Bartrell looking at her, but lust had dominated his expression. Owen's expression was different—it was one of affection.

"What are we doing?" she asked, laughing.

He smiled. "Nothing. There were too many people around. And we did not have the opportunity to finish our conversation in your uncle's study."

"No, we did not."

"I can't help but wonder what you thought of what I said."

Emboldened by the darkness, she stepped closer. His entrancing scent of forest and smoke intoxicated her, blending her sense of dream and reality. She leaned toward him. Her voice was barely above a whisper. "I thought—I thought I was in a dream."

He lifted his hand and brushed her hair from her face, letting his finger trail down her cheek.

Her knees weakened beneath her at his touch, and she rested her hands on his chest and leaned forward against him for fear her legs would not hold her steady. His chin brushed the top of her head, sending a shiver through her. She pressed her eyes shut.

Owen cupped her shoulders and ran his hands down her arms and then moved his hands to her waist, inching closer still. "But the more important question is whether or not you feel the same way."

She opened her eyes and looked up. His face was near hers. She should pull away, but his magnetism held her in a trance, unable to move. Unwilling to move. His nearness clouded her senses in a way she had never experienced. In that instant she knew her future belonged to him. "Owen, I do."

He grinned and then drew her close. He caressed her cheek again and then lowered his lips to hers.

Warmth spread through her. All that mattered was Owen. In

that moment it all made sense. This was what she had been searching for. This was what her heart longed for.

He released her, but as he did an angry shout rose above the
music.

Surprised at the suddenness of it, she jumped. "What was that?"

Owen drew his dark brows together. "I'm not sure. Come on."

The shouting intensified, and Owen took her by the hand, and
they emerged from the forest. Their steps hurried down the path
and back through the gate. Annabelle stopped short. Her hands
flew to her mouth as the origin of the shouting came into view.

Mr. Bryant was shouting at none other than her brother. Then
Mr. Bryant flung a punch at Thomas, the impact of which sent him
faltering backward.

Her blood ran cold.

"Stay here. Do not move." Owen rushed forward.

Panic seized Annabelle. She could not move. She could not
hear. All she could see was her brother. She lifted her gaze. Beyond
him stood Mr. Bartrell and Billy Crosley.

And her dream shattered.

Chapter Thirty-Nine

*O*wen pushed through the gathering crowd of villagers, women, and children and lunged forward to grab Simon Bryant by the arm. He dragged the flailing man backward to break up the fight, but Thorley charged Bryant and targeted his chest, the force of which pushed both Bryant and Owen backward.

Two villagers apprehended Thorley and peeled him off Bryant. Thorley struggled to maintain balance. Blood dripped from his lip, and his wide eyes were like those of a caged animal.

Owen glanced at Annabelle. Horror wrote itself on her face.

Langsby ran up, attracted, no doubt, by the commotion. His face fell at the sight of his nephew. It was clear he recognized the man who bore such a strong resemblance to Annabelle. "What is the meaning of this?"

Chest heaving, Thorley jerked his arm free from the man who held him. He cast a sheepish glance at his uncle before he wiped the blood from his lip with the back of his hand.

Langsby whirled around. "Mr. Bryant. What have you to say?"

Bryant pulled his arm free from Owen's grasp. Anger creased his eyes and reddened his expression. He ignored Langsby's question and stomped toward Thorley, his finger pointing directly at his foe's chest. "You will give me what is owed me, or I will take it, one way or the other."

Thorley huffed in arrogant dismissal, and Bryant leapt forward again and slammed his fist into Thorley's jaw.

Screams and gasps echoed from the crowd, and Owen jumped forward to detain Bryant once more.

Langsby's jaw trembled in anger, and a vein throbbed on his thin forehead. "Mr. Bryant, you will get your things and leave Fellsworth School immediately. You will not be allowed back on this property."

The magistrate, who had been in attendance, arrived and grabbed Bryant by the other arm. Owen dropped his hold and stepped back while the magistrate and Langsby removed Bryant.

The crowd began to disperse, but Owen closed the space between himself and Thorley. "You aren't welcome here," he hissed. "You need to leave."

Thorley snarled. "I'll not be told to leave by a gamekeeper."

Owen glanced up to see Bartrell and Billy Crosley approaching them. Dread squeezed his stomach. He had not wanted the festival to come to this. Not for the children. Not for Langsby. And certainly not for Annabelle. He glanced to where she had been standing, but she was not there. He pivoted to see her running toward them.

He turned back to Thorley, eager to keep as much distance between brother and sister as possible. "You have no business here."

But Thorley lifted his gaze past him to Annabelle. "Ah, Sister."

Annabelle stopped next to Owen, her hair whipping wildly in the mounting breeze. She tightened her shawl around her shoulders. Redness now rimmed her eyes, and she narrowed her gaze on her brother. She hurled words at him. "What have you done? What could you possibly be thinking?"

"I did nothing." Thorley shrugged. "I came here to rescue my sister from, well, *this*, and that man accosted me. I was merely defending myself."

Annabelle jutted her chin up. "Mr. Bryant said he knew you. What do you owe him? What have you done, Thomas?"

Thorley wiped his lip again. "You take his side without even hearing mine?"

"I don't need to hear your side." Annabelle crossed her arms over her chest. "Leave, Thomas."

The confidence in her expression slid to fear, and Owen jerked his head up to see why. Behind Thorley stood Bartrell.

Owen inched toward Annabelle, his muscles tensed and ready to intervene.

Bartrell stepped closer, and Annabelle withdrew ever so slightly.

"Annabelle." A greasy grin slid across Bartrell's sweaty face, revealing several missing teeth. He strolled forward calmly. "You left without saying good-bye. Is that any way to treat your fiancé?"

Annabelle's face paled. The fear in her eyes launched fire through Owen's veins. She drew a sharp breath but snapped her mouth shut as her uncle approached.

Owen was not sure he had ever seen Langsby so angry, not even when Owen had brought young Winter to him after catching him poaching. The older man stepped forward, his face red, his lips pressed into a firm line.

Thorley lifted his gaze over Owen's shoulder to Langsby and smiled as if nothing unpleasant had occurred. "Uncle. At last we meet."

Langsby stepped next to Owen. Despite his lack of stature, Edmund possessed a commanding presence. "Nephew. What is the meaning of this?"

"Mr. Locke tells me I am not welcome here." Thorley sniffed, ignoring his uncle's question. "Surely there is a mistake."

"You can return another time. Come tomorrow and we can talk then. But for now I think you have made quite an impression on Fellsworth School, and you need to leave."

Thorley flicked his gaze from his uncle to his sister and chuckled. "Ah. I see my reputation precedes me. Hardly seems fair, does it?"

Langsby stepped forward and eyed the three men. "Leave now, Thomas, before I change my mind and have the magistrate remove you and your friends. I've no tolerance for such boorish behavior."

Thorley slid his hands in the air as if admitting defeat. He shifted his gaze between Bartrell and Annabelle, then huffed in amusement. "If you so wish, Uncle."

Langsby's mouth remained tight as he spoke. "I think it best. Allow me to escort you to the gate. Since you have found your way here, I trust you can find your way back to Bancroft Park."

Thorley, Bartrell, and Billy Crosley, escorted by two of Langsby's men, disappeared into the darkness in the direction of the main gate. Nearby, music and laughter resounded, but the lighthearted mood had dampened. The group that had gathered dissipated, leaving Owen alone with Annabelle and Langsby.

Annabelle. His heart clamped at the sight of her. But it was the expression on her face—the downturned lips, the wide, frightened eyes—that pained him. He had failed to protect her—Bartrell and Thorley had made contact with her.

Langsby put a fatherly arm around her. "So that was my nephew. Charming fellow."

Annabelle looked over her shoulder in the direction of the gate. "Did Mr. Bryant say why they were fighting?"

"He claims Thomas owes him money from a game of cards. I've no patience for any of it."

Owen stepped as close to Annabelle as propriety would allow. "Don't give it another thought. Your brother is a spoiled child throwing a tantrum, 'tis all. His pride has taken a beating. Word of this will get to Treadwell, and he will not allow them to stay at Bancroft Park. Your uncle and I are here. No harm will come to you."

Langsby patted Annabelle's shoulder. "Mr. Locke speaks truth, but take heart, child. Have faith. This journey of yours is mapped out already. You just need to seek guidance to find your way through these shadows. All will be well in the end."

As the breeze intensified, Owen looked back to the forest. He found such personal solace in its dark beauty, but that very darkness could hide so much danger. But as he watched the three retreating forms, he noticed something odd. The men did not take the main road through Fellsworth and then on to Bancroft Park. Instead, they stepped into the forest, as if they knew where they were going.

He struggled to complete a puzzle with the pieces he possessed. The men were supposedly strangers. They should not know their way through Linton Forest. But they did, and they had contact with Bryant, one of the boys' teachers. Who else did they have contact with? Could they have had contact with Hemstead as well?

Chapter Forty

The next morning Annabelle's head throbbed. It was Sunday, and regardless of the festivities the night before, her presence was required at church.

She had been so tired the previous night that she had left her gown in a heap at the foot of her bed. She shook her head. She had been here for months and still hadn't gotten used to the idea that someone else wouldn't pick up after her. Gathering her discarded gown and slippers, she returned them to her trunk with a sigh.

The night had been a sleepless one, and now exhaustion tugged at her limbs with every movement. Jane, Louise, and Crosley had already quit their chamber for the day. It was Jane's day to oversee the girls' breakfast, and Louise and Crosley were tending other duties. Annabelle seized this rare opportunity for peace and solitude and skipped the morning meal.

Outside, a steady drizzle streamed from the heavens, and a dreary gray light lit the room. She looked to the empty fire grate, wishing a blaze was present now. Overnight clouds had moved in, bringing with them the damp breeze that permeated the window-panes and chilled the air. She shivered and reached for her black shawl and wrapped it around her shoulders before she sat on a bench next to the window.

Despite her efforts, her mind recounted the previous night's bittersweet events. Even now the memory of dancing with Owen brought warmth to her, and she smiled. Her stomach quivered at the recollection of how her hand brushed his. She tucked her knees up under her chin and looked to the foggy ground below. How different he was from Samuel. He was confident. Unguarded. Attentive. Unwavering. Never had she felt so protected or that her opinions held such value.

As excited as she was with the blossoming romance, the threatening reality of her brother and Mr. Bartrell's insistence persisted. All this time she had believed that Mr. Bryant was after her for some reason, but after last night it was clear his interest was in her brother. In truth, he had most likely been more interested in the value of the necklace she was attempting to sell than he was in her. Had they seen the last of Mr. Bryant? When Owen had been standing next to her, she had felt brave, but now, in the room's solitude, she felt terribly alone.

Next to her on the table sat Jane's Bible. Annabelle let her gaze linger on it for several seconds before she reached out to take it in her hands. It was worn, just as her mother's had been. She flipped through the pages. Some of the words were familiar, some not. She sighed and held it to her chest as she looked back out the window.

Her uncle had told her to have faith and that all would be well in the end. She tried to have faith, and she had borrowed her mother's prayers. Uncle Edmund had to be right, didn't he? That her journey was already mapped out and it was up to her to seek guidance to find it?

She pressed her palm to her forehead. She wanted to find peace in that statement, and her heart was almost ready to give in to it.

The bell rang again in its tower, and with a sigh Annabelle returned Jane's Bible to the table, then lowered her feet to the floor and shook out the black linen. She fastened her hair back from her face and gathered her resolve. At least Owen and Hannah would both be at service today.

She straightened her shawl, and the door flung open. Crosley stood in the doorway.

"Margaret!" Annabelle's hand flew to her heart. "You frightened me!"

Upon closer examination, Annabelle frowned. Crosley was soaked from head to toe. Her red-rimmed eyes were wide and filled with tears. Her breaths came in noisy gulps.

Concerned at the sight, Annabelle forgot their strained discord, dropped her shawl, and reached for Crosley's trembling hand. "Your hand is like ice! Have you been outside? What is wrong?"

A heavy tear plopped from Crosley's light-blue eye, and she sniffed and wiped her face with the back of her hand. "Where do I begin?"

"You will begin by shedding these wet clothes. You'll catch your death, then—"

"No." Crosley snatched Annabelle's hand. "We haven't time."

Annabelle tensed as the uncomfortable sensation that something was wrong flooded over her. "Haven't time for what?"

Crosley's lips quaked. "There has been an accident."

"One of the girls? Or—?"

Crosley shook her head. "No. Mr. Locke."

Annabelle recoiled. Surely she had misheard. Her stomach clenched. "Mr. Locke?"

"Oh, it's terrible," Crosley exclaimed as she met Annabelle's gaze before she stepped farther into the room. "We have not talked of it, but we must now. I know you are aware that my brother traveled with Mr. Thorley to Bancroft Park."

"Yes, yes." Annabelle suspended her breath, as if by doing so she could hear the words more quickly.

"I visited him early this morning to see him before he left. We met in the forest, just to talk. It had been so long since I had seen him. But while we were there, we heard shots. Then shouting. Apparently Mr. Whitten and Mr. Locke were in the forest hunting or something, and Mr. Locke has been shot."

Panic commandeered Annabelle's senses. "Is he all right?"

"He is hurt. Badly. Mr. Treadwell is with him, and a surgeon has been called." Crosley's voice wavered. "Billy and I were among the first there. It—it does not look good. I have never seen anything like it, but . . . he has asked for you."

Annabelle ignored the questions and possible scenarios already swirling in her mind. The only thing that mattered was getting to Owen. "Take me to him."

Chapter Forty-One

$\mathscr{A}$nnabelle's feet would not move fast enough. Each step slogged along as if in quicksand. The cold wetness numbed her feet as the horror pulsed through her.

Not Owen.

She followed Crosley through the woods—the very forest path where she had found Hannah all those weeks ago. "Hurry, Crosley. We must hurry."

Thoughts bombarded her as she stepped over the low-lying bramble and branches. Hannah. Mrs. Pike. Owen's dream of Kirtley Meadow. Each fresh thought urged her to move faster. She had to be there. To help.

"Oh, Annabelle, it was terrible. Just terrible!"

Annabelle took several deep breaths to calm the wild beating of her heart. "Where is he?"

"He was taken to an old cottage in the forest. They did not want to move him too far. I have never been there; I hope I can find it again."

"You must remember."

Farther and farther they scurried into the forest. Then Crosley's steps slowed. "There it is. Through the trees there."

An unfamiliar, dilapidated stone cottage stood in a modest clearing just past the path. The windows were broken and a tree had fallen over the thatched roof. She would have assumed it was uninhabited except smoke puffed from the chimney. Annabelle wiped the rain from her face. She gathered her skirts and bit her lip as if to summon strength. She would need every ounce of it she possessed.

Owen had been shot. There would be blood, pain. She had to be strong.

She exchanged glances with Crosley. How she longed for the old Crosley, who would listen to her, soothe her pain, take her side. In Crosley's red-rimmed eyes she saw pain and concern.

Crosley reached for Annabelle's hand. "Prepare yourself."

The smell of wood smoke tweaked her nose. Her body trembled with such violence that she wondered how she would make it inside.

Crosley gripped her by the hand, stepped before her, and pushed open the door.

Annabelle thought she might faint as she followed her through the doorway, preparing for the worst. Gathering her courage, she lifted her eyes.

And what she saw shocked her.

The door slammed shut behind her. Crosley dropped her hand. And Annabelle whirled around.

Owen was there, yes, but he was not injured. His eyes wide, he was tied to a chair, and a rag bound his mouth.

She froze and lifted her gaze. In the corner stood her brother, Mr. Bartrell, and Billy Crosley.

She opened her mouth to speak but then snapped it shut. Crosley moved toward the men and turned to face Annabelle. Gone were the sympathy and fear. A smug smile replaced any trace of concern.

Annabelle pivoted back to Owen. His upper arms and torso were tied, his fists gripped the chair, and his eyebrows slanted down in anger.

Terror clutched her. She had been tricked.

For several moments, no one spoke. Then Thomas left his perch and moved closer to Annabelle. She lifted her chin, refusing to retreat as he approached. "What have you done, Thomas?"

"It isn't what I have done," he said, calmly and coolly. "It is time you faced the consequences of your thoughtless actions."

Annabelle flicked her gaze from Owen to Mr. Bartrell and back to Owen. "This is wrong. Why have you tied him up? You must let him go. Immediately."

Mr. Bartrell shifted, revealing a pistol in his hands. She struggled to make sense of this. Why Owen? How was Crosley involved?

"You're not exactly in a position to be giving orders, Belle." Thomas circled her, and Billy Crosley shuffled toward her. "It's about time you realized you'll do as you're told."

Annabelle huffed. "I will not."

"You will, otherwise the gamekeeper here won't live to see another dawn."

Mr. Bartrell lifted the pistol and took aim at an invisible spot on the wall, then drew the weapon close, polished it against his sleeve, and fixed Annabelle with a pointed stare.

Annabelle could not control her trembling. She understood Mr. Bartrell's silent warning, and she didn't doubt that he was capable of such a dastardly action. Mr. McAlister's demise flashed before her.

Mr. Bartrell spoke. "I told you that I'd get my way and that I'd possess you. You will marry me, Annabelle. Today. Otherwise I'll kill your gamekeeper friend, who has caused enough trouble for me in his own right. And then you'll marry me just the same."

Annabelle looked to the door, wanting to run. It had been latched, and the lock bar had been lowered. Desperate for help, she looked to Crosley, but her cold expression conveyed she would be of no help.

Annabelle's mouth went so dry she could not even swallow. The glow from the fireplace created the room's only light, and it glistened on Owen's perspiring face. Her heart ached for him—ached for the fear he must be experiencing. But what frightened her most was the thought of never seeing him alive again.

Her mind begged, pleaded with God for knowledge of what she should do. But how did God answer prayer? Was it like a lightning bolt from the sky? A whisper? A feeling?

As Bartrell drew closer and shifted the pistol's aim toward Owen, she had no option. Mr. Bartrell would make good on his promise.

"Fine," Annabelle blurted. "But do not hurt him."

Thomas laughed. "So concerned. But we have other issues to address with Mr. Locke. You messed up trusting this one, Belle. You've no idea what you've done."

She did not have time to contemplate his words, for Mr. Bartrell stomped toward the door, pistol still pointed at Owen. "Your carriage awaits, Miss Thorley. And don't think about changing your mind. Billy here will be keeping an eye on our friend until he has been told our marriage has taken place."

Thomas jerked her arm, and her soggy shawl fell to the floor. He swung a cape around her shoulders before they went outside.

The air grew bitterly cold as she stepped behind the cottage to the carriage. The rain raked her face, and the raw wind bit into her skin. She had to find a way out of this. For now Owen was safe, and she prayed she was making the right decision.

Chapter Forty-Two

*O*wen yanked his arms against the ropes restraining him. The rough cords dug through his sleeves and burned against his arms, but they would not give. He grunted and thrashed as Annabelle disappeared through the doorway. Perspiration dripped from his wet hair and stung his eyes.

Billy Crosley crossed the room and smacked the back of Owen's head. "You'll knock that off if you know what's good for you."

Owen had been ambushed last night in the forest. In the span of seconds the men had been upon him. Against one or even two men he would have had a fighting chance. But with three armed men, he was easily overtaken.

What was even worse was that Annabelle had been tricked.

He had failed to protect her, and now she was in the hands of a monster. His lungs strained against the constraint of his rib cage. He was barely able to get enough air through his nose.

Thorley, Bartrell, and Miss Crosley had all gone with Annabelle. He had heard the carriage rumble away. He forced his breathing to slow. The only thing standing in his way, besides the ropes and ties, was the moronic Billy Crosley and the weapon he wielded.

He had to stay calm if he was going to not only get out of this alive, but find and protect Annabelle.

He assessed the cottage. He knew the structure. It had been empty since he was a boy—ever since a tree fell over the back roof. He passed it every so often but never gave it a second glance. But litter, bowls, and furniture implied that someone had been using it for quite some time. Rope and wire were stashed in the corner. Crates and trunks lined the back hall. And a pile of fur sat atop a roughly fashioned table. Even as he assessed the cottage's contents, his mind raced to put all the pieces together.

But what was even more shocking was what he'd learned from his captors.

Crosley paced the narrow space. "You picked a fight with the wrong man, Locke."

Owen could only eye him.

"He will destroy you, you know that?"

Owen refused to be intimidated by the smaller man. But he did not doubt the vicious nature of either Thorley or Bartrell.

After what seemed like hours, a noise caught Owen's attention. A dog barking. Not just any dog, but Drake. During the scuffle earlier that morning, he had become separated from Drake and was not sure what had happened to him. Owen had lost track of time, but no doubt Whitten would have noticed his absence by now.

He glanced to see if Crosley had noticed the noise, but he sat on the chair, pistol in hand. He was becoming complacent. Which was just what Owen needed.

His impatience mounted as the sound of barking grew closer. Drake was the best tracking dog he'd ever owned. If Drake was on the hunt, Owen would be found.

The rain started again, pelting the thatched roof and slamming against the panes of glass. The barking was growing louder, more erratic.

Crosley noticed the sound finally. The lanky man stood from his chair and moved to the window to look out. "Dog must be daft," he muttered, straining to see through the rain.

Owen's heart beat wildly and perspiration dripped in his eye again. He blinked it away and strained to hear over the rain.

Then someone in the distance called out, "Locke!"

Drake's barking sounded to be right outside the door. Owen forced himself to be perfectly still.

Crosley turned to the side as he regripped the pistol over and over, his motions clumsy and hesitant. He licked his lips and shifted from foot to foot. Perspiration dotted his brow and clumped his shaggy blond hair. Clearly he was not used to handling such a weapon, which made him even more dangerous.

Owen strained to see out the window, but the chair was too low to the ground.

Suddenly the door burst open and Crosley stumbled backward. Whitten appeared in the doorway, his thick frame but a silhouette against the dreary light outside, his weapon fixed firmly on Crosley.

Crosley fumbled with his gun and lost his balance, and Drake rushed into the room, snarling, and lunged onto Crosley's unsteady form.

A cry escaped Crosley as he fell, and the weapon clattered to the ground. It discharged, and the bullet flew through the cottage's back wall. Drake stood with his paws on Crosley's chest, growling with his teeth bared.

Whitten drew closer, his aim direct. His gaze did not leave Crosley's face. He stepped forward and kicked the gun away from the skittish man. "Not sure what all this is about, but I can't say I'm too happy to find Locke here tied up and you with a pistol. Get up, and if you try anything foolish, this dog will be on you faster 'n you can snap a whip."

Drake retreated, and Whitten made quick business of forcing Crosley into a chair. With Drake gnarling at Crosley's every move, the man did not dare move a muscle as Whitten secured him.

"There now." Whitten wiped his brow and turned his attention to Owen. He retrieved a pocketknife and cut the ropes. Owen pulled the rag off his mouth.

Drawing a deep breath, Owen scooped up Crosley's discarded weapon. "Where were they going?"

When Crosley did not answer, Owen intensified his voice and aimed his pistol at Crosley. "Where were they going?"

Perspiration dotted Crosley's brow and dripped to his chin. "They was going back to London, 'tis all I know."

When Owen did not lower the weapon, Crosley hissed, "I swear, that is all I know. He wants to marry Miss Thorley. That's it."

"That's not it, and you and I both know it." Owen's hand was steady as he continued to hold the pistol. "What were you doing out this morning?"

Crosley shifted, his gaze not leaving the weapon. "We were on our way back to Bancroft Park and got lost."

Owen let out a frustrated laugh and steadied his grip. "Now how about you tell me the truth."

Whitten stepped closer, and Drake snarled at his master's feet.

Owen whistled, and Drake inched toward Crosley. "I will ask you again. What were you doing in Linton Forest?"

Crosley could scoot back no farther. "I'll tell you, just get that mutt away from me."

Owen whistled, and the dog retreated.

Crosley fixed his eyes on the pistol. "We were looking for you. Bartrell said you had to be punished for what happened to Hemstead and said you knew too much. And when he thought you and Miss Thorley were together, he went mad."

Owen exchanged a glance with Whitten. The pieces fell into place: Bartrell and Thorley were behind the poaching, and they had been using their time on Bancroft Park property to make necessary connections for the game. And when they suspected Owen was on to them, they were going to prevent him from going to the authorities and exposing their activities.

That had to be it. That's how they knew their way around the forest. They'd utilized this very cottage to run their operation from. It had been right under his nose this entire time. It made perfect sense. Game needed to be sold someplace where its origins would not be questioned. And that place was London.

He now knew what he needed to know. Owen bent down and scooped up Annabelle's discarded shawl. The damp fabric felt heavy in his hand. Anger raged afresh within him. Annabelle was strong and feisty, but she would be no match for the likes of Bartrell and her brother.

"Make sure those ropes are tight," Owen instructed Whitten. "We've a carriage to catch."

Chapter Forty-Three

*W*ithin minutes Whitten and Owen had run to the stables to retrieve horses, pistols, and Walter Burley, the grounds-keeper. The rain continued to fall, but Owen did not mind. He had learned to use the elements to his advantage. He donned a greatcoat to protect himself from the weather and pulled his wide-brimmed hat low before he motioned to the other men to mount their horses. If he was going to overtake the two men, he needed to outnumber them. The more at his disposal, the better.

He knelt down to Drake and rubbed the dog's head. Drake licked his face and Owen scratched his ears. "Good boy. But your work is not done."

He placed Annabelle's shawl on the ground before him and gave the time-honored command, "Find her, Drake. Find her."

The dog sniffed the damp shawl and circled it twice. He barked wildly and ran around Owen.

Once satisfied the dog had the scent, Owen mounted his horse. "Let's go!"

They traveled the expanse of Bancroft Park land and made their way to a main highway. When Owen realized the direction they were traveling, he pulled the horses to a stop and shouted above the rain's patter, "This road leads to London, but there is a carriage inn about five miles away. From there the road juts in three different directions. Let's hope we can overtake the carriage. Everyone doing all right?"

Whitten, with ruddy face and excited eyes, nodded.

Burley, with blanched features and shadowed eyes, sniffed.

Owen and the men cantered down the road, passing forest and

vale, pond and field. He was beginning to fear they were on a cold trail when they rounded a bend in the road and a carriage could be seen in front of them.

The carriage did not appear to be traveling unusually fast, but the thought of Annabelle with Bartrell in the carriage sent fire surging through him. The carriage had an unusually large number of trunks fastened to it. Far too many for men eager to flee Fellsworth.

He wished he'd had time to touch base with Treadwell to find out if he knew anything, but if his suspicions were correct, Treadwell would have no idea what his guests had really been up to while staying at Bancroft Park.

Owen urged the horse into a faster gait, faster, faster, until he was within shouting distance. Bits of earth flung up with each pounding of his horse's hooves, and his horse stumbled in the thick mud on more than one occasion. He ran his horse up to the side of the carriage.

He ducked his head to the right just long enough to see Bartrell's face as he flew by. Owen urged the horse ahead, and the carriage driver and his comrade noticed him.

No doubt they thought him a highwayman. He glanced back at Whitten close behind him. Burley was farther back.

From the corner of his eye he saw the driver retrieve a weapon, but at his speed he could not stop to confirm it. His main priority was to get ahold of a rein to stop the horses. Fortunately there were only two pulling the carriage, but it would be a feat.

Finally he was close enough. He ignored the shouting and after two attempts grabbed hold of the leather lead. He pulled tight, the force slicing his bare hand.

He glanced back. The carriage driver and his partner were not there—they had jumped. No doubt they bailed at the first sign of trouble, especially if they suspected him to be a highwayman.

The horses eventually started to slow, their uneven hysterical gait eventually pulling to a halt.

Owen leaned forward in the saddle, gulping for air. He had not realized he was holding his breath until he stopped the animals. He looked down at his hand. Blood oozed from the gash.

He pulled his pistol from his saddle and turned to dismount, then froze.

Bartrell had exited the carriage and was pointing a pistol right at his chest.

Owen was but a few paces away. If Bartrell pulled the trigger, he would not miss.

Annabelle poked her head out of the carriage door, and at the sight of Bartrell with his gun drawn, her face grew ashen.

"What in blazes do you think you are doing?" Bartrell yelled. "What right do you have to stop my carriage?"

"You are transporting a lady against her will. And I have reason to believe that you have contraband game on your carriage."

Bartrell snorted and tilted his head as he noticed Whitten and Burley approach, their weapons drawn. "You're lucky I don't shoot you where you stand, Locke. You've caused enough trouble for me."

"Put the gun down, Bartrell," Locke ordered.

Bartrell huffed. "Or what? You'll shoot me?"

Bartrell started to pivot, but Whitten stilled him. "Don't move, Bartrell. I'll pull this trigger in a heartbeat. I'd love nothing more than to see a poacher like you put in his place."

Bartrell smiled, almost as if he were enjoying the game. "What if you miss? Miss Thorley's right behind me. Isn't that why you are here? Do you really expect me to believe that you would follow me all this way for rabbits and foxes?"

Owen flicked his gaze up. Annabelle was no longer visible in the carriage.

It was then Thorley rounded the carriage, with a firm grip on Annabelle's arm.

Her eyes were red, and her face was pale. Mud was splattered on her face. "Owen! Be careful!"

Thomas jerked her when she spoke, and waved an old-fashioned dueling pistol in his direction. "This is between you and me, Locke, as it should be."

They were three against two, and with Miss Crosley in the carriage, he had to act fast. With a sharp intake of breath Owen ducked low and ran himself into Thorley, and by doing so caught him off guard. The action broke Thorley's grip on Annabelle. She fell backward, and Thorley fell to the ground. Owen pressed his weight on top of him.

A shot fired.

The carriage horses jumped, and his own horse whinnied behind him.

A woman screamed.

Whitten shouted.

He could only focus on the battle he engaged in with Annabelle's brother.

Owen grabbed the smaller man by the coat and slammed his fist into his jaw. He was not expecting the fist that came back, striking him on the cheek. The blow fueled Owen's anger, and he landed another punch that knocked Thorley unconscious.

He lifted Thorley up by his lapels and turned to see blood streaming down Whitten's arm. But Whitten was not on the ground. He had his gun fixed on Bartrell, while Burley and Bartrell exchanged blows.

He was about to assist Burley when he noticed a flash of black streak through the forest. Miss Crosley.

Next to him, Thorley lay unconscious. Annabelle stood behind him. Before him, Burley was overtaking Bartrell and Whitten had his gun fixed.

Owen raced around the carriage, and within moments his long stride overtook Miss Crosley's. He grabbed her by the waist and easily flung the small woman over his shoulder to subdue her.

"Let go of me, you animal!" Crosley screamed and flailed. She pounded his back and kicked her legs.

He had no idea what role she played in this, but he would find out.

When he returned to the carriage, Owen retrieved a length of rope from the driver's box and secured Miss Crosley, despite her thrashing. She spit at him and cursed him, but he said nothing.

Once she was secure, Owen moved to Thorley's unconscious body, tied his arms behind his back, and propped him against the carriage wheel. Owen looked down. Blood trickled from his hand where he had stopped the horses. He climbed up in the driver's seat, set the brake, and then returned to the ground and motioned for Annabelle to stay where she was.

Burley had subdued Bartrell, and Whitten still had his gun pointed at him. Owen paced before them before choosing his words. He had thought that Thorley was the mastermind behind the plot, but after witnessing the conversation in the cottage, it was clear: Bartrell was the man behind this entire ordeal.

"It's over, Bartrell."

Bartrell laughed. "You'll have to kill me if that is what you want. I'm a gentleman, or have you forgotten? You'll be hanged for hijacking this carriage."

"Hijacking?" Owen stepped to the back of the carriage and released the trunks secured there. He used his knife to slice the leather bands holding them secure, and he pushed open one of the lids to reveal pelts. He slammed the lid closed.

Owen sauntered toward the man. "I must commend you, Bartrell."

Perspiration dripped down Bartrell's wide face. "How dare you speak like that to me."

"I must say you devised quite a plan. Using Thorley to befriend Treadwell to gain access to his land. Hiring a man at the school to carry out the real work. And how convenient for you that Miss Thorley chose to relocate to Fellsworth with her maid, whose brother just happened to be your scapegoat's footman. Interesting, indeed. So where were you selling the game? London? Bath? I suppose it does not matter now, does it? You will not be doing it again for a very long time."

"You can accuse me all you want," spat Bartrell. "You will never prove it."

"Oh, won't I?" Owen raised a brow. "What I can't figure out is how you got Thorley involved. We both know he does not have an original thought in his head. Hardly the sort of man to pull off something like this. But you—you saw his dire financial need and exploited it."

Bartrell threw his head back in laughter. "You have no idea what you are talking about."

Owen shrugged. "Maybe I do. Maybe I don't. Or perhaps that is what McAlister meant when he told Miss Thorley that her brother was in trouble. Maybe he was going to expose your little operation to Treadwell. Was that it?"

Bartrell's bloated face reddened at the sound of McAlister's name. "McAlister was a fool."

"A fool or a wise man, he still lost his life. I suspect that his loss had to do with the fact that he disagreed with you and your methods. You killed him, didn't you?"

At this Bartrell raged, and Burley struggled to keep the large man at bay, but Whitten stepped forward and Bartrell stilled at the sight of the gun.

Suddenly Bartrell jerked away from Burley, lunged at Whitten, and wrenched the gun from him.

Owen charged forward in response and jumped on Bartrell, then grabbed his arm and forced it up.

The gun fired.

Bits of fire stung Owen's arm, and the familiar scent of gunpowder wafted around him.

Bartrell hit the ground with a *thud*, and Owen landed on top of him. The obese man struggled and fought, but he was no match for Owen's strength.

Within minutes they had subdued him, and Whitten secured his hands with a length of rope.

With Burley and Whitten corralling the criminal, Owen jumped up, chest heaving, and turned to Annabelle.

It was time to get out of here.

Time to get these people to the authorities.

Time to get Annabelle home.

She stood at the edge of the road where he had instructed her to stay. Her hands were over her mouth, and her eyes were wide, unblinking. He reached out to take her hand. It trembled as she placed it in his.

Her clothes were wet. Dirty. Her hair streamed down around her face. Once her foot stepped on the road, she looked around, first at her brother, then at Miss Crosley, and then at Bartrell.

She turned her attention to Owen, and they stared at each other for several moments. As he moved toward her, she fell into him. He was not sure if she embraced him or if it was the other way around, but when they melded against each other, he knew this was where she was meant to be.

Relief flooded him. She was alive. Unharmed. Unmarried.

He pressed his lips to the top of her head. He could feel her tremble beneath his touch. He could feel the toll the fear and uncertainty had taken on her as she shivered in his arms.

"Shh. It is all right now. Everything will be all right." His words seemed so inadequate.

She lifted her head off his chest, the tears in her eyes making them shine even more brightly. "When I saw him point the gun at you, I thought . . . I thought . . ."

He brushed her hair from her face and let his palm linger on her cheek. He rubbed a tear away with his thumb. "Oh no. Don't you worry about anything like that. I'm not about to let someone like him kill me. After all, I have too much to live for."

She closed her eyes and leaned into his palm. She drew a shuddery breath and rested her hands on his chest. Her words were so soft he almost missed them. "Please never let go."

He tightened his arms around her and drew her closer. He slid his palm down the side of her face and tilted her chin toward him. Her kiss was even more tender, more sweet than he could imagine. He would have been content to stay in her embrace the rest of the day, but Whitten's cough caused him to turn around.

"We'd best get this motley crew back to Fellsworth." Whitten's voice was gruff. "I imagine the magistrate will have a thing or two to say to them."

Owen glanced at Bartrell's pitiful face before he turned back to Annabelle. He kissed her again and turned to return to the task at hand. But her hand on his arm stopped him.

She fixed her red-rimmed eyes on him, and a shaky smile trembled her lips. "There is something I didn't get to tell you last night at the festival."

He thought it an odd thing to say. "Oh? What's that?"

"I love you, Owen Locke. I love you with everything that I am."

Fierce yearning rushed through him, and he pulled her to him once more. "You will always have me, my Annabelle. Always."

Chapter Forty-Four

*A*nnabelle stepped into Fellsworth's small jailhouse.

"You don't have to do this." Owen ducked under the low threshold to step in behind her, followed by Treadwell.

Two days had passed since the incident at the carriage. Two days since Bartrell, Thomas, and the Crosleys had been apprehended. Two days since Annabelle became truly free.

But even though the physical threat had passed, her heart struggled with things yet unresolved. She looked to the cells that housed the men: Mr. Bartrell, Thomas, and Billy Crosley.

She gathered her courage. "I have to talk to them."

Owen squeezed her hand. "Treadwell and I will be just on the other side. We've business to tend to with the magistrate."

Annabelle nodded and smoothed her skirt, then knit her fingers around the hem of her shawl. She waited several moments for her eyes to adjust to the lack of light. Long, narrow windows allowed a small amount of light to permeate the darkness, but most of it came from the candles dotting the room.

She gathered her courage and turned to face Crosley, who was in a cell with one other woman. The sight tugged at her, and she could not help but bring to mind the years they had shared. The laughter. The secrets. But now, Crosley's betrayal, while not altogether surprising, seemed to cut almost deeper than that of her brother.

Annabelle was ready to leave this mess behind her, but she needed to make her peace. "Crosley."

At first Annabelle thought Crosley was not going to respond.

She did not have to. But after several moments, Crosley stood from the room's only chair and sauntered toward the bars.

The past two days had altered Crosley's appearance. Her usually tidy hair hung untethered to her waist, full of tangles. Gray circles darkened the area beneath her reddened eyes, and her black gown had a rip on the shoulder.

Annabelle cleared her throat and extended a bundle. "I brought you this."

Crosley eyed Annabelle's hand. "What is it?"

"Bread, cheese, and an apple."

Crosley sniffed and turned up her nose as if she was going to refuse.

"Take it. I don't want you to be hungry."

Crosley accepted it and tossed the bundle onto the table next to the chair and crossed her arms over her chest. "What are you doing here?"

"I want to talk to you."

"About what? To gloat? To prove that you were right and I was wrong?"

"I am just trying to understand what happened, that's all." Annabelle cut her eyes toward Owen and Treadwell, whose backs were to her as they spoke with the magistrate. "I've no wish to cause trouble for you. I only want to understand."

"Understand?" Crosley flung her hand in the air. "How could you possibly understand me? You, in your gilded, pampered world? No, Annabelle. You will never understand me."

"But we left London together. We could have helped each other. Why did you betray me?"

"I did not betray you. That is what you do not understand. Don't you see that this had nothing to do with you? It had everything to do with helping myself. I told you I never want to serve another person as long as I live, didn't I?"

Crosley paced the small space. "'Tis no secret now. I wrote my brother where I was after we arrived. After all, I had no secrets to keep. When he found out I was in Fellsworth, he told me that he worked with a man by the name of Mr. Hemstead, and he introduced us by letter. By the time I was fully aware of what they were doing, I was already in love with Mr. Hemstead. We were going to get married. The poaching was only supposed to be temporary, but Mr. Bartrell is so powerful. Nobody can get away from him. Even after Mr. Hemstead was sent to prison he would not let me out of the ring. Not with my life."

Tears rushed to Annabelle's eyes. She didn't know if Crosley was being truthful or not, but she knew all too well how terrifying Mr. Bartrell could be.

Crosley wiped moisture from her eyes. "He killed Mr. McAlister."

Annabelle winced. "Who did?"

"Mr. Bartrell. I heard them discussing it, and when they noticed I was there, Mr. Bartrell told me if I said anything he would kill both Billy and me. He's a monster, Annabelle."

Sympathy pulled at Annabelle. Crosley cleared her throat. "I thought Mr. Bartrell might give up the notion after Mr. Locke found Mr. Hemstead. But when he found out that you were in love with him, he became irrational. He was obsessed with you, wanting to marry you. He started to pressure Mr. Thorley all over again. That is when things began to crumble."

Annabelle heard her name, and she looked over her shoulder at Owen and Treadwell, who were waiting for her. She looked back to Crosley. "I'm so sorry, Crosley, but I have to go."

They stared at each other for several seconds. Then Crosley spoke. "I don't know what is going to happen to me. But for what it's worth, I am sorry if I hurt you. I see now that I was wrong, but I suppose I deserve what I get."

"You have my forgiveness, Margaret." Annabelle sniffed. Emotion was welling within her. She nodded. "Good-bye."

As she returned to Owen's side, she saw her brother from the corner of her eye. She stiffened. Whereas she had wanted to speak with Crosley to make peace, part of her never wanted to see Thomas again. He had broken their family bond long ago. The ties that bound brother and sister had been severed.

Still, when she looked at him, she saw the eight-year-old boy in the portrait her mother had painted, and sadness overwhelmed her. But the thought of how much this would hurt her mother compelled her. She garnered her confidence and tightened her grip on her satchel.

"Thomas." She stepped toward his cell, forcing her eyes to meet his. Stubble darkened his chin and cheeks, and his eyes were little more than slits.

He did not respond.

"Do I really mean so little to you, Thomas? How could you betray me like that?"

He leaned against the bars. "You're the one who betrayed me, Belle, not the other way around. Do you know how hard I worked to find a suitable husband for you after Goodacre? And you threw it away and ruined everything—*everything*—in the process."

He was turning the situation around on her. Would he never understand?

Annabelle sniffed. "And what of Eleanor? Do you know what is going to happen to you?"

"Thanks to your beau, my future is now uncertain." Thomas ignored her question about Eleanor and glared at Owen. "Can you live with that, Belle, knowing what *he* did to your brother?"

Annabelle followed his gaze to Owen. He was the only thing in her world that made sense. Nothing her brother could say would change her mind. There was something else she needed to clarify. "Crosley said you didn't kill McAlister."

"Bah!" Sarcasm laced Thomas's tone. "After all this, you think me guilty of murder?"

"What am I to think?" she shot back. "You were covered in blood that night. I heard the gunshot. Of course I was scared."

"It's no secret now. Miss Crosley has already told the magistrate of the murder, and her brother gave a firsthand witness. But no, it wasn't me."

"It was Mr. Bartrell."

Thomas looked to the ground.

"Why would you align yourself with someone like him?"

"I did what I had to do."

Her throat began to tighten. Tears would well if she was not careful. The pain of being brushed aside by someone she had known all of her life stung. She drew a steadying breath. She had come here for a reason. She reached into her satchel and retrieved a folded piece of paper.

"What's that?"

She turned the letter over in her hands. "Mama kept a prayer journal. You probably didn't know of it, but she did. I took it with me when I left London."

He huffed. It was no secret that Thomas shared their father's view on such things.

But Annabelle would not be deterred. "She wrote a prayer for you, Thomas. I thought you would want it." She extended the paper toward him.

After several seconds of stillness, he snatched the letter from her.

"She wrote one for me too. It has brought me comfort over the past several months. I hope it does the same for you."

He stuffed the letter in his pocket but said nothing.

Annabelle fretted with her shawl. She had done what she came here to do. "Good-bye, Thomas."

He nodded but still said nothing.

Walking away from him was harder than she anticipated. She did not know what his future held, but as she walked back toward Owen, she knew what hers held.

Owen took her hand. "Are you ready to go?"

She squeezed his hand and nodded as they stepped out of the jail's shadow and into the bright afternoon sunlight. "Yes, I am ready. Ready for so many things."

Chapter Forty-Five ————————

*A*nnabelle tucked her hand in her husband's. The sensation of it would never grow old.

Winter had passed, and now swallows swept from tree to tree and the spring flowers were opening their petals to greet the sun.

"Are you ready to see your new home?" Owen's eyes were as bright as those of a child about to receive a new gift. He gripped the gate to Kirtley Meadow and arched his eyebrow.

Annabelle laughed at Owen's eagerness.

Hannah, dressed in a new gown of cream satin with a wide pink sash, ran through the gate first, and then Owen held it open for Annabelle to enter.

She started to step through it, but he caught her hand and pulled her back. He wrapped his arm around her waist and kissed her playfully, the stubble on his chin tickling her face. "There was a time I thought I would never marry again, and here we are, Mr. and Mrs. Locke."

She still blushed from his flirtatious attention, and she hoped she always would. "I like the sound of that. Mrs. Locke."

He kissed her again. Longer. More passionately. "It suits you."

Hannah called to them from ahead, and Drake came trotting down the lane.

"Poor Drake." He released her hand. "I think it will take him time to get used to calling Kirtley Meadow home. He's an old man, stubborn and set in his ways."

Annabelle leaned down to pat the dog's head. "Come on, boy. Let's go home."

Owen tucked Annabelle's hand in the crook of his arm. She looked up at the green canopy of trees. Spring was here again. Another winter had passed and life was new. She was a bride. A mother to Hannah. She had a husband who loved her. A future free of the restraints of the past. And a home where she finally belonged.

"I can't believe it is finally ready." Annabelle smiled as they approached the cottage. She smiled at the thought of Owen playing here as a boy. He'd been working on repairing the cottage for months. She breathed in the fresh spring air and let her gaze linger on the stone cottage.

"Still needs a little work, but we'll make it home." Owen took her hand in his and pressed it to his lips as they walked the path. "And the best part? I have my very own portrait to hang on the wall. What other gamekeeper can say that?"

She laughed at the mention of the portrait she had painted of him the past autumn. "It looks much better with the frame you made for it."

Mrs. Pike appeared in the doorway. "Don't know what's keepin' you. If you want a hot meal, I wouldn't dally too much. I've said it before and I'll say it again. I'll not cook the stew all day."

Owen and Annabelle exchanged glances at the woman's odd ways, but in truth, Mrs. Pike was proving to be a true asset—and was becoming a friend. Annabelle knew nothing about keeping a house, and each day Mrs. Pike taught her something new.

"Do you think you'll miss the cottage at Bancroft Park?" she asked.

Owen gave his head a shake. "No. It held too many memories.

It was time to let them go. I want to focus on making new ones. With Hannah. With you. Besides, I still have my fill of Bancroft Park. After all, I am still employed there. It is in my blood, just as Kirtley Meadow is."

Someone called her name, and she looked to see her aunt and uncle coming up the path as promised to join them for the afternoon meal. Her heart was full. A family. A full family, just as her soul had dreamed.

The memory of her mother's nightly prayers for happiness crossed her mind. No, the prayers had not been in vain. God had heard them, and now, in this cottage in the copse in the woods, she was living in His answered prayers. It may have taken her a while to understand the truth behind her mother's faith, but she was beginning to, and she would say the same prayers for Hannah and maybe one day a child of her own.

She smiled and leaned her head against Owen's shoulder as they walked on the stone path toward the cottage. Their future spread before them, promising and full of hope. She filled her lungs with the crisp country air and turned her eyes on Owen.

She was home, and it was not only the structure of stone and thatch that made it so.

Her heart had found its resting place. Her soul had found peace.

And she had found true happiness—as the gamekeeper's wife.

Acknowledgments

Writing a novel is such a rewarding experience, and I would like to thank the following for sharing this journey with me:

To my family: It is because of your encouragement and support that I am able to follow my passion for storytelling. I am so grateful!

To my extraordinary editor, Becky Monds: Thank you for guidance and inspiration. And to the rest of the team at HarperCollins Christian Publishing—from marketing to design, from production to sales—you guys are amazing!

To my first readers, Ann and Sally: I love your insight! Thank you for helping me get the story just right.

To Tamela Hancock Murray: You are the agent who made this possible! Thank you for all you have done.

To my writing sisters Katherine and Kristy: I am blessed to call you friends.

To the "Grove Girls"—Cara, Katie, Melissa, Courtney, Katherine, Kristy, and Beth: Thank you for sharing your gifts and inspiring others to tell their stories.

To the incredible suspense writers who brainstormed with me when this story was just a glimmer of an idea—Colleen, Carrie, Michelle, Robin, Lynette, and Kristy: Your creativity helped me see this story in a brand-new light.

Last but not least, a huge thank-you to my readers. I am so grateful for each and every one of you!

Discussion Questions

1. Which character in this story do you identify with the most? Why?
2. If you could give Annabelle one piece of advice at any point in the story, what would it be? What advice would you give Owen?
3. Let's talk about Crosley. In the beginning she seems loyal to Annabelle, but as the story unfolds she grows cold. Why do you think this is? Was she ever really loyal to Annabelle?
4. In what ways is Annabelle different at the end of the novel from her character when the story opens? What about her faith—how does it change?
5. Same question for Owen: Does his personality or character change during the course of the book?
6. Even though Annabelle's mother died and is not present in most of the story, she still impacted Annabelle's life. In what ways did Annabelle's memories of her mother and her mother's prayer journal affect her?
7. Owen experienced great loss when his wife died, and he carried a great deal of guilt over the fact that he could not protect her. How do you think this loss impacted how he saw Annabelle? How do you think it affected him as a father?

8. Even though Annabelle grew up privileged, she was completely reliant on her brother. How do you think her encounter with Miss Stillworth early in the story impacted the decisions she made?

9. Pretend you are the author. What comes next for Annabelle and Owen? What would you like to see happen to these characters in the future?

About the Author

S arah E. Ladd received the 2011 Genesis Award in historical romance for *The Heiress of Winterwood*. She is a graduate of Ball State University and has more than ten years of marketing experience. Sarah lives in Indiana with her amazing family and spunky golden retriever.

FOREVER SMILING PHOTOGRAPHY

Visit Sarah online at SarahLadd.com
Facebook: SarahLaddAuthor
Twitter: @SarahLaddAuthor

328